Contents

Cover Art: Gervasio Gallardo

Fungi, Summer 2025, Volume 2, #25 is published in the United States by
Fungoid Press, Lowell, MA. All contents copyright ©2025 by Fungoid Press.
First North American rights reserved. Cover, illustrations, and reprinted
material belong to respective copyright holders. Visit Fungi
at www.pierrevcomtois.com. ISBN 978-1-63868-222-6.

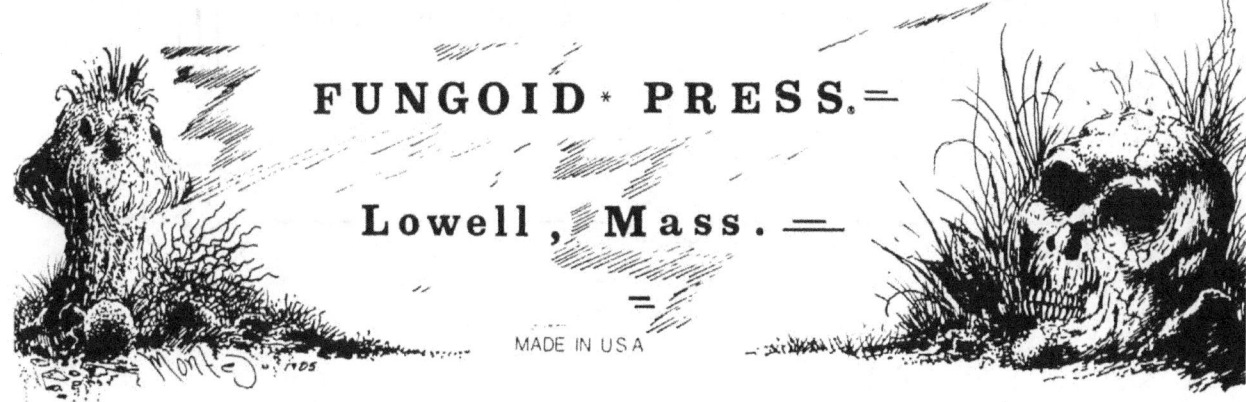

FUNGOID ⁕ PRESS.＝

Lowell , Mass. ＝

MADE IN U.S.A

Poetry

Art Pages

Alexis Comtois 37, 132
Joseph Wehrle, Jr 30
C.G. Porter/Gregorio Montejo 52

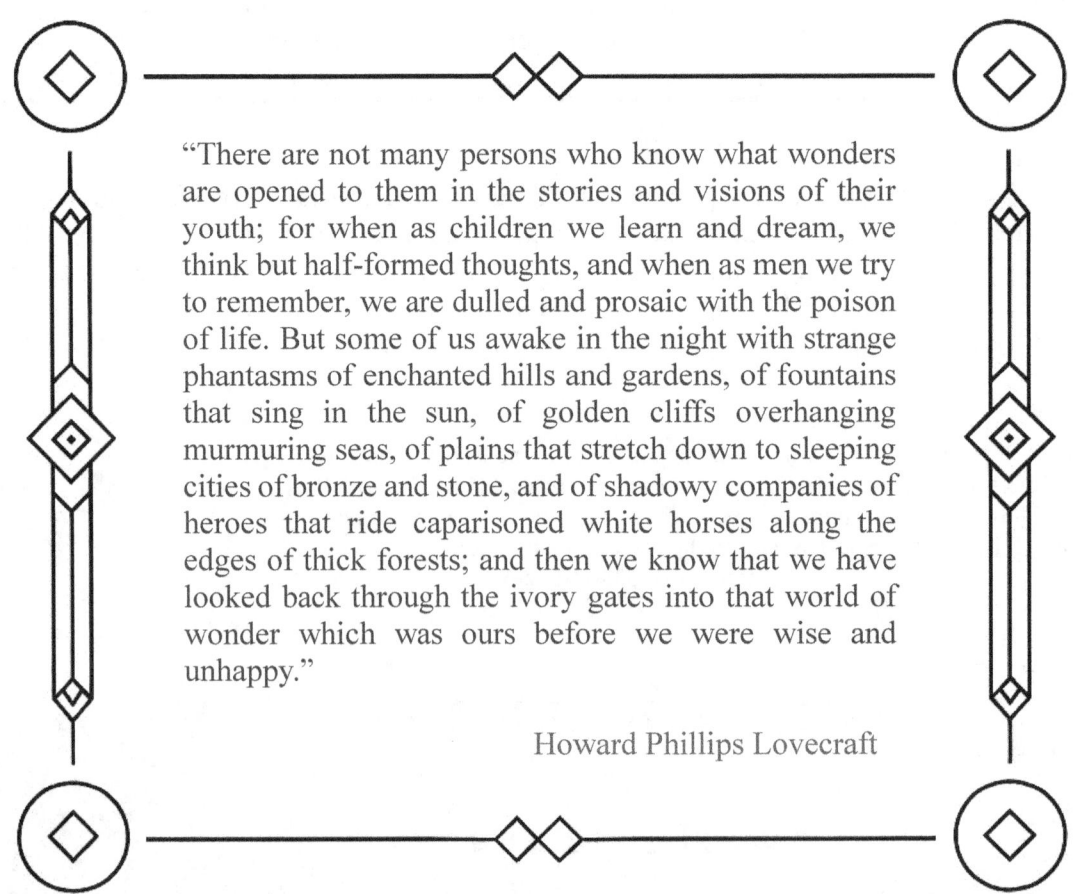

"There are not many persons who know what wonders are opened to them in the stories and visions of their youth; for when as children we learn and dream, we think but half-formed thoughts, and when as men we try to remember, we are dulled and prosaic with the poison of life. But some of us awake in the night with strange phantasms of enchanted hills and gardens, of fountains that sing in the sun, of golden cliffs overhanging murmuring seas, of plains that stretch down to sleeping cities of bronze and stone, and of shadowy companies of heroes that ride caparisoned white horses along the edges of thick forests; and then we know that we have looked back through the ivory gates into that world of wonder which was ours before we were wise and unhappy."

Howard Phillips Lovecraft

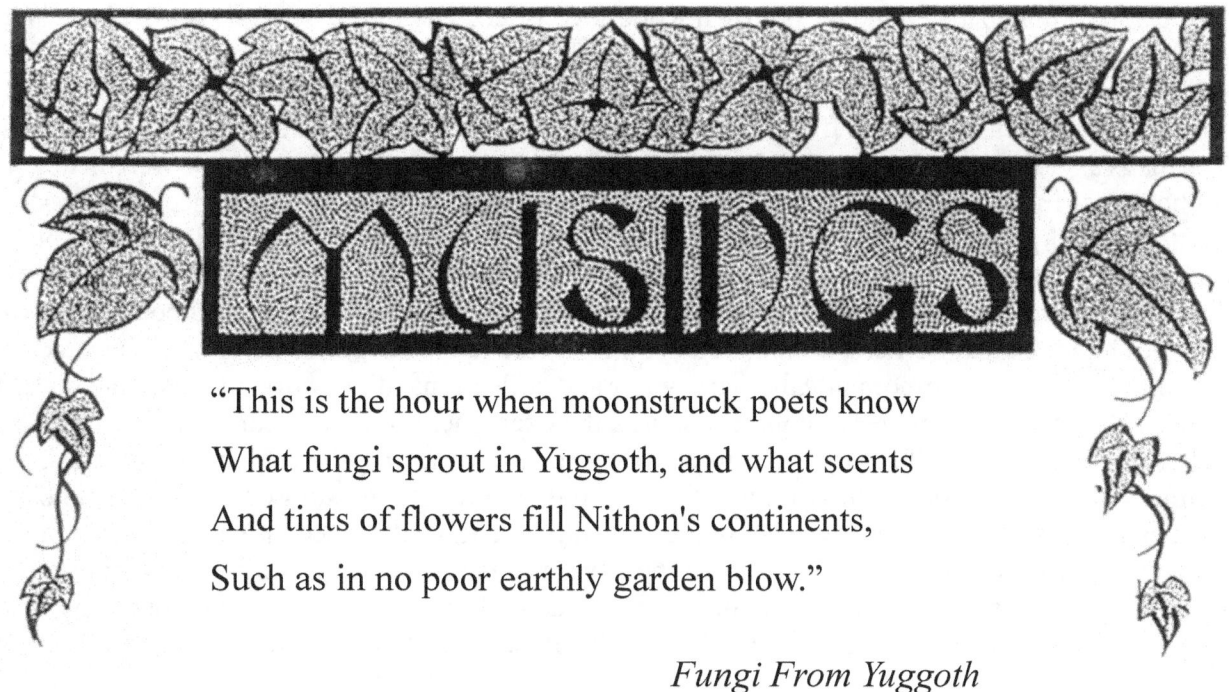

MUSINGS

"This is the hour when moonstruck poets know
What fungi sprout in Yuggoth, and what scents
And tints of flowers fill Nithon's continents,
Such as in no poor earthly garden blow."

Fungi From Yuggoth
By H.P. Lovecraft

Pierre V. Comtois
Editor/publisher

C. George Porter
Associate publisher/layout editor

Henry J. Vester III
Associate publisher

Welcome to *Fungi*'s 25th issue! The number is deceptive as it seems to suggest 25 years of continuous presentation of the best in new and classic horror, fantasy, and weird fiction and accompanying non-fiction articles, but actually the number covers forty *years* of publication, having been launched in 1984! And in part to celebrate that milestone, this issue of *Fungi* is dedicated to H.P. Lovecraft's alien cosmogeny, the Cthulhu Mythos. Now, some of you long time readers will wonder, "Why not a new issue of Fungoid Press' *Chronicles of the Cthulhu Codex*?" To which we reply: Good question! It was considered, but in the end the decision was made to stick with *Fungi* and allow the venerable *Codex* to rest in peace. It was just simpler to keep *Fungi* rolling along with all the latest self publishing tools now available that have made the last half dozen issues such good looking products.

So, once the decision was made to spotlight the Cthulhu Mythos, we were overcome with a rush of nostalgia for the subject, recalling those halcyon days of the early 1970s when an avalanche of Lovecraft's writings seemed to flood the paperback bookstalls. Ballantine Books included his Dunsanian fantasies in its Adult Fantasy Series, then the same company issued all of Lovecraft's remaining fiction in a series of reprints that also included two volumes gathering stories by his "disciples" who followed in his footsteps to dabble in the Mythos. After that, Ballantine also issued reprints of Arkham House volumes that included more work by such disciples as Clark Ashton Smith, Robert E. Howard, Frank Belknap Long, and especially August Derleth. Then, somewhere amid all that, Lin Carter published his *A Look Behind the Cthulhu Mythos.* All of which brought our initial interest in Lovecraft to a fever pitch. Things remained quiet for a while after that, with only Arkham House offering new material involving the Mythos until suddenly, late in the 1980s, Necronomicon Press was born and in addition to pamphlets collecting unpublished material from both Lovecraft and others, also began publishing the venerable *Crypt of Cthulhu* magazine edited by our own Robert M. Price. The long lasting *Crypt* evolved quickly from a thin pamphlet printing articles and occasional HPL pieces to thicker and thicker volumes that featured more and more Mythos oriented fiction both original and reprints from the full range of HPL disciples. But *Crypt* was not alone. It was quickly followed (or maybe in some cases, was joined) by such amateur mags as *Nyctalops, Haunts, Tekeli-li* and others (including *Fungi*!). Now those were heady times for Mythos fans! In fact, the *Fungi* staff at the time, journeyed to Providence, RI to meet Price and other contributors to *Crypt* (the "fun guys" from Yuggoth!) in a memorable visit that included a sightseeing tour of Lovecraft related sites including his burial place at Swan Point Cemetery. But all good things must end, and so did *Crypt* eventually, and again, it seemed that the sense of Lovecraft being everywhere fans looked, had receded. So here we are, nearly thirty years later. Lovecraft has finally been accepted by the literary world as an important American writer and collections of his work are available on Barnes & Noble store shelves as a matter of course, and yet, the excitement of those years in the 1970s and 80s has failed to be recaptured. The fight to win approval for Lovecraft has been won but, ironically, also taking much of the steam out of the Mythos. But as we mentioned at the start of this graph, a nostalgia for those early days of discovery overwhelmed us recently and thus, this special wayback issue of *Fungi* in which we hope to recapture the sense of fun the Mythos gave us in our youthful first exposure to the *Weird Tales* crew of writers. Yes, original tales in this issue will seek some new ground but hopefully the result won't be too far off the mark set by Lovecraft himself, while others will seek to capture more closely his style and approach, old houses with their moldering library of forbidden tomes and all. In short, it's all an effort to reach back to that primal time when Lovecraft and his work was reintroduced to the general reading public by Ballantine Books. If we've succeeded or failed, you'll have to be the judge!

And while you're doing that, here's another question to consider: Should all Mythos stories keep within the status quo established by Lovecraft? That is, should they be allowed make fundamental changes to the established Mythos "universe" that might forever alter the paradigm established by HPL? For instance, what if a story took a key Lovecraft invented element (whether a town such as Kingsport or an Old One such as Cthulhu) and blew it up so it could never be used again by future writers concerned with keeping their stories within the "timeline" established by Lovecraft? An event that would seem to be irreversible and one future stories would, if they were to continue the pattern set by HPL and his disciples, need to accept if the unfolding history of Lovecraft's "universe" were to continue in a single, linear direction? If this unwritten rule established by Lovecraft and his disciples in the early days of the Mythos (and somewhat picked up following generations of writers through the 1960s or so) were to be ignored, that linear history would be shattered and the Mythos legendry would enter an unfamiliar landscape and altered forever. One unsatisfying result might be the rise of "retro" stories that take place before the unalterable events (such as the destruction of Dunwich) thus freezing the Mythos forever in a pre-disaster time frame say, the twentieth century instead of moving forward to stories set in the 21st.

Seemingly catastrophic events were handled by HPL and his disciples in a way that the status quo ante was usually reestablished. For instance, Cthulhu might rise and menace hapless seamen but would eventually return to his prison without invading the mainland and causing untold and irreversible havoc. The reefs off Innsmouth could be dynamited, but Innsmouth would remain unharmed. The Old Ones, in short, would never rise and return to rule the Earth no matter the close shaves.

However, some stories have not done that. Perhaps the reader who doesn't want to accept the destruction of some basic Lovecraftian element might just imagine the story taking place in an alternate universe from that of the Mythos as established by HPL and his disciples? As such, it wouldn't violate the existing Lovecraft universe of which that element might form an important piece. If the idea behind such drastic stories is allowed to stand, then the internal logic, the progression of the history of the Mythos universe from that point onward, would be undermined and invite future confusion making it more difficult to decide which stories fit into Lovecraft's perception of a Mythos timeline and which might not.

Lovecraft himself never got around to tying his Mythos stories together into a coherent whole. He died before he could get along far enough to concern himself with a formal organization of his Mythos-verse with timelines, do's and don'ts etc., but he might have eventually. First string disciple, August Derleth, took it upon himself to do what Lovecraft might have done if he had had the time: putting it all together with Old Ones being trapped on Earth by Elder Gods following a war between the two sides. Derleth, we feel, was on the right track, at least in trying to bring order to Lovecraft's scattered tales and providing an outline upon which future contributors to the Mythos could hang their tales. Thus, the most effective and satisfying Mythos tales are those that remain within Derleth's framework. Stories that blow up part of that framework threaten the coherence of the Mythos universe and the literary milieu in which future tales can be laid.

That said, check out the contributions this issue by newcomer Arnden Christopher whose tales seem to postulate a major event in the Derleth/HPL Mythos that nevertheless ends with the status quo ante or at least a question mark. Does he succeed in having it both ways? You can decide for yourself, but for us, it works!

For us, as youngsters discovering the Mythos for the first time in the early 70s, the idea of a shared universe among multiple writers across the years, was a fascinating one. And even if a story only dropped a name or title of a book from another story it was enough in our minds to qualify it as belonging to the shared Mythos universe. Stories that might lie on either side of the equation described above are included in this special edition of *Fungi*. It will be up to the reader to decide for himself which to include in his personal idea of the Lovecraftian timeline.

On another, less academic, but no less effecting note, is this issue's special spotlight on interviews with classic authors conducted over the years by the *Fungi* staff. All have some connection with either Lovecraft, the Cthulhu Mythos, or one of his first disciples but as you'll see, these aspects were mostly de-emphasized at the time in favor of less discussed aspects of the authors' writing careers. A sad fact that binds them all, including E. Hoffman Price, Robert Bloch, Fritz Lieber, and Robert Elder, is that for most, if not all, these interviews were the last that were ever given.

We realize also with some sadness how few of the names mentioned by the interviewees were of people who are still with us. The *Weird Tales* group of writers including Clark Ashton Smith, H.P. Lovecraft, Robert E. Howard, Henry S. Whitehead, and Ray Bradbury of course, but also HPL disciples such as August Derleth, Frank Belknap Long, and Donald Wandrei. Lesser lights among the SF community mentioned include L. Sprague de Camp, Lester del Rey, Harlan Ellison, Terry Carr, and Clifford Simak. Coupled with the virtual disappearance of their collective work from book store shelves and thus from the culture itself, we can't help feeling that we've now entered a post fantasy lit era, where the institutional memory of the genre is fading if not already gone.

We are all the more proud to re-present our interviews here, scattered as they were over past issues of *Fungi,* all in one place.

As usual, this special issue of *Fungi* presents a healthy mix of fiction and non-fiction.

Also as usual, our list of writers includes both familiar names (including contributions by each of the original Fungi staff and editors emeritus) and new ones.

All of this beneath a wonderfully nostalgic cover image by the great Gervasio Gallardo executed for Ballantine Books' 1971 edition of HPL's *The Doom That Came to Sarnath.* Check out our tribute to Gallardo this issue, represented from issue #19 of *Fungi.*

Postscript: Since penning the above Musings, the publisher/editor has had strong feelings that this issue of *Fungi* may indeed be the last. And while he is aware of the adage "never say never," a definite air of disinterest in the classic writers of the *Weird Tales* era has made putting together even this all Mythos issue of the magazine somewhat of a chore. Originally intended to be published in a quick turnaround after #24, it turned into a longer grind than intended. Looking around, the reason for the slowdown it seemed to the editor, was a definite cooling down of the once thriving interest in the *Weird Tales* authors.

When *Fungi* was first launched, those authors were at their apogee with seemingly everything they wrote being issued in popular paperbacks and what was left, in small press books from such venues as Arkham House. Over the years, that availability has dried up. To be sure, much of it can be found on Ebay or Amazon Marketplace, but the level of enthusiasm that drove original research, discovery and publishing of rare or newly discovered writings, seems to have disappeared. Certainly, among *Fungi*'s founding members and regular contributors, the interest in new issues just doesn't seem to be there. And though the interest continues undimmed on the part of ye editor, the work in producing new issues of *Fungi* has become increasingly difficult when new material is not forthcoming. Thus, sadly, we must bid adieu to perhaps fandom's longest running amateur magazine, at least for the foreseeable future. Much thanks, of course, to all those who have contributed their creative energies to the magazine over the years or who have purchased a copy or twain along the way. For ye editor at least, the last 45 years have been a blast!

List of Contributors

Pierre V. Comtois is a former newspaper reporter writing from Lowell, MA who has been editing and publishing *Fungi, the Magazine of Fantasy and Weird Fiction* intermittently since 1984. Comtois' book *Goat Mother and Others* was released in 2015 by Chaosium Fiction. *Marvel Comics in the Early 1960s: An Issue by Issue Field Guide to a Pop Culture Phenomenon* was published in 2024 by Twomorrows Pubs. Earlier volumes include *Marvel Comics in the 1960s, 1970s* and *1980s*. In addition, Comtois has contributed fiction to many small press magazines over the years including *Haunts, The Horror Show, Thrilling Tales*, and e magazines such as *Planetary Stories*. Comtois' fiction has also appeared in various magazines for Cryptic Publications and Rainfall Books as well as such collections as *Lin Carter's Anton Zarnak: Supernatural Sleuth, Eldritch Blue,* and various Chaosium Books anthologies. The author has also written a number of books including novels such as *Strange Company* and *Sometimes a Warm Rain Falls*; non-fiction such as *Our Lives, Our Fortunes, Our Sacred Honor*; and short story collections such as *The Way the Future Was, The Portable Pierre V. Comtois, Different Futures,* and *Autumnal Tales*. Novels include *Scheduled for Extinction*, Desert Breeze Press (2018), and from Rogue Phoenix Press *Talismanic* (2018), *Extra Galaxia* (2019), *Novus Intelligens* (2019) and *Solve Gorgoni* (2023). Comtois has also found the time to contribute non-fiction articles to such magazines as *World War II, America's Civil War, Wild West,* and *Military History* which have been collected in *Hazardous History*. Sons of Liberty Press released *River Muse: Stories of Lowell and the Merrimack Valley* in 2011 to which Comtois has contributed a personal recollection entitled "I Was a Teenaged Bibliophile." More about Comtois can be found at www.pierrevcomtois.com

Dale Nelson, a longtime *Fungi* contributor, writes for *Beyond Bree,* a monthly Tolkien newsletter, and is the designated reviewer and columnist for *CSL: The Bulletin of the New York C. S. Lewis Society*. His work appeared in all nine issues of William Breiding's acclaimed fanzine *Portable Storage*, and he is a columnist for the lively online Arthur Machen site, Darkly Bright, operated by Christopher Tompkins.

David Daniel was born in Boston and now makes his home in the Merrimack Valley. He is author of many novels and story collections, including the prize-winning Alex Rasmussen private eye series set in Lowell (*The Heaven Stone, The Skelly Man, Goofy Foot,* and *The Marble Kite,* all from St. Martin's Press). His newest book, a collection of stories, is *Beach Town*, from Loom Press. He contributes essays and reviews to the *Boston Globe,* the https://artsfuse.org/and richardhowe.com. Contact him at daviddaniel67@gmail.com.

Robert M. Price, a fan of H.P. Lovecraft since the appearance of the Lancer paperback collections of 1967, began writing scholarly articles and humorous pieces on HPL and the Cthulhu Mythos in 1981. His celebrated semi-pro zine *Crypt of Cthulhu* began as a quarterly for the Esoteric Order of Dagon Amateur Press Association in 1981 and made it to an amazing 109 issues. In 1990 he edited a number of Mythos anthologies for Chaosium, Inc which also released a collection of his own fiction entitled *Blasphemies and Revelations*. A five-volume annotated edition of the fiction of H.P. Lovecraft is scheduled to be published by the author's own company, Exham Priory. The author also continues to issue new volumes to *Lin Carter's Flashing Swords* anthologies.

Henry J. Vester III, now retired from a career as a family therapist, lives in a crumbling shack in the high desert region of southern Oregon, where he communes nightly with the bats and coyotes. Long associated with *Fungi Magazine*, Vester has participated in interviews with such grandmasters as Fritz Leiber and E. Hoffman Price. The latter interview, translated into human glyphs by Gregorio Montejo, appeared in *The Book of the Dead* published by Arkham House. Besides appearing in *Fungi* and *Chronicles of the Cthulhu Codex*, the author's work has also been anthologized in *The Tsathoggua Cycle* and *The Innsmouth Cycle*, both released through Chaosium, in Rainfall Books' *Lost Worlds of Space and Time*, and (in collaboration with Ron Hilger) in *The Averoigne Legacy* from Pickman's Press.

Gregorio Montejo hails from the wilds of Minnesota by way of Florida and Massachusetts. A founding member of the *Fungi* editorial team, Montejo submitted countless stories, essays, and poetry to the magazine in all its incarnations but it is his art by which most in the fan community know him. Besides his many interior illustrations for *Fungi* and other small press magazines, the artist exceeded himself when he took up the paintbrush and executed a half dozen masterpieces for the covers of late edition *Fungis*. In books, his iconographic illustrations have appeared in *The Nightmare Factory, Lifting, and Prayer Wheels of Bluewater* as well as numerous covers for the Pulphouse Short Story Collection.

H.P. Lovecraft (1890-1937) lived most of his life in Providence, Rhode Island from which he drew much of the inspiration for stories of horror and the macabre. While most of his stories appeared initially in *Weird Tales* magazine, they also were featured in a number of small press publications. Though Lovecraft wrote many stand alone stories, it was those that fell within an invented cosmogony of alien beings intent on taking over the earth (known as the Cthulhu Mythos) that is his main claim to fame and the source of his enduring popularity among readers.

Alexis Strickland Comtois was born and raised in Florida. She has a love for all things art, with an emphasis on music and drawing. Her love for drawing began when her parents bought her the BIG box of crayons...you know the one. She finds her happy place in that spot where the lead touches the paper and finds that the world disappears when she's there. She has drawn everything from portraits and animals to still lifes and ships and everything in between. Ever the self critic, she pursues a beauty in her work that has to be seen to believe. Instagram.com/strictlysketchworks

Colleen Drippe lives in Kansas while indulging in several eccentricities including writing. She has had several children's books published, and several SF novels including *Godcountry, Gelen, Tree Light, Sunrise On the Ice Wolf* and *Vessel of Darkness*. Finally, Drippe has contributed many short stories and articles to various magazines and has been past editor of *Hereditas Magazine*.

Lin Carter (1930-1988) was a fan of science fiction and fantasy who made good. His name was a familiar one among the letter columns of early pulp magazines before he began writing himself. Influenced greatly by the likes of Robert E. Howard and Edgar Rice Burroughs, he unabashedly wrote numberless volumes in their style including his own barbarian warrior, Thongor. But it was in his role as anthologizer that he perhaps made his biggest and most original impact. In 1969, he began to edit the Ballantine Adult Fantasy Series bringing little known fantasists of the past to the attention of modern readers. In 1980, he also edited a number of volumes in a revived *Weird Tales* paperback. Carter's overall contribution to the SF and fantasy genre is inestimable.

R.J. Zimmerman writes from Dracut, MA and is an award winning Community Media Manager by day. One of the culprits that were in on *Fungi Magazine* from the start, the author was bitten early in life by the vampiric lore of *Weird Tales* and anything else that smacked of the classic era of horror lit. A yen for film studies, 60's psychedelic and garage rock, and assorted pop-culture ephemera has been tempered in recent years by an adoring wife and a trio of impish daughters. Luckily however, the two are not mutually exclusive allowing R.J. the occasional outlet for the once in a decade weird yarn or non-fiction piece.

Andrew M. Seddon is a retired urgent care physician who now calls Florida home after living in Montana for many years. With his wife Olivia, a veterinarian, he enjoys training his German Shepherd Baltasar, hiking and running marathons (knees permitting), and writing, for which there never seems to be enough time. Besides non-fiction articles and essays on various subjects, he is attracted to multiple genres, including science fiction, historical fiction, and supernatural/weird fiction which can be found in his books *What Darkness Remains*, *In Death Survive*, *The Deadliest Sins*, and *Tales From the Brackenwood Ghost Club*. *Bonds of Affection* and *Ranger's First Call* benefit German Shepherd rescues,and he edited the anthology *Wolf Wanderings* to benefit wildlife conservation.

Clark Ashton Smith (1893-1961) was a major poet and fantasist of the twentieth century with ties to California poet George Sterling. Smith, however, made his greatest impact not with his association with Sterling but with H.P. Lovecraft. Impressed by Smith's poem *Emperor of Dreams*, Lovecraft encouraged him to contribute to Weird Tales Magazine and together with Lovecraft and Robert E. Howard, became a favorite with readers producing scores of short fantasies stories of bejeweled detail. His unique style could never be mistaken for anyone else's.

Joseph Wehrle, Jr. (1941-2017) was, for several decades, an illustrator for such publications as *Galaxy Magazine, Worlds of If, Vampirella,* and the journal of Robert E. Howard studies, *Two-Gun Raconteur.* His cover art has graced publications from Arkham House, Mirage Press, and Hippocampus Press, among others. He was a master of the pen-and-ink technique of stippling, and much of his work is considered by many to be equal to that of Virgil Finlay and Lawrence Sterne Stevens. His most recent efforts have appeared in *Digest Enthusiast*, from Larque Press.

Arnden Christopher writes from the great state of Texas and has been a great fan of the Mythos since his teens. After a stint in the Navy and rereading many of Lovecraft's stories while serving on the USS Ashland, he was fired up to try his hand at some fanfic. His two submissions in this issue of *Fungi* are the result.

Beyond the Fields We Know:
An Appreciation of Gervasio Gallardo

by Pierre V. Comtois

No literary genre identifies itself with particular artists or illustrators as do those of science fiction and fantasy. And even in science fiction there are not that many, with only Frank R. Paul in the pulp era and perhaps Vincent di Fate and Kelly Freas in the paperback years. Fantasy, on the other hand, has had many, from J. Arthur St. John and Roy Krenkel (associated with Edgar Rice Burroughs) to Frank Frazzeta (Robert E. Howard's Conan) toVirgil Finlay (illustrator for *Weird Tales*) to Murray Tinkelman (with Matheson and Lovecraft). But of all these great talents, one artist stands out from the crowd, not simply by virtue of his unique talent, but by the very nature of his approach to fantasy.

Gervasio Gallardo never intended to become a straight fantasy artist. As a matter of fact, he began his career with an eye to fine art and only later found himself in the commercial art field. Born in Barcelona in 1934, Gallardo learned the rudiments of his craft and received his first assignments in the advertising field in his native Spain before going to Munich in 1959. Later, moving on to Paris, he found work there with the Delpire Advertising Agency for four years. Finally, in 1963, he made it across the Atlantic and arrived in the United States. Returning off and on over the next few years, Gallardo displayed his work in an occasional exhibition.

But this brief outline of Gallardo's career barely suggests the wonder and sheer imaginative power that would justly earn him a place among the great illustrators forever associated with the literary heritage of Western fantasy.

Even early in his career as an advertising artist, Gallardo refused to rein in his sometimes outré tastes and bizarre visions. Looking at some of his work in that period, one can only wonder and admire the courage of agencies (never mind their clients!) who accepted and used Gallardo's work which often included such recurring motifs as oversized eyes, human figures with the heads of birds or animals and weird, juxtaposed imagery such as a moonscape with dead butterflies, an insect eyed woman with butterfly net, a still life with body parts or creatures assembled with parts from different animals. But if his "public" work was strange, his "private" work, the pieces of art executed for his own pleasure, were even more far out. But no matter how surrealist his work became, it almost always remained grounded in some measure of reality with the artist's almost constant use of such common elements as flowers, fish, birds and other wildlife (even if their species and phylums remained unfamiliar to earthly botanists and zoologists!)

And so, Gallardo's distinctive style was firmly established by the time he was commissioned by Betty Ballantine to execute covers for her new line of paperbacks reprinting the classics of western fantasy. The Ballantine Adult Fantasy Series, which was to be edited by writer Lin Carter, was intended to take advantage of the growing boom for fantasy fiction generated by the unprecedented sales success of J. R. R. Tolkien's *Lord of the Rings* trilogy. In providing his share of covers for the line (which he executed from sketches prepared by Ballantine art director Robert Blanchard), Gallardo joined a handful of other imaginative artists that included Robert LoGrippo and Bob Pepper. But very soon, it was left in no question as to which artist's style was emerging as the line's definitive look.

"Very rapidly a Gallardo painting on a cover became a signature which fantasy fans recognized immediately," Betty Ballantine herself confirmed.

Among Gallardo's contributions to the Adult Fantasy Series were his extraordinary group of paintings illustrating the work of nineteenth century fantasiste William Morris. Wonderfully capturing Morris' medieval settings that never were, Gallardo brought just the right feeling of idle solitude to the hills of waving grass and distant trees dim in summer haze of *The Wood Beyond the World*; the meticulous detail of the fairy-land city on the cover of *The Sundering Flood*; the fatalistic otherworldliness of *The Well Beyond the World* and the strange, yearning beauty of *TheWater of the Wondrous Isles*.

For three collections of the short stories and poetry of Lord Dunsany, Gallardo seemed to have created a triptych of views from what might have been the same town as he takes the long view with *Over the Hills and Far Away*, the middle view in *Beyond the Fields We Know* and the close up of the very odd *Charwoman's Shadow*.

Another set of covers seem to show Gallardo still up to his old tricks of juxtaposing contrasting images as he does with the cover of G. K. Chesterton's *The Man Who Was Thursday* by having two gentlemen face each other as an oncoming train descends from the air between them. For *Great Short Novels of Adult Fantasy Vol. II,* a naked man rides on the back of a sea serpent and on the cover of George McDonald's *Evenor*, a winged fish takes flight. And what is the reader to make of the cover for *Great Short Novels of Adult Fantasy I* with its group of dwarves in the process of tucking a beautiful princess into their tree-trunk hideout?

The Ballantines must have been impressed with Gallardo's work on the Adult Fantasy Series, because they also managed to press him into service illustrating a set of paperback reprints of the work of H.P. Lovecraft. For these, Gallardo seemed to abandon all connection with reality and allowed his fertile imagination to run free. And so, unburdened by the constraints of reality (and apparently, of editorial control!) Gallardo proceeded to fill an elliptical cover layout with the most ghastly and grotesque inventions of his career.*The Spawn of Cthulhu* in particular

Gallardo's cover for Lord Dunsany's *The Charwoman's Shadow*

presents a menagerie of creatures as hideous and disturbing as anything found in Lovecraft's prose including a thorned plant adorned with human mouths; strange, filamented crabs, men with heads (adorned with medusa-like hair) too large for their undersized bodies and ghostly, mournful visages of the dead. For the cover of *The Survivor and Others*, a giant bird creature soars over a town with a naked body in its beak as vague, furtive figures flee in panic far below. And for Lin Carter's *Lovecraft: A Look Behind the Cthulhu Mythos*, reptilic creatures with avian style heads gnaw hungrily at bones in a graveyard even as bat-winged reptiles flitter past the moon and amorphic, rugose trees bend menacingly toward a nearby village.

Over the course of a few short years, Gallardo had launched himself from the anonymous world of advertising and the relatively rarified community of art dealers and buyers to the much wider circle of fantasy enthusiasts who lived wherever mass marketed paperbacks reached. But although Gallardo had success in the wake of his stint on the Adult Fantasy Series, creating paintings for such other markets as magazine publishing and record album covers, he soon retired to his native Spain to devote himself to more personal work.

There he remains today, continuing to unleash the weird fantasies of his ever-active mind, translating visions of the bizarre and the wonderful into mundane oil and acrylic for himself and the occasional connoisseur of the fantastic. But for all his accomplishments away from the literary field, it will be the evocative, visual doorways into the minds of writers such as Morris, Dunsany, MacDonald, Smith and Lovecraft for which he will always be remembered with fondness and affection by fellow travelers along the byways of imagination and that will stand as the greatest monument to his unique vision.

Mother of a Thousand Young

by Pierre V. Comtois

Benny Easton unconsciously pressed down on the gas as he watched the speedometer display in the dash climb to 65, ten miles past the local speed limit. Outside the Acura's passenger side window, the setting sun was just touching the top of a distant tree line. Around him on the lonely stretch of road, the forest crowded close to the shoulders, the trees towering overhead. The last streetlight had been back a few miles just outside the small town where he had stopped to gas up. When night finally fell, the only illumination would be from his own headlights and luminous strips of paint that divided the road and marked the shoulders.

Hunched forward toward the steering wheel, peering ahead for signs that would tell how far he had yet to go, he began biting a fingernail, but he'd already bitten it down as far as it would go. He'd been a confirmed city boy for a long time now and being back in the country, where streetlights ended and there was no reassuring glow of home lights twinkling among the trees for miles at a time, made him nervous. Was there a name for what he felt about the woods? Arachnophobia? Chemophobia? How about agoraphobia? Wasn't that the fear of open spaces? Was that it? He thought about it some more. Determining exactly what it was that he feared he decided agoraphobia wasn't quite it. In fact, he doubted there *was* a name for what he

feared. Because what had induced it, he was sure, was not anything in human experience so how could it be measured? Tabulated? Indexed?

Thinking about it, he began to shake again. His heart began to race. Deliberately, he leaned back in his seat and forced himself to calm down. It was why he'd moved to the city all those years ago. The bigger the city the better so he moved to the biggest one of all, New York. And to make sure he had an excuse never to leave it, he refused to own a car. In fact, he wouldn't have left the city earlier today if it hadn't been an emergency. His mother was dying and his siblings had insisted that this time, he had to leave and come back home to be at her side. He couldn't think of an excuse not to so ended up renting the Acura and hitting the road northward.

Now, with increasing trepidation, he found himself exactly where he vowed never to be again: out in the middle of nowhere with nothing but the trees for company. Again, he looked over and saw that the sun was lower in the sky and clouds farther off had a pinkish, purplish tinge. The sight took his mind back twenty years, to the time he was a senior at Dean's Corners Public High School…

That summer, he'd taken a job as a farm hand for old man Janders. His chores weren't anything he liked and in fact, consisted of the very things he wanted to get away from after he graduated:

slopping the hogs, baling hay, and getting up at the crack of dawn to milk the cows. But then, if he hadn't got up early on those mornings, he might have missed seeing Becca Stansfield. Even in his nervous state, a smile creased Benny's lips at the recollection. Becca was a college girl having entered Arkham University only that year and was a real looker! She had long, wavy hair the color of corn tallow and a perfect figure that made the halter top and cut off jeans she frequently wore look like a part of her. No doubt, Becca had grabbed his attention but good and he found himself seeking opportunities to see her as much as he could. Which weren't that many what with old Janders keeping him as busy as he did.

But now and then, he glimpsed her moving about the barnyard next door or in town where he met his friends a couple nights a week.

"Whoosh! Wouldn't mind getting' some of that action," said Curly Devens upon seeing Becca pass by the Breakfast Muffin Shop where the gang often gathered to shoot the breeze.

"Becca Stansfield?" asked Joey Dorp. "Dream on!"

"Don't think I could make it with her?" challenged Curly.

Joey snorted. "Ya think? Everybody in town knows how stuck up she is. And ever since she was accepted at Arkham, she's had her nose higher in the air than the tips of her boobs."

The others around the table all laughed at the joke, including Curly. No one noticed that Benny had not.

He was surprised at himself when he felt a bit of resentment at Curly's initial interest. Was he becoming interested himself? He knew Becca as well as the others and up until this summer, would have agreed with Joey's estimation of Becca. After all, Dean's Corners was small enough that every kid in town knew every other. And of course, Benny had known Becca from afar for years. Known her enough to have agreed with Joey's appraisal of her inaccessability. Still, this summer, his last in Dean's Corners he hoped, seemed to give him a different perspective.

Wondering where she was headed that morning, Benny made some excuse to his pals and left the cafe. Outside, he casually turned and walked in the direction Becca had gone, hoping none of the guys would notice. Reaching the corner, he caught sight of her as she rounded the next. She was wearing a short, flouncy summer dress that showed off a lot of leg and excited Benny deep in his gut. On her feet, she wore a pair of white sandals and closer examination revealed that her toenails hadn't been painted. Catching up to the corner around which Becca had disappeared, he peeked around and saw that she was just rounding the next one further up. Intrigued now, he dashed to that corner and looked after her again, admiring her retreating figure. At the third corner, she turned again.

Wonder where she's going? Benny asked himself.

Sure that she would enter one of the little shops that lined the street, he reached the next corner and was surprised to see that she hadn't stopped but turned again onto the street that would lead her past the Breakfast Muffin.

"Huh?" said Benny aloud.

More interested now in what Becca was doing than in Becca herself, Benny watched and this time didn't bother to stay out of sight. He stood there looking after Becca but she passed the cafe and continued on to the distant corner, rounding it again.

Benny hurried after her and at the corner, observed her following the same route she'd just finished. Over the next half hour, she walked the entire block four more times, neither looking into shop windows nor bothering with traffic on the roads.

Benny was perplexed. Had she been out for a day's constitutional of some kind? If so, she could have picked a better location to take a walk. There were a number of walking trails close by. Maybe she was frightened about walking in the woods by herself? Possible, but Benny didn't recall problems of that nature in the past. Girls were always running or walking dogs or somesuch along the trails. And like most girls in Dean's Corners, Becca was country born and raised. The countryside should have held no dread for her.

By the time Becca had completed her perambulations, the boys had left the cafe so Benny decided to make himself scarce. The next few days were bright and sunny keeping him busy at his job but Friday it rained. After milking the cows, Mr. Janders gave him the afternoon off.

After touching base at home, he wandered downtown to see what action he could dig up. He was still trying to hunt up any of the gang when he caught sight of Becca on the town common. At first, he wasn't sure it was her: she was bundled up against the rain with a hood pulled over her head. He debated whether he should go up to her and say hi, sort of break the ice between them but thought better of it. He was only a high school senior after all and she a college student. Better to bide his time and wait for just the right moment.

As before however, he couldn't help watching her, so he did so...discreetly. Pulling up the collar of his coat and pulling his hat down tight over his ears, he drifted over to the common and rushed up the stairs to the little bandstand at the center. Sheltered from the rain, he could follow Becca's movements in relative comfort. She was sitting on one of the park benches facing the town hall for some time which by itself struck Benny as odd. It was raining after all and that bench was soaked and yet there she was sitting there, looking straight ahead the way she did the other day when she walked around and around the block. Suddenly, she stood and began walking slowly along the sidewalk to the north side of the common where she sat down on a bench there. Now Benny was interested. Was she waiting for someone? Patiently, he waited to see what she'd do next, but nothing happened. She just sat there. He took out his cell and checked the time. So far as he could tell, she'd sat there for about a quarter of an hour without moving a muscle. He glanced around the park...no one around. Just the two of them. Then there was movement. Becca had risen and began to walk along the edge of the common until reaching the next bench facing east. Again she sat down. Again she sat rigidly, staring ahead. Benny guessed she'd be there for a good twenty minutes and sure enough, when the time had come, she stood and walked to the next bench, the one facing south. It occurred to Benny that Becca had sat at four benches all corresponding to the four points of the compass. Did that mean anything? And had there been a similar pattern to her walking the other day? He tried to think what walking around the block four times could mean but his imagination failed him. Presently, after about twenty minutes, Becca stood up, crossed the street and headed in the direction of her father's farm. He followed at a distance to make sure. By the time he saw her enter the front gate, the rain was really coming down and with the closing of the kitchen door behind Becca, he turned and sprinted all the way home.

Another week had passed. Benny never bothered to tell the other guys what he'd seen Becca doing. How could he? He didn't know what she had been up to himself. Tired of their banter, he left them in front of Daugherty's Pharmacy and wandered down Main Street. Heading vaguely in the direction of home, he passed the high school and found the unpaved access road leading into the woods and up hill to the water tower. He considered walking all the way to the top and shrugged. Why not? He didn't want to go home and his mind continued to turn over thoughts of Becca in her cut off jeans, in a swimsuit, in his arms...his fantasies were interrupted by a sound. Not a typical sound of the woods, of a chipmunk scrambling in the brush or a woodpecker testing a tree, a sound unnatural to the surroundings. A metallic sound, as if someone were mounting the iron ladder that went up the side of the water tower. It wasn't a sound he was unaccustomed to. Kids in town had always dared one another to climb to the top of the tower. In all probability, that was what was going on now.

He covered the last few yards of the access road as the tower loomed overhead; its spindly metal legs holding up the big tank high overhead. Benny's eyes found the ladder and followed it up to the top. No one in sight. Whoever it was must have reached the top already. He moved over and started to back up, trying to get a better view of the summit.

Suddenly, he stopped.

That was no stupid kid up there, it was Becca!

Shading his eyes against the sun, Benny could see her plainly. She was wearing a T-shirt and shorts and standing free in the direct center of the water tank...something that only the bravest of kids ever dared. There were no handholds there, no guard rails, nothing at all to grab hold of if you lost your balance. And yet, there she stood, bold and apparently unafraid. Her bare legs stood apart and she had raised her arms to the heavens. Benny didn't see if her lips were moving, but she definitely gave an impression of invocation, giving

Benny didn't see if her lips were moving, but she definitely gave an impression of invocation, giving the phrase "sun worshiper" a whole new meaning

the phrase "sun worshiper" a whole new meaning.

The whole experience was strange and vaguely frightful and kept Benny rooted to the spot, paralyzed as well as speechless. But he shook off the spell and decided to warn Becca to get off the tower hoping at the same time not to startle her and ending up being the cause of her falling instead of her rescue.

He started by giving her a little wave, to catch her attention. But it didn't work. She continued to hold her position, arms raised, eyes looking up to the sky.

"Becca," he called, in a low voice at first. It occurred to him that if he wanted to find a way to meet her, maybe this was it?

"Becca," he tried again, a little louder. But

clearly, she didn't hear him, or his voice just wasn't reaching her.

"Becca," he called, this time, loud enough that she couldn't ignore him. "Becca, come down from there. You might fall!"

That did it. She lowered her arms and stood there, at the apex of the tower, looking down at him. Through him. Then she turned and disappeared over the far edge of the tank, in the direction of the ladder. Presently, he heard the hollow metallic sounds of her descent.

But now that he'd finally drawn her attention, was about to meet her face to face, he found his belly filled with butterflies. What would he say to her? Should he introduce himself? That they'd shared a lit class last year when she was still a senior in high school and he a mere junior? No. Better not remind her of their age difference. In fact...where was she? She should have reached the bottom of the ladder and made her appearance by now.

Cautiously, Benny made his way around the hill to the base of the ladder. There was no one around. A narrow path, more a game trail than a path, opened at the edge of the clearing and he guessed that Becca must have slipped off in that direction. A feeling of disappointment came over him. Despite his nervousness about meeting her, he'd looked forward to the encounter. Now his chance was gone. He was back to square one. That, however, didn't change the facts of Becca's strange behavior. What had she been doing up there on the water tank? Should he mention it to anyone? Was it any of his business? But then, how would he feel if, in the course of a similar antic, she was hurt or worse? Could he live with the fact that he could have done something to prevent it and didn't? In the end, he chose the middle course: he would confront her about them and warn her that she could be hurt if she continued such dangerous stunts as climbing the water tower. *Yeah,* he thought, *that would be a perfect way to make contact with her!* And at the same time, express his concern. She was bound to be appreciative!

He was still in the positive mood his determination had put him in a few days later when he was finishing up his chores at Mr. Janders. The sun had gone down and dusk had settled over the farming community when he emerged from the barn, latching the doors behind him. As was his custom by that point, he looked over to the neighboring Stansfield place, hoping for a glimpse of Becca and got lucky. She was outside, having just finished butchering a number of chickens. She wore no cut offs or halter top now. Instead, to protect her from the often messy business, she'd donned a pair of worn overalls and long sleeved shirt. After depositing the newly slaughtered birds into a steamer, she washed her hands at a nearby water spigot before heading indoors.

On the spur of the moment, Benny decided to head right over and catch her before she could disappear inside. As he'd planned, he intended to remind her about the water tower and warn her about taking dares and endangering herself doing things of the sort.

Quickly, he ran to the split rail fence separating the two properties and just as he was about to call out, lost his balance and fell onto his face on the other side. Cursing, he rose to his feet, but now there was no sign of Becca.

Shoot!

Again, without much thought, he continued forward. Maybe she was still around. Suddenly a light went on at the back of the house and he instinctively gravitated in its direction. Unconsciously, he slowed, picking his footsteps with care. He knew what he was about to do was on the unethical side, let alone plain old ungentlemanly, but he couldn't resist.

He stopped in his tracks.

He could see inside the room with perfect clarity and with just as much clarity, could see Becca as she peeled off the overalls, stained with chicken blood.

And she didn't stop there.

Benny held his breath as she opened the shirt and prepared to shrug it off. Joey had been right in a way. She did have high breasts. High and tight. Benny forgot to breathe as she shed her panties and stood completely naked save for her socks. Then, somewhat belatedly, she went to the window and lowered the shade. Only then did Benny allow himself to breathe. She was every bit as beautiful as he always imagined. Maybe moreso! But even as he congratulated himself on his perspicacity, he noticed that Becca hadn't brought the shade all the way down. There still remained an inch or two gap between it and the sill. Benny licked his lips. His male hormones were up now, and he could no more resist looking than a moth could resist a flame.

Slowly, oh so slowly, his heart racing, he approached the window, his eyes wide. They grew even wider with what he saw in the room beyond. It was definitely a girl's room with its flowery wallpaper and frilly bed coverings, the vanity table and throw rug on the floor. The scattering of stuffed toys. But all that Benny took in without realizing it. What grabbed all his attention was Becca herself: still naked, still radiantly beautiful with her face framed in tumbles of blond hair as she casually balanced herself like a dancer, first on one foot then the other, and pulled off her socks. Bending over, she gathered her dirty clothes and walked out of the room. Presently, Benny saw another light come on in the corridor some place and guessed Becca was taking a shower.

He remained rooted to the spot, unable to tear himself away, hoping Becca would return so that he could feast his eyes on her some more. Sure enough, she came back, her damp hair evidence that she had indeed taken a shower. He continued to watch, not without feelings of guilt, as she dressed in clean clothes. She was putting on her sneakers when Benny heard the sound of a car pulling into the front yard.

Quickly, he ducked into the shadows as Becca left the room.

From somewhere, Benny heard car doors slamming shut and voices, all female, talking at the front door. Curious, he began moving in that direction when the group moved indoors and into the front parlor. There, the window was open and Benny paused to listen, curious.

"You're right on time," he heard Becca saying. "I just got out of the shower."

"Punctuality is a hallmark of Phi Omega Kappa," said one of two girls who had arrived in the car.

"We're happy to report that our observer confirmed that you performed all the required movements," said the other, whose voice Benny thought familiar.

"They weren't too hard to do," replied Becca. "Except maybe the one on the tower."

"They wouldn't mean anything if there wasn't some element of risk," said one of the girls. "Otherwise just anyone could get in to the sorority."

"And Phi Omega Kappa is the oldest, most exclusive sorority at Arkham," said the other.

"Which is why I'm anxious to join," said Becca.

So that was it! Now Benny thought Becca's strange behavior made sense. It was part of an initiation to get into this sorority at Arkham U!

"One problem though," said one of the other girls. "The observer noticed that you were being followed during some of your movements."

"I was?" There was a note of anxiety in Becca's voice. Did Benny inadvertently endanger her chances of getting into the sorority? "Who was it?"

"We asked around town and found out it was Benny Easton," said one of the girls. "He works next door at the Janders place. Know him?"

"Don't think so," said Becca to Benny's disappointment. But he was hardly thinking of that at the moment, more concerned that he'd been seen following Becca and even identified. He felt somewhat mortified now that Becca knew. What chance did he have with her now? His behavior would seem even more immature to her than his merely being in high school. Still, his being identified also alarmed him, made him more self conscious. Nervously, he looked around him, trying to pierce the surrounding dark. What if someone had been observing him all the time? Saw him at Becca's window? Now he really felt stupid! His immediate inclination was to slink away in shame, but curiosity once again seized him and he felt a desire to find out who the other two girls were who had identified him.

Reluctantly, Benny turned from the window and began making his way back to the Janders, thoughts of Becca dancing in his brain.

A few days later, he was still trying to figure out what to do about Becca and the whole initiation thing. He'd been looking over his shoulder ever since that night at the Stansfield place, wondering if someone was watching him even as he'd watched Becca through her window. Again, as he'd had almost every waking moment since, he envisioned Becca's naked form as she moved about her room and knew that while he wanted her more than ever, he was likely the farthest from ever having his dream fulfilled.

Just then, he was sitting in the Breakfast Muffin, drowning his frustrations in a large cappuccino when he recognized one of the sorority girls outside the window. She looked familiar and suddenly he had her: Jan, Janice Cordler! Her brother had been a star athlete at school some years ago and she had graduated right after him. That would have been about four years ago. Was it coincidence that the sorority girls who were in charge of Becca's initiation were also from Dean's Corners?

As Janice walked past the cafe, Benny made the instant decision to follow her. He had to know what was up with them. What more Becca needed to do to join their sorority.

Outside, he lingered in the doorway, peeking around its entrance alcove and catching sight of Janice as she continued down the block. Looking around to make sure that *he* wasn't being followed, Benny started walking. Soon, Janice had led him from the downtown area into a leafy residential neighborhood. She stopped in front of a house from which came the other girl he saw at Becca's. Was she from town too? If so, he didn't recognize her. Maybe she'd attended one of the two tony private schools in town. If she had, there was little likelihood that Benny would have known her. The public school students and those from the privates didn't mingle.

Now the two continued along the street as the distance between homes increased and farmland could be seen in the near distance. But they didn't go that far. Instead, they hopped a fence into open land belonging to the town's Conservation Commission. By the time Benny arrived at the spot, they'd disappeared into the woods. Luckily, however, they made no attempt to keep silent and he was able to follow them by the sounds they made.

He moved slowly so as not to make noise himself and breathed a sigh of relief when he fell into a trail. The girls' voices came from the direction leading away from the road so he moved cautiously after them. It had been near dusk when he spotted Janice from the Breakfast Muffin and by now the sun was fully down behind the surrounding trees. Benny had begun to wonder what the girls were doing in the woods at that time of day. Soon it would be dark, and the woods were no place for unaccompanied females, even in sleepy Dean's Corners. Nevertheless, they showed no sign of turning back but continued on deeper and deeper into the woods trending in a direction that Benny recognized as being unfrequented by local nature lovers.

What the heck?

Because of the increasing gloom, Benny had to slow down and watch each step he took in order to keep his silence. Ahead, the girls' voices diminished making it more difficult to judge where they were going or how close he might be approaching them. Suddenly, he sensed that he'd stepped into a clearing and quickly ducked back into the trail. Directly ahead, the two girls moved to the center of the clearing where others were waiting for them.

"You're just in time, the appointed hour approaches," said one of those who'd been waiting in the clearing.

"Is everyone here?" asked Janice. "The initiates?"

"Everyone's here," said another voice. "Or everyone who matters. I was able to recruit Samantha and Wanda from the Phi Omega Kappa house. They were the only ones staying there through the summer."

"No problem," replied Janice. "All we need is four made girls for the ceremony and we have five here."

"Becca, Constance, will you step over here, in the center of the Circle?"

From what Benny could make out in the gloom, lit only by a full moon overhead, the five "made girls" had assumed positions forming a rough circle into which Becca and another girl entered.

"Welcome to the inner Circle of Phi Omega Kappa," said Janice, who seemed to be the mistress of ceremonies. "The two of you have been privileged to join our sorority and learn its inner secrets which include the fact that it's a lot older than its association with Arkham U. The sorority's records, which you'll be privy to once you've been accepted, show that the children of Shub-Niggurath has existed for as long as there have been records in the state, and before that, the commonwealth of Massachusetts. Some sisters have speculated that it began with the local Indian tribes encountered by the first settlers but other evidence suggest it was the first settlers themselves that brought the knowledge from Europe where the tradition goes further back into pre-Christian times.

But whatever the case may be, the sisterhood goes on, as it ever has, in one form or another. I tell you all this in strictest confidence as you will be asked on your honor, whether ultimately chosen or not, to keep our secrets on pain of death. Do you agree?"

Becca and Constance looked at each other nervously before nodding their heads in affirmation.

"Good," approved Janice, apparently taking her office pretty seriously. "As you know, only one of you will be chosen to join us tonight. Both of you have performed the required movements which were a necessary precursor to tonight's ceremony."

Just then, there was the sound of a twig snapping but before Benny could turn to see what had caused it, he was struck from behind and fell unconscious. When he woke some minutes later and tried to rub his head, he found that couldn't. He was securely tied to the bole of a big tree, its rough bark digging into his back. He began to struggle, but the loops of rope holding him were too tight, the knot too well made. In fact, so tight were the cords that held him bound, he could hardly breathe.

Stupid, stupid, stupid! He thought to himself. How could he have allowed someone to sneak up behind him and conk him on the head? Who'd done it? Had one of the girls left the circle unnoticed? That must have been the answer because as he looked up in growing astonishment, he saw that there were the same number of girls gathered in the clearing; only now, Becca and Constance had both shed their clothes and stood like a pair of wood nymphs, their white skin glowing pale in the moonlight. Both lovely and otherworldly in attitude. To Benny, it seemed that they should have been garlanded in stars, blossoms at their feet.

But however he'd come to be tied up, the girls paid no attention to him. Instead, Janice read from a small, leather bound book she held in her hand.

"Becca, Constance, initiates both, having completed the required movements, do you freely and of your own choice agree to proceed with these ceremonies?" asked Janice.

"I do," Becca and Constance replied in unison.

Somehow, the whole thing struck Benny, never very religious himself, as being vaguely blasphemous. As not right. As being counter intuitive. That his adored Becca was participating in something that was far beneath her. Undignified.

That she was better than what this secret order was offering her. It was something he felt rather than articulate, something that prompted him to cry out, to tell her to stop, to step outside the Circle and reject the whole thing; but he couldn't. His tongue was as effectively frozen as if he were gagged.

"Then I'll proceed," Janice was saying. "The following words come to us down the centuries from the earliest made women whom we will never know but remain eternally thankful for preserving the Way and we, their inheritors, who continue to make sure the Link remains open and active against the day when the All-Mother will return in her glory and together with her offspring, Nug and Yeb, we'll see the rule of the Great Old Ones restored to the Earth!"

There were some general murmurings of ascent from the older girls forming the circle. Becca and Constance merely exchanged uncertain glances.

Did they know what was going on? Wondered Benny. Because it sure seemed to him that Janice and her fellows took what they were doing pretty seriously. Did they really believe all that stuff about their sorority being an extension of an age old cult? Tangentially, he recalled the stories kids in town had told each other about strange goings on in nearby Dunwich.

"I now read the opening passage taken from Chapter 12, canto 16 of the Necronomicon in hail to the All-Mother," Janice was saying. She began to read in singsong fashion: "Ever Their praises, and abundance to the Black Goat of the Woods. Iä! Shub-Niggurath!" Then louder: *"Iä! Shub-Niggurath! The Black Goat of the Woods with a Thousand Young!"*

The final lines were echoed by the other made girls who raised their arms to the sky as Janice continued to read from her book. But what she read proved incoherent to Benny, who failed to understand a single word. It wasn't English. Not even any recognizable language to his ear. Instead, it sounded like gibberish, the grunts and moanings of barnyard animals rather than sounds that could be uttered from a human throat.

Regardless, there was a reaction, or at least it seemed to be cause and effect to Benny as he noticed the air behind Becca begin to shimmer like a pool when the water is disturbed. Gradually, the disturbance became more agitated and the air began to stir, blowing Becca's blond locks about her head. She turned, mouth open in a soundless scream, as she looked at the disturbance. Did she see something there that Benny couldn't? Now Constance was shouting too as she took a step backward. Instinctively, she and Becca clasped hands in mutual support. Around them, the other girls stood, hair whipping about their heads and even Janice seemed to be taken aback.

Now the movement of the air increased and Benny could feel its pull even from his distance from the circle. He realized then that the wind wasn't blowing outward or around, but inward, toward the disturbance which had cleared so that he could see with disbelieving eyes that what was shown in the opening was not the woods that lay beyond it. It was like a doorway, a doorway to another place, another room, and in that room...Benny's tongue was finally loosened and he screamed, screamed like Becca and Constance had done and were doing as they struggled to keep themselves from being drawn into the opening.

And in that opening...Benny wanted desperately to turn away but couldn't...in that opening, was a thing; a monstrous thing that was indefinite in shape with eyes all over it and a hide that bubbled and rippled obscenely amid some shadowed, milky universe! He struggled to avert his eyes, but the thing held him mesmerized. Unconsciously, he pulled against his bonds...no use...as he tried to reach Becca, to pull her away from the thing.

"Behold! The Womb of the World!" shouted Janice in ecstasy as she reached her hands toward the thing. The other girls repeated what she said and lowered their arms to extend them instead toward the thing in the doorway. "One of you will be fortunate enough to be chosen by the All-Mother to join her in the Womb while the other is condemned to remain in this world! Choose Mother!"

Then, with horrible clarity, Becca began to be drawn to the doorway, screaming. This was clearly not what she thought would happen when she applied to join the sorority! Had she been lied to by the others? Or did she now regret her application when faced by the reality of the Mother? Her hand slipped from that of Constance and in a twinkling, she was gone! The last Benny had seen was her legs disappearing into the porous hide of the

Mother! He must have screamed then, shouted, struggled against his bonds, struck his head against the tree.

Dazed from hitting his head, it was a few moments before he could concentrate again and by that time, the attitude of Janice and the others had changed. The ceremony wasn't going as planned.

"No, Mother!" Janice was saying. "We did all as prescribed in the Book! We gave you the choice of two offerings! You've chosen one...no! No! It's not our fault! We caught him spying on us! We offer him to you!"

But whatever Janice meant by her words, seemed ineffectual as the reverse wind increased and first Constance was sucked into the doorway and then, before any of the others could move, a pair of hideous creatures oozed from the opening. A horrible stench filled the air and Benny couldn't keep himself from gagging. The things had no definable shape but changed and ovulated according to some internal logic of their own. Meanwhile, the girls had broken their circle. Janice's panic was contagious.

"What's happening?" asked one, as she saw one of the creatures leap on a fellow and hold her with a chitinous extension to its horny back. "What's happening?" she screamed again, now in sheer undiluted terror.

"Mother!" cried Janice. "Why do you send your sons Nug and Yeb? What have we done wrong?"

There were more screams as one by one, the other girls were seized and held onto the bodies of the two creatures who now began to close on Janice.

"No!" she cried, even as she lunged toward Benny, a knife in her hand. "No need to feel the ceremony defiled by his presence, Mother! I'll free him for you and you can take him into yourself! There's no need to sacrifice your obedient servant!"

Benny stiffened as Jance slipped the knife's blade beneath one of the cords that bound him but that was all she was able to do as one of the creatures, with two girls already semi-submerged in the noxious stuff of its body, took Janice into itself. With her head still exposed, the last thing Benny heard were her screams of inarticulate protest, saliva spattering from her mouth, slack with imbecility.

Himself stunned in near hysteria, he watched as

19

the two creatures, laden as they were with their female victims, retreated back to the doorway where the nebulous, bubbling thing waited...

With the clearing empty, the wind continued to howl and draw itself toward the doorway and Benny could feel his body being drawn in its direction. If not for the ropes that held him, he too would have been taken into the creature on the other side and even as he prayed his ropes would hold, he could sense the angry frustration of the thing when it failed to draw him to itself. Why it didn't send the other creatures for him, he could never understand; unless they had no way of getting past his ropes? As it was, the wind died down and the doorway began to shimmer again before finally fading out.

A pair of hunters found him a couple days later, drawn to him by the screams of nonsense he'd been shouting continuously since that night of horror. Local authorities could never make anything out of his babblings and finally gave him up to a state institution where he remained in therapy for years. No one ever believed his story about the events of that night, preferring an explanation involving a serial killer. At last, with doctors convinced that he was no danger to himself or others, he was released. But, of course, he was no longer the same. He retained an unreasoning phobia of the countryside and open spaces and a curious aversion to doorways. As a result, he couldn't bear life in Dean's Corners and fled to New York City which, if he avoided Central Park, was mercifully free of anything of a wooded nature. There he stayed, still apprehensive every time he needed to pass through a doorway but otherwise reassured in his concrete surroundings...until today, when for the first time since he left Dean's Corners, he was obliged to break his self-imposed exile and return home. Home to the familiar fields, barnyards, domed hills, and gloomy forests. With mounting anxiety, his hands tightened on the steering wheel as full darkness descended on the land. Ahead of him, the road stretched on interminably. *Where were those damn highway signs* he wondered, peering into the dark hoping to find the one that would tell him he had only a few miles to go before the turn off. Unconsciously, he pressed down on the gas, his speed increased. He had to spot that sign! His tires protested dully as he took a gentle curve. He tried to stay on the road, but he came too close to the shoulder. Gravel crunched under his tires as he swerved back to the center of the road. The Acura crossed the double yellow line and he quickly corrected. More speed. *Where was that sign? There it was! What was it?* His anger mounted when he saw that it was only one of those signs indicating a curving roadway ahead. He skidded again. Again he corrected. More speed as the road straightened out...70, 80, 90 miles per hour. He had to get away from the woods. Into town, any town! Suddenly headlights appeared ahead of him, coming right toward him. He was overcome with relief, feeling an overpowering urge to move in their direction...away from the dark...toward the comforting light. From outside the car, he heard the screech of brakes...*z*

Dreams in the House of Weir

by Lin Carter

"The hooting sounds are closer to the house tonight, and Elaine has glimpsed something huge and white squirming through the shrubbery under the walls..."

The following pages from the Journal of Hareton Paine were found amongst his papers, and may shed some light upon the mystery surrounding his *suicide.*

EXTRACTS FROM THE JOURNAL OF HARETON PAINE

February 16th, 1931

No progress was accomplished on the *Chauraspanchasika* today, due to virtually continuous street noise and frequent interruptions from neighboring flats and the accursed telephone. The technical difficulties of trying to translate the complexities of the Sandskrit *scholkas* into decent English verse are, of themselves, quite enough to deter any but the most indefatigable of scholars, but the almost incessant noise and requirements of domestic life render the deed not only impossible but an absurdity. I have taken to sleeping (or *attempting* to sleep!) during the day, reserving the nocturnal hours for my literary labors, which is a bit rough on poor Elaine. I begin to discover that a flat in Belgrave is not the place to work: these surroundings are intrinsically inhospitable, if not actively hostile, to scholarship. I must have solitude, and quiet, in order to concentrate. Bryce dropped in this forenoon and received my "whining" with a sympathetic ear: he suggests I let a place in the country for eight weeks or so, something remote and woodsy, devoid alike of close neighbors and, if at all possible, that infernal machine, the telephone. Candidly, it sounds like heaven, but doubt if my slender purse could afford such luxuries. However, at his insistence, I did speak with an estate agent who listened to a description of my needs, and promised to ring me back if he could find suitable accommodations among his listings. I felt rather dubious about the whole matter, and question whether I can afford the sort of peace and quiet I require; and then there is the problem of poor Elaine's condition. At any rate, the fellow did not call, so there's an end to it, most likely.

February 20th

Wharton, the estate agent, rang me up this morning with several listings which more or less met my principal requirements. One of these caught my interest, a place called Delaware House, up in the north country. It was the name of the place which appealed to me, as Elaine has relatives living in the American state of the same name. Further questioning elicited several interesting facts. It is a large, mostly empty stone house some miles out on the moors from the nearest village, built in the Thirteenth Century by a Norman baronet, one Sir Ranulf de la Weir (hence the name of the place, simplified over the years), on Saxon ruins believed to have been continuously occupied from the Eighth Century. If I remember my walking tours through that part of the country on holidays and vacations, no more somber and desolate surroundings are likely to be found. The downstairs rooms are still furnished, Wharton affirms, and village shops are near enough for weekly deliveries. It certainly sounds promising, I must admit. Elaine suggests I take a run up this weekend and look the house over. I am tempted to do just that, as the rental seems surprisingly moderate.

February 26th

We arrived early this afternoon at Weirton Station, books, clothes, papers, files and miscellaneous personal articles all bundled into a battered old steamer trunk. The village was small, the houses dingy and dilapidated, and the natives seem sullen and close mouthed, and eyed us mistrustfully, muttering amongst themselves. As we wish little contact with them at best, however, this may all to the good. At least we shall have no interruptions from visitors.

Wharton's local man, whose name I failed to catch, met us at the station, bundled us into his roadster, and drove us over the moors to Delaware House. At first and even second glance, the house appears to wear a forbidding, even sinister, look, squatting motionlessly amidst the dreary flat desolation of the moors, a somber and ugly pile of age-darkened stone. It is built in the pure Norman style, the cold angular walls unsoftened by ornamentation, spare and gaunt and lean. You can see it brooding over the level waste kilometers off. As we drove nearer it grew in size under a cold, wet, heavy grey sky, until it seemed to dominate the entire landscape. I could see Elaine found it oppressive and disconcerting, in truth, the place does look grim and inhospitable, so I kept up a cheerful running conversation, mostly one sided knowing she would relax once she saw the interior.

And, of course, she did. The rooms are huge and of immense extent, with lofty, vaulted ceilings and rather dark and chilly. But they are snug enough, and dry as a bone. The interior of the house was "modernized" a bit under the early Tudors, at least to the extent of paneling up the naked interior walls, covering the rough stone with quaint carved oak panels, now black with age. And the furniture, which is ancient enough to qualify as antique, is solid and comfortable enough, while drapery, bedding and toweling, although musty from long disuse, are clean and usable.

I pointed out these features to Elaine, who still seemed a bit dubious. The kitchen, huge enough to feed an army, and high-ceilinged, with smoke-blackened rafters, was equipped with an old iron range, and pots and pans of pewter, and old china. For heating, well, there is a huge yawning fireplace in every room and Wharton's man has had a copious supply of firewood cut and drawn, stacked neatly in the shed. There are even indoor bathroom facilities! Oh, we shall be comfortable enough here, as I assured Elaine.

March 1ˢᵗ

Settling in, nicely. Delaware House is less somber and hostile than it seems first, impressions are usually bad impressions, or however the old apothegm has it! Architecturally, the house is extremely interesting and unusual, and portions of it predate even the Saxon period, for there seems to have been a structure of one kind or another on this plot of ground from time immemorial. Wharton's man waxed voluble on its history while showing us around the enormous pile; the foundations are soldered stone to stone with molten lead in the ancient Roman manner, and the stonework in the crypt is considered Pictish by the vicar (who is by way of being the local expert on antiquarian matters), if not displaying traces of Phoenician.

I listened to this without further comment with the usual polite, social noises, but if it is actually true, it means that this site has been continuously inhabited by man for considerably more than two dozen centuries. Hard to take this sort of thing seriously, but, still, stranger things have been known to exist in this queerly desolate region of Britain.

Elaine seems subdued but comfortable. Dire and foreboding although this country seems at first exposure, the utter and deathly silence of the moors is most appealing. Believe I can begin my long delayed work on the Sanskrit tomorrow morning.

March 2ⁿᵈ

Rose bright and early after a deep, refreshing sleep which drained all of the tensions and nervousness induced by city life from my being, and left my mind clear and receptive.

The beds are really quite comfortable, as is all of the furniture, although it must be veritably ancient. The absence of the telephone is sheerly a blessing, however, it is a pity that the house of the de la Weirs was never wired for electricity. Candleabra or lanterns do little to lessen the dense gloom of the old house, where the shadows seem to be thick, like layer after layer of dust of darkness, settled over generations and centuries.

Still and all, the lack of interruption and noise is marvelous. The unutterable silence of this house would be positively oppressive to anyone less morbidly sensitive to sound than I; and Elaine, although she says little and never voices a syllable of complaint, must feel it. Today I at least made a sizable start on my work, armed with a photostatic copy of the Sanskrit text, and my armful of glossaries, concordances, dictionaries, and, of course, the text of the Powys Maters translation. No interruptions of any sort occurred to break my concentration, although after some hours I did become gradually aware of a faint distant hooting as of marsh-fowl. Over supper, Elaine mentioned glimpsing something in the underbrush near the house; the knee-high shrubbery grows right up to the outer walls. I should perhaps mention here, so if any wildlife inhabit the moor we are in an uncomfortable proximity to it. Nothing to worry about, of course, but Elaine seemed a bit jumpy and insisted on my closing the tall, narrow windows.

March 3ʳᵈ

A bit off my feed today, after rather an uncomfortable night. Bad dreams or something like that; indigestion, probably. Didn't quite feel up to tackling thorny old Chauras today, so wasted the morning poking through what remains of the de la Weir library. The family died out in the Eighteenth Century, I understand, and most of the collection was sold off to satisfy the creditors when the cadet line inherited the property, but recent owners or tenants have left a modest few shelves of odds and ends. Some popular novels, a few of those trashy romances women insist on reading, odd volumes of the Lake poets, and some interesting old Gothic romances from the following of Walpole and Mrs. Radcliffe. Grisly titles they have: *Buckets o' Blood*

penetrating through the dim window-panes.

Elaine says she does not like it here. When I pressed her for her reasons, she could give voice to none. But there is something about the old gaunt stone house lost in the immensity of the cold, windy moors that depresses her.

At first and even second glance, the house appears to wear a forbidding, even sinister, look, squatting motionlessly amidst the dreary flat desolation of the moors

and *Varney the Vampire* and one that particularly caught my eye, with the entrancing title of *Horrid Mysteries*. Any more of this brand of literature, and I would suspect Weir House (as I have come to think of it) as being the original Northanger Abbey!

March 4th

Accomplished little today. Hooting or honking of distant marsh-fowl kept breaking my concentration and the gloominess of the huge, echoing hall I have chosen for my work-room made me queerly uncomfortable. The day was grey and overcast, the wind wet and chill, the piercing dankness

March 7th

I have not been keeping up my journal, must remember to do so. Have been sleeping badly, terrible dreams., which I can never remember upon waking. The work is not going good. I am aware of the curious inability to concentrate, and keep starting up from the pages as if I half-heard a distant voice calling me.

The hooting sounds are closer to the house than ever, and Elaine has glimpsed something white squirming through the shrubbery under the walls.

March 8th

Last night I had a most peculiar dream which, upon awakening, I set down on the notepad I keep beside my huge, canopied bed. I shall copy the dream in my journal here, as I can still make out my hurried scribble.

I was in a room I have never seen before, with gleaming metal walls and floor, and queerly angled niches cut in the walls, holding stacks of plates of tablets. There was a nine-sided window in the wall but from the position in which I was sitting I could not see it clearly.

I was at a lectern or stand, also fashioned of glistening metal, perusing an ancient book written in a language not remotely similar to any writing I have ever seen before, not cuneiform or heiroglyphics, not Mayan pictoglyphs or Arabic curves, and certainly no Sanskrit. If anything, it looked like Chinese ideographs, but only vaguely.

The illumination was garish and livid, and emanated from a source unseen. Lost in the columns of strange charactery, my attention seemed to wander. Only my arms were within the range of my vision, and they were cloaked in some heavy woven fibre which seemed metallic. I could not see my hands, but my arms moved oddly, with a boneless and sinuous grace suggestive of more joints than the human arm possesses.

Suddenly, something caught my attention and I half turned towards the window. It was, as I have said, nine-sided, and through it I caught a dizzying glimpse of a strange, unearthly landscape, all steep black crags cleft with vertiginous chasms. Beyond the rocky heights soared bizarre metal towers, and beyond them, incredibly, a weird sky lit by *five* multicolored suns.

Then, quite suddenly, I awoke to find myself trembling violently, my night-clothes soaked through with cold perspiration.

What does it mean?

March 10th

Another of those unutterably bizarre dreams. I was again within the metal chamber, studying with feverish intensity a set of enormous metal plates inscribed in angular, vaguely runic, symbols. This time I seemed more "deeply" settled into my dream-body. I was even aware of its name, Kzoora, as nearly as I can reproduce the phonemes with my earthly tongue. I even knew what language was inscribed upon the metal plates, the language of the Nug-Soth.

Rising from my seat, which was a prism-shaped, metal crystalloid, I paced the chamber restlessly with an odd, fluid gait. I could hear the rasp of the hem of my robes of woven metal as they brushed the flooring, and the click and clatter of my shoes against the steely tiles. Or was it the clashing of hooves that I heard, or the scraping of claws? I ask this because it seemed to me in the dream that my nether limbs were curiously articulated, with more joints than are found in human limbs, and...yes, now I recall the sensation!...*that I possessed more limbs than are normal.*

Returning to my prism, I again focused my perception upon the metallic plates. They were, I dimly knew, the Tablets of Nhing. And it seemed to me that it was my task to search the Tablets for spells which would hold at bay the frightful Dholes (although what this strange term might signify, I do not know). But I was aware, as Kzoora, that I was but one of a vast cultus of wizards bound to the worship of the premier divinity of this world, a goddess named Shub-Niggurath, the Mighty Mother, prisoned here innumerable eons ago by the Elder Gods, her foes.

The Dholes were her servitors, I knew, even as we were her worshippers; but Dholes have certain...*habits*...which make them fearsome neighbors. Hence it was that those of my race, the Nug-Soth, who inhabit the surface of this planet strive endlessly to pen the terrible Dholes in those enormous and noxious burrows which they have tunneled beneath the crust of the planet. This world, by the way, is called Yaddith, and revolves around one of the many-colored suns, an orb of emerald radiance known to the astronomers of this earth as Deneb. The other suns are of various hues: one is the rusty dark crimson of drying blood, another a stark, livid blue-white sun, and there are two more whose colors are not in the spectrum of visible light known to my earthly eyes, and which are thus hues I can neither name nor describe.

Under the seering rays of the five suns the Nug-Soth and their ghastly neighbors had long striven in contention. But over recent eons the Dholes had grown in size as they had grown in strength, until by now their subterranean burrows threatened the foundations of our metal cities. And, with the puzzling and inexplicable defection of one of our most potent archimages, a certain Zkauba, our barriers of magical force which held the ghastly Dholes pent in their fetid warrens were perilously weakened.

These morsels of information were apparent to me as if they floated upon the surface of my Kzoora-mind: absorbed in his perusal of the tablets of Nbing, he was idly aware of them without thinking about them, as you or I are continuously aware of our identities and addresses and modes of occupation, without having to deliberately recall them to mind.

The dream ended quite suddenly. It seemed to me that the structure in which the metal walled chamber of Kzoora was situated shuddered as to waves of seismic disturbance. Curious objects of unknown purpose fell clattering to the floor, and Kzoora came swiftly to his feet with, again, that old articulation that seemed multi-jointed. As he did so, he turned and from the corner of my vision, I observed his reflection in a pane of silvery metal. The peaked hood of his metallic robes fell back, exposing a visage of horrible inhumanity with a proboscis like that of a tapir, and rugose, seven red eyes, and a squamous body, bipedal and human-like in design, but essentially insectoid in its several clawed limbs. It was all such that my earth-self recoiled in revulsion, and I awoke screaming, shaking like a leaf in a gale, and drenched in icy perspiration.

If these uncanny and disturbing nightmares persist, I shall have to seek an opiate from an apothecary in the village. But, please God, let them end.

March 11th

I went for a long walk on the moors during the late afternoon, my mental processes too numbed by the lack of normal, healthy slumber, and driven forth from the gloomy old house by a restless agitation of body and spirit. The gorse and heather which clothe the hillocks are of dull shades of rust and purple and dark, brackish pools lie hidden underfoot. There is something about this part of the north country which breeds ill-health; even the air seems stagnant and vitiated, as if intermixed with some poisonous miasma breathed from the pores of the earth…

For days I have been concerned by Elaine's pallor and lassitude. Her whining complaints get on my nerves, which are already frayed by those weird dreams which torment me nightly, and I become increasingly impatient and annoyed by her listless manner. Returning to the house, I caught her reading an odd little book, curled in her dressing gown on the window seat. I inquired (I think a bit too harshly) what book it was; easily distraught, she fled from the room as if, for some reason, frightened of me, the book falling from her hand. I took it up and examined it.

It was a manuscript, written in a fine Spencerian hand, the leaves sewn together with scarlet thread. The title page bore this inscription in hand lettering: *Visions From Yaddith*, and the name of Ariel Prescott. I bore the slim folio into my workshop with excitement and surmise. I had thought that strange name "Yaddith" to have originated in my dream disturbed brain, but here it was, affixed as title to this odd little hand made volume. And there was one other element in the discovery which contributed to my excitement. When I had been at Cambridge, the decadent verse of Ariel Prescott had enjoyed a mild vogue among the undergraduates, those of them given to sampling hashish and studying occultism and Theosophy, at any rate. I had looked into her work and found it to be puerile pseudo-Swinburne, seasoned with the dark perversities of Maldoror.

What I held in my hand might well be an authentic manuscript by the poetess, who had, I vaguely recollected, died raving in a madhouse. I opened the folio and read a passage at random:

My nine claws trace inexplicable hieroglyphics acid-etched in perdurable metal.
Through odd-angled apertures pour diverse solar colors in five distinct luminosities.
Crouched on my prism, I ponder cantrips to hold at bay the bleached and viscous swine-snouted
*   worms.*
On Nython and Mthura, my brethren barter for more potent ensorcellements.
For lack of these, must the Nug-Soth perish in the foundering of intricate metal cities?

Alas, the mother remains indifferent as to which of the races of her minions triumph!

I cannot describe the eerie effect these strange verses had upon me. So much of the poem seemed to tally with the details of my most recent dream, that I felt my blood run cold and my scalp tingle and crawl. *For the paw-like hand I had glimpsed in the metal mirror had borne nine claws...and the suns in the sky had numbered five.*

A shrill scream roused me from my tranced fascination with the little volume. A moment later, Elaine staggered into the room, panting of some apparition she had seen at the window: she virtually fell into my arms. I demanded exasperatingly what she had seen.

"A face...huge and white and bloated," she faltered. "With tiny eyes and a snout like a pig's."

I had little patience with her deliriums."Some local farmer's hog has broken loose and went rooting amongst the bushes," I said scathingly. "Surely, that is nothing to make a grown woman scream like a banshee."

"But...it as so *huge!*"

Changing the subject, I brusquely inquired where she had procured the little volume she had been reading when I had entered from my stroll on the moors. She said she had found it jammed behind some old books on the top shelf. I made her show me the place, but found nothing of further interest.

I must remember to ask in the village if Ariel Prescott had ever lived in the House of Weir.

March 14ᵗʰ

Doubtless because of my perusal of those weird verses in the little book Elaine had discovered hidden in the library, my dreams were again of the city of bizarre metal towers and dizzy black crags and labyrinthine streets of intricately-fashioned metal, under the burning rays of the five suns. It seemed to me that I squatted in a row of my fellow Nug-Soth as we hearkened to the thought-waves of our hierophant, Buo, the Arch-Ancient, him who was first among the servitors of the Mighty Mother.

These mental projections exhorted us to redouble our endeavors, for the monstrous Dholes had, only three day-fractions ago, broken through into the birth-crypts beneath the Ziggurat Z-12, to feast on the larvae of our young in a certain manner which was hideously indescribable. At this horrible news all of those ranked with me in the great amphitheatre became fearfully agitated, and raised a clamor of conflicting thought-impulses about which the dominant pulsations of him who was the prime servant of Shub-Niggurath soared: We must venture forth again in the light-beam envelopes, to plead stronger sorceries from the denizens of worlds yet farther off than any heretofore visited. That was the import of Buo's thought-message.

At that, we stilled timorously. Did the arch-Ancient think to dispatch us to trans-galactic Stronti, or the triple star Nython, or Kythamil, or even fear-haunted Shaggai itself?

Even as we trepidated, the surface of the planet shuddered under our nether limbs, and black cracks appeared in the sheeting of the metallic pave. *La! Shub-Niggurath!* we prayed, our mind radiations in flawless unison, as when we focused our pulsations together to sustain the barriers which held the Dholes in their grisly depths.

And again I woke screaming, drenched in perspiration. To still my perturbed mind, I groped on the bedside table for something to read, thinking to calm myself. I found the *Visions From Yaddith* pamphlet, and opened it to the following passage:

Sheathed in bent light, we drift to Kythamil or Kath.
The fungoid intelligences of Nzoorl repulse our entreaties.
Even should we migrate to a world remote from this,
The snouted worms can track us through our Dreams
Which call like beacons through the eldritch dark...

I cast the vile pamphlet from me, shivering uncontrollably.

March 17ᵗʰ

My only friend and, to some extent, intellectual equal in the sordid little village is, as I have earlier recorded, the local vicar, Dr. Minge. He prides himself on his knowledge of the vicinity, and assured me that "Arial Prescott" (the name was a pseudonym, it seems), did indeed once reside at the house Elaine and I now rent. When I mentioned finding the manuscript, he waxed voluble, if not enthusiastic, and informed me that the poetess had published her *Visions From Yaddith* in a small booklet issued from Charnel House Publishers in London in 1927, shortly before her mental derangement grew so noticeable that she had to be confined in Oakdeane.

He also informed me that her surviving family had all known copies of the booklet hastily bought up and burnt, for some reason, before hurriedly moving out of Weir. Which meant that my manuscript was perhaps one of the only known copies of the text in existence.

On my way home from the village, crossing the moors, I heard again that sound of honking or hooting which we now heard nightly, and thought I saw one of those hogs which poor, sick Elaine is always seeing in the shrubbery. It was albino-white, and its fat sides seemed to glisten curiously; also, it seemed extraordinarily huge for a hog, but the swinish snout was unmistakable.

By the time I had gotten up to where I had thought I saw the monstrously swollen hog, it had gone off. Nor did I find tracks of its hooves, although the earth was moist and oddly beslimed, there was nothing but a broad, shallow groove as might be left by a heavy body either slithering or being dragged through the underbrush. Odd, how these morbid fancies fill my mind these days! Those damnable dreams, no doubt…

And suddenly my flesh crawled and my throat went dry. It was just a thought that had flashed through my recollection, for no discernible reason; a line from that vile little volume of insane scribblings:

The snouted worms can track us through our dreams.

That night, drugged with a powerful opiate procured from the village apothecary, I slept heavily. And there were no dreams.

March 19th

Something strange happened today. I was on the roof, searching for dislodged tiles, for water or slime had been seeping into certain of the upper chambers, causing a particularly nasty stench. The day was leaden and grey, with dull light filtering through motionless, overhanging clouds. All was still as the proverbial grave, when I became aware of that annoying hooting or honking I had once ascribed to marsh fowl. We had heard it oft of late, weirdly distorted to a deeper timbre, doubtless due to the fog which has risen nightly from the moors.

Now I heard the irritating sound again, but louder and closer than ever before. The deep bass notes of it were like the grunting of foghorns, no fowl that ever lived could voice such ominous tones!

Peering over the ancient battlements, I saw something slithering through the dry bushes that grew close around the base of the walls; whatever it was, it seemed of an abnormal length, unless it was several creatures in a row. Again, I caught a glimpse of something albino white, bleached and glistening, and for some reason the breath caught in my throat and I felt the sick clamminess of fear. *Then, suddenly, the white thing reared up against the wall of the house, and I saw that it had no limbs, no limbs at all! And the size of the thing!*

The next moment, I found myself crouching behind the battlements, dizzy and shaking. I had momentarily blacked out. I, who had never fainted in my life! I crawled to my knees and peered over the edge, but there was nothing at all to be seen below that was unusual. And no trace whatsoever of the horribly immense, sluglike thing I had seen, or fancied I had seen.

In a moment or two, my head cleared. I realized, of course, that I had seen nothing. I had merely hallucinated the entire episode during my swoon. I forced a laugh at my gullibility, but my laughter sounded false even to my ears...and why was I trembling?

March 21st

Another of those accursed dreams I have come to dread almost nightly. Again Kzoora squatted on his prism, perusing the Tablets of Nhing; but unlike my previous dream visits to Yaddith, none of the several suns were aloft. Instead, the nighted sky was lit by uncanny aurorae, trembling curtains of vaporous colors, among them nine unfamiliar to my earthly eyes.

It seemed that I was even more deeply settled into the sentience of the wizard Kzoora than on my previous visits. I understood that these queer, uncouth runes held the key to the planes of existence, and that by means of them could barriers be erected or the pathways made clear. For there are gates between the dimensions of space, and strange paths that exist between them; it was by this mode that the minions of Shub-Niggurath negotiated the universe in their light-beam envelopes, and…

My hand shakes upon the page: almost am I loath to trace here the next thought-current that drifted through the intelligence of Kzoora. But record it I must.

Others beyond the Nug-Soth may tread the paths between the planes and among these are the horrid Dholes. And the runes which, even at that moment, the insect-creature was pondering, exposed to my shuddering consciousness a final, shocking revelation before which at this hour my soul sickens: for all intelligence has this mystery, that the mind is fragmented, with many sides, like the facets of a crystalloid. I was able to enter the mind of Kzoora, because the mind of the wizard was one facet of the many-sided mind, another part of which was my earthly self, Hareton Paine. And once one facet of the many-sided mind has entered another mental facet, though the gulfs traversed in dreams be wide and very vast, *the Dholes can follow the tracks and trace you to your lair.*

And now at last I know the peril which broods here on these empty moors. And the white, squirming things we have glimpsed in the shrubbery, the hooting, honking, abominably swollen glistening things, are not hogs…

Later:

They are all around the house now, making the night hideous with their baying. We have taken refuge in the upper storeys, but even through locked and bolted doors we can hear the splintering of timbers and the shattering of tall windows before thrusting swinish snouts. *This* was the horror that drove Ariel Prescott mad…and am I any the more sane?

I have oiled and loaded my old army revolver, but there is little that hot lead can do to injure shapes of flesh that can travel through the very planes.

At least, they will not feed upon Elaine, sucking the life-essence from her flesh with those obscene, quivering snouts. For she lies at my feet, shot through the heart by my own gun.

In a moment, I will terminate my own existence, how merciful anend is death, an endless sleep in which there are no…dreams.

I curse the day I ever came to the House of Weir. The damnable thing should be torn down, stone by stone, and the site purified by fire. God alone knows how long ago the psychic linkage between this monstrous pile of stones squatting amidst the moor and far, nightmarish Yaddith was established. And only God knows what huge, unthinkable and atrocious Act was done on this plot of ground ages ago, that makes it the nexus of evil contagion from alien spheres.

Not long to go now; even the stone walls shudder to the monstrous weight pressing upon them…

The window! Merciful God, that FACE! Can anything that lives be so huge...

(At this point the Journal breaks off and was never resumed)

From the Statement of Police Inspector Forster

…entering, found considerable damage to the doors and windows on the first floor, but no sign of theft or vandalism. The deceased was discovered on the fifth storey of the house, dead from a self-inflicted gunshot wound through the right temple. Near the body lay that of a young woman, later identified as wife of the deceased.

Could find no damage to the room, but the large window directly facing the two bodies had been smashed from the outside, as if by a powerful blow. Traces of peculiar slime on the woodwork of the broken window have defied analysis by police forensic laboratories.

No other signs of violence, other than the cause of death, were found on either of the bodies, but they are peculiarly shrunken and depleted, as though something had been drained out of them.

Forensic experts are unable to account for this condition.

Recommend that the crime be assigned to the work of unknown vandals, and the case be placed in inactive files.

Statement ends

Amidst Different Stars

by Andrew M. Seddon

How do we perceive the world and universe around us?

Is the glass half empty or half full?

Is Vaughan Williams' 1935 Fourth Symphony "the greatest symphony since Beethoven" (William Walton) or "I have never felt more depressed for English music" (Benjamin Britten)?

Are we seeing a vase, or two faces staring at each other? An old crone looking sideways or a young woman looking away? Which is real and which is illusion? Or are both real and both illusion?

Two people can see or hear the same thing and come to diametrically opposed conclusions. While some experiences are simply a matter of taste, our perceptions of reality can diverge greatly. While often this makes little or no difference, there's the same amount of water in the glass either way. And whether one likes or dislikes Vaughan Williams' symphony is hardly critical to existence. Other divergences can have more profound effects. As Henry David Thoreau said, "It's not what you look at that matters, it's what you see."

Take, for instance, the nature of the universe and the human place within it. What have people seen when they raised their gaze heavenward into the sky, blazing with sunlight in the day and speckled with stars by night?

Who first attempted to make sense of the changing patterns of the sun, moon, and stars, the days and the seasons? By the time of the neolithic, people erected massive monuments such as Stonehenge and Newgrange aligned to the winter solstice to mark and celebrate the changing seasons.

Early star gazers saw patterns in the stars; a depiction of Orion found in a cave in Germany is estimated to be 32,000 to 38,000 years old. A bull constellation (Taurus) has been known since the Copper Age (2500-2200 BC) or even earlier.

The Babylonians, who noticed Auriga about 1000 BC, gazed skyward with precision, keeping extensive astronomical records, while on the other side of the Atlantic, the Maya and the sun worshiping Inca did the same/ Curiously, the latter's Intihuatana stone in Machu Picchu marks the equinoxes (when the sun stands directly over the stone) and not the solstices.

Western civilization is indebted to the account in the book of Genesis: "And God said, 'Let there be lights in the firmament of the heaven to separate the day from the night; and let them be for signs and for seasons and for days and years, and let them be lights in the firmament of the heavens to give light upon the earth'...and God made the two great lights, the greater light to rule the day, and the lesser light to rule the night; he made the stars also." (Genesis 1:14-16).

The Hebrews looked up with theological eyes, seeing the hand of God in the heavens. King David (reigned c. 1000-960 BC) wrote: "The heavens are telling the glory of God, and the firmament proclaims his handiwork. Day to day pours forth speech, and night to night declares knowledge" (Psalm 19:1-2). The book of Job (c. 3rd-7th century BC) records God as saying, "Can you bind the chains of the Pleiades, or loose the cords of Orion? Can you lead forth the Mazzaroth in their season, or can you guide the Bear with its children? Do you know the ordinances of the heavens? Can you establish their reign on the earth?" (38:31-33).

This view of the heavens continued into the Christian era. The wise men from the east, probably Persian astrologers, followed the Star of Bethlehem (whatever it was). And in the 13th Century, St. Francis of Assisi composed his *Canticle of the Sun*, featuring Brother Sun and Sister Moon.

Meanwhile, the ancient Greeks populated the heavens from mythology, with heroes and animals and objects: Hercules, Orion, and Perseus; Leo; Taurus, and Pisces; Lyra, Argo Navis, and Libra.

In about the year 150 AD the Greek astronomer Claudius Ptolemaeus (Ptolemy), drawing on Babylonian, Assyrian, Egyptian, and Greek records wrote his *Almagest*, listing 48 constellations (including the familiar 12 of the Zodiac) and 1,022 stars, as well as the Ptolemaic system of geocentricity.

Howard Phillips Lovecraft

Also originating in ancient Greece, and associated with Pythagoras, was the notion of *musica universalis*, or the music of the spheres; the philosophical concept that proportions in the movements of the sun, moon, and planets was a form of music. Centuries later, Johannes Kepler took this a step further, believing that this music, though inaudible, could be heard by the soul, that it was a harmony designed by the Creator. In his scheme, Saturn and Jupiter were basses, Mars a tenor, Venus and Earth altos, and Mercury a soprano. Truly a celestial choir!

And so H.P. Lovecraft was following in ancient and varied footsteps with his love of astronomy, discovered at the age of 12, and which became a determining factor in his worldview. Although he wrote a considerable number of astronomical articles and started his own magazines, a professional career was doomed by his lack of mathematical proficiency.

What did Lovecraft see when he gazed into the night sky? What was his view of the starry heavens?

Early in life he renounced the moralistic Protestantism into which he was born, calling it "sombre greyness," and duly "resigned all vestiges of Christian belief." Much more attractive to him were legends of the Orient and Eastern religions, followed by a fascination with Graeco-Roman paganism. But then he discovered "the myriad suns and worlds of infinite space," and thrilled by the grandeur of the universe, plunged into the study of astronomy. Doing so impressed on him man's "impermanence and insignificance" and formed his lifelong "pessimistic cosmic views" and the "futility of all existence." For Lovecraft, the spiritual was "a wholly illusory system of thought." Lovecraft was now an atheist, a "cynical materialist" as he called himself, and remained so through his life.

And so it was with the eyes of unbelief that Lovecraft observed not only the universe, but the human species inhabiting planet Earth. When he wrote of "the infinity, eternity, purposelessness, and automatic action of creation, and the utter, abysmal insignificance of man and the world" he could hardly be further in spirit from King David, who wrote:

> "When I look at the heavens, the work of your fingers,
> the moon and the stars which you have established,
> what is man that you are mindful of him,
> and the son of man that you care for him?
> Yet you have made him a little less than the angels,
> And you have crowned him with glory and honor…"
> (Psalm 8:3-5)

Granted, King David's knowledge of the observable universe, like that of all ancient people to whom some 6,000 stars were visible to the naked eye, was vastly inferior to our own. But more than sheer size alone mattered to them; what mattered was the importance given to humanity.

For Lovecraft though, human beings were "crawling, miserable vermin." "...it is just as sensible to assume that all humanity is a noxious pest which should be eradicated like rats or gnats for the good of the planet or the universe. There are no absolutes, no values in the whole blind tragedy of mechanistic nature; nothing is either good or bad except as judged from an absurdly limited point of view. The only cosmic reality is mindless, undeviating fate; unmoral, uncalculating inevitability." Human life is "sardonically purposeless" and "the cosmos holds nothing worth wanting." Lovecraft "looked on man as if from another planet. He was merely an interesting species presented for study and classification." The doctrine of an immortal personality he considered absurd.

The First World War hardly improved his opinion of the human species. Had he lived longer, the atrocities of the Second World War might have degraded it still further; and perhaps the actions of various godless regimes which both preceded and followed that conflict ("godless" not only in the sense of explicitly atheistic regimes such as the Stalinist USSR and the Kim dynasty's North Korea, but the "practical atheism" of acting as if God did not exist as with Hitler in Nazi Germany, Vladimir Putin in Russia, and various others) would have reinforced his negative opinion of humanity.

Rather than being a home for humanity, this mechanistic universe was not even hostile, it was indifferent: "It does not matter what happens to the race; in the cosmos the existence or non-existence of the earth and its miserable inhabitants is a thing of the most complete indifference."

In other words, the universe couldn't care less. People simply don't matter. This bleak, nihilistic conception prefigures that of prominent scientists of today. For example, Richard Dawkins: "The universe we observe has precisely the properties we should expect if there is, at bottom, no design, no purpose, no evil, no good, nothing but blind, pitiless indifference." Lovecraft would have approved.

Physicist Steven Weinberg: "The more the universe seems comprehensible, the more it also seems pointless." And cosmologist Carl Sagan: "The universe seems neither benign nor hostile, merely indifferent." And as for humanity, "Who are we? We find that we live on an insignificant planet of a humdrum star lost in a galaxy tucked away in some forgotten corner of a universe in which there are far more galaxies than people."

Indifferent and ultimately meaningless, this is the universe that Lovecraft the cosmicist conceived and that contemporary atheists endorse.

It lay to Lovecraft, though, to create the genre of "cosmic horror," to look into this black abyss of stars and craft his stark vision into prose.

He did more than this, however. He populated this nightmare vision with nightmare creatures; not deities, but hideous extraterrestrials as indifferent to humanity as the universe itself. Beings that once ruled the earth but that now, in a state both dead and undying, wait for the time when they will be released to bring a reign of madness and destruction to the Earth. And for the human characters in the stories that attempted to look into these forbidden, hidden realms, to know things that weren't meant to be known, only insanity awaits. Visible "reality" was only an illusion; beyond it lay only the horror of an unseen, incomprehensible, "true" reality.

I read these stories decades ago, and remember thinking that they were the most chilling stories I had ever read, replete with ghastly, malignant creatures with hideous names that burrowed into the mind like malevolent earworms. The "oldest and strongest kind of fear is fear of the unknown," Lovecraft wrote in *Supernatural Horror in Literature*, and this is what he set out to create, to cause us to "tremble at the thought of the hidden and fathomless worlds of strange life which may pulsate in the gulfs beyond the stars, or press hideously upon our own globe in unholy dimensions which only the dead and the moonstruck can glimpse."

After Lovecraft's death, his disciple, August Derleth, a Catholic, attempted to structure these extraterrestrials into a pantheon, formulating the "Cthulhu Mythos," in which Lovecraft's malign "Great

Old Ones" (representing evil) were opposed by the benign "Elder Gods" of Derleth's fashioning. He also attempted to connect these beings to the four elements of earth, air, fire, and water. But this struggle between good and evil was alien to Lovecraft's conception, because for him, as for Richard Dawkins, there is no universal concept of good and evil. There is no divine justice, purpose, or destiny.

Lovecraft, who died in 1937, may not have heard of Schrödinger's cat, that famous 1935 thought experiment. (Lovecraft, had he known would probably have selected a dog, since "Dogs, then are peasants and the pets of peasants; cats are gentlemen and the pets of gentlemen.") In the experiment concerning quantum superposition, "a hypothetical cat may be considered simultaneously both alive and dead while it is unobserved in a closed box, as a result of its fate being linked to a random subatomic event that may or may not occur." Can we detect a hint of dead Cthulhu who lies dreaming in sunken R'lyeh?

And what of the "music of the spheres?" Possibly the modern equivalent is "string theory." Physicist Michio Kaku writes, somewhat imaginatively, "In string theory, all particles are vibrations on a tiny rubber band; physics is the harmonies on the string; chemistry is the melodies we play on vibrating strings; the universe is a symphony of strings, and the 'Mind of God' is cosmic music resonating in 11-dimensional hyperspace."

Lovecraft was apparently not much of a music lover, limited to pop tunes of the day. Music in Lovecraft's stories was typically dissonant and unsettling. For instance, at the center of his universe (in language reminiscent of Dawkins) and representing primordial chaos, dwelt Azathoth, the "blind, idiot god," a "monstrous nuclear chaos beyond angled space" who "bubbles and blasphemes" "amidst the muffled, maddening beating of vile drums and the thin monotonous whine of accursed flutes." So much for the harmonious music of the spheres! One wonders what there is to blaspheme against in a godless universe.

Lovecraft's genius lay in personifying this chaos at the heart of infinity, looking it squarely in the face, and realizing that if all is chaos and insanity, then our own sanity is merely an illusion or a dream. Is there even such a thing as reason when confronted with unreason; rationality with irrationality? C.S. Lewis pointed out that, "If the universe has no meaning, we should never have found out that it has no meaning: just as, if there were no light in the universe and therefore no creatures with eyes, we should never know it was dark. Dark would be without meaning."

Unlike the atheist scientists who simply write glib words and carry on life as normal, Lovecraft painted an unforgettable portrait in words of a purely materialistic universe. Russian artist Wassily Kandinsky phrased it thusly: "The nightmare of materialism, which has turned the life of the universe into an evil, useless game, is not yet past; it holds the awakening soul still in its grip."

Lovecraft showed us what a universe without God is really like: a universe without hope, goodness, beauty, love, joy, morality, truth, reason, meaning, reality, justice; because these things are simply illusions, ephemera to be consumed by the madness of a blind, insane, meaningless universe. A Godless universe is one of infinite horror, against which we cocoon ourselves in vain by distracting ourselves with a myriad of petty amusements. We close our eyes and refuse to look beyond our daily lives. We don't appreciate the awesomeness of the universe, and whatever lies beyond the purely material (in Lovecraft's view nothing lies beyond the material; hence the horror). It's no wonder that Lovecraft's stories and the entities they contain are so chilling.

Lovecraft was not afraid to follow this indifferent universe to its dismal, despairing conclusion. "It is good to be a cynic...it is better to be a contented cat...and it is better not to exist at all. Universal suicide is the most logical thing in the world..."

And yet Lovecraft, despite claiming not to have a fear of the dark, did not commit suicide, not even in his last year of life when suffering from the intestinal cancer which ultimately killed him at the age of 46. For he could still recognize "beauty as the one living force in a blind and purposeless universe," and believed that pessimism produced kindness, agreeing with German philosopher Arthur Schopenhauer about "the most necessary thing in life...the tolerance, patience and regard and love of neighbor, of which everyone stands in need, and which, therefore, every man owes to his fellow."

There is a certain irony in that Lovecraft's pessimistic, cynical outlook brought him to an awareness of beauty and love of neighbor; and tragic that it fell ultimately short of returning him to a worldview that would embrace such virtues.

Arthur Machen

His cosmic horror differs from the redemptive sacred terror of Arthur Machen, a writer Lovecraft regarded highly. Machen also saw the horror of the unknown, but clung to hope, whereas Lovecraft could only despair and say that, "I no longer desire anything but oblivion." Lovecraft might raise a symbolic, though futile fist to the universe, "a calm, courageous facing of the infinite by the resigned, disillusioned, unhoping, unemotional atom," whereas Machen could avoid despair and kneel before the good God who created the cosmos. Though both authors desired to create feelings of horror, and both encouraged us to think more deeply about the nature of the universe we inhabit, they did so from different perspectives, and reached opposing conclusions.

"The role of the artist is not to look away," wrote Japanese director Akira Kurosawa. And Lovecraft didn't. Enjoy his fiction or not, he forces us to confront the universe and ask: What do we see? What kind of a universe do we believe in? What lies behind the veil? Do humans, as small as we are, have value or not?

Do we share Lovecraft's vision of a mechanistic, uncaring universe, lost on a pathway to nowhere amidst indifferent stars? Or one like that expressed by Presbyterian Nobel Prize winning physicist Arthur Compton (1892-1962) who wrote, "It is not difficult for me to have this faith, for it is incontrovertible that where there is a plan there is intelligence; an orderly, unfolding universe testifies to the truth of the most majestic statement ever uttered: 'In the beginning, God?'"

NOTE: H.P. Lovecraft quotations are from his essays, *A Confession of Unfaith, Nietscheism and Realism, Cats and Dogs, Idealism and Materialism – A Reflection*, and *Supernatural Horror in Literature*.

"Schrödinger's Cat" from Wikipedia.

Other quotations can be found on Brainy Quotes.

Scripture quotations from the Revised Standard Version.

Rockhound

by Colleen Drippe

Back where I come from, when the road takes a curve, you might see just about anything: an old house half buried in weeds or a tiny church still in use. People used to be very specific about their religion when I was growing up. Free Will, Primitive, First, Second. The congregations were small because all it took was one kink in the doctrine to make someone split off and start a new church.

And they knew things, those people, remembered things that northerners have forgotten. That dogs draw the lightning for instance. Or that a large shape moving through midnight woods might not be a bear...or a man. And I remember how just about any boy of a certain age could shimmy right up a loblolly pine and get himself back down again. And most of the counties were dry.

Up here the roads are straight and cottonwoods grow along the creeks and the rest of the land is corn or soybeans. Or pasture. Nothing has changed since I came in 19-- and I don't expect it to. It is I who have changed. When my cousin Joe Bob first invited me to check things out, I had never heard people talk like they do here. It sounded like someone had sat on their heads. But now I expect I sound just like them.

So I stayed, got a wife and lost her, and now it's just me and Henry, my blue tick hound. You don't amble your car from place to place like they did back home because up here it's just a lot of empty space between places. You drive through it and it all looks about the same and you don't always see it. A lot of the time you don't worry too much about

the speed limit either. Henry likes to stick his head out the window and let his ears blow back.

So I don't stop much between my road and town or wherever I'm going and I really don't look around much at the country I'm passing through. It was Joe Bob who once drew my attention to a stretch not all that far from where I live and shook his head. "Ain't no people along here," he said. "They say things don't grow right."

It just looked like dried up pasture to me, only there were no cows and the fences didn't seem to be in good repair. On a slight rise to the left I saw a chimney sticking up where a house had fallen down. Beside the ruin, a couple cottonwoods reared leafless branches and a crow, or something like that, flew off with a loud croak. Henry wasn't with us that day or he'd have had something to say about that.

But the way Joe Bob said what he said made me think of things I had seen back home, deserted farms, houses and trees taken out by tornadoes and places we kids were told not to go. I remembered going to one of them when I was out hunting and I also remember suddenly deciding to hunt somewhere else. But that was *there*, where old things lingered and shadows were, well, shadowy. This was the bright, flat Midwest and there was no place for shadows like that to hide.

We went on about our business that day and no more was said. As I passed and repassed that stretch and didn't hardly see it, I forgot what my cousin had told me. In fact, I didn't think about it again until early one fall when I saw a pickup stopped beside the road. I pulled over. That's when

I saw the chimney and the dead cottonwoods and it sort of came back to me.

The truck belonged to a neighbor of mine. I saw him down in the ditch, though I couldn't remember his name right off. Kevin maybe? Something like that. He was a science teacher at the high school and he raised chickens. I heard the rooster sometimes.

"Need help?" I called.

He came up to the road and grinned at me. "Matter of fact, I do," he said. "There's a rock in here I spotted last winter. Limestone mostly, chert and quartzite. But its got some great colors. Probably left here by the glacier."

I waded through the weeds, watching out for poison ivy. I don't do good with that stuff. And then I stopped. A rock, he said. The thing looked more like a boulder. From the glacier; yeah.

He is a big guy and I am no midget, but this looked like a challenge and no mistake. As I got closer, I saw that he was right about the colors. Red, green and blue were mixed in with what I guessed was quartz. I don't know a lot about rocks, but I don't think I had ever seen anything like this before. "You want to take that *home* with you?" I asked, still wondering how he was going to move it.

He gave me a sidewise look. "Well, that's what I had in mind."

I didn't ask him what he would have done if I hadn't come by. I could guess. He was a fanatic rockhound and no mistake. Probably he would have waited for someone else to come along.

He turned back to his find. "Let's see if we can roll it up to the road," he said, taking my offer for granted.

The thing was netted with vines, I looked real careful at their leaves before I touched them, and it sat in its own little nest of stunted weeds and dirt. As I got a closer look, I suddenly didn't want to put my hands on it. I know this sounds strange, but it put me in mind of some kind of animal disguised as a rock. Must have been the angle of the light.

Well, my neighbor was already working on it and I forgot my silly notion and gave him a hand. The hardest part was to get it loose and started, but once we did that, it wasn't too hard to get the thing up onto the road.

"Inertia," he said and I remembered he was also supposed to be the physics teacher.

I grunted. There was still the matter of lifting it onto the bed of the pickup. I wondered what his wife would say when he brought it home. I could imagine what the inside of his house must look like, piled everywhere with the "treasures" he had collected. But that was his problem. Most likely he just wanted it for his yard anyway.

Well we got it onto the truck finally. By that time, I had come to hate the very sight of the thing. All those streaks of color, closer and closer to my face as I struggled to hold up my side of the rock; they almost seemed to move. But I knew that had to be the sweat running into my eyes. Even so, I felt a little woozy when we finally put up the gate. That truck was going to ride pretty low on the way home.

Well he thanked me, but we were both so winded after loading the rock that I just said, no problem and that was that. I watched him drive off, wondering if I would see that thing in his yard next time I went by, thinking it should be easier to unload than it was to load. He could just back up to where he wanted it and roll it off the truck.

But the memory of those colors, patterns it looked like, must have stuck with me. As I shoved my supper into the microwave, I could still see them. Like the memory of that glacier that had probably carried the rock here. But what did I ever know about glaciers? Yet when I closed my eyes, I seemed to see the towering ice, moving slowly over the land, grabbing up whatever got in its path, carrying rocks and dirt from God knows where, only to drop them when the great melt came.

From God knows where. That phrase kind of stuck.

I woke myself later in the night, yelling. Woke old Henry as well. He sat up on the rug and actually howled for a moment.

"Hey, hey," I said when I had got myself oriented, "it's okay, boy. I didn't mean to scare you."

But he was shivering. After a moment, I let him jump up on the bed where he shivered some more. I tried to remember what I was dreaming.

At first, nothing came clear. Then I thought I remembered the glacier I'd been picturing to myself when I went to sleep. Only it wasn't just an ice mountain in my dream; it reached right up to the stars, snatching its freight of rocks from who knows where, as it moved relentlessly across the cosmos. In my dream, I had been standing at the base of the thing and its very hugeness was crushing all the spirit out of me. That was when I woke up. It seemed to be telling me what a nothing I was and that I should just give up.

Needless to say, we didn't sleep very well the rest of the night. Once Henry had to go and I headed for the back door to let him out. And then, when I had the door open, he seemed to change his mind. I felt him shove up against my legs, still shivering as I reached down to mess with his ears. "What is it, boy?" I asked. "Coyotes?" There's been some howling earlier, but Henry had never seemed to be bothered by them before.

In the end, I had to go out with him, just like when he was a puppy. We stayed close and he did his business right in the back yard before running back to the porch where he waited for me, pressed up against the door.

The moon was out, not full but working on it and its light was kind of silvery. The shadows of my raspberry row and the side of the garage were so deep they looked like cut out pieces of the night itself. Somehow, those blots of darkness made me uncomfortable.

I don't know what made me turn to look out over the half harvested soybean field beside my place. Maybe I saw something from the corner of my eye. As I gazed, the moonlight set its gentle glow all across the landscape. Everywhere, that is, except in the direction of my neighbor's place down the road. Over there, the light had taken on a slightly different hue, or rather set of hues. Pale beams of red, blue and green seemed to wash over the distant fields and into the sky, moving like reflections off a lake or some other body of water.

It had to be the distant lights of town. You could see them on a cloudy night, reflecting from the clouds. Gas stations, liquor stores, a shopping center. Only thing was, this night was clear. Way too clear after my nightmare. Each star was like a piece of glowing crystal, the milky way a cold and sweeping streamer in the sky.

I turned around and opened the back door.

*

The fall came on and I picked apples one weekend and froze them. Jack 0 Lantern time came and went. There were not many trick or treaters out here in the country, but this year there weren't any at all. I was faced with eating or throwing away a bag of Jolly Ranchers.

The weather was heavy and it rained some. I woke up with aches I hadn't had before and at the end of a day at the plant, I was a lot more tired than I had been. I even wondered if it might be time to retire. I looked down at Henry. He seemed to be thinking along those lines too.

Henry had fallen off in the past month or so. He had lost weight and he no longer went exploring as he had done before. In fact, he didn't go out at all unless I went with him. I suppose it was the coyotes. Certainly the howling was a lot worse than it had been.

Each morning I saw my neighbors heading out to work. The school bus passed me as I drove into town to my job. Sometimes I glanced at the teacher's house as I went by, Kevin Butler, that was his name, but everything looked okay. The boulder was a greyish hump in the yard, barely visible in my headlights. Once in a while on my way home, I saw Butler out there, but he never waved and neither did I. I had the funniest feeling he only had eyes for that rock of his.

As for me, I stopped looking in the direction of his place at night.

So that was how things went on. My arthritis got worse, my dog began to spend his time lying on my bed and a couple people I knew down the road didn't call or come out much anymore. Maybe they were getting old, too.

Sometimes I would sit in my chair in the evening and turn on the TV. But reception wasn't as good as it had been and anyway, my concentration wasn't what it had been either. It was hard to stay awake with the screen all fuzzy, lines of blue and green and red and the sound it made sometimes: static noises that almost sounded like talking in some language I didn't know.

I think things could have kept going on that way all winter, if it hadn't been for the possums. There were three of them in my yard one morning, all dead. At first I thought they were just playing possum, when I went out with Henry, but they didn't move when I toed one of them. And Henry gave one sniff and ran back to the door, scratching to get in. I'm afraid he had an accident on the kitchen floor later that day.

Meanwhile, I couldn't leave three dead possums in the middle of the flower bed, so I went back out to clean up the bodies. The trash people could deal with them, I thought.

I fetched a garbage bag and picked up the first one gingerly by the tail. The tail came off in my hand. With a yell, I sprang back, throwing the nasty

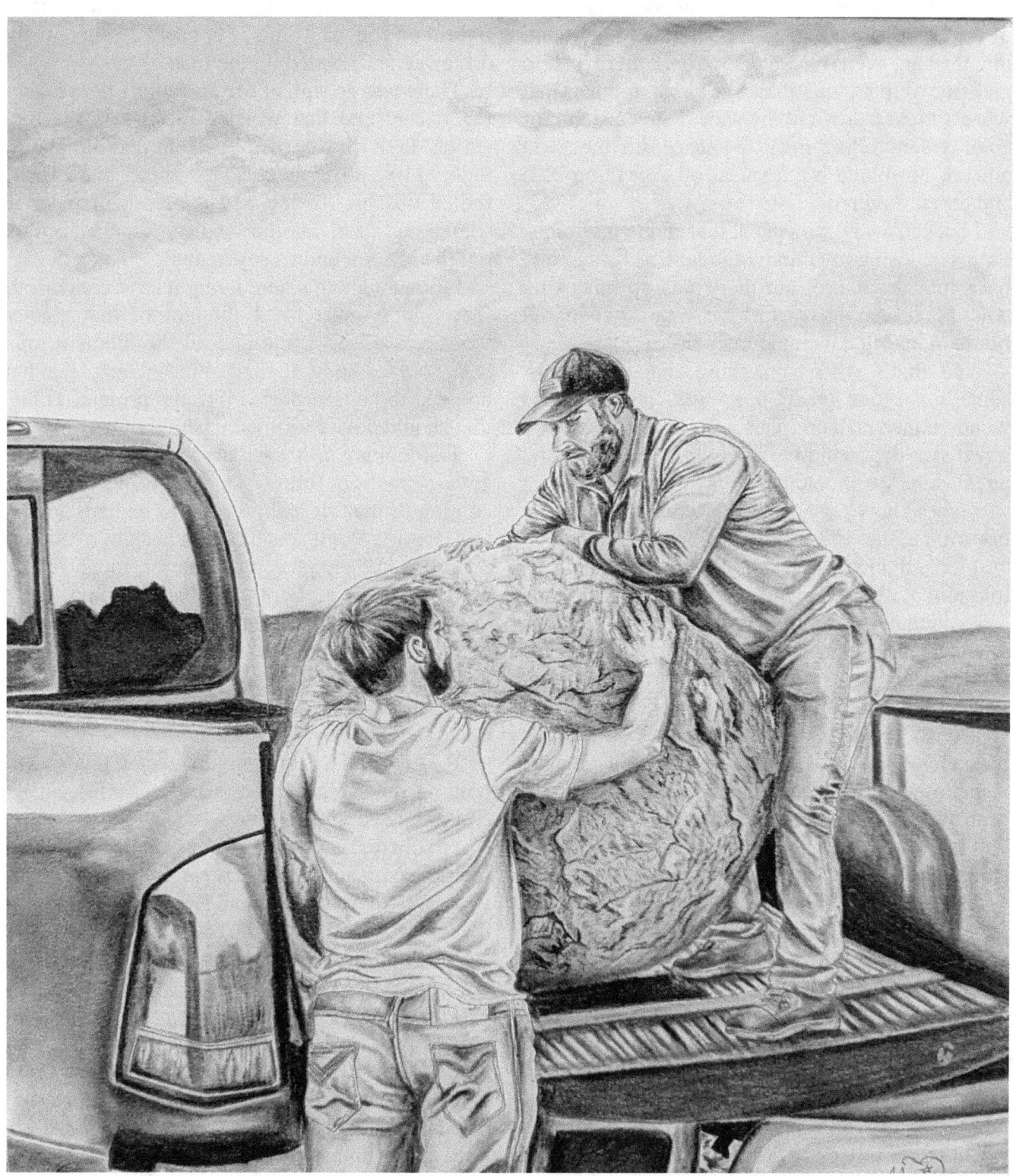

Well we got it onto the truck finally. By that time, I had come to hate the very sight of the thing.

37

thing as far as I could. It took a real effort to come back, kick over the body...and find that it had been ripped in half. There wasn't much blood.

The other two were the same only worse as some sort of decay had set in: a fungoid crumbling of the flesh which made it impossible to get them into the bag, even if I could have brought myself to pick one of them up. I think the worst of it was that when I looked down at my shoe, I saw a streak of color where I had made contact with the dead animal; not blood but a smear of something blue and green. And red.

I backed away, wincing at the pain in my joints. I must be losing my mind, I thought, as I staggered back into the house, but there was no mistaking what I had seen. Henry met me in the kitchen, tail between his legs, whimpering a little.

And that's when something changed. It just came over me that this was no midnight woodsrunner, no haint. This was real dead possums, a real sick dog, and him barely five years old, and a real stone we should never have moved!

I don't know why I made that connection. It just occurred to me. But it felt right.

I looked down at Henry. "Enough is enough," I told him. "We are going to put it back!" But even as I said that, I heard from down the road, a distant howling. Howling in broad daylight! I had a sudden vision of bloodied teeth, of eyes that flashed the colors of that damned stone. Was it the soul of the thing? Or just some poor dog that got too close to it sometime and...well maybe something happened. Whatever it was, it was probably guarding the stone right now.

I knew I was thinking crazy stuff, but I couldn't stop.

"But I'm no Yankee," I told myself, "even if I have been living up north. I know what's what and no damn rock is going to mess with my dog!"

Across the field, I heard again the howl like an answer to my challenge. I wondered how things were going with my neighbor. I thought about giving him a call, but then I decided I'd better head over there. First I stopped to load my 12 gauge and add a handful of shells to my jacket pocket. It might not be any good against a stone, but it could sure take out whatever killed those possums.

Henry followed me to the door, whining a little and looking up into my face. Would he be safe here without me? Poor dog, he was so far gone now he didn't have much to lose. I decided to bring him along. When I lifted him up into the car, he licked my hand and wagged his tail a little.

"That's right, Old Boy," I said. "We'll go down fighting, you and me." I backed out of the driveway and headed up the road.

There was no sign of life at Butler's house when I got there and that worried me. I saw the rock sitting in a flower bed, half buried in leaves, looking like it had always been there, but I wasn't fooled one bit. To me it was as out of place as something from another galaxy dumped in the middle of somebody's soy beans.

I thought about where it might have come from. How old it must be. I thought of that glacier, thousands of years ago and all the things it must have scraped up in its final retreat. Things that had no right to be transported into the present. Things that should have remained where they were.

Just looking at it gave me the willies. It hinted at vast epochs of time. Vast, empty eons before the coming of man. It had no right to be here now, in this century. But it was. It was a heck of a lot older than the human race and...maybe more real? I dunno. It was better not to look at the thing.

I left Henry in the car but I took the shotgun with me as I walked up to the door. I rang the bell and knocked, wondering what I would find. When there was no answer, I gave the door a push and it opened right away.

It was kind of dim in there and I hesitated, holding the shotgun ready. But ready for what, I couldn't have said.

"In...here," a hoarse voice called from an interior room and I moved down a short hallway to what must have been a den. Just as I had guessed, the place was filled with rocks and all kinds of scientific stuff. A telescope lay partly assembled on the couch.

I saw Butler half sprawling in a chair. We looked hard at each other for a moment. I don't know what he was looking for, but I gave him a good, long stare before I decided he was probably okay. Not changed, I mean. That's how crazy I was thinking by then. His face looked drawn and one leg was wrapped in a messy bandage, but it was still him.

"Are you alone?" I demanded.

He stared at the shotgun. "Yes. My wife is visiting relatives."

Carefully, I set the gun against a bookshelf. "I guess you know why I'm here," I said.

"I...I think so."

"We have to take it back," I told him. "You and me."

He stared at me in surprise. "There's a dog," he said. "A stray. But I don't know where it lives."

I frowned at him in impatience. Of course there was a dog. Something had ripped up those possums. But didn't he realize I was talking about the rock?

Or was I?

I came closer and got a good look at his leg. "Did it bite you?" I asked, remembering the possums and how they sort of broke apart. It took all my courage not to grab my gun and head back out the door.

He got a kind of confused look on his face. "I...I don't think so. I fell. Tripped over something in the yard and..." He tried to focus on me. "I don't feel so good. I'm not thinking clearly."

I swallowed and moved closer. "Let me look at that leg," I said, though it was the last thing I wanted to do.

Slowly I unwrapped the bandage, all the time expecting something out of a nightmare. But all I saw was a very nasty scrape. Red and swollen flesh, but nothing like those possums. "You'll do," I told him, trying to keep a tremor out of my voice. "And now we have to take care of that rock."

But he still didn't understand and in the end, I had to explain about how some things belong where you find them, that there are places where different laws apply and those places are not a part of the everyday world. That not all of the earth belongs to us and it never did. I told him about the glacier and how it scraped up something that should have remained where it was, wherever that was. Now it was out of place. Kept where it belonged, it was harmless, but having been moved...well...

I think he would have scoffed at this, him being a man of science and all, and he had just opened his mouth to say something when we both heard a howl out in the yard. I remembered Henry and, grabbing the shotgun, I ran for the door.

I had left the windows of my car open a crack but I couldn't see Henry. Maybe he was lying down on the seat. What I did see...but I'm not sure what I saw. I had an impression of eyes and teeth, flashes of colors no dog should have and...

There was no dog in the yard. Only the rock, half exposed in its nest of autumn leaves. The thought of touching the thing made me physically sick. Half turned so I could keep an eye on it, I ran over to my car.

On the seat, Henry looked up at me, trembling a bit, but his eyes steady on mine.

I looked around and saw Butler in the doorway, clutching the frame. "Where's the dog?" he asked.

"No dog," I said firmly. "Except Henry here."

He wavered. "You really want us to take back the stone? To put it where we found it?"

"You got any extra gloves?" I asked him.

"I...we can't," he said. He wasn't looking at me as he said it. "It's...mine. Do you understand? Mine!"

"You weren't listening," I said. "Things like that...they're out of place. We have to let them go."

He stared at me for a moment, kind of dazed, and then he limped over to the garage and got into his truck. I held my breath as he pulled it out into the driveway. When he had got it angled right, as close to the stone as he could, he stopped and just sat there. I fetched a pair of gloves from my car.

"Come on," I said and I could feel the thing pushing on my will. I pushed back. "Give me a hand," I told Butler.

He looked at me a moment and then he got out of the truck, moving real slow like he was half asleep and trying to wake up. I went straight over to the rock and he joined me.

I wasn't feeling too spry, as you can imagine, and now I wondered if we could even get the thing back up into the truck bed. He was staring at it doubtfully.

"I don't know," he said, and then he stopped, unable to take his eyes from it.

I set down my shotgun once more and put on the gloves. As I did so, I saw something run past and collapse in the yard. It was another possum. They don't usually come out in the daytime unless they're sick, but this one was more than sick. I watched it crumble onto the grass, leaking a multicolored fluid that might have been blood. I glanced at my neighbor in sudden dread.

His face was as white as anyone's I had seen,

like he really was sick. Was he going to collapse and go the way of the possum? And what would I do if he did?

But he didn't. There was more to him than that. He reached for the rock instead.

"Put on some gloves," I said, pointing to a pair he kept in the back of the truck.

He did so, clumsily. "It...it talks to you," he mumbled. "Inside. Tells you to give up. To go the way of the trees back there, and the animals. To let it in..."

"I know," I said. I started pushing on the stone, loosening it from its new home, flexing my aching muscles as I prepared to lift my side of it. The colors were dancing wildly and I didn't know if I could force myself to do this. Sometimes it was a rock and sometimes it was something else. Something warm, almost hot. Alive. I tried to look away while I waited for my neighbor.

At last he reached over and took his share of the burden. "It was so beautiful," he murmured. "So beautiful."

"Don't look at it," I warned him.

In my car, Henry was making a low, whimpering sound that made me want to shoot the damn rock or smash it into crumbs. In my rage at the thing, I forgot my aching joints and together Butler and I got it back onto the truck bed.

"I'll follow you," I said as I went back to my car.

He put up the gate and limped over to the driver's side. I still didn't like the way he was moving, sort of clumsy and stiff like any minute he would break apart like some kind of fungus. I wondered if he could even drive.

But he managed to pull out onto the road and I followed him as close as I dared. There was no other traffic. For the first time, I realized I hadn't seen another car all morning. It was Saturday. No school bus. Everything seemed dead around us, like we had slipped sideways into another dimension. Even the sky was kind of dark and more clouds were piling in.

As we neared the ruined chimney, the first thing I noticed was a new carpet of green growing where the dried out pasture had been. Even the cottonwoods were leafing out...in November. But as I got a closer look, I could see there was nothing healthy about that green. It was the color of pond slime with tints of blue and red.

The pickup pulled over beside the road. I followed and parked behind it. I saw my neighbor open the door and get out. As he did so, something howled. Henry gave an answering howl that sounded more like a groan.

I forced myself to walk over to the pickup and open the gate. Butler came to stand beside me while the stone looked back at us. I knew it saw us...but it was beautiful. Even I could see that and I could imagine how it must look to a man who loved rocks like he did.

"Let's roll it off," I said, donning my gloves once more. But neither of us moved. We might have stood there all day, not able to tear our eyes from the thing, waiting for it to speak to us...to tell us how small we were, how fragile.

It wasn't just the colors, it was the patterns they made. Sometimes it seemed more like a living thing; something with long, dense fur and shining eyes. Red and green and blue were in those eyes.

It was something that had once loped across the starways, lifting its muzzle to howl at new formed suns and infant worlds. Something older than the world and a whole lot more real.

I thought I loved it.

And then I heard another howl; the sound of a real dog in the world I lived in. I hadn't latched the car door and Henry had fought his way out, using the last of his strength to stagger over to my side. He started barking.

At this, I looked up at Butler and saw the struggle in his face. I knew he loved the stone more than I ever could.

But I hadn't reckoned on his own grit. With one sweep, he brought one hand down on his wounded leg in a blow that made him half lose his balance. He staggered, set his shoulder to the stone and heaved it to the road. As it hit, I saw the hound start to take form.

But before it could get to its feet, Henry's jaws closed on its leg. He hung on. Even while the thing struggled to rise, even when it opened its muzzle, teeth flashing toward Henry...he hung on.

I moved with the stiffness of a man far older than my sixty years as I picked up my gun and swung it at the thing's head. The shock ran up my arms, the gun went off; Thank God, nobody was hit. Then it was a rock once more. Ignoring the pain, I reached down and began rolling the thing back to its place in the ditch. My neighbor came over and helped me.

When we had it in place, I looked all around the wasted land. Would our offering be accepted? Were we pardoned for having moved it? I knew there were forces here greater even than the stone or the hound or the things that had stalked the woods back home.

As I watched, the clouds thickened and the blighted trees danced in the wind. I was being dismissed; sent away from where I had no business being. Beside me, Henry tugged at my pant leg, steering me to the car. As the first thunder sounded, I saw Butler climb painfully back into his pickup, turn it around, and head back the way we had come. I followed.

Not too many days after that, my arthritis passed away and Henry got back his spunk. Butler recovered too, but I'm afraid his faith in pure science was shaken a little. Not too much, just enough to be healthy.

Which is to say, I'm sure he didn't get rid of all his rocks – but I bet he was a lot more careful about what he took home.

I know we both must have passed that cursed stretch of road more than once as we went about our lives in the years to come, fearful that I might see others fooling around there, kids maybe. But I never looked too closely at the barren trees or the crumbling chimney. I didn't want to know if there were. It was just a place to pass by.

We humans are relative newcomers on this our world and it's only right to respect whatever came before us. To mind our own business and pass it by.

The Shattered Room

by Robert M. Price

Young Andy Sawyer, about nine years old, had been off visiting his grandparents in nearby Ipswich when something had torn through the Dunwich countryside like a tornado. He wondered what on earth had happened. None of the grown-ups would tell him when he asked. Tornados and storms were plenty scary while they were happening, but afterward? You'd think the adults would never get tired of telling and retelling their stories of the big event, and their stories grew as their memories faded. But not this time. It must have been pretty bad because, among many others, a couple of his best friends were nowhere to be seen. He had to go fishing all by himself, and it wasn't near as much fun that way. He'd never caught any fish anyway, so why bother anymore?

Andy was looking for other stuff to do these days. He couldn't spend the day in school because the ramshackle one-room school house had been completely flattened by whatever had wrecked most of the countryside. So he whiled away the lonely hours ranging over the barren, burned-over district that was Dunwich. Ma and Pa didn't know where he was by day, nor did they much care, staying drunk most of the time. They hadn't used to be that way, not until the unmentionable Thing that ruined Dunwich, which wasn't much to begin with.

Every day Andy would venture farther and farther from home. He wanted to see for himself what was left of the countryside. He had crisscrossed the landscape many times in his young life, but now he hardly knew where he was. There wasn't much left to recognize. Finally he spotted a steep hillside with a lattice of weathered and splintered boards propped against it. Wasn't that where the old Whateley farmstead used to be? He'd many times been soundly warned not to go near the place, but that was when there *was* a place. If he went over to explore the heap of rotten lumber, who'd blame him? Who'd even *know*?

What must once have been a barn was the closer of the two demolished heaps. Though a small boy, Andy knew enough to step carefully. He thought of a game of pretend he and his friends used to play in the woods. They'd found a clearing with a neglected tree house. One day they'd pretend it was a house, the next a store, and after that a pirate cave. As Andy looked around at the interior (which now was mostly the same as the exterior), he couldn't think of anything to play, especially all by himself.

Hmmm...it seemed the broken shell of the place was not entirely empty. He moved closer to a sagging, half broken shelf to scrutinize a dented and rusty coffee can. If nothing more fun came to mind, he could always just kick the can around. The tin cylinder bore a crudely scrawled label which he could not read. But if he could have, it wouldn't have meant anything to him anyway, for it said POWDER OF IBN GHAZI.

He sneezed. The fine, brown powder started up in a small cloud. It didn't dissipate as readily as a careful observer might have expected. Then it seemed to gravitate slowly toward a corner a few feet away, and there it stopped drifting and settled. But upon what? Andy thought momentarily that the powder was clinging to a spider web, but no. There was something under there. Some *thing* under there. Something residual. Something that *lingered*. Something that had *waited*. Waited for *him*.

*

The scene shifts now to the depths of Cold Spring Glen, a ravine that looked like some giant

had plunged a great ax into the earth. Rumor had it that the odd sounds that floated upwards from there were a kind of groaning human speech, though none who claimed to have heard it could understand it. And who dared linger for long at the precipitous edge of the Glen? But the rumors were well founded: there were indeed people living down there, though some might have quibbled at the term. Light seldom penetrated into Cold Spring Glen, which was just as well: the sights that might have been revealed were better not seen.

The large and notorious Whateley clan was even larger than generally thought. The troglodyte population of the ravine was a long forgotten branch of the family. To classify them as members of the "decayed" Whateley kin would not even begin to describe the degree of their degeneration, having lived for generations like blind minnows in a subterranean grotto. The scarecrows, surprisingly, were still able to reproduce, though the results were not exactly favorable. These poor beings had sufficient to drink from the Cold Spring. For food they had the slimy creatures that regularly emerged from the earthy walls of their habitation, and when these failed, there were always the older, weaker members of the group. There were, however, scarcely enough of them to spare.

This rag tag band of creatures dimly understood that their time was short. They possessed a vague sense of purpose and expectation, inherited from their forbears, though with each generation, knowledge of it eroded with every repetition. They felt, almost by mere instinct, that some great change was at hand, and this change they associated, they knew not why, with the standing ruins of the old Whateley place. Periodically the stronger among these ultra-decayed Whateleys would climb up from their wormy hell and shamble their way toward the abandoned farmstead, whose only harvest had been chaos. Not knowing what they sought, their poor brains were capable only of a kind of adventurous expectancy. Had anyone else been present, they might have shuddered at the plodding silhouettes against the enormous moon.

*

Andy watched with a mixture of eagerness and fear as the powder gravitated to whatever lay in the corner. Though more and more of the dust now coated it, the underlying object remained unidentifiable, amorphous. The boy wondered if the problem lay with his eyes: had more of the dust got into them than he had felt? Was he just having trouble focusing?

But no. The image was becoming more distinct, more definite. He *could* see it clearly; the mystifying shapelessness was a predicate of the thing itself. There were ropey tentacles or tendrils. There were bulging eyes, gaping mouths. And it was moving. It was even *growing*. Already roughly the size of a curled-up sheep dog, it was rapidly assuming the proportions of a youngish bear, though it resembled one in no other respect. It resembled nothing else.

The tentacles were now shifting, the rheumy eyes blinking, some rapidly, others slowly. Mouths, gummed with dripping strings of mucus, opened and closed hungrily. What made the thing grow? What energized it?

Andy.

It was Andy himself. Finally he noticed what he had not felt: a long tentacle had snaked its way to his arm, fastening upon it, opening its vampiric suckers, painlessly transferring the boy's tissue into itself. It must have infused him with a paralyzing agent, like that used by some predatory insects. Still oblivious of the violence of the thing's attack, he nonetheless felt acute nausea, weakness, and dizziness inside. Of course he blacked out with the shock. His clarity of thought evaporated so rapidly that he had not time even to wonder if he were dying.

But he wasn't.

Not exactly, anyway. Andy lived, or *it* lived. Lived and thrived. In his new form, the changing form of that which had absorbed him.

*

They knew it when they saw it, the ravine dwellers. Somehow they had an awakening quasi-memory of the recent events that had overwhelmed the Dunwich invader. After all, some of them had shared Cold Spring Glen with the invisible behemoth which had been housed here in the recent past. And though the bulging sack of slithering matter was quickly fading from visibility,

they sensed the link between the creature and themselves. What was it doing here? Something had kept it here when the giant creature shattered its confinement and went a-ravaging. Now it appeared that the remnant could replace the vanished whole, as if the ocean would grow from the sole remaining rain drop. But it had to absorb and convert other life in order to do it. The Whateley monster had waxed great and powerful on an endless supply of beef and blood. But human tissue was apparently adequate, whether Andy Sawyer's or that of the Whateley cavemen. This was the change. It had come. And they didn't mind at all.

But it wasn't enough, not by a long shot. If the new Dunwich colossus was to fulfill its inherited mission, which it had now begun to recall, more humans would have to jump aboard the bandwagon. *Many* more, and the Thing knew just where to find them.

*

The sun was clearing the horizon when the elderly farm couple Ezra and Matilda Hanford flinched at the sound of a sudden massive crushing of wood. Some of their neighbors, now absent, had heard the same sounds in recent days. They had not survived the hearing. And now Ezra and Matilda, who had earlier counted themselves blessed by God, realized their number was up. Their ceiling fell in as they managed to make a run for it. Bent over and panting, they looked around them frantically for the engine of destruction, but saw nothing. But of course neither had Elmer Frye and his doomed family. But the Hanfords found themselves at the end, not of a hammer but of a syringe, sucked into the quivering mass.

Once assimilated, the completely disoriented husband and wife, though lacking their accustomed senses, found themselves somehow aware of one another, of their thoughts. And not only the two of them. They recognized the terrorized consciousness of their neighbor boy, little Andy Sawyer. And soon many more as most of the populace of Dunwich, then Aylesbury, then Wilbraham and Monsen joined them. The juggernaut had almost reached Arkham when it realized it had amassed enough. Then it reversed course and headed back to Dunwich. That's where its mission awaited.

*

The Dunwich region was now completely depopulated. The few who had managed to escape absorption fled the towns, some putting as much distance between themselves and Dunwich as they could. Some few even took refuge in ill-rumored Innsmouth. All of Arkham heaved a deep sigh of relief when the shadow of their mysterious destruction retreated, they knew not why. But at the Miskatonic University, the faculty met to consider their options in case the danger surfaced again. It had, after all, hit Dunwich twice. All knew that their colleague Henry Armitage had been instrumental in combating the Dunwich Horror, as it had come to be called; a vague term because few had any idea what had really happened those months ago. This time Armitage was no help, as he was these days a resident in the Danvers Asylum, seriously shaken by whatever had transpired atop legended Sentinel Hill. Professors Morgan and Rice, Armitage's allies in the final confrontation, had never really understood Armitage's plans or his eccentric methods. But such efforts would not be required this time. It wasn't going to come to that.

*

The new Dunwich behemoth possessed virtually no mind of its own. It was guided by a deeply imbedded, one might even say programmed, purpose. What flickering gleam of intelligence it did have it owed to the stockpiled minds of those whom it had devoured like a whale ingesting krill. But of these minds or souls it remained unaware. It was a complicated relationship. The absorbed victims were little more than passive passengers, like barnacles on the underside of a ship. However, they could not but be aware of the Thing's purpose. It became clearer as their hulking host neared the Dunwich region. It became crystal clear as the monster started to plod invisibly up Sentinel Hill.

The creature was going to open metaphysical gates to another world into which this familiar earth would be sucked. The captive consciousnesses of the dwellers in the devourer suddenly sparked, sending flashes of memory across the synapses wired throughout the titan form. At once each one shared a cascade of fond images of spring blossoms decorating the Dunwich hills, the sunset beauty illuminating the hill-crowning menhirs, lakeside family picnics, times of good fellowship around the pickle barrel in Osborne's General Store, and many more. Even in Dunwich life could be good, often *had* been good.

Interspersed amid these visions other, quite different, images erupted: picturing horrific hellscapes of cratered deserts under acid-oozing skies. Thunder crashed with sufficient force to shatter mountain peaks beneath. Things identifiable as living entities only by their animation collided and ripped each other asunder. Dimensions were confused; strange hues baffled perception. And bellowing bestial screams filled the air. Worse yet, in the distance nightmarish shapes very like the monster of which they now counted as constituent cells roamed the scene.

Was this, then, the destination to which the Dunwich chimera sought to drag the unsuspecting Earth? Those absorbed into the ravaging monster already existed in a hell but dreaded unleashing a worse one upon all mankind. They knew it was time to resist, time to confute the monster's nefarious aims.

The Thing had almost gained the summit, then hesitated. Its prisoners shared a telepathic understanding that the creature found itself stymied. It did not know what its predecessor knew: the formula from the *Necronomicon*. The dying Wilbur Whateley had transmitted it to his invisible sibling. It would have been effective to pry open the dimensional portal had not the cursed bipeds interfered.

In this crucial moment, a chorus of inner voices commanded the Dunwich entity to turn back, to give up. There was no thought of freeing themselves. That, they sensed, was impossible. But that hardly mattered now.

*

But the Gates *were* opening! Was it all in vain?

Perhaps not, because the Earth was not moved from its proper place. Nor did a hideous flood tide of mind-shocking monsters come crashing through to our world.

Instead, a single gigantic maw protruded and swallowed the Dunwich creature. As for the wretched souls aboard that awful ark, they were simply snuffed out, which was a mercy. Or so you and I may hope.

OFFERINGS

by Henry J. Vester III

I drift like fear in London's fog
And stand, night-shrouded,
In her alleys, her doorways, and her rubbish-choked yards.
These streets are black as Hell's gaping maw.
There is no white chapel here.
I have no face. Even as I pass beneath
A lone gas lamp I am invisible.
A starving cat casts its bright yellow eyes
Upon me, and vanishes.

I am many, and I am none.
They call me Leather Apron and Red Jack.
They say I am a doctor, a Jew,
A lascar, even a policeman.
I am none of these.
I know who I am.
I am the right hand of Death.

My slim, bright friend does his work so well.
One after another, after another.
I drink their terrors as I would fine wine.
I store them within,
Cherishing them as priceless shining jewels,
Toothsome offerings for
The One who waits.

I know not who or what He is,

But I see Him in my dreams.
He comes to me ravenous, demanding...
Kthulu, the One who sleeps.
I offer Him my precious jewels,
One after another, after another.
These are my gifts, my sacrifices, my worship.
He feeds upon the terrors and is pleased.
He feeds, and then rewards me
With dark and terrible ecstacies beyond imagination.

Again the night descends, and again
I become darkness.
The clock of St. Mary's tolls once.
The hunt continues.

The Devout Derleth

by Andrew M. Seddon

August Derleth.

Surely no name elicits such passions in the realm of H.P. Lovecraft studies as his. Praised on the one hand, for preserving the works and legacy of Lovecraft, abhorred on the other for putting his own interpretative gloss on the stories. Admired and derided. His detractors, like S.T. Joshi, many; his defenders, like John Haefele, few. Arguments rage back and forth about what exactly Derleth did and why, and those interested can consult the works of Joshi, Haefele, and others for in-depth explorations. But it is not my intent to enter into this argument, rather to explore a different aspect.

Derleth's reimagined Lovecraft's cosmos by adding to Lovecraft's bleak atheism wherein humans were merely an irrelevant sideshow, an eternal conflict of good vs evil in which humans were involved, and by imposing a structured order onto Lovecraft's chaos. This is typically asserted as due to his being a "devout Christian" or more specifically, a "devout Catholic." But how accurate is this, and how did his Catholicism affect his writing, particularly his weird stories? What evidence is there for this assertion?

Without having access to Derleth's correspondence, my analysis is based upon the single biography *Derleth: Hawk...and Dove* by Dorothy M. Grobe Litersky (described on one website as being a "rather problematical and questionable book by a former student of his") and the weird short stories themselves; some 136 of them (excluding duplicates) collected in eight volumes: *Someone in the Dark, Colonel Markesan and Less Pleasant People, Mr. George and Other Odd Persons, Dwellers in Darkness, The Derleth Mythos, The Watchers Out of Time, Not Long for This World,* and *Something Near.*

Let's begin with the biography.

August William Derleth was born into a Catholic family in Sauk City, Wisconsin on February 24, 1909. He was presumably baptized soon after birth, and received Extreme Unction (Last Rites) at the early age of five after sustaining a head injury in a fall. He lay unconscious for two days before making a complete recovery. He attended parochial school at St. Aloysius Catholic School. While Litersky tells us about Derleth's literary efforts and romantic entanglements, there is no further mention of religion until 1940 when we learn that he took a young assistant friend to church regularly.

August Derleth

He was, however, not above criticizing the Catholic hierarchy, as he did in 1949, when he wrote to former First Lady Eleanor Roosevelt (a lifelong Episcopalian) in support of her opposition to federal funding for parochial schools, which she considered to be a violation of separation of church and state. (Derleth even made sure that the newspapers received a copy of his letter). Francis Cardinal Spellman accused Eleanor of anti-Catholicism. Derleth in turn claimed that Cardinal Spellman's response was bigoted and narrow-minded and denied freedom of opinion to others. Derleth assured Mrs. Roosevelt that not all Catholics or Catholic priests were like Cardinal Spellman.

As well as disagreeing with the hierarchy, Derleth also disagreed with the Church's stance on sexual morality, as Litersky relates. For example, in addition to his own lifestyle, (Litersky asserts that he was bisexual and had lovers of both sexes), he was in favor of sterilization to prevent the birth of defective children, a position he first articulated in 1939. He was unswayed by Pope Pius XI's encyclical *Casti connubii* (*On Christian Marriage*) of 1930 (Litersky mistakenly refers to an encyclical of December 1929) and reiterated his position in 1953 and again in 1964.

He became engaged to Sandy Winters, a young woman 26 years his junior, and when she was found to be pregnant (the child may or may not have been his) demanded she procure an abortion. However, the doctors determined the pregnancy to be too far advanced, and so Derleth agreed to proceed with the marriage as long as the child was given up at birth. The wedding, on April 6, 1953 was performed by Fr. Sylvester Van Berkel at St. Aloysius Church.

The marriage did not last, and Derleth and Sandra divorced in 1959, Derleth receiving custody of their two children. He seems not to have sought an annulment, but instead wrote an article complaining that wealthy people were able to buy their way out of the sin of divorce, whereas the poor were excluded from the church's good graces. Litersky writes that "apparently Derleth was not able to get re-instated as a Catholic unless he could afford a substantial donation to make him welcome in church again." Given that sexual morality was not Derleth's strong point, one wonders just how serious this gripe was to be taken. He had other lovers, and near the end of his life was pondering marriage again – albeit to a married woman who desired a divorce from her husband. Derleth would surely have known that without annulments for both parties a church wedding would have been out of the question.

The year 1969 saw him receive the Last Rites for a second time, following complications from gallbladder surgery. Yet again he survived, but his energy and stamina never really recovered and he began to believe that his time was short...and perhaps even that death would offer him an escape from a relationship that he felt would overwhelm him. He passed away on July 4, 1971 of an apparent heart attack. A requiem Mass was held at St. Aloysius Church with five priests in attendance.

Although Lovecraft was known to have commented on "little Augie's Christian tendencies," Litersky's biography does not leave the impression that Derleth was particularly devout. Apart from that initial comment she tells us nothing further about Derleth's attendance at Mass or Confession. John Haefele (*A Look Behind the Derleth Mythos*) appears to reach the same conclusion: Derleth "was never so dogmatic as one might think...though he would probably acknowledge the Catholic Church as a positive component of modern society, Derleth personally adopted a modified Scientific Humanism as his social philosophy" (p. 20-21). He also quotes a letter from Richard Tierney who wrote after meeting Derleth, "I got the impression that intellectually he was an atheist or close to it. He also thought we were on this earth one time around and that was it." This is, however, an impression only and not a definitive statement, and impressions, as we know, can be in error.

J.S. Mackley, in an essay in *Theology and H.P. Lovecraft* edited by Austin M. Freeman, quotes Derleth as referring to himself as an "anticlerical Catholic," and that "the Catholic faith is one thing, and...the men in it are another." Mackley concludes that, "All this suggests that Derleth opposed the institution of the Roman Catholic Church when expressing or seeking worldly power, but supported the fundamental teaching of the Bible and Roman Catholic doctrine and sacramental practice" (p.83).

So the picture we receive of Derleth's supposed "devoutness" is rather mixed. It is perhaps reasonable to conclude that he accepted Catholic belief in general without necessarily holding to all of it or being particularly devout; a not uncommon position. He certainly considered himself to be a Catholic, and there is no suggestion that he ever thought of leaving the Church.

What can we learn, then, from his writing?

It is important to note Derleth's own view of his writing, which he explained in an essay in *The Book of Catholic Authors* in 1960: "I have never thought of myself as a Catholic author, but rather only as a writer who is a Catholic, and apart from a novel in progress (*The Lock and the Key*) and juveniles, have made little attempt at Catholic writing." He lists St. Augustine and Jacques Maritain as Catholic influences, and expressed admiration for Hilaire Belloc, G.K. Chesterton, Francois Mauriac, and Monsignor Ronald Knox.

From this statement we may conclude that Derleth saw himself primarily as a writer who happened to be Catholic; that is, someone who looked at life and the world from a Catholic viewpoint but whose writings might or might not reflect that outlook, rather than one who wrote from a distinctly Catholic viewpoint with the intent of infusing his writing with Catholic sensibilities; that is, someone deliberately promoting Catholicism.

Primarily, that is, but not exclusively, because in 1943 his novel *Shadow of Night*, part of his regional Sac Prairie Saga, was chosen by the Cardinal Hayes Literature Committee as one of the best Catholic books of the year. And in 1955 he wrote three historical juveniles: *Father Marquette and the Great River*, *St. Ignatius and the Company of Jesus*, and *Columbus and the New World*, the first two of which are still in print from Ignatius Press. Although he indirectly received a papal blessing for these from Pope John XXIII 1959, as the blessing was for the publisher, Vision Books, and the authors of the series, Litersky claims Derleth felt bitter at the need to write these, as they took him away from his saga and his poetry.

Indeed, with these exceptions (and possibly the Mythos discussed below) it is difficult to see any overwhelming Catholic, or even Christian, influence in Derleth's weird fiction, which to be fair, he did not rate highly, as he wrote these stories for pulp magazines as a source of income.

Derleth's stories were often formulaic: someone does something bad (John murders his Uncle Bob for an inheritance) and receives retribution from beyond the grave (Bob's ghost returns to exact revenge; Derleth seems to have a fascination with malefactors being strangled). Or a person comes into possession of an object with evil powers and suffers the consequences. Or someone seeks forbidden knowledge and comes to a bad end. Derleth's fertile imagination crafted many variations on this basic premise: evil doesn't pay.

In my survey of Derleth's non-Mythos stories, I came across four characters who were Catholic priests:

Those Who Seek: A priest gives information.

The Return of Andrew Bentley: The good, strong priest Fr. Burkhardt of Sac Prairie successfully combats a revenant and its familiar.

Eyes of the Serpent: A bishop declines to help because he doesn't want to make concessions to superstition.

The Occupant of the crypt: Fr. Napier helps a professor dispose of a vampire.

Out of these four, two successfully combat evil. This is not exactly a stellar showing for Catholic clergy, perhaps reflective of Derleth's anti-clericalism. Other religious types are few and far between: an Anglican vicar who comes to a bad end in *Here, Daemos;* Mass-going Mr. Larkin who cannot escape from evil in *The Pacer,* and a disbelieving minister (presumably Protestant) in *Nellie Foster*.

One might also have expected from a Catholic more in the line of "bell, book, and candle." But of crucifixes there are few: a blessed crucifix wielded against a vampire in *Nellie Foster*; Fr. Burkhardt using the power of the crucifix in *The Return of Andrew Bentley*; and a medallion and crucifix "blessed by St. Augustine" in *The Occupant of the Crypt*.

There are few other things that jump out as specifically Christian: a reference to ultimate justice in *The Telephone in the Library*; a quote from the Beatitudes in *Blessed are the Meek*; and a single reference to God in *The Occupant of the Crypt:* "…evil things fear only good and the source of all good which is God."

In these stories written for *Weird Tales* and other pulp magazines, Derleth apparently did not see the need or desirability to insert much in the way of Christian elements, whether or not he intended to promote either a Christian message or support a Christian worldview. But still, these few are enough to at least imply belief on Derleth's part.

What, then, of Derleth's Mythos stories?

In *Ithaqua*, Fr. Brisbois discusses legends of malign elemental spirits and compares them to Christianity: "After all, have we not our own Biblical legend of the struggle between elemental Good and Evil as personified by our deity and the forces of Satan in the pre-dawn era of our world?" A similar sentiment is expressed in *The Return of Hastur* of "our legendary Genesis" being an explanation of his mythos. In *The Shadow out of Space* ancestral memories become the Christian mythos. *The Gable Window* becomes even more explicit when the narrator remarks, "Did it matter whether you called it God and the Devil, or the Elder Gods and the Ancient Ones, Good or Evil…" before launching into a list of gods including Nodens of the Elder gods and Azathoth of the Ancient Ones.

The House in the Valley describes the Elder Gods as residing on Betelgeuse, against whom the Ancient Ones (aka the Great Old Ones) rebelled in a "legend pattern paralleling the rebellion of Satan against the archangels of Heaven."

Rather than the cosmic indifference of the creatures in Lovecraft's mythos (creatures which, it should be noted, are not supernatural in any sense, but simply extra-terrestrial beings of the material realm, although ones endowed with awesome powers) Derleth refashions it as a battle between good and evil. "One may not need to see the embodiment of evil to believe in it," we are told in *Witches' Hollow*. And in *Watcher from the Sky*, "Evil is the ancient enemy of all good whether as we who are Christians understand it or whether it is understood in some prehistoric mythos."

But the weapon against this evil is not the Crucifix, or anything else Christian, but the five-pointed star, the symbol of the Elder Gods, which appears in various stories: *The Horror from the Depths*, *The Gable Window*, *Witches' Hollow*, *Something from Out There*. I do not recall encountering a single instance of anyone praying for Divine aid.

Something from Out There references the potentially deranged monk Clithanus who told a story of St. Augustine. But the story with the most Catholic elements is *The Gorge Beyond Salapunco*, in which we find Fr. Andrada: "a priest, a missionary among the Indians of the interior. In his own way he is a great man, possibly even a saintly man, though the

August Derleth at his writing desk

Church hesitates to recognize him as such...the Church is exceedingly careful in such matters, as no doubt you know, and that is well-advised, since it is presumably infallible in spiritual matters, and it cannot afford to be in error." The good priest is killed, however, and his form assumed by an evil creature preaching the return of Cthulhu, a being "who was as 'old as time' before the teachings of Christ were made known to mankind." This creature, in due course, is not killed by any spiritual or supernatural means, but by a bullet.

The Black Island contains an expansive description of Derleth's conception of the Mythos, as well as a list of great catastrophes affecting the earth, several drawn from the Old Testament, and one referencing the (real) Spanish priest, Fr. Bernadino de Sahagun, a pioneering ethnographer.

But, as Mackley writes, "Arguably there is nothing in either Lovecraft or Derleth's writings reflecting the Christian concepts of God or Heaven and Hell. Derleth systematized Lovecraft's pantheon of cosmic chaos and replaced it with forces of cosmic good and cosmic evil and aligned these creatures with the four elements all of which are motifs in Christianity" (p.81); that is, earth, air, water, and fire. And yet Mackley writes, "For Derleth, the Creator, who loves, sustains, and nurtures us, remains in control of the destiny of the universe. The fact that the Great Old Ones exist means, in the way Derleth presents the Mythos, that they are part of the Divine Plan" (p.86).

In short, Derleth brings in Christian imagery and creates a parallel heavenly pantheon to oppose Lovecraft's beings that then represent Satan and the evil orders, all of which are subject to God's will. God, however, is noticeable by His absence in Derleth's mythos. The Derleth-created Nodens, chief among the Elder Gods, is not the Creator God of Christianity; a more appropriate analogy would be with St. Michael the Archangel.

And there is no Messiah or Savior in Derleth any more than there is in Lovecraft. The Elder Gods help humanity out from time to time, but there is no mention of God's saving action. Humanity remains fairly irrelevant, invested with no cosmic significance. On an individual level there's no sin, no need for repentance or redemption; there's no living, breathing Church animated by God's Spirit performing His work in the world.

Despite this, it is surely evident that Derleth, for all his admiration for Lovecraft and commitment to preserving Lovecraft's work and legacy, has no truck with his mentor's nihilistic atheism. For Derleth, good and evil are real, predating humanity and hence not simply human societal constructs.

The way that Derleth recast Lovecraft's Mythos provides evidence that Lovecraft's atheism was not for him. Underlying Derleth's own Mythos, and demonstrated in the (admittedly few) stories showing the power of the Crucifix over evil, Derleth implies that God exists. God is there, even if He is not seen.

And yet there is nothing in either the biography or Derleth's weird fiction that would lead to the definitive conclusion that he was particularly "devout." Catholic, he was, but the depth of his conviction and faith is not discernable. Perhaps his letters and other writings tell a different tale. Or perhaps we are best left with Derleth's own conclusion that he was not a Catholic writer, but a writer who was Catholic.

Before my murmured exorcism, The world, a wispy wraith, shall flee

The Song of the Necromancer

by Clark Ashton Smtih

I will repeat a subtle rune
  And thronging suns of Otherwhere
  Shall blaze upon the blinded air,
  And spectres terrible and fair
Shall walk the riven world at noon.

The star that was mine empery
  Is dust upon unwinnowed skies;
  But primal dreams have made me wise,
  And soon the shattered years shall rise
To my remembered sorcery.

To mantic mutterings, brief and low,
  My palaces shall lift amain,
  My bowers bloom; I will regain
  The lips whereon my lips have lain
In rose-red twilights long ago.

Before my murmured exorcism,
  The world, a wispy wraith, shall flee;
  A stranger earth, a weirder sea,
  Peopled with shapes of faery,
Shall swell upon the waste abysm.

The pantheons of darkened stars
  Shall file athwart the crocus dawn;
  Goddess and Gorgon, Lar and faun,
  Shall tread the amaranthine lawn;
And giants fight their thunderous wars.

Like graven mountains of basalt,
  Dark idols of my demons there
  Shall tower through bright zones of air,
  Fronting the sun with level stare;
And hell shall pave my deepest vault.

Phantom and fiend and sorcerer
  Shall serve me...till my term shall pass,
  And I become no more, alas!
  Than a frail shadow on the glass
Before some latter conjurer.

Editor's note: Here, in a trilogy of tales, the author presents a Derlethian scenario in which the Old Ones manage to break the bonds of their eons long imprisonment and confront the Elder Gods in a cosmic rematch! Who will be the victor? Read on and find out!

Slaughter House

By Arnden Christopher

You try to remember but it gets harder all the time. Slowly, however, it comes back to you...

It all started the day your office received a call from Cal Thompos out at Cow Hill Farm. You were busy on another call and so didn't have the time to get out toward Dunwich till the following Tuesday. By then, the evidentiary trail might have grown cold but then, as the county's only full time agricultural agent, you were spread pretty thin what with regular livestock inspections, tracking avian flu, and testing rivers and streams for use of illegal fertilizers and sprays, you had plenty to keep yourself busy. But finally, Tuesday came around when you were scheduled for a produce check at the Dean's Corners farmers' market. When you'd finished there, you trucked the few miles down 113 to Dunwich.

You already knew where the Thompos outfit was located having visited there a number of times over the years. Thompos operated a slaughter house and meat packing business at his farm, popular among livestock producers all over the Miskatonic Valley. In your experience, you'd never received any complaints about Cal's operation so you were curious as to the nature of the call you'd received the previous week, not least because it had come from Cal himself. It wasn't often that your office was called upon by farmers themselves when something was amiss. Usually they were anxious to keep prying eyes as far away from their operations as possible. And if necessary, were willing to slip you a little something to keep quiet.

As always along Dunwich's badly maintained roads, you had to take your time or risk breaking an axle in one of the many potholes that dotted the crumbling tarmac. Trees crowded the side of the roads, their untrimmed branches threatening power lines that snaked overhead. Ordinary residences and housing developments were few in town; Dunwich being one of the last townships in Massachusetts that retained a mostly agricultural profile with forest and farmland dominating the countryside. You passed a number of farmsteads in varying states of disrepair including Jed Comer's pig farm and Zekiel Dormer's dairy on the way to Old Brookside Road along which the Thompos place was located. There, the trees crowded even closer overhead and the late summer's sunshine barely penetrated the gloomy forest that almost choked off Oddy's Brook as it passed through a culvert beneath the road. Finally, you reached the Thompos place, designated by a faded sign secured to a big oak. It was hard to believe that heavy trucks came and went down here all the time, delivering stock to be slaughtered or carrying off dressed meats to local supermarkets and restaurants.

You hauled off on the steering wheel and brought the aging GMC Sierra to a halt, brakes squeaking. You hardly had time to step from the cab when you were met by Cal Thompos.

"Sorry it took so long to get out here, Cal," you said, holding out your hand in greeting.

"S'all right, Bob," said Cal, taking your hand in a firm, calloused grip. "Wasn't exactly an emergency but definitely puzzling. I might even say unnerving."

You raised your eyebrows at that. "Unnerving"

wasn't the kind of vocabulary you expected from Cal or many other farmers you knew.

"Sounds mysterious," you said.

Cal shrugged and led the way toward the rear of the plant's main facility. Passing by the various loading docks, you wrinkled your nose against the smells wafting through the open overhead doors. Inside, the stench became more intense and the noise of processing and conveyor machines coupled with workers shouting to each other to make themselves heard assaulted your senses. Luckily, Cal didn't linger there. Instead he continued on to the far side of the work floor where the big walk in refrigerators were located.

He stopped before one of them and pulled on the heavy latch. The thick, insulated door swung slowly open and he motioned for you to step inside. Cal left the door ajar as if reluctant to be sealed inside the space with whatever was kept there. But as you looked around, you noticed that the 'fridge unit was empty but for a single wooden crate.

"Seems a bit of a waste of space," you said.

"Maybe," agreed Cal. "But you'll see why I didn't want to keep anything else in here with that."

You wondered what was up. Meat from a diseased animal?

Placing a handkerchief over his nose, Cal lifted the lid of the wooden crate and said, "Come over and take a look at this."

Warily, you approached the box and peered in.

At first glance, it was hard to make out anything; but as you continued to look, disquieting details emerged. Whatever it was, it was no animal you had ever seen before. It was gelitinous but with rigid appendages that were obviously legs and fore arms but jointed in the wrong places, as if the thing were an insect rather than an animal. The smell it emitted soon became too strong for you and you were forced to back away.

"Seen enough?" asked Cal.

All you could do was nod as you buried your nose in the crook of your elbow.

Cal let the lid drop and led the way out of the 'fridge.

Outside, where you and Cal could catch your breaths, you asked: "What is it?"

"Hoped you could tell me," said Cal. "My men found it among a flock of sheep they herded into the factory."

"It's a sheep?"

"If it is, it's the most deformed specimen I've ever seen. No. Can't be a sheep. It's...something else. You saw it. You think it's a sheep?"

You shook your head. "It was in among a flock of sheep you say?"

Cal nodded. "Want to talk with Lucas? He was in charge when the flock was brought in."

"Definitely."

Cal disappeared into the floor of the rendering plant and soon returned with Lucas, a stocky fellow wrapped in bloody coveralls.

"Tell Bob what happened the night you brought in that thing," instructed Cal.

"Nothing much to tell," said Lucas. "We fetched the flock from the holding pen and herded 'em to the plant. It was after dark by then so we didn't notice anything wrong. It was still on the gloomy side when the animals were directed into the shute. Jimmy started in on the stunning, whacking one animal after the other. The usual. But one that he hit collapsed too easy. The bolt buried itself in its head and wouldn't come loose. That never happened. He had to remove the bolt from the gun and then drag the carcass out of line to make way for the rest. That was when I noticed there was something weird about the animal. I went to the switchboard and turned up the main lights and that's when we saw that the thing was no sheep. It was like a huge bug or something. The other guys backed off, scared. I was too but being in charge, couldn't afford to just let it sit there. I got one of the wooden crates and managed to stuff it in. Showed it to Cal the next morning but by then the stink was really bad. That's when we put it in the 'fridge until you could come by and take a look."

"You say it was mixed in with the rest of the sheep?" you asked.

Lucas nodded. "Yeah. Acted kind of funny come to think of it. Jimmy thought it acted like it knew what was comin'. Like it knew what the hammer was for."

Cal laughed nervously.

This was usually about the time Cal would slip him a few hundred dollars to look the other way, as he'd done in the past, but this time he had no interest in skirting the law.

"I don't know what that thing is, but you've got to take it off my hands," said Cal. "I don't want it around here any longer. I can't risk my operation here. If word gets out about it, it'll hurt my reputation and my business."

Recalling the thing in the box and its smell, you weren't anxious to take it off of Cal's hands yourself but you knew it had to be done.

"I'll take it to the state lab," you said. "Maybe they can make something of it."

Cal wasted no time in getting a couple men to haul the crate out and place it in the bed of your truck.

"Before I go, can you tell me whose flock of sheep it was that the thing came in with?"

"Betty Dorn," said Cal. "She brought them in only a few hours before Lucas herded them in to the plant."

"She delivered in the middle of the night?" you asked. "Is that unusual?"

Cal shrugged. "Unusual, but not unheard of."

Cal was familiar with the Dorn place but decided to get the specimen to the state agrilab as soon as possible. The way it smelled, it might not be long before there wasn't anything left to examine.

It was a few days later when you found yourself back in Dunwich, driving its narrow roads leading to the Dorn place. You knew you were getting close after passing the remains that marked the old Whateley lot. You'd heard vague stories of the explosion that had destroyed the house and barn there decades ago but nothing you'd paid much attention to. The Dorn farm was another mile or so back where the forest had been cleared for open fields and pastures made suitable for sheep grazing.

You spotted the familiar mail box that leaned dangerously off kilter and pulled in to the long, rutted drive that led up to the house. Cutting the engine of your truck, you stepped out into the hot summer sunshine and looked around. Everything seemed quiet with the pens behind the barn empty of livestock. The barn doors were open so you decided to check there first.

Just inside the doors, stacks of hay bales towered to the dim rafters and the smell of shorn grass was heavy on the air.

"Is that you, Bob?"

You spun around at the voice to find Betty Dorn, looking manly in overalls, straw hat, and work boots, silhouetted against the sun.

"Hi, Betty," you greeted her. "Did Cal tell you I was coming by?"

Betty nodded, removing the stalk of grass she'd been gritting between her teeth.

"Did he say why?"

"Something about another animal among the consignment of sheep I sent him?"

"Right. His men found...something mixed in with them, something no one could identify."

"Really?"

"You saw nothing like that when you rounded up the sheep for shipment?"

Betty shrugged. "It was dark out so if there was, we didn't notice."

"You did it after dark? How come?"

"Well, there's been some kind of predator out here," said Betty. "Must come down from the hills looking for easy prey. Whatever it was, it got a couple of my sheep. Tore them apart. After that, I wanted to get my livestock out of here and over to Cal's before I lost any more."

You recalled then reports of livestock found dead in other towns in the area; cattle, poultry, pigs, as well as wild animals such as deer and local black bears. Even coyotes, which eliminated the only suspects, as rare as it was for a coyote to attack anything bigger than themselves. You'd briefly considered wolves, but there hadn't been a wolf sighted in the valley for a hundred years. That left only one possibility; one you'd hoped was wrong: human beings.

As with most heavily wooded areas in Massachusetts, the valley had its share of hunters but none, so far as you had ever heard, gave any reason for local farmers to worry would present any danger to their livestock. In any case, hunters were pretty strict about their own code which involved field dressing their kills for later consumption.

But the kills you'd been hearing about, confirmed by Betty's description of what she'd found among her sheep, didn't involve systematic skinning and quartering, but outright dismemberment with odd body parts taken away. That could still suggest humans, but humans of a more disturbing variety.

"Did you take any pictures of the carcasses?" you asked.

"Right here," said Betty, pulling out her cell

phone. After fooling around with it a bit, she handed it over to you.

You scrolled through the images and they confirmed your suspicions. Just like the others reported over the last several months. Handing the cell back to Betty, you used your own to make a note of their locations.

Back at the office, you began a long delayed project of marking the reported mutilations on a wall map of the valley. You were surprised at how many there were. But when you'd finished, there were enough to make a rough guess as to the epicenter of the occurrences: About three miles farther back from the Dorn farm, deep in the third growth forest of Dunwich around a hill known by the locals as the Devil's Hopyard.

While a plan of action was forming in your mind, you took some time to drive in to Boston for a visit with Chris Samkin, manager of the state's agrilab where you'd left the remains given to you by Cal Thompos.

But there, you ran into a surprise.

"Chris quit yesterday," said the assistant lab manager.

"Really? How come?"

The man shrugged. "He didn't say. He was upset over something, I'm sure of that. I'll never forget the look on his face when he told me. Just said he was quitting and walked out."

"What about that job he was working on for me," you asked.

"What one was that?"

"The specimen I brought in from Dunwich. The one from the Thompos integrated rendering plant."

"Not familiar with it. Let me check the files."

The assistant manager retreated to a computer work station and scrolled through a number of windows. He shook his head.

"Nothing here," he concluded. "You sure you brought it in?"

"Of course I'm sure!"

"Well, there's no record of it here...wait one." He did some more checking. "Funny. All of Chris' files have been deleted. That's a big no-no."

"You think Chris did it himself?"

"Must have. But he knew that was against policy; against the law, actually."

Suddenly you knew that if you didn't reach Chris first, he would surely be tied up in a departmental investigation and once that happened, he'd be forbidden to talk about his case to anyone.

"Where does Chris live?" you ask, trying to keep the desperation out of your voice.

"Outside the Beltway someplace. Billerica? Yeah, I think it's Billerica." He pulled out his cell and did some checking. "43 Delton Place, unit 12."

"Thanks."

You wasted no time in returning to your truck, inputting the address into the GPS function of your cell and finding your way back onto the highway and out of town. Forty-five minutes later, you were in Billerica and on the grounds of the condominium development where Chris lived. But would he be home?

You found the proper building and pressed the button beneath Chris' name: Christopher Samkin.

There was a reply.

"Who is it?" asked a tired sounding voice.

"It's me, Bob, Bob Quincy. Can I talk to you for a minute?"

There was a pause at the other end and then the buzzer sounded allowing you to push through the entrance door.

Upstairs, Chris let you in to his unit. He seemed nervous or worried about something but you chose to ignore it.

"I just came from the lab," you said. "They told me you quit?"

Chris nodded wearily. "Yeah. And it was on account of you."

"Me! How?"

"That specimen you brought in," he said. "I tried to reach you about it for days."

You took out your cell and checked for messages but found none from Chris. No phone logs either. You told him so.

"Never mind," he said. "What I want to know is where the devil did you find that thing you brought in?"

"You didn't identify it?"

"No, I didn't!"

"Okay; calm down," you said, holding up your hands. "I got it at the Thompos rendering facility in Dunwich."

"A slaughter house!"

"Yeah, it came in among a flock of sheep and was killed in the shute before anyone realized it wasn't a sheep. It was in among the sheep, gathered in by accident from the originating farm. No one knows anything about it."

"Hard to believe a mistake like that could happen."

"It was before dawn and the floods hadn't been lit."

Chris ran a nervous hand through his hair before throwing himself into a chair.

"Well, I don't mind telling you that thing had me stumped," he said. "The lab ran the remains through every test in the book and so far as we could tell, it was neither animal nor vegetable nor anything in between!"

"What are you talking about?"

"What I'm saying is that whatever it was, it was unidentifiable. We even sent out samples to the physics lab at MIT to run it under their electron microscope. They couldn't figure it out either. Even on the molecular level, nothing about it was familiar. The closest they could come to a comparison were certain elements found in a meteorite that fell in Antarctica millions of years ago."

You laughed then but Chris wasn't joking.

"So you've got nothing for me?"

"Literally," said Chris. "The remains decomposed into an inert slurry then even that disappeared, leaving us nothing but our notes."

"There were no notes," you told him. "The assistant manager I spoke to said all the files were deleted. Chris, you're in hot water. You've broken the law."

Chris laughed then. Not in good humor but the kind you hear from someone at the end of his rope.

"You think I care about that?" he said, when he'd finally stopped. "Bob, this thing whatever it was, was like nothing found on Earth. It violated every known law of biology and chemistry." He shuddered. "When I think of those deep backwoods out there where it came from. The brooks and streams that no one ever sees or knows where they originate, or where they drain. Some of them, I understand, start from deep underground. Maybe that's where…"

"Stop it, Chris," you ordered when he began to ramble. "Is that why you quit? Because you were stumped?"

Chris laughed again and said, "It was just…it made no sense! It threw everything I thought I understood about the natural world into a cocked hat! It forced me to admit that I really knew nothing at all. That everything science tells us is a lie. All based on perception, not on reality."

"And what reality…?"

"I don't know! I just don't know! I just know that suddenly I felt like I was living on the edge of a cliff. One more step and oblivion! The only way I could save myself was to step away from the brink. So I quit. Maybe I'll get a job shoveling manure somewhere. Or sweeping the streets…"

You realized then that you were not going to get any more help from Chris. Something had rattled him but good. And recalling the thing as you first saw it in that crate…well, you could almost understand how someone could just throw up their hands and walk away in despair.

It was all you could do to keep from sinking into melancholy yourself but by the time you returned to your truck, you had recovered from the spell, determined on a new plan of action.

You were no closer to resolving the mystery of the specimen found by Cal Thompos but that didn't mean there were no avenues you could pursue. Back at your office, you again studied the map of Miskatonic Valley, noting the places where mutilations or slayings of livestock had occurred over the past few months with its epicenter in the vicinity of the Devil's Hopyard. The only thing you could think of doing next was to go out there and look around. But that seemed too aimless. You could wander around the woods back there and never find anything suspicious. If there was something stalking the wildlife out there, you had to find some way to make it come to you. That meant bait.

Some days later, you pulled your truck off a little used road back of the Devil's Hopyard and cut the engine. You pulled out the backpack you'd prepared and shrugged into it. Next, you lifted out the sheep you'd bought from Betty Dorn and made sure the leash was secure. From there, you entered the surrounding forest following a game trail you'd learned about from local hunters. It was faint, but obvious as it wound among the undergrowth. On your right, the land began to rise quickly as it formed the hill atop which was located the Devil's Hopyard. Presently, you reached the little brook you were told of and followed it up stream. The

Slowly, you reached for your rifle, cradling it in your arms, trying to pinpoint the exact location where you expected the predator to emerge.

going was fairly easy until about a mile in, you found the grassy clearing you'd been looking for. Looking around, there was no sign of recent activity by wildlife or anything else.

Setting your pack down behind some trees at the edge of the clearing, you shoved a metal stake into the ground in the center of the clearing and, taking the leash in hand, secured it to the stake. The sheep didn't seem to mind the hike or the limitations on its movement as it immediately

began to graze.

Returning to your pack, you found a cozy spot beneath a big pine tree whose branches swept the ground and screened you effectively. A thick carpet of needles made a natural mattress and you settled down for what was likely to be an extended stay. You checked the chamber of your Henry .22 rimfire rifle to make sure the gun was loaded. It was. You set it aside where you could reach it quickly if you had to. By then, the sun was going down and you were hungry. Breaking out one of the MREs you brought with you, you started the heating element and settled down for a hot supper and a long night.

As evening came on, a full moon slowly rose from among the surrounding trees, finally breaking into the open above the horizon. It was late in the season and the cold nights kept down mosquitoes and other insects making your vigil a not uncomfortable one. Around you, there were other night sounds: the distant howl of the occasional coyote, the hoot of owl and call of night bird, the snapping of the occasional twig from the step of some nocturnal animal. None of it was anything to draw your attention in particular. But when those other sounds arose, you had no trouble recognizing them as something out of the ordinary. They came as slight shuffling noises from the woods on the far side of the clearing. They came and went as if whatever was making the sounds was moving in fits and starts. A predator? You looked at the sheep to see if it sensed anything amiss but it continued to sleep where it had curled up for the night. Clearly, the animal wasn't bred for the wild otherwise it's every sense would be on alert.

Slowly, you reached for your rifle, cradling it in your arms, trying to pinpoint the exact location where you expected the predator to emerge. Your guess wasn't far wrong. Something that shone whitely in the moonlight poked from the dark underbrush. You strained to make out more detail, but failed. Hesitating at the edge of the woods, it moved forward again on what seemed like a jointed set of legs protruding from a gelid core, a sight that froze you into immobility. Your hands gripped the rifle more tightly. All you could do was stare as the thing moved relentlessly toward the sheep. Why didn't the creature wake up? You wanted to warn it but your throat remained constricted as you watched. At last the sheep stirred. It's head lifted as it listened. Such was its innocence that when it spotted the creeping thing, it made no reaction. The first sound it made was its last as it screeched in sudden pain when the thing leaped the remaining distance and seized it. You crouched there, beneath the pine boughs, and watched as the thing dismembered the sheep and eviscerated it. It gathered odd bits of its carcass that it held up in a number of its limbs as it used others

to retreat back into the woods.

It was gone for some minutes before you remembered to breathe. It took a physical effort to relax your frozen muscles and pull your finger from the trigger of the .22. Trembling, you sat there, thankful for the cover of the pine branches. The thing you'd glimpsed was clearly related to the one you first saw in the wooden crate at the Thompos plant. Your original intention had been to shoot the predator when it revealed itself but that plan was now moot. But to trap it or kill it, you'd need to follow its trail, something you were not eager to do in the dark of night. In fact, you found yourself not eager to follow at all. Only your duty as an agricultural officer and your self-respect as a man, kept you from turning back.

The rest of the night passed slowly as the memory of the thing prevented sleep. At last, however, the moon went down and the sky began to brighten. Such was your fear however, that you waited until the sun had fully risen before gathering your things and stepping out into the clearing. You took only a moment to examine the remains of the sheep, noticing that one of its legs and its head were missing. If any of its internal organs had been taken as well, you couldn't immediately tell. Turning away, you made sure of your grip on the rifle and ducked into the woods at the spot where you saw the thing disappear.

In the bright morning light, the trail left by the thing was plain: broken twigs and bent branches were obvious, but mostly it was the sheen of something slimy that was the most obvious, making your efforts to follow an easy one.

As the morning waned, you noticed the terrain had been trending upward with the creature's trail moving steadily in the direction of the Devil's Hopyard. Looking up through the trees, you could make out the crest of the hill where the group of megalithic stones poked from the ground like broken teeth. Was that where the thing was headed? There was only one way to find out, so you continued following the trace left behind, instinctively avoiding the bits of slime so as not to smear your boots. It was about then that, slowly, bit by bit, a strange story began to unfold in your mind. Or did it come afterward? Or had it been all your imagination?

It went like this: the thing you were following,

like the creature in the box, was called a Shinth. It didn't have a personality or even a will of its own, but was one of many, mere extensions of a larger entity that called itself Mog-Sooth.

It was Mog-Sooth's purpose to collect certain body parts of any living creature, absorb them, and acquire their latent evolutionary energy, an energy the impossibly ancient Mog-Sooth had some relationship with from the dawn of time. This evolutionary energy was needed to fuel Mog-Sooth's escape from its Earthly prison and travel to a planet called Yuggoth there to assume its rightful place among the hierarchy of the Old Ones: Yog Sothoth, Azathoth, Nyarlathotep, even great Cthulhu himself as they gathered to prepare their long awaited retributive assault on the Elder Gods who were the cause of their exile and imprisonment of eons.

All over the Earth, gathering momentum over the past few centuries, Mog-Sooth's fellow Old Ones have been doing the same in their separate ways, gathering followers, dispatching servitors, exciting the ether across time and space, all in preparation for that climactic moment when they could break free of the bonds imposed on them by the Elder Gods and seek their long awaited revenge on those who had dethroned them from their places on high.

With the revelation completed, your mind returned to the present and you discovered that you'd continued to follow the trail and now found yourself at the base of the hill, a stone face rising steeply before you. But at its base there was a low, dark opening swathed in a tangle of underbrush. There, the trail of slime led so you pushed the brush aside to expose the opening. Strangely, you felt no hesitation about getting down on your belly and worming your way through the opening. You squirmed onwards for some minutes, the ceiling of the cave brushing your head, the trail of slime grown from a faint trace to thick streak that soiled your clothes. But you continued on until the opening widened and you were able to stand. Faintly, you wondered where your rifle had gone but it didn't matter, you were in the presence of Mog-Sooth now. Again, you wondered why you were not repulsed by its stench, revolted at its appearance: a monstrous, gelid mound that pulsed and glowed and nearly filled the cavern beneath the hill. At its edges, the spindly legged creatures you were familiar with were formed and detached to run off independently and skitter away into the tunnel leading to the outside even as others entered, returning from forays where they had collected the parts of animals and even plants that they then fed to Mog-Sooth by the simple expedient of being reabsorbed into its bulk.

Then you noticed that the surface of Mog-Sooth's bulk was somewhat clear and just beneath its outer skin, objects, moved and darted. Then, one of them broke the surface, then another, and another. They continued to extend outward, swaying on stalks of fibre with the ends resolving themselves into great, glaring eyes. They studied your frozen figure up and down until, apparently satisfied, retreated somewhat.

Still you didn't panic. You didn't back away in revolting horror. Your mind seemed a blank as you simply stared ahead. Finally, the eye things retracted back beneath the gelid mass of Mog-Sooth and were replaced by great, disjointed arm stalks that pushed their way from the mass and in moments, you'd been torn to pieces and you realized, too late, that, like the animals that had been dismembered, collected, and absorbed, humans were little different to Mog-Sooth.

But now, your the memories began to fade again. But more immediately, you remember a strange quickening of your consciousness within that of Mog-Sooth and your understanding of his purpose. You are among the million favored ones and will share in the triumph of the Old Ones when they have their revenge on the Elder Gods and resume their rightful place in the cosmos.

And yet, some part of you still cries out: *If there is such a thing as a soul, I hope that somewhere I am free, if not, then whatever this consciousness is, is trapped forever in this living hell!*

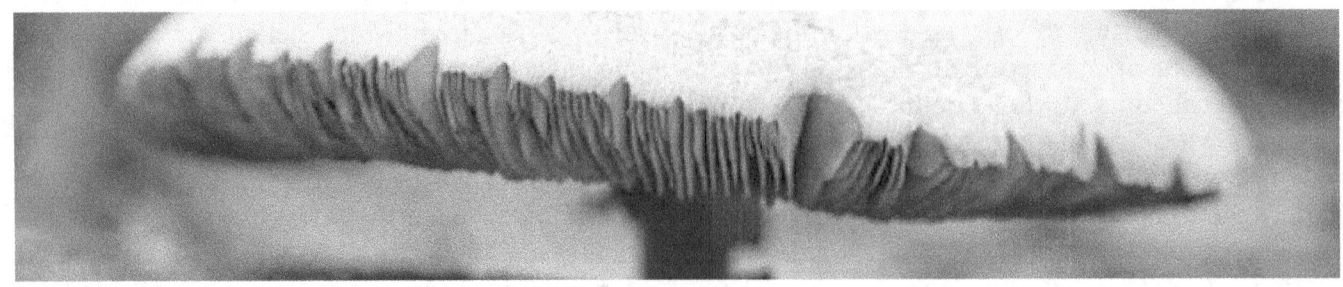

Top Secret: Incident #A0098
Report for Commander in Chief

Compiled by Arnden Christopher
Special Assistant to the President

Captain David Lunberger
United States Army Corp of Engineers
Op Warren AFB, Wyoming
May 21, 20--

To Whom It May Concern,

 After consulting my superiors I was instructed to forward this request to the Department of Agriculture, Wyoming Field Office.

 On May 1-19, I was placed in command of a unit with orders to lay down a hardened field line of comm filament in the area of the Chilicote Forest. In the process, we had cause to enter an area with apparent tree blight with a good percentage of the forest already dead. Soil conditions seemed normal at first, but upon reaching approximately 121 centimeters (4 feet), a non-soil/biological element was encountered. Test bores in the surrounding area all encountered the same material. After reporting the situation to headquarters, I was instructed to make the following request: that the Department look into the matter in a timely manner and apprise me immediately of your findings. My orders to lay down a secure landline is of the utmost urgency re national security. Your early reply to this request will be appreciated.

Thank you,
Capt. David Lunberger

*

Lawrence Kearney
Lead Mycologist
Department of Agriculture
June 17, 20--

To:
Robert Turich
Area Supervisor
Midwest District

As per request dated June 10, I led a team into the Chilicote Forest Preservation Area upon reports of extensive deforestation in northwest Wyoming. This message confirms the report with direct observation finding a ratio of 4/1 in the area. After consulting departmental actuarial tables for this rate, I've determined that there is indeed an out of nature event in process. Consequent to this finding, I attempted to mag the area of blight and have found that it extends well into two adjacent states including Idaho and Montana. With visual limits of blight measured by initial drone survey, extent of blight is estimated to encompass at least 50,000 acres. Although fusion tests from the Cheyenne forensic laboratory have not been completed, I'm confident that cause of the blight will turn out to be *Armillaria ostoyae.* As you know, if such proves to be the case, it will be the largest such find to this date...by far. I await further instructions pending laboratory results.

Larry

*

Robert Turich
Area Supervisor
Midwest District
June 20, 20--

To:
Lawrence Kearney
Lead Mycologist

Larry,
This message is to acknowledge receipt of your report of June 17 and to thank you and your team for responding to my request in good time. Consultants at the lab agree with your assessment re *Armillaria ostoyae* and advise proceed accordingly. Please continue your field survey to confirm *Armillaria ostoyae* and determine its size. As you know, department policy at this time is to leave such natural phenomena as is, especially in light of its slow rate of growth. However, if the phenomenon threatens the health and safety of local inhabitants, measures will be taken. Thus, recommendations covering different contingencies will be welcome.

Thank you,
Rob

*

Lawrence Kearney
Lead Mycologist
Department of Agriculture
July 11, 20--

To:
Robert Turich
Area Supervisor
Midwest District

This report is to confirm the presence of *Armillaria ostoyae,* or at least something resembling it pending confirmation of laboratory fusion of paired fungal samples. Assuming support from lab findings, and taking into account up to date survey results, my estimation of the size of the fungoidal growth is the largest ever found. As per report of June 17, I had estimated its size to be in the area of 50,000 acres. That estimate will have to be revised upward considerably. I'm sure your office will be as surprised as members of this team were when it was discovered that the growth in question covers almost 100,000 acres or 156 square miles and encompassing portions of Wyoming, Idaho, and Montana. The entire structure is buried beneath accumulated topsoil of at least three (3) feet and in many places as much as ten (10) feet. As to be expected, over the years, human habitations have been built, mostly ranches and farms that did not require deep bores. In a few places small towns have been established. However, in those cases, topsoil had been so deep that even basements could be dug without striking the biological strata. My guess is that this mushroom is at least 10,000 years old. My intention is keep investigating but will require some heavy equipment in order to dig through the topsoil and reach the biological strata for a more detailed analysis.

Larry

*

Associated Press dispatch
Wyoming Daily Advertiser
July 15, 20--

...world's largest mushroom.

According to mycologists working for the Department of Agriculture, an amazing discovery was made recently in the tri-state area. The largest mushroom in the world has been found in the area. Lying from three to ten feet beneath the ground, the mushroom covers nearly 156 square miles and may have begun growing before the arrival of human beings on the North American continent.

The Department of Agriculture was first alerted to the discovery with reports of a blight that was killing a number of trees in the Chilicote Forest Preservation Area.

Lead mycologist for the Department of Agriculture, Lawrence Kearney, has reassured residents that the presence of the mushroom does not present any kind of threat to the local population.

Early testing from the department's Cheyenne laboratory indicate that the mushroom is indeed a single organism that feeds on tree roots, explaining the die off of nearly one in four trees in the forest.

Department policy, said Kearney is to leave such organisms alone unless they pose a threat to human life, which he does not see in this case.

Research, however is planned to continue with heavy equipment to be used to remove topsoil and expose portions of the mushroom for examination...

*

Robert Turich
Area Supervisor
Midwest District
July 20, 20--

To:
Lawrence Kearney
Lead Mycologist
Department of Agriculture

Larry,
    Laboratory tests of samples of biomass you provided confirms fusion of paired fungal samples, however, there was a failure to identify the material as being from *Armillaria ostoyae* or any other known fungi. Further testing is ongoing, but in the meantime, continue on site investigations taking suitable precautions. Hazmat protective gear will be delivered along with heavy equipment (trailer trucks with backhoes and bulldozer) scheduled to be on site by 7/24. In addition, a team from the Cheyenne lab will accompany the equipment for on site testing and chemical analysis. Be assured that you will retain site management control.

Rob

*

To:
Robert Turich
Area Supervisor
Midwest District
Aug 8, 20--

From:
Dr. Ephraim Zolsker
Laboratory director
Department of Agriculture
Cheyenne Office

Arrived at work site on August 6 and met with field leader and chief mycologist Lawrence Kearney. He filled me in on the discovery and work in progress. A series of twelve (12) test holes were dug using back hoes that revealed the surface of the bio mass layer lying between four (4) and ten (10) feet below the topsoil layer. My team chose six (6) from which to withdraw tissue samples with subsequent testing in the mobile lab unit. As of now, I can only report that the composition of the bio mass material is completely unknown to me. Molecular breakdown reveals no known relation to Earthly fungal plant life. I come to this conclusion with great reluctance but can only report the facts as we have found them. Our team will continue with testing using polymerase chain reaction, immunochromatography, DNA sequencing, whole exome sequencing, and transcription-mediated amplification testing. Frankly, however, I have to admit my belief that this bio-mass material is like nothing ever categorized before.

Dr. Ephraim Zolsker
Laboratory director
Department of Agriculture
In the field

*

Associated Press dispatch
Wyoming Daily Advertiser
August 10, 20--

...two buildings collapsed with no injuries.

Elsewhere, in Idaho's Jefferson County, the earthquake seemed to strike with greater force. Several barns and silos are reported collapsed and a number of structures in Clarkstown as well. Again, no injuries reported.

According to the US National Seismic Network, an earthquake registering 2.6 on the richter scale was recorded in the tri-state area.

"Although earthquakes in the region are rare, there is evidence that they have occurred as far back as pre-historic times," said Prof. Isaac Jorson, of the Seismic Network. "In fact, one of the most powerful earthquakes ever to have struck the continental United States took place in 1812. With its epicenter located at Madrid, Missouri, it literally changed the course of the Mississippi River."

Although the quake that struck the region yesterday was relatively weak, such tremblors can still cause damage to some structures.

As to what may have caused yesterday's quake, Jorson was reassuring.

"Earthquakes are a natural function of the Earth and are caused when tectonic plates that compose the surface of the Earth, come together. When sufficient pressure builds up, one or the other slips, causing an earthquake."

According to Jorson, though there is a possibility of smaller after shocks, he sees no cause for general alarm.

*

Wyoming Daily Advertiser
Aug 15, 20--

Cheyenne—Scientists from the Department of Agriculture currently working in the Chilicote National Forest report possible sabotage of their efforts to study a record sized mushroom in the tri-state area.

A number of earth moving vehicles including backhoes and excavators were disabled after it was discovered that sugar had been poured into gas tanks clogging fuel injectors and fuel filters.

Contrary to popular belief, the presence of sugar in a vehicle's fuel lines presents no danger to the engine itself so long as the vehicle is not operated at length. However, spokesmen for the Department of Agriculture acknowledged that the vehicles could not be run in order to prevent the sugar from spreading throughout the vehicle's engines.

As a result, gas tanks would have to be completely flushed and cleaned possibly necessitating their removal and replacement. Depending if the work can be done on site, it will involve some delay in the department's ongoing study of the mushroom that covers many square miles beneath the tri-state area.

According to the Cheyenne Sheriff's Office, the tactic of using sugar to disable construction vehicles is a common one employed by environmental activists. As such, the police are investigating known activists and climate fanatics in the area...

*

FBI report:
Gmail intercept
FISA #9585764F
8/10/20--

Joel, Walter, Mara, and officers of the Society of the Great Rising, *Ia!*

News reports of tremors in the area of western Wyoming have come to my attention. As you know, this is one of the deterministic nodes where the sleeping gods dwell, waiting for the great day in which they will arise and we, their loyal servants, will receive our reward as marshals of the human dregs. However, our destiny cannot be fulfilled should the sleep of ages be disturbed outside the fore ordained plan of the Old Ones but more importantly without the proper performance of the rituals of Mnar and the Dhole Chants before hand. I am sure you realize the gravity of the situation. I have been in contact with Brother Alexie in Boston who has consulted the Xanthu Tablets at Miskatonic University that seem to confirm that the western Wyoming area is indeed a node of importance perhaps even being the resting place of Oukranos, brother of Lord Cthulhu. With these facts on hand, I am sure you will agree with me that the time for the Great Rising is not yet here and all must be done to prevent Oukranos' premature disturbance from his slumbers. All must be done to halt further disruptions in Wyoming by the Department of Agriculture for which it has been suggested we resort to simple sabotage of the earth moving equipment. This can be done very easily. This message however, is not the proper venue for discussion and planning. May I suggest the Westernmost Motel on I80 outside Cheyenne?

Brother Kendall (aka N'gorah)
Ia! Ia! Cthulhu fhtagn

*

From:
Federal Bureau of Investigation
Thaddeus Venlius
Field Agent, Cheyenne Office
Aug 21, 20--

To:
Michael Sanders
Special Agent in Charge
Headquarters,
Washington, D.C.

Interrogation of the suspects involved with the sabotage of construction equipment belonging to the Department of Agriculture on 8/15/20-- was completed on 8/20/20--

As detailed in my previous communication, this office was notified of the sabotage by department personnel on the scene. Evidence suggested it was performed the night before. Following standard procedure, this office contacted all motels, hotels, and rooming houses in the tri-state area and got lucky. The Westernmost Hotel outside Cheyenne reported a group that had rented a number of rooms just days before the incident. Furthermore, the proprietor described them as "a bunch of weirdos." Though not usually enough of a description to help much, this time it turned out to be pretty accurate.

What's more, according to the manager, the group had not checked out. Immediately, a tac unit surrounded the rooms identified by the manager and I made contact myself. As it turned out, the unit I visited held the leader of the group who offered no resistance and suggested to the others not to offer resistance.

Among the arrested were four men and two women all in a wildly disheveled condition and all humming an unidentified tune in unison. However, they stopped when asked.

At the office, standard interrogation procedures were followed, questioning each of the suspects separately. Their stories, such as they were, matched with the leader, one Kendall Abrahamson, freely admitting to their performing the sabotage.

Although Kendall Abrahamson was the leader's real name (discovered through fingerprint checks and a long list of offenses, mostly public nuisance) he insisted on calling himself N'gorah.

As to their reasons for the sabotage, Abrahamson claimed they were members of a religious sect (he claimed freedom of religion as his defense against the charges) and believed one of their 'gods' was being disturbed by the activities of the Department of Agriculture and that it was forbidden for anyone to interfere with its rising. Seems this group believed that the giant mushroom discovered by the Department of Agriculture was actually self aware and was on the cusp of rising from the Earth ahead of some cosmic event to take place somewhere called 'Yuggoth." From there, they claim, the "Old Gods," "gathering in their might," would make the final assault on the "Elder Gods." It was all a bunch of gibberish that I'm inclined to believe is a smokescreen either for an insanity or freedom of religion defense once they're indicted.

Since the group has freely admitted to their guilt in the matter of sabotage, this office recommends they be charged with felony and handed over to the proper authorities for prosecution.

Thaddeus Venlius
Field Agent, Cheyenne Office

*

Department of Agriculture
Cell phone transcripts
circa Aug 25, 20--

...evacuate area immediately! This is not a drill! Repeat, evacuate all excavation sites!

...going on? Why the panic?

...dozer tipped over, crushed the operator!

...whole area is trembling! Trees toppling! Vehicles tipping over, rolling over! Run! Run!

...Rob! This is Larry! Everything's going crazy down here! The whole area is rocking and bulging! I can actually see the landscape rippling, the topsoil sloughing away...

...Larry! Repeat...!

...It's gigantic! Eeeyah! Run! Run!

...get pictures...look out!

...Oh, my God! It's looming higher, taller than the trees, scraping the clouds!

...get ahold of yourself, Jorby!

...Run!

*

Department of Agriculture
Cell phone transcripts
Lawrence Kearney/Lead Mycologist
Robert Turich/Area Supervisor
circa Aug 25, 20--

...Larry, been trying to get ahold of you...
...Bob, it's the most incredible thing I've ever seen! People are running everywhere, just out of their minds! Some just ran into the woods, don't know if we'll find them again. Just out of their minds!
...Take it easy, Larry! Catch your breath.
...I'm...I'm okay now. Heart still pounding though. Bob, it's the *Armillaria ostoyae,* or whatever it is. If it's a fungi, it's like no other I've ever seen. It's alive, Bob! No, not just alive. It's *awake*, like it was

"If it's a fungi, it's like no other I've ever seen. It's alive, Bob! No, not just alive. It's awake, like it was dormant and we somehow woke it up with our equipment. This is a thing like we've never seen. A holdover from some unimaginably long time ago, before mankind, something old."

dormant and we somehow woke it up with our equipment. This is a thing like we've never seen. A holdover from some unimaginably long time ago, before mankind, something old. And Bob, I think it knows what it's about. I saw it deliberately kill some of the men! And it's enormous! Covering parts of three states!

...Take it easy, Larry...

...It's okay. I'm not insane. I'm perfectly lucid. Those lab results, Bob. Those lab results were inconclusive, right? They found that the fungi was like nothing ever categorized before? This thing is either a whole new species or not of this Earth. You hear me, Bob? Not of this Earth...

...Let's not rush to conclusions, Larry. Stay calm. Regroup as many of the team as you can find and get clear of the danger zone...

...Easier said than done! That thing is still growing, Bob! It's almost as high as the Pachuso Hills. Don't know what it's intentions are, but we can't let it be. It has to be destroyed! You hear me, Bob? Contact the Army, the Air Force...

*

From:
Department of Agriculture
Office of the Secretary
Manfred Jones
Aug 26, 20--

To:
Office of the President
Chief of Staff
Gerald V. Overhoffer
Urgent!

Gerry,
This message is classified red alert M-12.
I'm not making the following request lightly.
See attached documents for details and reports from the field for the full picture.
But here, I'll just say that some weeks ago a department field unit discovered in the Chilicote Forest area of western Wyoming what they thought was a giant fungoidal growth. They were wrong. Upon using heavy equipment to study it further, they apparently woke it up. That's right. This thing is not a plant nor a fungi, but some kind of living creature. So far, estimates are that it covers at least 150 square miles. You read that right! The thing continues to rise up with latest report that it towers over nearby hills and its movements have leveled nearby towns. The entire tri-state area is now being evacuated. Gerry, this thing must be destroyed as soon as possible! For that reason, I'm writing to you to get the President to authorize some kind of strike by the military. Whatever form it may take, I leave up to your advisors, but for Heaven's sake, don't waste any time with this!

Manfred Jones

PS See attached video of the creature as captured by field units.

*

From:
Office of the President
Chief of Staff
Gerald V. Overhoffer
Aug 27, 20--

To:
Department of Defense
Secretary of Defense Chester Glaude
cc: JCS Chairman Gen. Victor Agee
re: OFR #256

This Presidential Memo is to authorize military strike against crisis situation developing in the tri-state area of Wyoming, Idaho and Montana. This action is designated Most Urgent. The Department of Defense is now authorized to take whatever action it deems necessary to eliminate the cause of the emergency after first assuring the safety of civilians in the area. Repeat, action to be taken immediately.

President Daniel Morgan Toomsby

*

Air Combat Command
Mountain Home AFB Idaho
Gen. Clarence Sholter
Comm #68122A
Aug 29, 20--

per order of Air Force Chief of Staff Gen. Alan Wetherton
per Presidential OFR #256

Your command is being issued this Strike Order for Tri-State area as detailed in conference brief of 2100 hours, August 28. Your command is to release up to twenty-four (24) GBU-43/B units (Massive Ordinance Air Blast [MOAB]) on authorized target. Your command will then conduct aerial survey to study effects and report back to this office as quickly as is feasible. This strike to be affected IMMEDIATELY. Repeat: IMMEDIATELY.

Air Force Staff HQ
Gen. Alan Wetherton

*

From:
Air Combat Command
Mountain Home AFB Idaho
Gen. Clarence Sholter
Comm #68122A
Sept 1, 20--

To:
Air Force Staff HQ
Gen. Alan Wetherton

This is to report that twenty-four (24) sorties of C-130 aircraft each delivered GBU-43/B units onto designated target in Tri-State area after all clear was given that civilians had been evacuated. All units struck target at calculated points and as expected, resulted in massive damage to target. Follow on surveillance craft observed effects of strike and though it was considerable, did not have any lasting effect. Repeat: DID NOT HAVE ANY EFFECT. Within minutes, damaged areas began to "fill in" and "heal" so that within several hours, target had returned to status quo ante and had resumed its activity of northward movement. Currently, civilians are being evacuated from outlying farm and urbanized areas. This command awaits orders.

Air Combat Command
Mountain Home AFB Idaho
Gen. Clarence Sholter

*

Transcript:
White House
Washington, D.C.
Situation Room
Sept 3, 20--
President Daniel Morgan Toomsby presiding
In attendance: Relative Cabinet members, Chairman JCS, Staff members Dept of Agriculture

...
    "Can anyone tell me what the hell we're dealing with here?"
    "There's no concensus on that, Mr. President."
    "What does that mean? Is this thing animal, vegetable, or mineral? You can tell me that at least?"
    "Believe it or not, Mr. President, our lab tests indicate that the thing is made up of all three, even though a number of its elements have never been identified before. All we know for sure is that it's definitely alive."
    "Does it think, Bob? We've heard some reports that it might show signs of intelligence."
    "Sir, that rumor is unconfirmed."
    "Some cultist characters arrested last week seemed to think it is."
    "Cultists?"
    "Oh, come on! Let's stick to facts, shall we?"
    "The fact is, this thing is big, it's old, and it seems to be moving with a purpose."

"It's going somewhere?"

"Heading north so far as we can tell. Luckily, the population is sparse in the eastern Idaho/western Wyoming area."

"That's one good thing anyway. If we have to go to the next level, at least we won't have to worry about having to evacuate large populations."

"Which has already begun in anticipation of the next level."

"That level being…?"

"The nuclear option, I'm afraid, sir."

"Just wanted to make sure we were all on the same page. But as long as we are, is nuclear our only option?"

…

"Looks that way, sir."

"This thing is huge, and conventional explosives have had no effect."

"What about napalm?"

"No effect."

"Biological means? Insecticides? Defoliants? Herbicides?"

"Unfortunately, the elements that compose its diverse molecular structure work to defend each other from various forms of attack. Structurally, it's the perfect living organism."

"So what? All that's left is to drop an atom bomb on the thing?"

"In short, yes, Mr. President. However, work being conducted at Los Alamos might mean more than a simple nuclear explosion. Perhaps Doug can better explain what the lab boys at the Department of Energy have come up with?"

"Doug?"

"The idea is very simple. In fact, it's an old one. Our scientists are proposing to build a special bomb along the lines of Little Boy…"

"The first bomb dropped on Hiroshima?"

"Correct. That bomb was triggered with a gun type explosive device in which a slug of uranium was shot into another slug of the same element then bombarded with neutrons that triggered the reaction resulting in an explosion. However, this Little Boy will be slightly modified so that the uranium slug will be shot into one of the newly identified elements comprising the body of the thing. Luckily, this element's molecular structure was a simple one allowing our scientists to come up with the new bomb quickly."

"So, if I'm getting this right, the uranium slug will hit the new element…"

"…and begin a chain reaction all through the thing's bulk instantaneously, resulting, of course, in a massive explosion. In effect, the creature itself will provide the fuel for its own demise"

"But the big question is: will the thing be able to come back from that as it has after conventional bombing?"

"No guarantees but we believe not."

…

"Then what are we waiting for? Doug, tell your brain boys to get that bomb ready toute suite. General, put your Idaho command on stand by alert. Bob, can you conduct the evacuations? Good. Gerry, prepare the necessary OFRs. Gentlemen, I expect everyone to do their duty and work together with full cooperation. Gerry, get hold of my speech writers. I'll be needing to address the nation before we drop the bomb."

End transcript

*

Washington AP – At a press briefing today, the United States announced that an agreement had been reached with Russia and China to allow an exception to the Nuclear Test Ban Treaty permitting the United States to detonate an above ground nuclear device in western Wyoming.

Reason given for the unusual request is the emergence of a massive living creature in the Wyoming/Montana region.

The creature, which covers a purported 150 square miles, was awakened by construction equipment digging in the area earlier in July. Since then, the creature, which officials at first supposed to be a giant fungi or mushroom, has lifted itself high enough to tower over nearby hills and begin to move in a northerly direction.

So far, three people have been reported dead and another sixteen missing. Everyone in the tri-state area has otherwise been evacuated. However, the evacuation zone has been further expanded to prevent harm to the public from the expected atomic blast and resultant fallout…

*

To:
Office of the President
President Daniel Morgan Toomsby
Sept 10, 20--

From:
Secretary of Defense Chester Glaude
cc: JCS Chairman Gen. Victor Agee
re: OFR #256

This Office is pleased to report complete success in Operation 512. Final on scene report indicates complete dissolution of creature. Atomic device worked as advertised with nuclear "bullet" fired from gun directly into contact with creature whose own atomic structure reacted according to theory. Process of decay took 0000.2 mili-seconds, virtual instantoniety. Fallout will require the tri-state area and many square miles around it (exact danger zone to be determined by 9/15/20--) However immediate threat to the nation is over. Repeat, the threat is over. Post action Op Committee to convene by the end of the week for final briefing and discussion.

Secretary of Defense Chester Glaude

*

Warning!
Top Secret
Eyes only
National Security Agency
Dispatch series AAA2057894
To: Office of the President of the United States

SigInt report of 12/3/20-- confirmed. Messages intercepted from People's Republic of China (PRC) indicating activity in Shaanxi Province similar to recent incident in tri-state Wyoming area. Cities being evacuated, military taking action which so far have had no effect. Prognosis: all efforts will be useless in containing the problem. Question for President and command staff: does the United States share knowledge of how to end threat?

End message
NSA Dispatch series AAA2057894

Fungi Out of Time

by Arnden Christopher

Listen, I don't know how many times you want me to repeat my story. There's not much time left! In fact, there might be no time at all! Of course, I admit I had those explosives in that rental truck. I was headed for Algonquin Peak in the Adirondacks to seal in Yanyoth, an Old One identified in my uncle's papers. I thought that if I could prevent him from joining the others, their plans for war could be disrupted somehow. And if other Old Ones could be prevented from leaving the Earth, the ensuing devastation that I saw in my dreams could be averted completely or at least mollified. I can tell that you don't believe me. But you have to! The fate of the world, of mankind depends on it! All right, all right! I'll calm down. There, you see? I'm all right now. You want me to repeat my story? Again? But there's no time... All right, then! I'll repeat it one more time. But this has to be the last time because there won't be any left when I finish. Now listen carefully...

For me, Steve Falkner, the nightmare began on a dull and dreary November when I was at last able to take possession of the house on Peekskill Road, on the outskirts of Arkham.

The house had belonged to my uncle who'd disappeared some years before Massachusetts'

adverse possession law kicked in. Arkham officials, interested only in collecting taxes on the abandoned property, had contacted me as soon as the law allowed, demanding to know if I planned to claim possession and how soon could I pay up the back taxes?

News of my uncle's disappearance and the situation with the old house came as a surprise to me as I'd not seen or heard from my uncle since I was a boy. Unfortunately, town officials had no information on Uncle Alec's disappearance and could only direct me to a real estate firm that had acted as property manager for my uncle until its remit had ended some years before and the tax payments had dried up.

With fond memories of visiting the big old Victorian style house in company with my mother when I was a youngster, I couldn't help but consider seriously the notion of keeping the house and perhaps staying there to enjoy the long New England summers and colorful autumns. As it was, I was a mere cliff dweller in New York City where I worked as a stock broker, employment that could be conducted from anywhere with the miracle of the internet. As a matter of fact, the more I considered it, the more I liked the idea of working from the old house that I recalled, sat in a woodsy, edge of town location with enough landscape to provide plenty of screening from the neighbors.

Newly determined, I made an appointment with the real estate company that had handled my uncle's property, packed a duffle bag for a few weeks' stay, and began the long drive to Arkham. As the city gave way to the Connecticut countryside, I tried to recall what I knew about Uncle Alec. He was my mother's older brother. He never married. He was always somewhat unkempt with his hair askew as if from constantly running his fingers through its thick, silver strands. He was kindly, not aloof, and not in any way resentful of playing host from time to time. Nevertheless, I recalled his impressive, well stocked library, the strange objets d'art that littered rooms and hallways, the detritus of the many overseas trips he'd taken over the years: tomb artifacts from Egypt, Inca idols from Central America, miniatures of the giant heads of Easter Island. Reminded of the artifacts, I realized that many of them might be valuable and that it would have been worth it to visit the property if only to secure them.

But what my uncle did to earn a living, to be able to afford his world travels, I, then as now, had no idea.

So it was with mounting interest overall, that I finally left the freeway and found myself dumped on Main Street in Arkham. From there, it wasn't far to the real estate office. I'd made good time driving north arriving in town about lunch time and decided to get a bite to eat. Best not to conduct business on an empty stomach, something I'd learned long before. It wasn't hard to find a diner in the downtown area so I pulled in at a likely place and looked forward to some home style local cooking.

After asking the waitress for directions, I found the real estate office with little difficulty, happy to find the building had its own parking lot. Inside, a number of desks in the storefront style ante room were vacant, but I sensed movement in the private office in back. There, I found a smallish, balding man going over papers. I knocked lightly on the door frame.

"Mr. Wopitz?" I inquired.

Here, as throughout my recitation, I'll try to recall various conversations as accurately as I can.

The man looked up, startled, pushing the glasses on the end of his nose more firmly into place.

"That's me," he said. "Who may I…?"

"I'm Steve Falkner."

"Oh! Right!" said Wopitz, rising and extending a hand. "I lost track of the time."

"No problem."

"Please have a seat."

I took the chair he indicated.

"I assume you haven't changed your mind about claiming the property at 182 Peekskill Road?"

"You assume right," I told him.

"Well, then, let's get some of this paperwork squared away and I'll show you out to the house."

"Fine."

The next few minutes were taken up with signing ownership transfer forms, taxpayer notifications, and insurance forms in duplicate and sometimes in triplicate.

"As I told you on the phone, although this office has arranged for some maintenance of your uncle's property since his disappearance, it was necessarily of a minimal nature," Wopitz warned me when the formalities had been concluded. "You'll find that there'll be some landscaping that needs attention. The lawn has been kept mowed and the leaves picked up but shrubs and trees will be a bit shaggy. Indoors, dust covers were spread over the furniture and I've engaged a woman to keep the place somewhat presentable. In fact, knowing of your coming, I had her give the place a last going over before you arrived. The gas and power have been turned on but you'll have to do some grocery shopping on your own."

"That all sounds good," I told him, pleased. "I appreciate it. Do I owe you anything for all that…?"

"Naturally, as with the back taxes, whatever maintenance this office has done over the years was done in the expectation of being reimbursed upon either a claim on the property or its sale by the state."

"You'll send me a bill then?"

"Fine. Now, is your car out back? Then you can follow me out to the house."

So saying, Wopitz motioned me to the door. By that time, other employees had returned from lunch and were working at the outer desks. "I'm going to show Mr. Falkner out to the Falkner place."

"Yes, Mr. Wopitz," said one of the women, her eyes shifting as if checking me out.

We left the office, each taking to our respective vehicles. It wasn't a long drive. Arkham was a small city, mostly a college town dominated by nearby Miskatonic University whose campus we passed on our way to the suburbs. Or what used to be the suburbs when my uncle's house was first built. Back in the day, it was a more tony part of town, noted for its big Victorian or red brick homes located on large tracts of land. Set on high ground, the Miskatonic River could be seen from parts of the neighborhood as it slowly wound its way through the nearby hills and out toward Kingsport and the sea.

Unfortunately, since the nineteenth century when the big homes had been built by successful merchants and mill owners, land had been sold piecemeal by successive owners so that the neighborhood had become more crowded and with far less attractive capes and split level houses. In short, it had become a typical bedroom community. I'd imagined the house to be as it was in my memory: big, lonely, and still somewhat isolated from any newer additions in the neighborhood. And to my relief, it turned out to be little changed. My uncle, as well as previous owners, had resisted reduction of its property and except for the roof of a ranch home around the corner, there was little evidence among the thick gathering of trees and shrubs that filled the property of encroaching civilization. In fact, the house itself was barely visible from the road but soon after turning into the long, curved driveway, the turreted tower at the corner of the building hove into sight soon followed by the arched front doorway still nestled under the shelter of a portico. The house itself consisted of three stories counting the full attic space and was fronted in fieldstone that yielded to clapboard in the rear.

Getting out of the car, I looked around and was satisfied with the landscaping that had been done. Not much work would be required to get the yard in shape. Work that I kind of looked forward to doing myself. As for the house itself, it looked all right. No peeling paint, no broken windows.

"The lock is a little resistant," Wopitz was saying as he jiggled the keys in the door.

I mounted the short flight of stairs leading to the front door and arrived there just as Wopitz got it open. There was a musty smell inside, but nothing to be concerned about. In fact, there was the hint of a familiar scent in the air that, in a flash of nostalgia, instantly reminded me of my uncle. A combination of pipe smoke and the cologne he habitually wore.

As Wopitz had said, the furniture was all covered in sheets and the sunlight that streamed through the tall windows in the front parlor and sitting rooms caused the white sheets to glow against the dark mahogany of the wainscoting.

"As you can see, once the sheets are removed, the house will be ready for occupation," observed Wopitz. "I think you'll find that you'll have to do little housekeeping at least to start. Back here's the dining room and kitchen."

As we proceeded through the house, I found my dim memories of those long ago visits begin to be rekindled. I remembered those rooms. Meals in the kitchen with my mother and uncle. Formal Sunday dinner in the dining room. The little den off the dining room still had the TV set that occupied my evenings, the set that was more a piece of furniture than today's flat screens.

But it was the big library at the very back of the house that was the clincher.

Stretching up through the first two floors of the house, the walls covered floor to ceiling in shelves, they were all still there, the rows and rows of books with the colorful bindings that had attracted my attention when I was a boy. The big, expansive desk and its plush swivel chair set against the room's tall, paned window. I could almost see my uncle sitting there, as it seemed he almost always was on my visits.

Here, the sheets had been removed from the furniture and the big desk gleamed in the sunlight, clean of the papers, books, and charts that used to cover it when my uncle was alive. *Where did it all go?* I wondered. All of it so important at the time but now replaced, put away, perhaps even thrown out. And just what was it that Uncle Alec did? For the life of me, I couldn't' remember or if I ever knew. He had money I was sure. All that world traveling. But what had he done to earn it? I had no clue.

"Do you know what happened to all of my uncle's papers and notes?" I asked Wopitz. "He used to conduct a lot of business and correspondence with acquaintances around the world."

"I have no idea," replied Wopitz. "Maybe the housekeeper knows. I'm sure she wouldn't have thrown anything out. She had no authorization for that kind of cleaning up. Maybe it's in the desk drawers…?"

He circled the desk and began yanking open drawers.

"Yes, the drawers are full of papers and things."

I went over to look and confirmed that the drawers were crammed indiscriminately with papers and file folders. When I had the time, I'd go through them. At least I could get some idea of what my uncle's business was.

"I suppose you haven't heard anything about your uncle's whereabouts? No news?"

"Nothing, I'm afraid," I said. "But he did like to travel, often to areas I'd consider dangerous. The Himalayas, the Brazilian jungles, the Gobi Desert. It's possible he might have met with a fatal accident somewhere and we'd never know."

"You don't say? Well, despite all the trouble he's left us, I hope he's safe and maybe even shows up again some day."

"That would be nice," I agreed, and meant it. There was every chance that, like Dr. Livingston, he survived some place under the care of natives but too sick or injured to make his way back to civilization.

The second floor was taken up with a number of bedrooms from which I decided to use the familiar one I'd stayed in when I visited as a boy. It was plenty big and gave a good view out the rear of the house and the hills and river beyond. In the master bedroom, everything was in order even to the various objects and figurines from odd places around the world: Tibet, Yucatan, the Ponapes. Idly, I remember picking one up, a weird piece of sculpture and noticed a label stuck to the bottom: *Azathoth in Repose,* Clark Ashton Smith, 1934. Odd, the things you remember.

"Seen enough?" asked Wopitz at that point.

"I have. Thanks for coming out with me. And thank the landscaper and housekeeper for me. They did a great job keeping things in shape."

"I will. And here are your keys. The other ones are for the garage and the storage shed out back."

"Thank you. Think I'll get my things from the car and move right in."

"Fine! Everything with the town and the state is squared away. The house is yours free and clear."

With that, Wopitz left and I watched until his car disappeared from the driveway.

I spent the next several days settling in, reestablishing my routine, making plans that would leave the house empty part of the year while I attended my job back in New York. I considered seriously relocating to Boston and making the house my permanent residence. Then one day, the possibility of another reason to stay appeared on my doorstep.

I'd started to look through my uncle's desk, looking through his papers, when the door bell chimed.

Not knowing anyone in town as yet, I wondered who it could be. Mr. Wopitz? A neighbor with a house warming casserole? But when I opened the front door, it was neither. Something better, much better, in fact.

I realize that the following might sound like a digression, but bear with me.

"Mr. Falkner?" asked the young lady standing on the front porch. A late model Ford was parked in the driveway at the foot of the steps.

She was only a few years younger than myself, and though wearing wire rimmed glasses with her blondish hair tied back in a girlish pony tail, I could tell by her trim figure and fresh appearance, that she was quite attractive.

"That's me," I admitted in as friendly and welcoming a tone as I could muster. "Can I help you?"

"I hope so," said the girl. "I've come from the Miskatonic University Library. The library administration heard that a new owner had moved in to the property and hoped that there might be a chance to reclaim some valuable books lent to the previous owner some time ago."

"That would've been my Uncle Alec," I said. "I'm the new owner. If there are books here that don't belong to my uncle, I'll be glad to hand them over."

The girl seemed relieved at my cooperative tone. "Oh, thank you. We were afraid that we might never have got them back."

"No guarantees, I'm afraid. When I arrived here, there was nothing out of order. I found no stray books about. Only the books already on the shelves. But then, the housekeeper who'd been taking care of the place before I arrived might have put them away. Won't you come in and look for yourself. Maybe you can recognize them on the shelves."

"Thank you," she said, stepping inside. "Oh, by the way, my name is Sheila Banks. I'm assistant to the assistant librarian at Miskatonic."

She said it in such a light hearted, self-deprecatory manner that I couldn't help liking her even more.

"Hello, Sheila," I said, extending a hand. "My name's Stephen Falkner," but I asked here to call me Steve.

Closing the door behind her, I led the way deeper into the house. "The library's this way."

"Wow, this is an impressive home," she said, looking around at the ornamental woodwork, winding staircase, shiny floors, antique furniture, and paintings. "No wonder you decided to keep it."

"Is that what you were told?"

"Why, yes. The real estate person…"

"Mr. Wopitz?"

"That's right. He said you decided to keep it as a vacation home or something."

"I did. It would've been a shame to sell it and see all of my uncle's things scattered to collectors and auction dealers."

"It would!"

"Well, here we are," I said, standing aside to usher her into the library.

"I'm impressed all over again," she said, craning her neck to the topmost reaches of the book shelves. "I wanted to come earlier to retrieve the university's books, but couldn't get access to the house while it was caught up in legal limbo. We had to put a lien on the house to make sure the university could reclaim its books before any sale"

"Sorry that the university was inconvenienced," I said. "But if you don't mind my saying so, glad in a way, otherwise we wouldn't have met."

Her cheeks reddened and I quickly apologized.

"Sorry if I was too personal," I said. "I know we just met, but you see, I still don't know anyone in town and…"

"That's all right. I'm flattered."

Breathing a sigh of relief, I returned to business. "Well, as you can see, there are a lot of books in here. Do you have any idea where to look for yours?

They were borrowed, you say?"

"Yes, some years ago, so you can imagine how anxious the university is in getting them back. They were kind of rare."

"What kind of books were they? Maybe my uncle kept them with others on similar subjects?"

"The kind that the Miskatonic Library specializes in I'm afraid," she said, scanning the shelves.

"Which is?"

"Most people would characterize them as books about the supernatural but really they're not that at all. Technically their science based but so out there that the difference between science and supernaturalism is hard to determine."

"You mean something like alchemy?"

She shrugged. "I guess so, but I'm not really sure as I don't really have that much involvement with the library's special collections."

"So can you give me any titles," I asked her while I began poking through the big desk. I thought that maybe Uncle Alec kept the borrowed books off of his own shelves.

"One is called *The Prophecies of Kadath*, another *A Dhol Chant Hymnal*."

"Huh?" was all I could muster.

"Told you they were offbeat."

"Yeah. Anything else?"

"*The Book of Iod* and *Possible Translations and Interpretations of the Pnakotic Fragments*."

"That last was a mouthful. Any more?"

"A book called by the Comte D'Erlette called *Cultes des Ghoules*."

"Ghoules? I hope there aren't any more…?"

"No, that's it. But the last two especially, are very hard to find anywhere in the world I'm told so the library is especially keen on getting those back. I sure hope they're here."

Spotting a cabinet across the room, I went over to take a closer look and through its protective glass doors, I was able to identify one of the missing books from the title on its spine.

"I think I found them," I called in triumph, pulling open the doors and pulling out *The Book of Iod*. Hard covered, it was well worn with thick, yellowed pages. With a shock, I realized the Latin text was hand printed and illuminated like those old time books transcribed by monks. "How old is this, anyway?"

"Very is all I know," said Sheila, taking the book from my hands. "It might date back to the Middle Ages."

"And they let my uncle take it home?"

She shrugged again. "It does seem strange, but I gather your uncle was well respected by the administration. I don't know."

With somewhat more trepidation, I began removing the other missing books, which left a few remaining that were unaccounted for.

"You're not looking for those others?"

"They're not on my list."

"I wonder if my uncle borrowed them from other places. After all, they're kept in the same cabinet as yours."

"Could be. Check the flyleaves to see if there are book plates, or librarians' stamps."

I did that, but found nothing.

"Let me see that one," said Sheila, taking one of the books from my hands and looking at the title. "*The Ponape Scripture*. I'm sure this is a really rare volume. I mean, really rare! Makes me wonder what other books your uncle had on his shelves."

"Or why he was so interested in this stuff," I said.

"Different shakes, I guess," said Sheila as she gathered her own books.

"Let me help you with those," I offered.

Together, we made our way back through the house and out to the driveway where we carefully deposited the books in a special valise that Sheila had brought for the purpose.

"Thanks," she said, slamming the car door.

"Hate to think this is the last I'll see of you," I said, rather boldly I'm afraid.

Sheila smiled though, without embarrassment that time. "You know where you can find me."

With that, she slipped behind the wheel, and drove off. I have to admit, I stood there watching until her car disappeared from view.

With some reluctance, I returned to the house and after a brief hesitation, decided to return to the library and take a closer look at my uncle's books.

The first place I checked was the enclosed cabinet where the borrowed books had been. There were a few others there as well and I wondered if they'd been lent too. Again, they seemed like older books but these at least, had copyright notices inside: 1913, 1932, etc: *Apocraphies of Nuth,*

Possible Orders of Battle on the Interdimensional Scale, Smithson's Index to the Old Ones.

I had no idea what the books were about.

Replacing them, I turned to the shelves that ranged the library walls.

Although most, as I quickly discovered, were ordinary encyclopedic, legal, or classical in nature, most of the lower shelves were filled with books that echoed the esoteric nature of those I'd found in the cabinet including such titles as *Sky Phenomena and Other Less Obvious Atmospheric Questions, Commentaries on the Cthaat Aquadingen* from the University of Thuringia, Olaf's *Visitors in the Night Sky, Could Earth Survive a War Involving the Elder Gods?*

The only thing I could conclude was that my uncle had an unhealthy obsession with obscure cults and Erich von Daniken UFO claptrap. I replaced the volume in my hand and turned to the desk. Earlier, when helping to find the books Sheila had come for, I'd noticed its drawers had been filled with various papers and fat file folders. Curious now about my uncle's interests, I decided to look through them.

It took the remainder of the afternoon just to sort it all out but by evening I had several stacks of folders and papers neatly sorted out on the desk. By then, my stomach was telling me it was time for dinner, so I walked away from the work for a while. But all through my meal I wondered about what I'd found: extensive correspondence between Uncle Alec and similar seekers around the world, newspaper clippings with a similar international tinge, and log books and journals of his thoughts and feelings about this strange work that obsessed him. Luckily, my uncle hadn't seemed to make the transition to the digital age and all of his researches were confined to hard copies so that I didn't have to worry about finding passwords and such to access a computer. Or was it part of the paranoia that also seemed to be an element of my uncle's makeup? Was it a deliberate choice to stay off the grid? To keep him and his work secret? To remain invisible to others? At the time, I shrugged off the notion. There were plenty of people who tried to leave as small a digital footprint as possible without being pathological about it. The bottom line though was that it did make it easier for me to follow up on my uncle's interest and hopefully even find a clue to his disappearance. Although Wopitz did say that the police, early on, had gone through my uncle's things seeking clues to his whereabouts but without success.

Well, no harm in giving it a try myself. That was my thought at the time. That maybe I'd stumble across something that only a relative would recognize as significant.

It was in such a mindset that I returned to the library after dinner to begin going through the paperwork. It took longer than I thought. In fact, it was several days later that I finally cleared the loose papers and files to finally get to what I considered the heart of the trove: the journals and notes.

It was then I began to piece together what my uncle's concerns were all about. Sure, by any normal standard, they could be judged as paranoid, even slightly mad. After all, what would you call a belief in some kind of pre-historic religion or belief system involving a cosmic war in which the losers were exiled and imprisoned in out of the way places on Earth? And according to my uncle's findings, these imprisoned beings were still able to exercise a malign influence outside their prisons, drawing weak willed humans into their orbit as acolytes and worshipers. These acolytes, always a small minority, worked in secret to allow their masters to escape their prisons. But it seems that my uncle had developed a theory of his own, one he'd been running past others who were aware of this Cthulhu cult as it was called, and finding some in prestigious universities who agreed with him. In short, my uncle theorized that all this secret activity, conducted over tens of thousands of years, was aimed at an eventual escape of the imprisoned beings, called the Old Ones, the allying themselves with other forces opposed to the Elder Gods, and mount a second challenge to their supremacy in the universe.

All of it, the notes, the files, the journals, kept by my uncle seemed to lead to a single conclusion that I could see: Uncle Alec, convinced of the veracity of his research, and the correctness of his theory, had been ready to take a kind of final step. That step seemed to involve an altering of his consciousness, the only way a human being could transverse this limited plane of reality, and enter that of the Old Ones. At that point, it was unclear

to me (and possibly my uncle as well), what happened next. What exactly was my uncle trying to do? Observe the actions of Old Ones and their adversaries? Understand the scope of the Cthulhu cult? Or merely to dispel any doubts in his own mind that his suspicions were correct and that he wasn't after all, himself insane?

In not so many words, my uncle indicated how he expected to breach the barrier between this world and the cosmic plane. He didn't set it down with any clarity. He was vague and even metaphoric in his explanation but that, no doubt, was the reason that the police, in their investigations, never caught on. But it was likely that the police never really applied themselves to understand my uncle's obsession. On the surface, it all seemed mad. However, my own diligence paid off. From what I could gather, my uncle had learned of a potion or drug distilled by cult members somewhere among the Himalayan Mountains, an area called the Plateau of Leng. To my amazement, I learned that at great expense, my uncle had actually traveled there, hired Sherpa guides, who led him to a certain monastery and then promptly abandoned him. The monastery apparently had an evil reputation but actually it was an important hub in the Cthulhu cult. But it wasn't the end of Uncle Alec's quest. From there, a monk led him deeper into the mountains where snow and ice had been packed for untold centuries and the wind howled incessantly. At last, his journey ended in a cave whose interior was carved everywhere with vast and unidentifiable figures and scenes. The cave was dimly lit from a source located in what appeared to be a bottomless pit in which, the monk claimed, lay imprisoned one of the Old Ones. It was from some liquid that bubbled up from the pit that the monk filled a tube stoppered with a piece of dirty cloth torn from his robe. Returning to the monastery, the monks created the final distillation before handing the results to my uncle. They demanded no payment. The effort my uncle had expended in reaching that place was apparently enough to convince them of his sincerity and identification with their cause.

My uncle waited until his return to Arkham before doing anything with the potion. His notes

Sherpa guides...led him to a certain monastery and then promptly abandoned him. The monastery apparently had an evil reputation...

indicated that he'd intended to examine it to determine its composition but I couldn't be sure if that was ever done. Apparently, it was soon after my uncle arrived home that he disappeared.

That said, did he ever try the potion on himself?

Did something happen to him before he could? Even though there wasn't any evidence of it, I wondered if members of the Cthulhu cult were more dangerous than my uncle thought? Were they responsible for his disappearance? Did those

83

monks in that questionable monastery have second thoughts about him? The only hint that I could ever find regarding his disappearance was a note in one of his journals that stated something about "using Carter's key" to escape. Leading me to wonder: was my uncle's disappearance of his own volition after all?

It was with such questions in mind that I visited the police station to find out first hand what detectives knew about Uncle Alec's disappearance. But they knew no more than I did. Yes, there were strangers in town around the time my uncle disappeared but that wasn't out of the ordinary as the University hosted many foreign students and faculty. Furthermore, there was no evidence that my uncle had entertained any guests. They'd questioned his house and grounds keepers and neither knew of any visitors to the house.

With the issue of the disappearance and my uncle's obsessions somewhat settled for the time being, I continued to make myself at home, exploring the grounds and going over the interior spaces with more attention. In between, I continued to think about Sheila and decided that I needed to contact her soon before the warmth of our initial encounter began to cool.

It was while I was poking around the house that I revisited the basement, something I hadn't done since the first day. Lit only by the occasional dangling light bulb, it consisted of the expected items: the big black oil tank sitting in a corner, the old fashioned furnace and boiler with their insulated pipes and conduits snaking across the ceiling and disappearing into all parts of the house, old pieces of furniture, window frames that had once been used to enclose the rear porch, a mouse trap or two, the door leading to a bulkhead that in turn led outside. But in a distant corner, hidden in the shadows, was the suggestion of a work table. On my first inspection, I had assumed it was a typical woodworking area with vise and tools hanging over the table. But when I pulled the cord that lit the overhead bulb, I saw that it was more than that. Yes, tools were hanging from a peg board, but the table itself was covered with chemistry apparatus: a bunsen burner, centrifuge, racks of test tubes, chemicals of various sorts. There'd been no indication that my uncle had any inclination toward scientific experimentation so the

equipment's presence in the basement was somewhat of a mystery. That is, until I remembered my uncle's notes that suggested his intention of studying the potion he'd acquired in the East. I'd assumed my uncle intended to take the stuff to a lab, not to work on it himself. Looking more closely, my eyes stopped on the rack of test tubes. The half dozen tubes were all empty, except one: one stoppered with what appeared to be a dirty bit of rag. With mounting excitement, I reached out for the tube and held it before my eyes. There was a label on it that simply read: Leng. A chill ran down my spine as I realized I was holding the very potion that had been given to my uncle by the monks in that remote, and mysterious monastery, with its evil reputation among the natives. The potion distilled from the fluid that had leaked from the pit where an Old One was said to reside.

Experimentally, I removed the bit of rag from the tube and gave its contents a tentative sniff. I smelled nothing. It was odorless. I took a strong whiff. Still nothing. Replacing the cloth, I determined to finish what my uncle had started. I'd take the potion to a reputable chemist to have it analyzed. In fact, it would make the perfect excuse to visit Sheila at the university. I'd ask her to recommend a professor on the faculty who might volunteer to do it or at least assign one of his students to do the job.

The potion rested on the dresser in my bedroom when I retired that night, happy with the thought of seeing Sheila the next day and perhaps wrangling a date with her. But, as it turned out, my slumbers were not to be untroubled. I tossed and turned all night, snatching only a few minutes sleep here and there. It was still only dawn when I finally gave up trying to sleep and left bed to have some breakfast. When I finished, it was still too early to go to the college, so I killed some time by puttering around the property. Despite my plans, I found myself following a trail that led through the woods behind the house and by the time I returned, my eyes had grown heavy and I was yawning prodigiously. I decided to make it an early night and went to bed.

Unlike the evening before, I fell immediately to sleep and dreamed…of something.

I awoke suddenly and in a sweat. For a moment, I was disoriented, not knowing where I was. Then things began to come into focus. The real world reasserted itself...but why did I think of it in just that way? Why the "real world" and not the "waking world"? Tossing aside the damp sheets, I looked around. All was as it should have been. Outside, it was late and the full moon shone, its bright, silver light throwing crooked shadows across the room as it streamed through trees outside and through the room's windows.

I breathed a long sigh of relief. It'd only been a dream, a nightmare really. Trying to pierce the cobwebs of sleep from my mind, I failed to call up any memory of what had driven me to wakefulness. All I could remember was panic and stark fear. In fact, my heart was still racing and it took a conscious effort to calm myself down. Dragging myself from bed, I availed myself of the decanter on the night table and poured myself a stiff shot of bourbon. It seemed to help. Reluctantly, but with resolve, I returned to bed and determined to sleep. I succeeded. And when I rose in the morning, the anxiety of the night before had dissipated. Still, I felt too shaken to visit the university and Sheila that day. I decided to go the next day.

All that same day however, as a slow fog rolled in from the distant sea, I was plagued with visions that teased the edge of my mind. More than once, I tried to remember my dream but failed. Only a vague echo of fear remained, an echo that prevented me from enjoying whatever I was doing or making plans for the day beyond preparing a simple meal.

The next night, the scenario repeated itself: the dream, the restlessness, the awakening in the night, the bourbon, dawn. In fact, the sequence repeated every time I shut my eyes for some sleep. Not only at night but naps during the day. By the end of the week, it was really beginning to worry me. They were becoming more insistent, more vivid. Of vague impressions of titanic things rising, causing climatic catastrophes and disturbances in the atmosphere and even the immediate solar system. It felt as though I was on the verge of some kind of a breakthrough in understanding.

But I had no desire for understanding, only a good night's sleep, without interruption. Examining my immediate past actions, I thought back to anything that might have triggered the dreams. Was it something I ate? What I'd been reading in my uncle's study? Could it even have been a change in routine? This last gave me an idea. Maybe I'd unconsciously set myself a new routine at the house that invited the dreams. If so, the way to disrupt them was to do something out of the ordinary. And the first thing I thought of was to follow through with my planned visit to Miskatonic and asking Sheila for a date.

As usual, I woke that morning after another restless night but with a new determination to bull my way through the day and shake things up in my life. By mid-morning then, I was ready to leave for the university. I carefully placed the vial with the potion in my shirt pocket, the one that could be secured with a flap, gathered my keys and wallet and went out to the garage. It was the first time I'd taken the car out in over a week but it coughed to life with no hesitation. Pulling out, I tooled around the long curve of the driveway, and entered Peekskill Road for the short drive to the university.

There, I found my way to the library and asked for Sheila. She was on duty and soon appeared from somewhere in the stacks.

"Well, hello," she said when she saw me. I was relieved to hear the welcoming tone in her voice.

"I wanted to see where you worked," I lied. "What kind of place stocked the sort of books my uncle borrowed."

Sheila laughed. "No Addams Family library here. Sorry to disappoint you. Aside from the books locked away in the special collections, there's nothing here any other college library might have: some fiction but mostly reference material and faculty notes and records."

I looked around and verified Sheila's testimony. Except for the vaulting ceilings and fancily carved woodwork, the old fashioned desks and tables with their reading lights, a glass display case here and there...and a suit of armor in the corner, there was nothing out of the ordinary.

"It could use a swordfish with a man's leg sticking out of its mouth to brighten up the place," I commented and wondered if Sheila would pick up the reference to the old TV show.

She laughed good naturedly. She got it, all right.

"So how have you been?" she asked. "All settled in at the house?"

"Oh, yeah. Got a routine going now. But I'll have to be getting back to New York soon. Have to make a living you know."

She nodded.

"But…" I hesitated then. Should I have bothered her about my sleepless nights? Would that be getting too personal at that point?

"But?" she prompted.

"Well…it's silly to even bring it up really, but I just haven't been sleeping well of late. I've been having nightmares."

I tried to keep it from sounding too serious of course, but couldn't prevent an undertone of concern in my voice.

"Is that unusual?" she asked. "I mean for you?"

I shrugged. "Yeah. I've never had nightmares before."

"What do you dream about?"

I remember hesitating. At that point, I didn't know exactly what my dreams were about. I only had impressions. Nothing concrete. I didn't want to make more of them to Sheila than they were.

"Nothing I can nail down," I said, finally.

"Have you been reading any of those books in your uncle's library?" she asked. "Some of those could disturb anyone if they were in a receptive mood. We've seen it sometimes here when people research stuff in the special collections…where your uncle borrowed his books."

I admitted that, yes, I'd been reading some of the material.

"There you go," she said. "I've heard stories from others here that often just from reading that kind of thing can give a person nightmares."

I laughed off her concerns.

"Yeah, right! Listen, I've read every Stephen King novel there is, so I don't scare easy."

But did I really believe it?

Sheila rolled her eyes and looked at me skeptically.

"Famous last words," she concluded.

"Well, maybe it's only something I ate," I suggested. "I'm not the best cook in the world. In fact I do most of my eating from cans and Healthy Choice frozen dinners. Maybe I'm due for some real cooking. Want to help me out? Maybe you can suggest a good local restaurant. If you come with me, I'll treat!"

"Big spender!" Sheila said, laughing. "But I'll take you up on that."

"Great! Now all you have to do is point me in the direction of the science department where I can find someone who can analyze something for me."

"What is it?"

"Just a compound I found in my uncle's basement. He had a little lab there believe it or not. I'll tell you more about it when we have dinner."

"You can try the chemistry wing of the Armitage building. It's just behind the library."

"Thanks. I'll call you later," I promised after she'd given me her cell number.

I had no problem finding the chemistry department and to have a graduate student assigned to do the analysis. I had some trepidation about leaving the vial at the lab but after I was assured by the director that it would be treated with the laboratory's full security protocol, I let them have it.

The dreams seemed to increase in intensity and even clarity over the next few nights, perhaps brought on by concern and conjecture about what the lab's findings would be regarding the compound I'd left there.

Despite the increasing pace of the dreams, my well being was reinforced with anticipation of dinner with Sheila, sometimes it seemed to be the only thing I had to look forward to. Up until then, I hadn't noticed the toll my dreams had been having on me. Then one day, looking in the bathroom mirror, it struck me how gaunt I looked, indicating loss of weight, there were bags under my eyes indicating loss of sleep, a loss of color to my skin. My clothes hung loosely on my thinning body and I felt a loss of energy.

Finally, one day, I called Sheila to arrange for our date, and it seemed she noticed something different in the quality of my voice.

"Are you all right?" she asked. "You sound tired."

I brushed away her concern. "I'm fine. Just built up a good appetite for a decent meal."

"Your voice sounds weak."

"Does it? Bad reception, I'm sure."

She agreed to a time and place and gave me her address.

I'd no sooner ended the call when I received another. I didn't recognize the number.

"Yes?"

"Mr. Falkner?" said the voice.

"That's me."

"This is Jones, the lab director at the Armitage

building?"

"Oh, yes! Do you have any results for me?"

There was a noticeable hesitation from Jones before he cleared his throat.

"Well, that's the issue, Mr. Falkner. You see, the lab was broken into last night. The grad student was struck unconscious...he's recovering in the hospital right now…"

"That's too bad…"

"Yes, well, the problem is, though nothing else was disturbed or removed, the only item we can determine that *is* missing is the sample you left with us to analyze."

"The vial is gone?"

"I'm afraid so. And since it was the only thing missing, the police naturally are curious."

"Do they know who took it?"

"No. They were hoping you'd have some notion of who might have been interested in the compound other than yourself."

"I have no idea…" But did it, I wondered, have anything to do with my uncle's disappearance?

"In any case, the detective in charge said that he'd be giving you a visit soon about the incident."

"All right. Please keep me informed if you learn anything else."

"Of course."

It was soon after that that the police arrived. Questions were asked, but aside from the story of finding the mysterious vial of fluid in the basement, there was nothing new I could add to the mystery save a suggestion that my uncle's disappearance might be connected. Could he have been kidnapped, forcibly taken, by the same person who broke into the college lab? Was the vial the connection between the two incidents? I had no idea, but the police appeared to consider the connection.

After they left, I was left to wonder if my own safety was in danger? Would the unknown thief strike again, this time with myself as his target? Perhaps he'd stayed away up to now thinking the vial wasn't around. But now that its presence in the house had been confirmed, might not the thief return to make sure I hadn't divided its contents and still had some on the premises?

It was with some trepidation that I made sure all the doors and windows in the house were locked before I went to bed that night, trepidation that somehow triggered the recurring nightmares, drawing me deeper into them than ever before.

The details would evade me upon waking, but in broad terms, their content couldn't be misinterpreted: the gigantic, looming presences that had been touched upon on previous nights became more concrete. They figured in some titanic, sprawling contest between two powerful forces contending for mastery of not Earth but the entire universe. In the dream, my consciousness was a weak, trembling flame that threatened to gutter out at the slightest gust from the collision of the powerful forces whose battle see sawed across time and space. An interdimensionality that cared little for the sane laws of earthly science and physics.

Fearfully, I felt myself falling between the countless dimensions that made up non-Euclidean space, from realities made up entirely of gasses or fluids or ever shifting solids all with insane, non-sensical points of view where up was down and down was sideways and directions that could not be defined as direction at all. It was all happening across multiple levels of existence and could have lasted a million years or a few seconds as men measure time.

Dimly, the readings I did of my uncle's notes and files, the books in his library, (and, I now suspect, the fumes I'd inhaled of the stolen potion) allowed my consciousness to ground itself in terms that I was able to grasp. What I became witness to was a war between ancient enemies including the Elder Gods who resided on the farthest edges of the universe where the first galaxies continued to rush away from the Big Bang. They were old, old, beings of infinite evolution so far removed from the norms of the governing forces of the universe, that they long since had seized to identify with any other form of life, including intelligent life, or even to notice it, least of all the intelligent life that infested an insignificant speck its inhabitants called Earth.

Coterminously in time, I saw the original revolt of some of the Elder Gods against others, their struggle for self-determination, their failure, and the rain of their now corporeal selves into a lone reality, a single dimension, a particular solar system; to lay trapped and harnessed for uncountable time in remote prisons on a frozen planet called Yuggoth and an uninhabited ball of swirling magma and steaming mist that, in eons yet unborn, later inhabitants would call Earth. There, they festered and raged, laying their plans to free themselves and confront the Elder Gods once again, this time in triumph. These were some day to be differentiated from their victorious brethren as the Old Ones, known to the earliest primordial races of Earth and their successors among the branches of mankind whom they used to further their cause with empty promises of power and glory.

And the visions continued, the nightmare went on, as I saw things with names like Azathoth and Chaugnar Faugn and Hastur and Cthulhu emerge from their prisons and rise, drawn up like filings to a magnet. In rising, the Old Ones left behind devastation, annihilation, and loss that left their prisons, Earth among them, wasted balls of apocalyptic death and climatic inundation. Man was left to scramble as best he might in scattered bands of brutish hunters, as he did ten thousand years before. They marshaled their forces beyond the orbit of Yuggoth, in the cold wastes of space, formed their order of battle, and as Yog-Sothoth opened the way, swarmed outward and inward at the same time to take the Elder Gods by surprise on the infinite planes of non-existence.

The Old Ones succeeded and at first, the struggle was all one sided as they celebrated key victories over the Elder Gods on different planes of existence, outside time. With no manner of measurement possible, the battle could take place over billions of years or none at all. Whatever it was, it proved elastic enough for the Elder Gods to recover from their complacency, and react, to devastating effect. First, the Old Ones' great general, Azathoth, was cast off across numberless dimensions. Then, great Cthulhu himself was sent reeling, causing a ripple effect among the others. Something that could only be described as panic ensued and the lesser Old Ones began to retreat. Briefly, Cthulhu rallied them on an abysmal plane in some uncharted sub-dimension. They counter attacked, and once more the Elder Gods were taken unexpectedly.

But Nodens, first among the Elder Gods, refused to be troubled. He gathered his strength and assaulted the Old Ones from multiple directions at once. Now it was Cthulhu that was thrown back and this time, he could not control the fear that gripped his mighty host. By contrast, the rest of the Elder Gods were emboldened and added their power to those of Nodens and together turned the tide of battle. The Old Ones fled, seeking the safety of their former prisons and, seeing that their enemies were defeated and understanding their own inability to destroy them completely, the Elder Gods allowed them to go only making certain that the Old Ones could never again rise to threaten them anew. They laid a great Sign over the obscure solar system which was their prison and determined never again to let their own guard down.

It was then that I awoke with a start and a long scream that filled the empty rooms of the house and only ended when all the strength left me and I collapsed back amid the damp sheets. my mind was frantic with impossible thoughts that yet were frighteningly real. Desperately, I wanted to forget, forget especially the sights of men, like ants, scrambling over a blasted Earth seeking a means of survival that didn't exist.

Shouting again, I leapt from bed, clutching my head, pounding it in a desperate attempt to drive the thoughts from my mind. My actions seemed to succeed as the vivid imagery faded away leaving me exhausted. Slowly, I performed my toilet and dressed. I retreated to the kitchen and fixed myself breakfast and, as was my habit, took it into the TV room and turned on the news.

There were the usual political controversies, trouble in the Middle East, murder and mayhem at home, the weather. It was under the heading of weather that something caught my attention. There was a report from Central Asia of a strange phenomenon, of a "reverse meteor" where an object broke through the Earth's crust and rose in the form of a fireball, into the sky and disappeared into the stratosphere. There was general disbelief among Western scientists, but a film of the event existed that indeed showed what looked like a meteorite falling in reverse. Analysts rejected the idea some eastern nation was experimenting with a new kind of rocket but it's eccentric trajectory continued to baffle the experts.

I sat immobile, a slice of toast half way to my mouth. I'd seen a phenomenon like that in my dreams. Suddenly, I broke out in a cold sweat. It was *just* like in my dreams! I was seized with an inexplicable sensation of rising panic. This was only the first, I realized. As the Old Ones launched their long planned assault on their ancient tormentors. And with the rising of the rest, the world would be left destroyed and mankind virtually extinct. Then it hit me full force as I was struck by the meaning of the backwards meteor: What I'd assumed from my dreams was a prophecy of some distant event was in reality a warning of impending disaster. So you, see, I'm not out of my mind. We need to keep the Old Ones from escaping! Stop! Don't do that! Let me go! Don't you feel them? Those distant rumblings? It's the Old Ones! We have to stop them! Keep that needle away! You don't know what you're doing! You're condemning the human race to obliteration! Let go! Let go! Stop!

(The recording ends here)

The Fungi Interviews

Editor's Note: This special section re-presents interviews with Mythos related writers and individuals that first appeared in earlier, now hard if not impossible to get, issues of *Fungi.* So far as the editor knows, all of the interviews were possibly the last given before the subjects passed away. Sadly, fandom has lost the entirety of their generation, the second immediately following the deaths of Robert E. Howard, H.P. Lovecraft, Clark Ashton Smith and the rest of the original *Weird Tales* alumni. The *Fungi* staff, which conducted the following interviews over a span of about ten years, wish to thank posthumously E. Hoffman Price, Fritz Leiber, Robert Bloch, and Robert Baker Elder for making themselves available to admiring young fans. They were among our literary heroes.

The Fungi Interview: Robert Baker Elder

Transcribed by Henry J. Vester III

Editor's Note: Robert Baker Elder was born in Auburn, California on July 7, 1915 and died there on June 18, 2008. After working for a local newspaper and military service, he wrote articles for *National Parks Magazine* and wrote a number of novels including *The Sheriff of Sycamore Flat* (1952), Whom the Gods Destroy (1953), *Rattlesnake Dick* (1954), and *Banner House* (2002)

The following interview was conducted by the author on October 12, 1984 at the subject's home in Auburn, California. This small, ex-mining town located in Placer County, had been the longtime home of the poet Clark Ashton Smith. Locating Mr. Elder and then boldly calling upon him, the author was graciously allowed an extended visit at the former's home. Himself an author of many pieces regarding the history and ecosystems of the western United States as well as the novel *Whom the Gods Destroy,* Mr. Elder has given the readers of *Fungi* a rare opportunity to perhaps know more intimately the life and influences of one of the world's premiere fantasistes.

Robert Baker Elder

Amid the shining lights which comprises the genre of fantastic literature, no sorcerer's lamp shines more brightly than that of the California poet and prose author, Clark Ashton Smith. So rarely does the student of the outre find such scintillant clarity of unearthly vision wedded to such masterful command of evocative language, that the works of Smith stand almost unique as a monument to the all but infinite capacity of the human imagination to transcend the boundaries of the commonplace. The writings of this altogether remarkable individual (who wold have felt more at home in Zothique than in Auburn) have enjoyed merely a rather sparse and sporadic readership since the publication of his first book of poetry in 1912. However, due to the laudable efforts of a handful of Smithian enthusiasts, many of his short stories, at least, are still in print and appear to be gaining an ever widening circle of devotees. It is the hope of this writer that the appreciators of his profound and otherworldly poetry will not be far behind.

Elder: I can remember Clark all my life, but I never really got to know him very well until maybe the last five or six years of his life. As a boy, I can remember Clark walking around town, a very individualistic looking character; you could pick him out on the street more or less. He was not a sociable person, and I was in my middle life before I really got to know him. He read a book that I wrote and became convinced that I was writing about him! (*Whom the Gods May Destroy*, Robert Baker Elder, Comet Press Books, New York, 1953). So he invited me out to his place one day. I didn't know if he'd be easy to talk to or not, but after I got to know him I found he was very friendly, and we became quite good friends the last years of his life. I can remember him walking around town. He carried a little satchel. I don't know what was in it. Maybe he carried his papers in there. Somebody said he carried a wine bottle! (laughter) I really don't know.

He read this book that I wrote and said "He's writing about me!" So he sent me an invitation to come out to lunch at his place, and I was completely flabbergasted! All my life I'd more or less known who he was, and then I got this note out of thin air. I couldn't imagine why! Must have been the late fifties sometime. I had read some of his stuff and though I'm not a science fiction fan, I could see that he had a good style and that he was a capable writer. And I had read some of his poems I'd liked. So I went out wondering what I'd talk about and then he told me, "I read your book, and I think you're writing about me."

Vester: Did he seem upset about it?

Elder: No! He was quite pleased, and that's strange because Clark didn't like people to write about him. He told me "They don't understand me. I don't like these things they say about me." But strangely enough, this book, which I was really writing out of own head, he liked very much. He said "This is me down to the core." I never told him one way or the other that I was or was not writing about him. After a while we became quite friendly, and we would exchange our writings and discuss his poems. He wasn't a person who looked like he'd be easy to know. He lived in his own world, but I found him to be very friendly and affable. After I got to know Clark, I wished I'd become acquainted with him sooner. He was an interesting person, and certainly had a vivid imagination. Do you prefer his prose or his poetry?

Vester: I think I like his poetry better.

Elder: I do too. So many people know him only for his stories...not a lot of people read his poems. I think they're infinitely superior; he thought so too. He thought of his prose as a way to make a living. He had to make a little money somehow, so he began to write for these pulp magazines, and he told me it was a very unsure way to make an income. Sometimes they paid, sometimes they didn't, sometimes they sent a note saying I.O.U. (so much). Half the time those were never paid, so when he did get a check from them he felt very lucky. They were very small, sometimes around twenty, thirty dollars.

Vester: How did Clark first break into print?

Elder: Some lady in town here, a school teacher, I think, sent some of his poems to George Sterling. He wrote Clark a letter saying how much he liked his poems, and thought they ought to be published. And it was soon, in that manner, that Clark's first book was published. Sterling had a good deal to do with it. And Clark got some quite good reviews. In fact, I think it was the *San Francisco Examiner* that carried the

Clark Ashton Smith

headline on the front page: "Remarkable Poet Discovered in the Wilds of Auburn," or something like that! And so Clark and Sterling became very good friends. And Sterling was very close to Jack London, so Sterling told London about him, and London sent Clark an invitation to come to the Valley of the Moon (near Santa Rosa, California) for a visit. But Clark wouldn't go! He was very poor, and had nothing but very threadbare clothes. He wouldn't tell him why he wouldn't come...he just made excuses. So he never go to meet London.

Vester: How frequently did you and Clark have contact after you met him?

Elder: Oh, not too often...maybe once every five or six months or so. After he invited me out to his place, why, I wanted to return the favor, but I was no cook so I wanted to take him out to a restaurant. But he didn't want to go to a restaurant with a lot of people around him. But there was an old hotel in Auburn. In years past it had been Auburn's finest hotel, but it had gone downhill until it was practically unfrequented. Very, very few people went there, so we agreed we'd go there. We had almost the entire dining room to ourselves, and we had a real nice dinner. He told me he just didn't like people around him. But to visit, like you and I are, why, he enjoyed that.

Vester: Did he and his wife ever live in the cabin after they were married?

Elder: Yes, she was out there for a while, but there was no plumbing in it. There wasn't even a toilet. It was pretty primitive.

Vester: What was Clark's sense of humor like?

Elder: Well, he had a subtle sense of humor...it wasn't a loud sense at all. But he wasn't without humor. There are a few of his poems that show a little humor.

Vester: What seemed to be Clark's own attitude toward his writings?

Elder: Well, as I say, he sort of dismissed the stories as just a way to make a living, but he thought that some day he would be a recognized poet. And as he grew older and recognition never really came, I think it saddened him a great deal. When they (the poems) first came out, they were well-reviewed...remarkably well-reviewed...but the public never took to them much at all...they were too out of the ordinary, I guess. About the only people who appreciated them were the occasional literary people, and as far as getting any public reception, I don't think they ever did. But he always thought, like most poets, "Well, after the years, I'll come to be recognized," But that time has hardly ever come as far as I can see. There are people who like him, but they are few and scattered. Maybe he'll have to wait another hundred years or so before he'll come into his own. As far as he was concerned, if he had any right to fame, it was through his poetry. That was what he thought. Although I've read some of his stories that show a remarkable command of prose, the type of prose that was written maybe a hundred years ago...not the Jack London newspaper style, but more or less the perfected style between poetry and prose.

Vester: Do you have any sense of his philosophical or spiritual leanings?

Elder: He certainly had that side to his nature. I don't think it's what we would call the typical religious person, but he did definitely live in another sphere. I'm sure he did believe in other spheres and other worlds and things of that sort. I don't think he was an anti-religious person really, sometimes he would get a little sarcastic, I guess lots of people do that.

Vester: I seem to pick up Buddhistic and Taoist references in his poems.

Elder: Yes. In fact, Carol said that after they were married they used to read some of the Indian Vedas and about Buddha. He was acquainted with the Bible, because he quotes it in lots of places. He was acquainted with the Greek and Confucian beliefs and he liked the Arabian Nights, the Eastern character to them. I think he was well acquainted with all the religious cults and the philosophical ones. I mentioned Emerson to him once and he seemed to have a kind of an anti-feeling toward the New England school of poetry and writing. I always liked those, so I didn't get into that with him. I thought we'd get into an argument. Clark didn't like modern writing at all. I can't think of any modern writers that he liked, at least none of the "accepted" ones. He liked Lovecraft, and the science fiction people he corresponded with, but he didn't like the style of present-day writing very much. That's why I was surprised that he liked my book, but then, he thought he had a special reason to like it. Anything that had to do with the old alchemists or magicians, he loved something like that...

A Bit of the Dark World

an interview with Fritz Leiber

by Gregorio Montejo

Editor's Note: Fritz Leiber was born on December 24, 1910 and passed away on September 5, 1992.

Fritz Leiber was born in Chicago in 1910; Both of his parents were actors. Leiber attended the University of Chicago, where his interests shifted from "chemistry and physics to psychology," He received a Bachelor of Philosophy in 1932. It was during this period of time that he and his good friend Harry Fischer created two characters which would prove to be of lasting endurance: Fafhrd and the Gray Mouser. These two swashbuckling adventurers, and the magical world they inhabited, were the product of two fertile imaginations inspired by wide and varied reading. Their influences ranged from Gustave Flaubert' *Salammbo*, Henrik Ibsen's *Peer Gynt*, and Robert Graves' *I, Claudius* to the *Elder Edda*, E.R. Eddison's *The Worm Ouroboros*, and James Branch Cabell's "Poictesme" novels.

Since first breaking into print in 1939, Fritz Leiber has found himself equally at home in both the science fiction and fantasy genres. In his first decade as a professional writer he produced a number of short stories which have become classics. Among these are "The Automatic Pistol," "Smoke Ghost," "Wanted: An Enemy," "Sanity," and "The Man Who Never Grew young."

All throughout the 1950s and the early part of the 1960s, Leiber continued a steady output of fiction. Among his most memorable creations from this period are a series of dark satires which reflected the pensive and neurotic atmosphere of the Cold War. The most celebrated of these stories is "Coming Attractions," a nightmarish piece which was voted one of the "best science fiction stories of all time" by the Science Fiction Writers of America. Equally remarkable was *The Big Time* a unique science fiction novel which takes place continuously in one setting, an experiment inspired by Leiber's theatrical background, and Joyce Cary's "Gully Jimson" trilogy. In the past two decades, Leiber has written less profusely, yet with no apparent attenuation of his literary prowess. In recent years he has given us such masterful short tales as "Belson Express" and also the superlative short novel *Our Lady of Darkness,* a fantasy about the supernatural and literary denizens of San Francisco. Since 1970, Leiber has lived in a bustling and crowded section of San Francisco, full of small shops, used book stores and Depression-era hotels converted into apartment buildings.

Mr. Leiber graciously allowed Henry J. Vester, R.J. Zimmerman, Pierre Comtois, and I to interview him at his home in August, 1986. His apartment looked very much as one might imagine: replete with crowded bookcases and various literary awards. The fruits of a long and productive love affair with the written word.

Montejo: I saw your father in a movie just a few dayus ago, a historical picture with Frederick march; your father played the hero's side-kick.

Leiber: in the last part of his life, between 1935 and 1949 (when he died), he played many relatively

93

small roles in about 50 or 60 movies. Things like "The Life of Emile Zola" with Paul Muni, "Anthony Adverse," "The Prince and the Pauper," "A tale of Two Cities" with Ronald Coleman, and so forth.

Zimmerman: Have you ever done any acting; on the stage or in the movies?

Leiber: Oh, yes. I acted in my father's Shakespearean company for a couple of seasons, when he went out on the road, including the last season: 1934-1935. We had played Los Angeles toward the end of the tour, and from then on my father lived on the west coast.

Comtois: Did you ever make it to celluloid?

Leiber: Well, I played a small part in the Greta Garbo/Robert Taylor *Camille.* I'm in the cast in the role of Valentine, I think it is.

Montejo: So you met Garbo?

Leiber: No, I just acted in a scene with Robert Taylor, so she wasn't around. Then there was a much later film called *Equinox;* that was originally done as an amateur film, but later it was expanded into a longer witchcraft film. I played the character of a professor who gets killed about halfway through; I was chased by a demon and I die in a stream. I remember in the shooting I had to lie there in the running water.

Fritz Leiber

Comtois: How did you get involved with the movie, *Tarzan and the Valley of Gold*?

Leiber: At that time, Ballantine was issuing the paperback Tarzan series, and they got together with Edgar Rice Burroughs, Inc...the youngest of the Burroughs sons was the manager of the company at that time...together with the producers, Eagle Productions I think it was called, and they decided that they wanted a novelization of the movie. I'd been writing quite a bit for Ballantine at the time, I had a few books published by them, so I was chosen. And they decided to authorize a 25th volume (in the Tarzan series)

Montejo: Which has been out of print for quite a while.

Leiber: Yes, they don't reprint that one; and that's partly because too many people are supposed to make money out of it: the movie people, Eagle Productions, ERB Inc, and Ballantine.

Montejo: And eventually even you.

Leiber: I did it for a lump sum. So I wouldn't stand to profit by it.

Comtois: Did you write from a script?

Leiber: Yes, I wrote from a script.

Comtois: Were you able to deviate from it?

Leiber: To some extent I had to. For one thing, the picture was supposed to be set in the Mato Grosso province of Brazil, but it was all very inaccurate. The Brazilians all spoke Spanish instead of Portuguese. There weren't any South American animals, or any Indians except for a few people who were supposed to be Incas who had survived. That part of the film was shot entirely in Mexico using an old Aztec ruin. Actually the script I worked from was quite different from the finished picture itself so there are quite a few differences between my novel and the motion picture. I followed the story, but provided a lot of authentic Brazilian detail: the food, the coinage, the Indians, the animals, etc.

Vester: This may be a question from which you've been asked all too frequently, but which of your books have you been happiest with?

Leiber: I'd say with the books about Fafhrd and the Gray Mouser, because they've gone on since the beginning. They were in the first story of mine which got published; just at the start of World War II, in *Unknown*, August 1939.

Vester: That was "Two Sought Adventure?"

Leiber: The story was called "Two Sought Adventure" when it was first published. I later used that title for the first collection of Fafhrd/Gray Mouser stories from Gnome Press. I changed the title of the story itself to "The Jewels in the Forest," so that's the title you'll find it under in the Ace volume *Swords Against Death*. I wrote the Fafhrd/Gray Mouser stories for various magazines; the first four or five for *Unknown*. Then there was a period of about ten years when very few were published, then I started to write them for *Fantastic*. It wasn't until 1967 that Ace started to publish them, beginning with the novel *Swords of Lankhmar*. Right now I'm writing a very long story, a short novel really, called "The Mouser Goes Below." That will round out the seventh Fafhrd/Gray Mouser book; which will probably be called *The Knight and Knave of Swords*.

Montejo: Didn't you publish an amateur magazine sometime in the late 40s or early 50s?

Leiber: I published an amateur magazine for the first half of 1949 called *New Purposes*.

Montejo: Did you begin this magazine because some of your markets were closing at that time; basically to publish your own work?

Leiber: (laughter) That's usually the reason for starting a magazine.

Comtois: Sounds familiar!

Leiber: I didn't actually know much of anything about fans and fanzines, you see; although I'd been writing and selling for about ten years. I was acquainted with a few people who appeared in the magazine. There was one story and a number of articles by Robert Bloch; and one story by Henry Kuttner and various friends of mine. Kuttner and Bloch were a couple of the people I happened to know through my correspondence with Lovecraft towards the end of his life.

A wonder novel of Fafhrd the Barbarian and the Gray Mouser by the foremost master of sword-and-sorcery science-fiction...

FRITZ LEIBER
the SWORDS OF LANKHMAR

Montejo: Some critics have said that after you began the magazine your science fiction stories began to be slightly different. They dealt with more dystopian topics.

Leiber: That's true. That was partly because I went to my first SF convention in 1949, the World Con in Cincinnati. That was when I met the New York writers, especially I became acquainted with the writers who would be featured shortly in *Galaxy*. Writing for *Galaxy*, it was natural to get into a more dystopian mood.

Vester: (Reading from the first issue of *New Purposes*); "The sick world is obsessed with means, here we will speak of ends. The machine breeds monotony, here we will have excitement. The mass media of communication inculcates uniformity, here we will have diversity. Religion is cloaked in dark myths, here we will strip her whether she be beautiful or ugly. Science is preoccupied with matter, facts and generalities, here we will demand of him spirit, drama and generalities. The prophets of doom worry us with warnings of atomic war, here though heeding those warnings, we will dance in doom's mushroom shadow. Modern puritans urge sobriety and fear the wild spirit of man, here we will get wisely drunk and nourish the wildest fantasies. Elsewhere pleasure is a goddess, here she will be a friend and ally. Elsewhere money, possessions and success are displayed, and minds plot feverishly to gain more, here we will show off our wealth of ideas and experience, and lay plans for their increase and not hesitate to talk of failure. The Age of Anxiety is smothering us, but here we will breath freely. The guilt of ages is on our shoulders, but here we will laugh and look toward the future." *New Purposes*, January 1, 1949.

Leiber: That sounds very new to me.

Vester: Did John Campbell discourage you from writing these more pessimistic stories?

Leiber: No, I wouldn't say so. All of my earlier science fiction stories were written for Campbell, including the novel *Gather, Darkness*. As I was writing for *Galaxy* in the 1950s, I also wrote "The Lion and the Lamb," "The Enchanted Forest" and others for Campbell.

Montejo: Was *Gather, Darkness* based on Robert Heinlein's *Sixth Column*?

Leiber: Oh, yes, I sort of carried on from there in a way. He had the same idea of people founding a religion based on a new science.

Montejo: Did Campbell suggest the idea to you?"

Leiber: No. I just liked the idea of a religion with fake miracles based on newly discovered science. I'd just written my first, and only, witchcraft novel *Conjure Wife* for *Unknown*; which was also Campbell's magazine. So I thought if you can have a novel based on the idea of a religion whose miracles are worked by science, what if there were witchcraft worked by science? That would be one way of mounting a revolt, have their "miracles" also be managed by advance technology.

Montejo: I guess that really appealed to Campbell?

Leiber: In a way that was a natural after *Sixth Column*.

Zimmerman: How do you feel about L. Ron Hubbard's Scientology?

Leiber: Well, that all went along with the feeling that we were in a lot of trouble. We were worrying about the atomic bomb. The period when Scientology started was just at the beginning of what we now call the McCarthy era. The feeling that Campbell shared with Hubbard, and a lot of others, was the ideal that people had to get straightened out very fast or we'd destroy the world, and what was needed was for everybody to be psycho-analyzed in record time. That was what gave it such a strong appeal at the time.

Zimmerman: But doesn't Scientology have a lot to do with technology? They use machines to "test" people…

Vester: It's just a simple galvanometer.

Zimmerman: Isn't that strange?

Montejo: They use technology to solve the problem of technology run rampant.

Leiber: But that is what made it sound so logical, so appealing. It's been very successful at establishing itself.

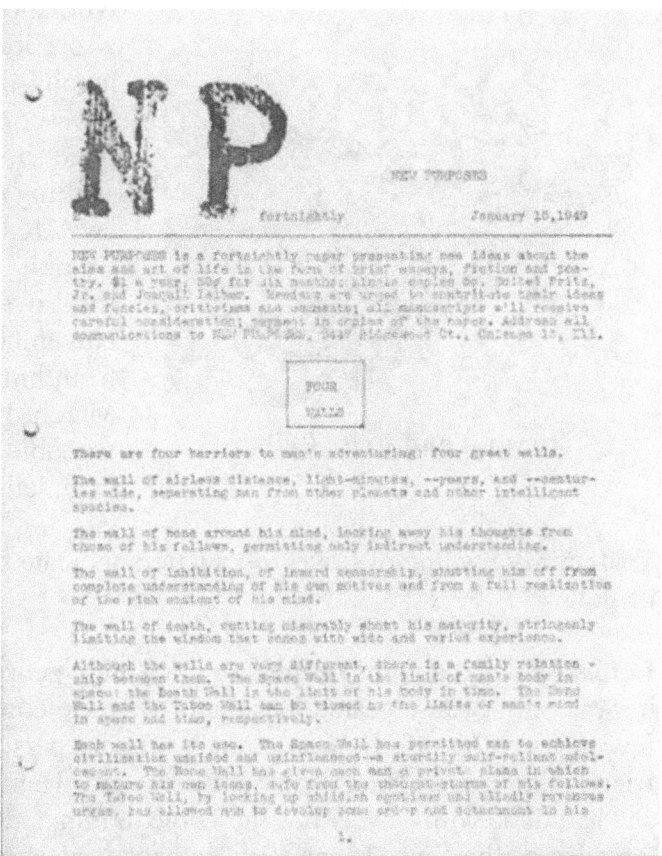

New Purposes #2

Montejo: You've met many interesting writers during your career, including Thomas Mann. Do you have any anecdotes you could relate?

Leiber: I'll begin by saying that I would never have gotten in contact with Lovecraft on my own; because I wouldn't have had the nerve to write. That wasn't the sort of thing I did, write people I was interested in. I was always being modest and holding back, and being shy at that time. So, actually my wife wrote Lovecraft a letter. She didn't write care of *Weird Tales* because Lovecraft had just had two stories, "At

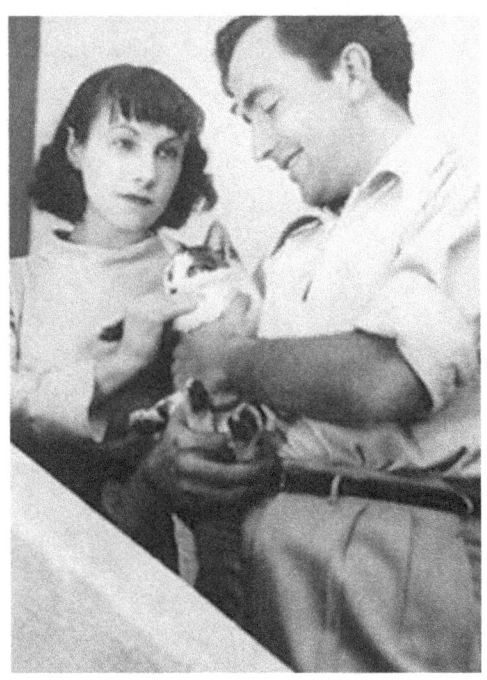

Jonquil and Fritz Leiber

the Mountains of Madness" and The Shadow Out of Time,"published in *Astounding* just before Campbell became editor. So she wrote to Lovecraft care of Street & Smith Publications, telling him about my being such a big fan of his, wondering if his stories were available in book form, and so on. He wrote a very nice response, and that gave me my chance. From then on, for the next several months, both my wife and I wrote him letters. I wrote very long ones, and he wrote long replies. It was a chance for me to tell him how much I liked his work. And to send him the first Fafhrd/Gray Mouser story; which was "Adept's Gambit." He read and liked it, and made minor suggestions, mostly correcting spelling mistakes. That was how I came to meet Robert Bloch and Henry Kuttner, because Lovecraft circulated "Adept's Gambit" to them, to August Derleth and a few other people in the Lovecraft circle. The correspondence went on through November and December of 1936. The last letter I received from him was in February of 1937, and of course he died in March. It was utterly amazing that a man who was that sick was able to take on two new correspondents; and to write them huge letters.

Vester: My reading of Lovecraft's letters indicate that he became more and more fully human the older he got.

Leiber: He met a lot of people; mostly young people. He thought of himself as an old man even though he was only twenty years older than I was. He could have lived for many more years. But yes, the last few years of his life he was a much broader person, more tolerant. He had a number of good Jewish friends like Robert Bloch and Sam Loveman. Then my wife did the same thing with Thomas Mann that she had done with Lovecraft. She wrote to him and made a date for me to see him. He was living in Los Angeles at the time. I was very embarrassed about it, sort of mad at her for doing that. I saw him eventually, and it went off perfectly, except for one thing. I had read *The Magic Mountain*, "Death in Venice," "Mario and the Magician," "Tonio Kroger" and other things. But I hadn't read his first novel *Buddenbroooks*. Mann thought that *Buddenbrooks* was his best novel. So here was I, supposed to be a big fan, and I hadn't read his best book. That's pretty embarrassing.

Zimmerman: Do you know Harlan Ellison Well? You wrote the story "Gonna Roll the Bones" for his anthology *Dangerous Visions.* Is he as volatile and unpredictable as everyone says?

Leiber: Well, ever since I wrote that story we've been very friendly. At the upcoming World Con in Atlanta, Harlan will with an auction, to help Mrs. Wellman pay off Manly's medical bills. I contributed a little ruby glass mug that was a present from Lovecraft. His aunt returned my letters to Lovecraft after his death; she also gave me this mug that has "H.P. Lovecraft, 1900" inscribed on it. He had received it as a present when he was ten years old. But Harlan is very active. He'll do things like write a story in the window of a book store, in order to promote the story, and to attract attention in general.

Montejo: One of your stories which I find particularly interesting is "Dark Wings." A story in which you use Jung's concepts of the anima and the animus."

Leiber: He's always been very good about science fiction. In the concept of the anima especially; he's very much up on H. Rider Haggard's *She*, which he uses as one of his examples of the anima. Also, the character from William Sloan's *To Walk the Night*, another portrait of the anima which Jung recommends to readers who want to understand the concept. I wrote an article about the anima in science fiction for Terry Carr's magazine, *The Lighthouse,* giving other examples: "The Thing on the Doorstep" by Lovecraft, the woman in Clifford Simak's *Way Station* and a few others. I'd say that in the last 20 or 30 years the stories I've done have been written with some knowledge of Jung and his archetypes.

Montejo: There's also the subject of chess, which appears in a number of your stories, including "Midnight by the Morphy Watch."

Leiber: I've played chess all my life. I learned to play it when I was thirteen years old; fairly well along. I played it in college at the University of Chicago, I used the play on their team. In the years between 1958-1968 I played quite a bit of chess out here. I only won one tournament, that was the Open Santa Monica tournament back in 1959. And I played in one tournament in San Francisco; after I came here in 1970. It was on the basis of the tournament that I wrote "Midnight by the Morphy Watch." I was always fascinated by that watch Morphy was presented, with the chess pieces on the dial. I wanted to write about it, make it more real.

MEETING ROBERT BLOCH, AUGUST, 21 1993

An interview conducted by R. J. Zimmerman

Editor's Note: Robert Bloch was born on April 5, 1917 and passed away on September 23, 1994.

On a balmy late August wind the NecronomiCon: First Edition blew into the serene community of Danvers, Massachusetts, pitching its metaphorical tents at the unsuspecting Sheraton Tara Hotel. This convention was the first of what is hoped to be an every other year event, in honor of author H. P. Lovecraft and his literary legacy concentrating on his infamous Cthulhu Mythos stories. Held on August 20-23, 1993 (August 20th being Lovecraft's birthday), convention planners chose Danvers as an appropriate location for the event. After all, it was next door neighbor to witch haunted Salem (referred to as Arkham, in many of Lovecraft's stories) Also, Danvers itself had once been part of Salem, known as Salem Village, where much of the witch hysteria of 1692 originated.

This first convention had the good fortune to line up two extraordinary special guests: author Robert Bloch, who should need no introduction to readers of this magazine, and artist Gahan Wilson, who has long entertained Lovecraft and *Weird Tales* fans with his humorous and witty mythos related drawings and cartoons.

A month before NecronomiCon's arrival in town, I had started a new job working as an Associate Producer at Danvers Community Access TV. One of my first assignments was to create a monthly news and magazine style program. The timing was perfect; I would contact the organizers of the event to see if I could videotape highlights of the convention with the goal of putting together a video short for my new magazine show. To my surprise and delight, I was not only granted permission to videotape the activities in the convention halls but I was also offered the opportunity to interview both Mr. Bloch and Mr. Wilson.

And so, on Saturday, August 21, with camera equipment in hand, I arrived at the NecronomiCon, nervous and anxious about meeting one of the original members of the storied Lovecraft circle. Assisting me that day was a certain local author named Pierre Comtois – another name that should be familiar to anyone reading this magazine! In short order two of us were introduced to the legend himself. Casually dressed in suit jacket and button down shirt, Robert Bloch was relaxed and sociable. He immediately made me feel at ease and even cracked a few jokes as I was setting up the video equipment. The questions I had prepared were not meant to be particularly probing or esoteric as this was ultimately going to be viewed by an audience who, most likely, had never even heard of Robert Bloch. (Although they may have heard of *Psycho,* the Alfred Hitchcock film based on one of his novels) Still, Bloch's answers were very detailed and revealing.

Robert Bloch

It's a pleasure having you here Mr. Bloch and I'm very appreciative of the time you're giving me for this interview so without further ado, let's begin...

Fungi: When did you begin your writing career?

Bloch: I began my writing career just about exactly 59 years ago. I sold my first professional story and several times since then I've debated working for a living but decided against it.

Fungi: How did you become interested in the fantasy horror genre and the writings of H.P. Lovecraft in particular?

Bloch: I acquired my first copy of *Weird Tales* magazine in which Mr. Lovecraft was appearing when I was ten years old. I began to read it and I became an avid fan. When I turned sixteen I wrote my first and only fan letter asking where I could find some of those stories. Since in those days there were no paperbacks, this type of fiction was not reprinted in hardcovers and you had to get back issues of those magazines. And, he not only replied and offered me the loan of any of those magazines but we also entered into a correspondence. Very shortly thereafter he suggested I try my own hand at writing. And I did. And it was that simple and I'm indebted to that man who, sixty years ago, changed my life.

Fungi: Most fans know that Lovecraft was the creator of the Cthulhu Mythos but could you elaborate on some of your own contributions to the Mythos?

Bloch: What I did primarily to the Mythos was invent a few magic volumes, books on sorcery and necromancy that became part of the Mythos and utilized some of Lovecraft's own concepts. I didn't add very much directly to it but I did write, as most of us did, in imitation of his style for a while. He was a tremendous influence on all the horror and fantasy writers of that generation and succeeding generations for that matter.

Fungi: On that same note, at that time in history were people like Lovecraft, Howard, Smith, as well known then as they are now?

Bloch: *Weird Tales* wasn't the typical run of the mill pulp magazine. It was unique and called itself the unique magazine, and it was. It printed the type of fiction that other magazines wouldn't touch. Of these three writers you mentioned, Clark Ashton Smith was a gifted poet in his own right and he had a small but devoted following; Lovecraft had a somewhat larger following of people that were interested in scholarship. Howard probably had the largest following because of his Conan character. But between the three of them they might have had a grand total of 2,000 fans in the U.S. And that was the extent of their influence. Their main influence was on other writers and readers, like myself, who decided to become writers. It would be ironic and astonishing to them today if they could see what happened in terms of the renown they've won. Andy Warhol's fifteen minutes of fame certainly arrived for them but far too late unfortunately.

Fungi: How do you think Lovecraft would have felt about his posthumous acclaim?

Bloch: Lovecraft would have been greatly amused and I think greatly flattered because he never realized that there would be this much interest in him or in his work. He was a very modest man and this type of mass media influence was something he wouldn't have dreamed of.

Fungi: Did you ever actually get to meet Lovecraft or was your friendship strictly through correspondence?

H.P. Lovecraft with Frank Belknap Long: Although Bloch never met Lovecraft in person, he was among the many young proteges that the author made friends with through correspondence and encouraged in their writing ambitions

Bloch: My relationship with Lovecraft was strictly through correspondence and that was the case with the majority of the people that formed the group known as the Lovecraft circle. We all corresponded with Lovecraft but we all lived during the great depression at which time neither we nor Lovecraft could travel unless we wanted to go by freight car.

Fungi: I'd like to talk a little bit about you as a writer. You're probably best known as the author of *Psycho* which was made into one of Alfred Hitchcock's most famous films. What did you think of his translation and how did it boost your popularity as a writer?

Bloch: I'm glad you mentioned that [affects a mischievous grin], I'd forgotten the name of the director! Hitch's film followed the book very faithfully and for that reason it was extremely flattering to me that he would do so. In terms of boosting my popularity...what it did was put a label on my forehead, for better or worse, so that I had something to be identified by. But by that time I was already out in Hollywood. Not because of the film...the film had not been produced. I was writing for television and I had received my first film assignments on my own. But it certainly didn't do any harm and, ever since then of course, I've had to be very careful and very persuasive to get any young ladies to shower with me.

Fungi: As a screenwriter you've written for *Thriller* and *Star Trek* and some Hammer pictures I believe; were you asked at the time of *Psycho* to contribute to the screenplay or weren't you in Hollywood yet?

Bloch: At the time *Psycho* was done as a screenplay, I was living 2,000 miles away in a little town called Weyauwega, Wisconsin. Mr. Hitchcock didn't know of my existence, [and] asked if I were available as a screenwriter. The man he asked was with MCA, the [talent] agency, and the man at MCA said "no, he's not available" and recommended one of his own clients. It was probably just as well because I don't think, first time out, I would have been that equipped to do justice to the screenplay though of course, naturally, I would have enjoyed the chance. But I had already embarked on my own thing by then.

Fungi: Do you have a favorite script that you've written?

Bloch: I would say that my own favorite, and there aren't very many of them, would be in television; the *[Alfred] Hitchcock [Presents]* shows or the *Thriller* shows that I did. There were about a dozen of each, most of them adapted from my own short stories. In films, I guess the first segment of a film called *Asylum* which was a British made production [from] Amicus [productions].

Fungi: Do you have any favorite stories? I know you've written for many different genres and of that enormous canon do you have any particular favorites that stand out?

Bloch: Well, I'm afraid I've published between 400 to 500 short stories in my misspent life and some 24 novels so it's difficult for me to choose favorites. They're all my children and you know how people are about their kids! I'm that way too. Right now, of course, I'm plugging my autobiography *Once around the Bloch* which has just been published by Tor books and that would make a wonderful screen story but I don't think that Sylvester Stallone is available for the lead.

Fungi: Well maybe Schwarzenegger then?

Bloch: (laughs at the notion)

Fungi: As a fan of your work, I've noticed that your books are notoriously difficult to find, at least in newer bookstores. Do you know if there are plans to reissue or reprint any of them?

Bloch: I think I have about a dozen titles presently in print and available at least in paperback from Tor books. I'm just going to have my first two collections, originally done by Arkham House back in the 1940's, printed as an Omnibus volume: *Opener of the Way* and *Pleasant Dreams* and that will be out in a couple of months. I've just finished editing my second anthology called *Monsters in our Midst* which will be out from Tor. I have some new short stories in that. And, at this convention, the letters that Lovecraft wrote to me have been collected and reprinted in a volume of their own. When I get back I will have to look at my desk and on my desk there [will be] a contract and the contract says I have to write a new novel. So, I guess there will be more. There will be more.

Fungi: That's great news! What do you think of today's horror stories and are there any current authors you particularly admire?

Bloch: There are many writers I admire. I hesitate to pick out one or two at the expense of the others but I would say of course people like Stephen King and Robert McCammon and Ramsey Campbell in England and Dan Simmons and Jonathan Carroll and a number of the other people whose work I asked to be included in the anthology I spoke of. I'm not too much in favor of excess gore. I think that it's very good for the ketchup industry but bad for the movie industry.

Fungi: I agree completely. Do you think yesterday's writers had to be more creative than today's writers due to the stricter censorship and public standards of the time?

Bloch: Yes, they were limited and unable to cut loose as it were, pardon the expression, and probably just as well [since] their motivations were different. They centered on characterization and the actors. You must remember, the actors were the stars of the horror film: Lon Chaney Sr., Boris Karloff, Bela Lugosi, Peter Lorre and, more recently although still ancient times, Peter Cushing and Christopher Lee. Today the stars of horror films are the special effects and that makes quite a difference. It's much easier I think, in one-way, but much more difficult for the writer to do characterization, in print or in film, if he or she is writing about the living breathing human being. But it's not too difficult to do characterization for a dinosaur.

Fungi: Of all the different genre's you've written is there one particular favorite or, like your stories and novels, are they all your children?

Bloch: I think my stories start to run together. I started out writing supernatural fiction because that's where I thought that area of horror was and now I might write more psychological fiction because I think the horror is not in the great beyond but in that little secret world inside our own skulls.

Fungi: One last question, Do you have any plans to tour this area?

Bloch: Not at the moment. I'm hoping to go back home and, as soon as I can get hold of a decent size shovel, to get the bills off my desk. [Then] I will tackle that contract and the novel.

Fungi: Thank you very much Mr. Bloch for participating in this interview. It was truly a pleasure.

As I was changing the camera shot for a wide angle of the two of us, Bloch mentioned that, of the Lovecraft circle, the only other author who was still alive was Frank Belknap Long. Several months later, Frank Belknap Long passed away on January 3, 1994. Sadly, Robert Bloch passed away shortly after this on September 23, 1994, only about a year after this interview was conducted. It's likely that it marks one of the last times he was interviewed on camera.

A Conversation With E. Hoffman Price

Transcribed by Gregorio Montejo

Editor's Note: Robert Bloch was born on July 3, 1898 and passed away on June 18, 1988

E. Hoffman Price was born in 1898 near San Jose, California. As a young boy he was first introduced to the pulps, and his interest and love for this form of fiction has flourished for more than three quarters of a century. As a young man, Price first saw the world outside of California when he joined the Army during World War I. It was his return to civilian life in the early 1920s that finally gave him the incentive to begin writing stories. During the next three decades, Price became one of the most successful and highly paid writers in the pulp market. When the pulps began to fold in the early 1950s, Price retired from writing. And for the next two decades he preoccupied himself at a number of professions such as micro-film technician, astrologer, and photographer. In the 1970s, Price returned to the writing field with renewed enthusiasm; writing and selling four science fiction and two fantasy novels to Del Rey. Captivating a whole new generation of readers with his talent and imagination.

In August of 1985, Pierre Comtois, Henry J. Vester III, R.J. Zimmerman and I were invited to Mr. Price's home in northern California. The house is situated atop a high promontory, and once inside one is awed by the wonderful library and the Oriental objets d'art and rugs from the Middle East, which adorn the floor and the walls. Mr. Price proved to be an eloquent and vivacious orator, as well as an entertaining and hospitable host. The *Fungi* staff spent a wonderful afternoon listening to Mr. Price's episodic account of his life, and the accumulated insights and wisdom of almost ninety years of life. The following pages present some of the highlights of that memorable conversation.

Mr. Price began by relating an anecdote from his days as a pulp fiction writer:

Price: Now I used to send my stories on 16 pound bond paper; after all the postage was less. My agent suggested that I get back to 20 pound bond. He told me that a certain editor would often take stories home to read. He would stretch out in his tub, full of hot water, to relax from the day's work. And in that position, the lighting in his bathroom would be such that the light would go right through the 16 pound bond and it would make for difficult reading. I'm just giving you some of the inner secrets of the business.

Comtois: (laughter) I'll have to remember that...reading in the tub that is...

Price: Well, let's begin this interview, you've traveled a long distance.

Montejo: Could you talk about how you became a writer?

E. Hoffman Price

Price: All right. I began reading pulp magazines in Uncle Alesander's barn. I don't know who left the pulps. There was one blood and thunder Chinatown terror. Also some adventure magazines, mystery-suspense stories. For their day and age they weren't badly written by any means; at least I liked them. I also used to read Sax Rohmer. Years later I read reprints and I wondered how I ever read such silly stuff. I read a biography of Rohmer which Edmond Hamilton had in his library in 1976...a few months before he died. He recommended it highly, and I got around to reading excerpts here and there. It seems that Sax Rohmer always admitted that he knew nothing about China, the Chinese, or their culture. And furthermore, he didn't want to ruin a good thing by learning anything about them.

I also read westerns. I read quite a few fifteen cent paperbacks, not four dollar paperbacks, the fifteen cent ones! Buffalo Bill and other westerns. I preferred magazines; the adventure stories were always my favorite. Some years later, when I was an usher in the Liberty Theater in San Jose, in 1914, the assistant manager, a man of a certain amount of serious thinking, asked why I read such "junk." My answer to him was, "Because I hope to write 'junk' like that someday."

Now getting back to how I became a writer: When I was less than seven years old...well, instead of "Jack sees Jane. Jane sees Jack. Jack sees Spot. Jane sees Spot. Run Jack! Run Spot!" we didn't have that garbage. Before I entered school I had read the Odyssey, a junior grade fictionalization of the adventures of Odysseus. My second grade neighbor across the irrigation canal, she had a picture in her reader of Odysseus with the sirens on the beach piping away, skulls and thighbones scattered on the sand. Odysseus strung to the mast, struggling to break free and dive over and meet the young ladies. The oarsmen with wax stuck in their ears so they couldn't hear anything.

In a first grade reader I saw a picture of Henry Wadsworth Longfellow: a writer, wearing a beard and a University graduate. I also saw a picture of John Greenleaf Whittier: a poet, wearing a beard. I had always wanted to be a writer so I decided to grow a beard and go to school a bit.

At that age, I also decided to collect Oriental rugs, we call them Turkish rugs. I also decided that I would become an astrologer. At Sunday school I got so tired of the prophets, always predicting gloom, long faced, unpleasant fellows. The Chaldeans sounded much more appealing. They served the sun, the moon, and the stars and they impressed me as being a lot smarter. So I was going to be an astrologer, and I did practice astrology professionally.

Somebody wondered how I became a Buddhist. I don't know, I must have been born that way. In spite of going to Sunday school, and planning on becoming a Chaldean and an astrologer. I used to sit in the family orchard which had peaches and apricots and some of everything. I would carry a small bucket of whatever fruit was in season, and sit under a prune tree and practice a very childlike, juvenile, rudimentary imitation of what, in Zen temples many years later, I learned was what the Occidentals call meditation. But what the Zen masters simply call sitting and facing the wall. Meditation is something you'll hear in theosophical circles, but that is not really what Zen meditation is; but I won't get into that.

That was one of my notions. Living in a fundamentalist Christian family atmosphere, I don't know where I got that idea. But that is how I started. That was probably the first manifestation of Buddhism.

I've given you the origin of the fiction, the Buddhism and collecting rugs. Getting back to the fiction. When I was about sixteen, I read the stories of H. Bedford Jones and...his name always slips my mind. H wrote about India.

Montejo: Talbot Mundy?

Price: Yes, Talbot Mundy. Well, I decided I needed a pen name hence E. Hoffman Price. I had cards engraved with my name, that was in 1914. It wasn't until 1924 that I wrote my first story. However, I had a by-line waiting for me ten years in advance, until I had the time and the occasion, and the stars were right. So, in 1924, I wrote two stories, I was working at Union Carbide, I bought a typewriter and some paper. Every night, on the job, I would write a couple of pages of "The Rajah's Gift" and one or two pages of "Triangle of Variations." My first sale was "Triangle of Variations" not a mathematical story. I sold it to one of the sophisticated, risque magazines, *Droll Stories*. Jack Shaw, of *Black Mask*, rejected "The Rajah's Gift," it was a wild chance in selling it to him, but there was no harm in trying. It came back in no time. I then sent it to Farnsworth Wright (editor of *Weird Tales*) and I got an acceptance. And only a year later I got my check. Well that was how I started writing.

I had always wanted to be a writer, but I never got around to writing; I was busy traveling. I went into the Army in 1917. There was a war on, in those days any young man that had any spirit of adventure joined. Never mind whether it was just or unjust war, win the war. When you have won it, then find out if it was just or otherwise.

That was the first time that I was significantly far away from home. Instead of going to fight in France, eighty of us were sent to the Philippines. We were assigned to the Fifteenth Cavalry. We embarked at transport dock, Fort Mason, San Francisco. After nearly a week at sea we pulled into Honolulu, Pearl Harbor, to discharge some of the troops. We had shore leave for the next day. It was at this time that I began to train my memory; this was the first time that I had been outside of the state of California. Then we steamed for two weeks more to discharge a detachment of Marines at Guam. Then another week at sea, heading northward towards Manila and Fort William McKinley.

I was training my memory because I wasn't keeping a diary, which in time of war isn't advisable. Still, I figured that one of these days I would get around to writing. Anyway, we left the Philippines six weeks later. The entire regiment, the Fifteenth Cavalry, was ordered back to the States. We were back in Fort Mason in October 1917. We had left in early July, right after my birthday. We had had an interesting sightseeing tour: eighteen days on the China Seas, dry-dock in Nagasaki, on the way back. On our return, we were stationed at Camp Fremont in Menlo Park, near Palo Alto, for several months, going through drills. Then we were sent to Douglas, Arizona; near the Mexican border. In March, 1918, we were sent to France at about the lousiest, nastiest season for crossing the Atlantic. I don't pretend I enjoyed that trip one bit. Well, we finally made it to France. The sun was shining. The coastline of France was one of the most pleasing sights I have ever seen.

In France, there was more sightseeing. We were sent south, to Bordeaux. Then we were ordered out of that area, They didn't want the Fifteenth Cavalry to be harassed by enemy fire, we were valuable. So they sent in the Marines. They got us all the way down to Bayonne. Bayonne was a real home. If you have read any of my *Weird Tales* stuff, you will note how frequently Bayonne features. The Cognac region is only a short distance away, in a slightly north-easterly direction. The Armagnac brandy region is about forty miles east of the cognac region. My son and I have spent many a happy hour, right here, and in his house debating if we were marooned on a desert island, and were restricted only to either the Armagnac or the Cognac, which would we select: Robinson Crusoe had spirits on his island, rum I believe. Now, all that is part of how I became a writer.

Another thing. I once received a critical letter for one of my Oriental stories. A reader wrote to me and said that my Oriental stories were a mishmash of about every culture of the Near East. A combination of Turkish, Syrian, Iranian, Indian, with touches of Malay, the Far East and China. But, he said, don't worry, your readers won't know the difference. That was a good letter. However, I dug in and bucked up my studies to build up authenticity in my stories.

I believe I've given you a fair picture of how I started writing. I had an urge, even when I was young, to write. I could also read at an early age. My father, who used to run a country store in what is now San Jose, learned German fluently. In that area most people either spoke Spanish or German. If they spoke English, it was rather rudimentary. My father had a large Spanish dictionary, and a small, elementary Spanish grammar book. It had pictures in it, and I found out that Spanish was fairly simple. I guess I had heard so many names like Los Banos and San Jose and whatnot, and words like *tamales*. In the book there would be a picture of a tree: *el arbol*; there was a picture of a chair: *la silla*; a table: *la Mesa*. So I learned more words just by looking at the pictures. And the phonetics of Spanish made sense. The phonetics of French absolutely bugged me; there were no pictures, and how were you supposed to pronounce it, anyway?

So I didn't learn any french until I landed in France, and then there was no problem at all. I had a French phrase book: what to say in a bar, in a drugstore, in a grocery store, in a bus station; and the phoneticization was by no means bad. It was hardly the French pronunciation for addressing a learned gathering, but one could make himself understood.

Mr. Price then spoke about his policy toward amateur publications:

Price: I will write a letter, just for good fellowship's sake, to an amateur magazine. But I do not, under any circumstances, write an essay or anything of that sort. I have no moral scruples against granting interviews. It's just this way, If I start popping up all over the place in amateur publications, my publishers will begin to get the idea that, since I am addicted to giving away fiction, or any other writings, why should they increase my rates?

I returned to business about six or seven years ago. I had been starved out by the pulps folding. Jessica Amanda Salmonson asked me to write something for her amateur magazine and I agreed. I sent it to her, But, I said, you may not use my name in the byline, use a house name or "anonymous." She sent it back with regrets, Well I wrote back to her and said: "My name is valuable. Apparently it must be because you don't want my writing unless it had my name on it."

Mr. Price went on to discuss his recent work:

Price: I went to a cocktail party held by Lester and Judy-Lynn del Rey in San Francisco. We discussed what my next book would be. I couldn't get Lester or Judy-Lynn to commit themselves. All right, I said, I will decide whether it will be a fantasy or a space opera. My two fantasy novels have not earned their advances, but both of my space opera novels have been paying me royalties, and one is in its second printing. When I got my royalty report, I decided what to do. I wasn't going to write another Chinese fantasy unless *The Jade Enchantress* had earned her advance. If so I would do a space-age Chinatown novel, with an Occidental protagonist. The plot would be about the Moon-goddess, who is getting very unhappy about the landings on the Moon. But I won't be writing it because I got the report. I earned royalty on *Operation Misfit* (1980). I earned royalty on *Operation Longlife* (1983), but I didn't even get a report on the two T'ang fantasies.

I love the T'ang dynasty; it was China at its best. But the American public apparently does not like the Chinese fantasy stories.

Vester: Is that why you had intended to make the protagonist of your planned novel an Occidental?

Price: Yes, exactly. Ch'ang-an, now Sian, was the most important city in the world, in its time. Rome had fallen. The barbarians had dictated the peace terms. About 450 AD, the Rome we think about was gone. There was Byzantium, I am not downgrading it. But they were fighting a losing battle. They had Caesars, but it was not the Rome of Gaius Julius Caesar, or of Augustus. Now Byzantium, around 750 AD, may have been as big as the capital of the T'ang empire. But Ch'ang-an was undoubtedly the most civilized city in the world at that time. China's great disaster was when mechanical weapons; high powered ammunition, displaced the Mongol arrow which was deadlier than firearms for quite a few generations. As a center of culture, and of elegance, the T'ang dynasty, I think, was a peak. That's just one man's opinion.

Now the T'ang dynasty was not the only peak of civilization in China. There was also the early Manchus. The diaries of one of the Manchus has survived. I can't think of his name. A most remarkable ruler. The Manchus were not quite the barbarians they are represented as being. But, like every other dynasty in China; they eventually declined. The Manchus though, had the greatest system of elections. When the son of Heaven, perhaps the tenth successor to the founder, got too obstreperous, and too un-Heavenly, there was merely a nation wide revolt, exterminating the entire dynasty, and setting up a new one. I believe that if we had that system in this country, we would be in a much better shape today. Chinese culture is the most durable that I know of.

Comtois: Why is it that Chinese culture remained so static over such a long period of time, while European culture evolved more quickly?

Price: That is a very hard question to answer. All I can do is give an evaluation through comparison. Around the eleventh century, Lady Murasaki, a Japanese baroness, wrote a novel that is a classic. And there are many Occidentals who value it as a literary work. Charlemagne, at around the same time, couldn't even write his own name. A few monks could write. As for the matter of a European lady writing a novel; the idea is too preposterous even to be the subject of laughter. Where did the Japanese derive their culture from? From the T'ang dynasty. The Japanese kimono is taken from the T'ang. Some say that the Japanese are imitators, that is rather superficial, they improved the kimono and stylized it. I think they borrowed the tea ceremony from the Chinese and made it a uniquely Japanese institution. But, I just can't give you a simple answer to that question.

One of the predominant cliches about the Orientals is that they are grave, sober, and poker faced. I have prowled Chinatown for the last twenty-two years, as a sort of honorary mayor. I've been associated with numerous Buddhist groups. Neither the Chinese nor the Japanese are grave or poker faced when they are at home or with friends. They are about as stoical as an Italian wedding when the fourth case of champagne has been expended.

Vester: Then that's justs the face they show to Occidentals.

Price: I went to a Chinese gathering lately. When I entered, I was told to sign my name in Chinese. So I took the pen and wrote Tao Fa in Chinese characters. Now forcing a foreign devil to sign in Chinese is the kind of joke that tickles them pink. Well, when they saw my signature, they couldn't help laughing.

Tao Fa is not a translation of E. Hoffman Price. It is a dharma name given to me by the venerable Yen-Pei of Singapore.

Montejo: I'd like to know why you stopped writing. And how you began again.

Price: When the pulps folded, I stopped writing, I got gainful employment. I bailed out in 1952. Before that I was very happy, in a fool's paradise, receiving two and half cents a word. Anything over two cents was deluxe, and very few were getting even that. You had to have a good agent to get publishers bidding. The highest paid name in the entire business was only getting five cents a word. The top western writer at the time was getting that, but he bailed out. Then they got me for two and a half. I didn't know about that until later. It was a very prestigious magazine, a Street and Smith.

Before I go on, I should recap a bit of my career up to that point. In 1924, I knew nothing about the fiction business, so I wrote two stories and sold them. In 1932, when Union Carbide fired me, I decided to turn to full time writing. I acquired an agent and I got married. The first thing the agent said was: "You sold twenty stories to *Weird Tales* and *Oriental Stories* and *Golden Fleece*. Why don't you get out of that market? You can't make a living selling to those magazines."

I had not attempted to write SF. They paid worse than *Weird Tales*. At least *Weird Tales* paid you some day; you never received any money from Hugo Gernsback unless you threatened him bodily. He knew you couldn't afford to sue him, not for one-fourth of a cent a word, or whatever his swindle was! I will never win a Hugo, I am too old, but if it *were* awarded, I would decline it. I will not have anything to do with a shyster, a chiseler, and a crook, even if he *was* a pioneer!

109

Because of my agent's advice, I began to learn how to write crime stories. I also wrote for the spices. *Spicy Adventures* and *Spicy Western*. The silliest stuff I've ever written in my life. Eventually I sold stories to *Top Notch* and *Argosy*. Then I made *Short Story* and *Adventure*. *Adventure* was the peak of prestige. *Short Story,* I think, was fully as good, but of a slightly different flavor. *Blue Book* I did not make. The story went that you first had to make *The Saturday Evening Post* before you qualified. Eventually, I ended up in the *Street and Smith Western.* But by then the pulps were dying and I quit.

I got two jobs. I was 54 years old, and, having spent twenty years as a full time writer, I was very much out of date. I got a civil service job as a microfilm technician. The job wasn't called that, but I made it so. I photographed a faded document that was barely legible to the naked eye. It was a faded yellowish-green ink. By using different filters, I finally found the right contrast filter. I made an 8 x 10 blowup in black and white. And it was far more legible than the original.

Then I got a job across the street for a commercial microfilm operation. At age 70, I retired. I got a good enough retirement plan so that I had a good income. In my spare time, I practiced astrology and filmed weddings. At that time I decided to get back into writing. I wrote *The Jade Enchantress* (1982). It took ten years to sell it; I couldn't find a market.

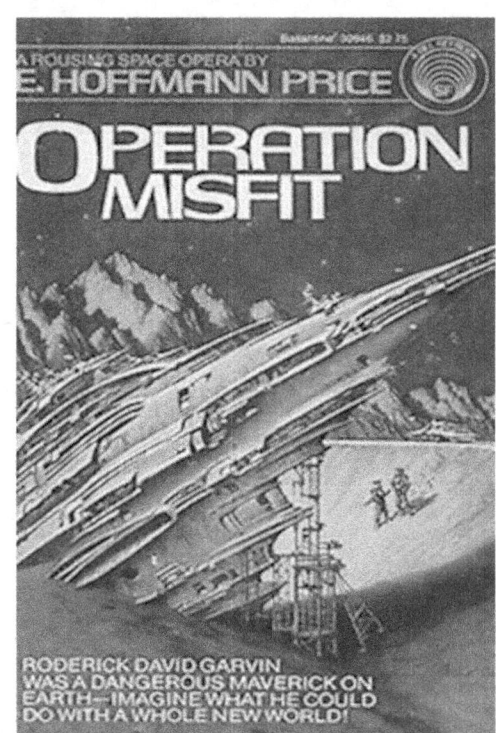

Vester: Are your short stories still in print?

Price: I'm against any more reprints. It's just that I don't care to have the stories written a half century ago competing with my modern stuff.

Zimmerman: I read somewhere that you collaborated with Clark Ashton Smith on a story.

Price: No, not really. That story has been circulating for many years, but it's not true. Clark was in a deep and sour mood. I remember the occasion. I had gone up to Auburn. He had two stories, which he asked me to read. He was fed up with the stories because they had been rejected. I told him that if I was collaborating I would make certain changes. He told me that if I could do anything with the stories, that I could keep them. I thought they were saleable, so I made a few minor changes, sent them out, and they both sold. But they were not collaborations.

The four novels in the Operations series were among the last fiction produced by Price before his death

Comtois: You were acquainted with Otis Adelbert Kline. Do you know anything about his feud with Edgar Rice Burroughs?

Price: I don't know too much. That's a very controversial thing. All that I have to say about it is purely conjectural. I think that Burroughs and his publisher disagreed about money. They parted company. I surmise that the publisher then asked Kline to do something in the same vein. I don't think they asked Kline to imitate Burroughs. Kline was very popular in the late twenties and thirties. Today you couldn't give his stuff away.

Robert E. Howard around the time Price visited him at his home in Cross Plains, Texas

Zimmerman: What style of story do you enjoy most? SF, crime, Oriental…

Price: Well, I enjoy the Oriental stories the most. While researching them I found many Oriental philosophies and some of their social views very fascinating. I found the people interesting. In fact sometimes I have viewed our culture through the eyes of an Oriental, and our culture seemed quite grotesque in some ways. I found through my Islamic studies some very interesting things. The first thing that most people turn to when they find both the fundamentalist and the conventional Christian viewpoint inadequate is Islam. Islam seems to be the next step. Then one, sometimes, sees through the Islamic philosophy to the Oriental philosophies. One finds these Oriental cultures a very refreshing improvement on the stereotypes of western cultures.

Asiatic history has impressed me more and more with the provincialism of our historians. It is only in recent years that our gross misconceptions about Genghis Khan and Tamerlane have been rectified. Our gross ignorance of Oriental societies has led us into some of the most disastrous situations.

I'll give you an example. Some of you are probably familiar with the classic Persian miniatures. They are elegant, exquisite. The greatest artists of Iran specialized in these miniatures. There is one of these miniatures that characterizes the Oriental in a way that many books seem to fail in doing. It is a depiction of Tamerlane and his staff, riding the most elegant and beautiful of horses. They are on an inspection tour. All around them are pyramids of decapitated heads. Tamerlane was not loved, but he was respected and revered.

Another example is that of Douglas MacArthur. At the end of the war, MacArthur had three Japanese generals executed. That's because MacArthur understood the Oriental mind as few, if any, in this country have ever understood it. It was a matter of politics. If you have the three generals executed, then you are a great and mighty man. The Japanese would feel less humiliated surrendering to a man who hangs generals. MacArthur, lordly, elegant, commandeering, they could respect him. Just as they could surrender after the jA-bomb without losing face, for it was a force of nature that destroyed them, actually. I never knew MacArthur personally, but from all I can gather, I see he knew what he was talking about. Truman, of course, did not. Very few Americans did.

The question of the Beirut hostages comes to mind. I would have stationed a battleship off shore, aimed the big guns and said: "Deliver the hostages at once, or I we will destroy the city, shot by shot, until it is a hole in the ground." If they knew it wasn't a bluff, then the same could have been done in Iran. It is our weak attitude which has won us nothing but contempt.

Vester: Absolutely. Derision all over the world.

Comtois: When we passed through Cross Plains, Texas, we spoke briefly with Lindsey Tyson. Did you meet him when you visited Robert E. Howard?

Price: No, I didn't. I was the guest of the Howards in 1934; on my way from the Osage Indian country to the Pacific coast. They were very hospitable people. I thought Robert was amiable, a very nice guy. But He was certainly very eccentric.

Comtois: What did you think of *Dark Valley Destiny,* L. Sprague de Camp's biography of Howard?

Price: I thought it was very good. I thought that it rung true, overall, despite a few flaws. As for his psychological explanation of Howard, I never tried to explain Howard. He was a nice guy, and undoubtedly a little bit crazy. He certainly wasn't mentally balanced. If he were, he would probably be living today. Sprague, I think; had more psychology in his life of Lovecraft than was necessary. I will say that overall, Howard was a weird character, but I found him a very likeable person. And if he was a bit off the beam, he was still a man of good will.

I remember one incident. They had shallow oil wells in that part of the country. I told Bob that I had written some things about the deep oil wells in Oklahoma, but I had never seen these type of wells. He invited me to take a closer look, We were walking through town, heading for the wells. And some of the townspeople were greeting him. All of a sudden he said to me that he was proud I came to visit him. He said, "These people in town don't think I amount to anything, and I'm glad when someone important comes to town to see me."

We arrived at the oil wells, and we looked around. After a while he turned and asked if I had any enemies. I said I couldn't think of anyone and he got an incredulous look on his face. Well, I said, there was one guy I clobbered with a pickaxe handle. But I wouldn't call him an enemy. He was too chicken to be on the list of what I would call enemies. That made him happy..

Later, he took me for a ride in the countryside. There were no sights to be seen. We drove past a small clump of brush, he stopped the car and drew a handgun. Then he got out and inspected the clump of brush. He came back and told me he really didn't think there were any enemies there but there were so many idiots in the country, a fellow couldn't take any chances. Sprague thought that Howard was just trying to give a tenderdoot a few thrills. I told him I thought he was wrong. It was against Howard's charactter to do something like that.

Sprague consulted me on the book and I was very glad to help. He is one of the most worthwhile and engaging characters in this business. He has a wonderful sense of humor. That's very rare. Most fantasy writers are very humorless.

Vester: Would you take that as an indication that they take themselves far too seriously?

Price: Not in person, but in their writing. Now Lovecraft took *his* writing far too seriously. He wrote a few good things, but some of his stuff...it's unfortunate that it was printed. A few of his things I like. "The Silver Key," which some have downgraded as juvenile; I always had an affection for that story. It's one of his stories that I like to reread.

Lovecraft and Bob didn't live long enough to learn the business. Bob wrote some stories that I admire. Some of them were perfectly impossible, especially his adventure stories. But there is a certain charm, a magic, to some of these utterly improbable tales.

Unto Us a Child

by David Daniel

And then, almost overnight it seemed, the uncanny occurred. The seagulls, always so vivid and raucous a presence in Slate Harbor, were gone. — from the *Kingsport Sentinel* Oct. 17, 1934

"Richard. Did you find the Christmas stuff?"

Anji O'Dowd stood at the foot of the hinged staircase that unfolded on heavy springs from a trapdoor in the third floor hallway ceiling, her head cocked upward in an attitude of listening. Long drawn-out *skreeks* were issuing from the attic above.

"There's a draft down here," she called.

Overhead the creaking went on, joined by an occasional banging. And now a muted *thump*.

"Richard?"

Anji climbed a few tentative steps, feeling the staircase settle. Obviously, this wasn't the original attic entrance; folding stairs hadn't been a feature of housing design a century and a half ago. Once, a steep fixed flight of steps led to the attic, but that had been sealed off, the access door paneled over, all of this long before the O'Dowds bought the house. When they moved in four months ago, Richard had asked about this and the Realtor had no explanation.

The house was one of the oldest and largest in Slate Harbor. Built in the years after the Civil War, the Bancroft House, as it was known, had been the summer residence of Capt. Ezra Bancroft, whose forebears had made their fortune in commercial shipping. Anji and Richard O'Dowd had discovered Slate Harbor by chance, in a *New York Times* piece about the once-active fishing village on an island north of Boston being re-vitalized after long years of near-abandonment. Working professionals in their late thirties, childless, and feeling cooped up in their non-rent-controlled Manhattan apartment during the depths of the Covid lockdown, the O'Dowds had been ready for change. Anji was a freelance writer for magazines like The *Atlantic* and *Vanity Fair*, Richard an instructional designer. Since their work was largely remote they could live anywhere they chose.

In April, following up on the *Times* article, they took a weekend trip up from the city to Slate Harbor and almost immediately wondered if they'd made a mistake. The place was more rundown than they'd envisioned, one stretch of the downtown waterfront comprised of sagging piers and dilapidated fish shacks, and they might well have taken the ferry right back to Kingsport on the mainland, except it ran only twice a day and the next run was hours away. Richard, ever a glass half full guy, said that maybe it was a sign, and Anji, setting aside for a moment her tendency to pessimism, agreed. It was a bluebird-blue spring day with an east wind spanking lines on small boats moored in the protecting cove and sending cherry and crabapple blossoms fluttering like spindrift, and they determined to the place a chance. By day's end they'd decided to look for a house.

Anji climbed to where she could poke her head through the ceiling opening and peer into the attic. She had ventured up here only on one previous occasion: a half dozen trips on a day not long after they had moved in in August when the attic was full of trapped heat and the buzz of wasps nesting in the outside eaves. Energetic as Sherpas, eager to settle into their new home, they trundled up unopened boxes and bins into haphazard storage with some notion of coming back in the cooler days of autumn to sort through the accumulations of a decade and a half of marriage. But island life had taken swift hold, and that had not happened. Now the attic was dim and drafty cold. A single overhead bulb threw spidery shadows into the December gloom.

"Richard?"

In the months since their relocation, upgrades and repairs on the house had consumed them. And there were work transitions: Richard adjusting to his new workspace and the island's wonky electrical grid, which sometimes went down with no warning; Anji reading proofs of an extended piece about the failing U.S. water supply, which had become *The Atlantic*'s cover story in October. And now here it was five days till Christmas.

She heard creaking again and swiveled her head toward its source. A light was shining in a far corner of the attic, beyond the massive central chimney. The chimney was one of the features of the house she'd fallen in love with, with its four fireplaces, one in each of the bedrooms, and an enormous brick hearth in the living room.

"Richard."

She climbed the remaining steps to stand on the planked floor, her breath white puffs in the cold. The headroom was just adequate to stand upright. Treading carefully on the wide planks laid across the joists, she picked her way around the chimney.

Her husband was on his knees under the sloped angle of the roof. He had set up a table lamp (a wedding gift from an aunt, she recognized), minus a shade and was using the claw end of a hammer to tug nails from a thick rafter. In a mimicking shadow he yanked one out now and a patch of the plaster knee wall crashed down in a bloom of dust.

"*Richard...*what the hell..?"

He turned, face flushed and eyes beaming behind his tortoise shell horn-rim glasses. "Hey

you."

"I've been yelling for you. There's an arctic blast coming downstairs. What are you *doing?*"

"Check this out." He was excited. "Here's where the original stairs came up." He spanked his palm on the plank flooring.

She frowned at the spot. "Okaay. So..?"

"So the Realtor told us he didn't know anything about that."

"Well, then he probably didn't. Does it matter?"

"Not really. He did say the original plans are long gone. The point is this knee wall is old, too, but it's not original."

She gave this a patient five count. "What about the tree ornaments? I send you up for one thing and it turns into the Big Dig."

"Stay there a sec. Watch."

"Richard."

"Just let me show you." He levered the hammer and there was a godawful *screech* as a nail pulled loose followed by another small avalanche of plaster and dust. Anji covered her nose and mouth. "Damn, is that safe?"

"You mean am I breathing asbestos or something?"

"God forbid. I mean is the roof going to cave in?"

The Realtor, Carl, had made a virtue of the "ship quality" construction, meant to withstand the Nor'easters the Atlantic sometimes battered against the island. As for breathing anything, it was only dust and, as if to prove this, he sneezed, and then again. "No wonder the upstairs rooms are drafty. This is old lath strips and horsehair plaster, and not a scrap of insulation. I'm going to cut this out with a saw and order some fiberglass rolls and snug this up."

"Fine, a good project for the new year, but we've got Carl and the Gayles coming tonight for dinner, and we're supposed to be decorating. So...the tree ornaments?"

"Yeah, no. I found the stuff." He waved toward a clutter of storage crates beyond the chimney. He had gone so far as to pull out the three red and green boxes that held the ornaments they'd been accruing since their first Christmas together sixteen years ago, just out of college. Trimming the tree was a seasonal custom the O'Dowds had maintained over the years, along with watching

114

The Bishop's Wife and taking in the holiday show at Radio City. They had not given up the idea that they might one day share the traditions with children, but so far this had not happened. This year, however, the Rockettes would have to high kick without them. Manhattan was four hours away.

"I'll take one of the boxes down with me," Anji said.

"I'll bring the rest."

"Don't be long, I told the guests seven, and these locals are prompt."

"Be right down. Careful on those steps. And Anj, Carl probably just forget about the blueprint question, no need to make an issue of it tonight."

Shaking her head, she waved over her shoulder. "Course not. What do you think I am, Scrooge?"

*

The guests *were* prompt. Rev. Tom Gayle and his wife Evelyn, and Carl Reed. Tom was the Congregational minister, a likeable man who had taken on the small island church as an interim after the former pastor had left abruptly the previous spring. In their mid-seventies, the Gayles were a benign, energetic couple, whom Anji and Richard had only just met. Long-time summer residents, they had moved over permanently when they'd retired. Carl Reed, a youthful fifty, was the Realtor who'd sold the O'Dowds the house. Richard and Anji had got the tree trimmed and an array of *hors d'oeuvres* and drinks ready and they all settled before a fire in the central hearth.

"I'd *seen* this house my whole life," Carl Reed was saying, "but until it came up for sale this year I'd never been inside." Which explains his not knowing about the sealed staircase, Anji realized. Carl had his own agency in Kingsport, on the mainland, but lived here on the easternmost side of the island, an ocean stretch called the Reach. "I almost came in once...friends and I daring each other when we were about thirteen. It was abandoned, had been for years. But we chickened out. Threw stones, instead."

"I love what you've done with your decorating, Anji," Evelyn Gayle said.

"It's a team effort. Richard has some restoration projects in mind."

"I understand you write for...is it the *New Yorker*?" Tom Gayle asked.

"Actually, that's a market I haven't cracked yet though not for want of trying. I had a feature recently in *The Atlantic*."

"Exciting. Are you assigned what you write about or do you come up with your own ideas? I've always wondered."

"It depends. Mostly, I smoke out an idea and pitch it to an editor, and they might help me get the right slant. I'm between projects now, starting to look for a new one. Possibly something about Slate Harbor?"

Carl Reed nodded encouragingly. "Though not something too cute, I hope," Tom Gayle said. "We get those 'best lobstah roll in New England' pieces, every summer. Not that I'm complaining, mind you. The tourist revenue is good for everyone, but we'd like to see more folks like the two of you, who want more than a just a drop in...who're looking to set down some roots."

"Is that what we're doing?" Richard said, and they all laughed.

Anji picked up the theme. "I'd be interested in doing a story with a bit of the area's history. It's culture."

"Well, Slate Harbor's got plenty of that," said Tom. "Even a splash of the bohemian in its past, wouldn't you say, hon?"

"Oh yes. There was a lively scene back in its heyday. Before our time, of course. There was a speakeasy, and a dockside nightclub during Prohibition. The Harbor is nicely sheltered, so boats would come in. Fancy yachts, even. Locals got to mingle with the glitter people. All very.high time. There are stories. Things changed, of course after the fishing ran out. Alas."

"Those were tough times," Carl Reed said darkly. "It killed the local economy." There was a silence, then he smiled. "But we like to highlight the resurgence we've had since. The island's wholesomeness and charm. *And* the best lobstah rolls."

Dinner was old fashioned baked ham with pineapple. After, regathered around the brick hearth with drinks and dessert, Anji asked to know more of the history of the family who'd originally owned the house. Carl had the details ready.

The Bancrofts were seafarers since Colonial times. Through the mid-19th century, Bancroft

Trading Co. had a fleet of clippers that ran from Salem to China and Japan. Though by the time the family line reached Ezra Bancroft the trade had gone away, eclipsed by European steam ships. "Seeing opportunity here, he got into commercial fishing and did well. He built this house and moved out here—one of the earliest residents, not counting the Indians. But the fishing, which was the backbone of the island's economy, died abruptly in the early 1930s and never came back."

"Abruptly." Anji's curiosity was aroused. "Why?"

"No one's got a definitive answer. Government studies have been done, theories advanced. You hear 'overfishing,' or the Atlantic acidifying due to climate change. Some people want to talk about an old curse. But all that's above my pay grade. Bottom line was the fish were gone, and the island took a hit."

"So, a mystery," Anji mused.

"Uh oh," said Richard. "Beware. Her right brain is lighting up. I know the signs."

She swiped playfully at his knee. "Seriously, though."

"Oh, do tell," Evelyn encouraged. "Are we at the dawn of a new creation? Is this how your muse works?"

Anji laughed, slightly embarrassed. "Nothing so romanticized as that. Mostly, it's sausage making."

"Oh, listen to me go on about something I know nothing of. I'm sure it's easier said than done. But, supposing, could you *really* write a story about why fishing ended here?" Evelyn seemed enchanted.

"When she's in flow," Richard said encouragingly, "she can cook up a spellbinder about almost anything."

Anji darted him a "thanks a lot" glance, but went on amicably. "Well, stories *are* everywhere, but not all ideas are good ideas. Could this be one though? Possibly. I'd need to research to see what's what. And then I'd have to make it interesting."

"Juicier?" Tom Gayle laughed. "More of a grabber? 'Something fishy in Slate Harbor'?"

Anji joined in the laughter. "But you are all giving me ideas, though let's not dwell on that. As Carl says, it's the Harbor's rebirth that's important, and we're happy to be here, glad to be part of it."

It was in the second round of drinks that Clara Bancroft's name returned. Evelyn brought it up. "She was Ezra and his wife's only child. A sprite, I'm told. Right from an early age, Clara loved being outdoors, loved the sea. In her teens she got a little daring, would arrange swim parties on those remote beaches out on the Reach, swimsuits optional." Evelyn smiled a moment, then grew serious. "Sometime in her twenties, word got about that Clara was pregnant. Wasn't married, didn't even have a beau, so far as anyone knew. Naturally, there was curiosity about who the man might be. A seafarer who'd come on one of the ships, and left the same way? A local Ezra didn't want part of the family and paid him off? There were theories. Always are. Though what business is it of anyone's, then or now?"

There was a lull as Anji served coffee. Evelyn picked up the thread.

"The Bancrofts were secretive, maybe on account of their lineage. Most people hereabouts were simple fishing families. In the end, Clara apparently miscarried. Wasn't so long after that before, poor thing, she kind of...what would you say, Tom? Carl?"

"Lost her marbles?" Carl provided.

"Is that part of the lore, too? Madness?" Anji leaned in. She wanted to separate wheat from chaff.

Tom's brow furrowed. "Post-partum depression we'd probably say now. Though mental problems did run in that family. Ezra's wife spent her last years in the asylum over to Arkham. And Ezra himself, well that's another story too. *Whatever* Clara's case, she did change. Wasn't the lively young woman she'd once been."

"It was sad," Evelyn expanded. "There was teasing, small kids, you know how they can be. 'First comes love, then comes marriage, and here comes Clara with a baby carriage.'"

"That's sad," said Richard.

"It was. But she did get...odd. She took to wandering around town pushing an old wicker perambulator."

Anji gasped. "With the dead child in it?"

"Oh, gosh, no. Selling cut flowers from it. When Tom and I first started coming out here, fifty

116

years ago, can you believe it? there were still folks around who recalled Clara, pushing the baby carriage stuffed with pussy willows and wildflowers from her garden. And if you wished to buy a bunch, she might sell you some or not. You never knew. At times she seemed to look right through you."

"Just out there," Carl pointed to one of mullioned windows, "was a beautiful garden. Long gone now." He brightened. "There's a project for you two, come spring. Flowers really pop out here. The salt air."

The Gayles stayed with the past. "There were stories, of course," Tom went on. "Always are. It's easy to weave them about folks we consider different from us. The rich, who seem to live in a bubble, and the less fortunate, who've no platform from which to explain themselves. The Bancrofts knew both ends of that spectrum. They'd been the 'royals,' Ezra's forebears made a fortune in sea trade, but by the time things came to him..." Tom clicked his tongue. "He did make a go with fishing for a while, as Carl said, but that died. They wound up practically paupers, living in this house, no more connection with any of the locals, who were struggling, too. Some blamed Ezra."

"Why?" Anji wondered. "*He* didn't make the fish stocks dwindle."

"Another puzzler. So, with his wife over in the asylum, it was Ezra and Clara, and his odd assortment of folks who'd once worked for the family. The history gets fuzzy." He waved a hand, as if bidding goodbye to a trail that peters out.

The conversation took other directions and the fire crackled companionably in the hearth. At nine o'clock, Carl said he had a property showing next morning and bid goodnight. Anji was glad the Gayles stayed. She was enjoying the evening. Since the move from New York, between settling in and adjusting to island life, there had been scant time for friendship building.

"All this good talk," Tom said, "*I've* just remembered something."

And he told it.

When he was a boy, his grandfather had an insurance agency in Boston, where Tom would visit in the summers. Bancroft Trading Co., still one of the largest commercial marine enterprises on the Atlantic seaboard, was a client. "Marine insurance underwriting is complicated, reams of international maritime regulations, indemnities against this, that, and the other. All hand-entered in big ledgers in those days. Like something out of Dickens. One of the Bancroft senior clerks used to bring their paperwork. He was a yakker. I think everyone else rolled their eyes when he was around, but me. Picture me all of ten at the time. I *loved* his tales of the tall ships, exotic ports of call: Shanghai, Ceylon, New Guinea, places where there were still headhunters and cannibals. And there was the baby story."

Rev. Gale's years in the pulpit had made him a good raconteur. He paused dramatically, then leaned back, remembering. "Out on the Reach there used to be an encampment of some of those ship hands left over from earlier days who'd stayed loyal to Ezra. They'd be around a while, living in caravans out there. But when the fishing went away, they did, too."

"Some of this is coming back to me," Evelyn said. "The caravans, yes. Old wooden affairs with wagon wheels."

"They kept to themselves," Tom went on, "but you'd see them in town on occasion. Odd-*looking* folks: short, wiry, stoop-shouldered. Kept to themselves, didn't get into talking with locals. Again, before our time. But what's made me think of it now is something that chatterbox clerk told my grandfather. He implied those people were connected some way to Clara Bancroft's baby."

"Really?" Anji sat up. "How?"

"According to him, Clara *had* lost her baby, but not in the sense of being stillborn or aborted or anything like that. Literally *lost* is what I understood the man to mean. Taken out of its carriage."

"Kidnapped?"

"Gone."

A stick snapped in the fireplace, freeing sparks to twirl up the flue. Tom sat back as if conscious of the spell he had cast, embarrassed by it. "Well, I was ten," he concluded. And I don't say any of this is true. You know how stories go around. But I will say that the idea of it...well, being an impressionable kid myself, it spooked me. And, I never tried to learn more."

And it seemed enough for all. Energies were running down, and the busy holiday season called.

Very near the shore, something shattered the sea. It was upright, man-sized, but clearly not human, and in the moonlight, glistening green and brown, it churned forward, seawater streaming from a scaled body

The Gayles thanked them for a delightful evening. "Next time we'll do it at our place," said Tom, adding neutrally, "and if the spirit moves you, there's a candlelight service at the church Christmas Eve."

"No proselytizing, Dear," Evelyn said.

"No, no, just being neighborly."

Richard walked them outside to their car.

"Thank you for a great evening," Tom said as he closed his wife's door. "I hope we didn't gang up on Anji tonight. It's exciting is all, a real writer.

And I'm sure she's got plenty of fine story ideas of her own."

"When she gets one, she's all in. I tease her. I hope Carl didn't take that wrong."

"A word about Carl." Tom's lowered voice implied confidentiality. "Carl's a booster, all in for the island. The Harbor saw lean times for decades when he was young, but it's finally turning around. Carl's going to be cautious about anything that might chill it and, well, he worries a bit about some of those Ezra Bancroft stories."

"Worries how?"

"Let's just say his own people have been out here a long while and maybe that's a past that needs to be forgotten."

Richard mulled this, not quite sure what the minister meant, but said nothing. Tom shook his hand. "But don't misunderstand me. It's great having you and Anji here. And, truthfully? There're stories about Slate Harbor that probably *should* be told."

When the Gayles had driven off, Richard stood a moment. Stretching overhead the night sky was a cold spangle of stars, many more than were ever visible from the mainland, and certainly from Manhattan where even the moon sometimes struggled to be seen. He still wasn't entirely used to living out here, as if something in the vastness of sky and sea frightened him a little. He went inside.

*

On Tuesday, two days until Christmas, Anji took the morning ferry to Kingsport. The city was bustling. Old brick warehouses, sail lofts, and ships chandleries had been repurposed as gifts shops and galleries, restaurants and a craft brew pub called Lovecraft's. The old Federal Customs house, with its imposing façade, was a mall of shops and galleries. In one she bought a replica of an antique map of Slate Harbor. Absolved of having to mail gifts to their nieces in Oregon (Santa's sleigh this year would have an Amazon swoosh on it), Anji aimed to do some groundwork. She was looking for an idea to pitch to her editor, and the other evening's talk about Clara Blanchard had intrigued her. Some brief online searching at home hadn't produced much.

The Kingsport Public Library, was an impressive granite structure, with a fan of stained glass, 1840 *Anno Domini,* over the door, and inside, lots of elaborate woodwork and bookshelves rising several floors around a large open reading room. At the circulation desk she introduced herself to the young woman there, Nessa according to her nametag, and asked about getting a patron's card and was given a form to complete. "You're on the island," Nessa remarked was she reviewed the form. "Welcome." She issued Anji temporary card with full borrowing privileges. "Is there anything in particular I can help you with?"

Anji said she was interested in local history generally and the Bancroft family in particular. She made no mention of living in the Ezra Bancroft house, or that she was a writer. Nessa said the library had some holdings and she showed Anji where she could get started.

With so much data about everything available at one's fingertips, it was easy to forget what was on the internet was only the tip of an enormous iceberg. There were vast amounts of data that never had been (or likely ever would be) catalogued. There were handwritten journals, and oral accounts, tales dependent on memory, passed on and altered in the telling and retelling and ultimately lost. But there were sources too, archaic mechanisms which dwelt in a nether zone, as Anji conceived it, between cyberspace and oblivion. Journalism training had taught her how to find them. She asked Nessa about microfilm, and was taken to a room with a reader and directed to make a written request, and soon a tray of small plastic cannisters appeared.

It would be the work of several sessions to plumb the material, nothing she would undertake today. However, she could get an overview and gauge the scope of such a project, so for more than an hour, using a reader, she skimmed images of old newspapers and historical records. Property rolls did show a number of Bancrofts going back many decades. The lone photograph of Ezra Bancroft, taken when he was quite old, showed a man with a tangle of beard and pale eyes staring severely into the camera. There was a brief feature on Clara Bancroft and her "perambulator." Clara herself was not interviewed, so the piece relied on the remembrances of others. What emerged was a not-unkind portrait of a lonely, eccentric woman. There was no mention of madness or a dead child. In one file was a gallery of sepia-toned images of Slate Harbor in its early days: rows of fishing boats, town parades and picnics on the beaches, people in archaic bathing costumes, an image of the wooden caravans the Gayles had mentioned, all of these from before the fishing went fallow and over time the harbor front fell into disuse. After two hours, her vision beginning to blur, Anji was questioning whether there was enough *there* there for a story.

Maybe Carl Reed's suggestion that she write something seasonal and "wholesome" would be the best she could do, though that was hardly a magazine piece.

The library was quiet. Mothers reading to preschoolers, retirees using public computer terminals, occasional shabby individuals napping in chairs. At the front desk Anji inquired about possible other source materials. Nessa produced some old directories of Slate Harbor's Congregational church, where Tom Gayle was currently interim pastor. A quick survey turned up some Bancrofts way back, but none on the member rolls since the 1940s.

It was going on two-thirty, she'd been at it three hours. She would sample the brew pub for a bite, Lovecraft's, quaint name, and then take the four p.m. return ferry home. As she was gathering her things, a faded manila envelope fell on the table before her. "I found *this*," Nessa said.

There was a number on the envelope, handwritten in pencil, nothing more. Inside was a single old photograph of a woman. A yellowed note attached by a rusty paperclip identified her as Clara Bancroft, circa 1935. Partially obscured in shadow, she was standing in a garden and gazing off to the left of where the camera would be. Anji could make out most of her face, but in the shadow and the haze of the photographic emulsion, it wasn't possible to read with certainty what emotion underlay the woman's expression, but Anji thought it was alarm, or no, terror.

*

At home that evening, Anji created an e-file for her notes, little more than an info dump at this point. Often, as she approached a project there came a moment when, even though the full scope and shape of a story remained unknown, she began to sense its outlines. Now, narrowing her search to two fields: Slate Harbor history and the Bancroft Trading Co., she began to browse the internet.

She was disappointed almost at once to discover there were no living Bancrofts whom she might approach for an interview. The last descendant, a police detective in Lowell, had died in 1972 at age 41 of a self-inflicted gunshot wound.

She gleaned details about the family overall, admittedly a vague tissue of information from scattered sources, some of which she was able to weave together with strands she'd heard the other night and from that day's session at the Kingsport Public Library. What emerged was that Ezra Bancroft had been a stern, standoffish man who, over time, developed an interest in the occult. Never a member of the island church, he was apparently nevertheless strict in keeping his own "sabbith." When his wife Prudence was committed to the asylum in Arkham, twenty miles inland, he signed the papers and, to anyone's knowledge, never saw her again. He occupied the house on the island with his daughter Clara, shunning social contact with any but a group of people who had once labored as crew on his ships. Bancroft rarely ventured from the house, though he was known at times to set out at dusk and drive a wagon to a stretch of beach on the open Atlantic, the area known as the Reach. Anji found it on the map and was able to calculate it was about two winding miles from the house. The facts of what might have happened with his wife and daughter would likely have been closely kept from gossiping tongues, and the truth made impossible to find. For instance, there was mention that possibly "jippsys" [sic] had helped deliver Clara's child; but on the matter of its father, or its being stillborn, or birthed and stolen, the information superhighway had no traffic.

When Clara Bancroft did finally emerge in public, in her late thirties by then, she was to be seen at odd hours, a forlorn figure pushing a wicker baby pram full of flowers around the streets of Slate Harbor.

From the *Kingsport Sentinel* in a piece from 1934, titled "When Fishing Failed" Anji came across a tantalizing quote: "And then, almost overnight it seemed, the uncanny occurred. The seagulls, always so vivid and raucous a presence in Slate Harbor, were gone."

Uncanny, indeed. She put the quote into her notes.

"Tracing the line" her first editor had called it, the act of finding some essence of a story, posing it as a question, and following the breadcrumbs that might lead to an answer. If, as the *Sentinel* article claimed, the gulls had followed the fish stocks, what had happened so suddenly to the fish? Had something poisoned them? Wiped them out? Scared them away? And, tantalizing to ask: was this tied up somehow with Ezra Bancroft?

"You in flow?" Richard was in the doorway.

"Just mulling."

"Mull this." He handed her a glass of wine "Dinner will be ready shortly."

*

On Wednesday, Christmas Eve, Anji returned to Kingsport. The town square had a merry mood, with lights on in the decorative trees, carols playing, and the bustle of people looking for last-minute gifts. The library would close at 3 P.M. Aside from some of the tattered sleepers of yesterday the reading room was not busy. With her laptop, she set up at a table. Soon, Nessa appeared and laid down a magazine. "This is you." She said it with suppressed excitement, part statement part question. It was the October issue of *The Atlantic,* with Anji's cover story.

The woman seemed thrilled to have a writer there. She confessed to being an amateur poet. Anji took a chance and revealed she was researching the history of her own house. Nessa looked around guardedly. In a voice pitched even more softly than a librarian's customary hush, she said, "Do you know about the Miskatonic University Archive?" Anji didn't. "It's a trove of holdings accessible only to scholars. Much deeper than we have here."

Anji angled her laptop so the librarian could access the keyboard. "How do I get there?"

Nessa typed in a URL, went through MU landing page to the university's library. She frowned. "It requires confirmed scholarly credentials. But I think you can qualify." She keystroked, then turned the screen back to Anji to set up an account, which Anji did. Almost immediately she got provisional acceptance and, pending full approval, was granted temporary limited access. "If you need me," Nessa said, "you know where I am."

There was a lot of regional historical material on the site, mostly obscure, pedantic stuff of more use to academic researchers than to her. There was a history of Bancroft Trading Co., which added to what she knew. The shipping enterprise had been hugely profitable for generations of Bancrofts, starting before the American Revolution and continuing for another century before seeing its power reduced as the China trade declined. Domestic manufacturing in the rapidly industrializing northern states supplanted imports, and European shipping introduced steam ships that could outperform U.S. clippers. By the early 20th century, the company had gone from global trading giant to a small commercial fishing operation. For years, unmarried and headstrong, Ezra had resisted being a captain of business in favor of being a ship's captain traversing the world; now, only reluctantly, he took on the leadership role.

And he married, this too with pressure from his family. He wed Prudence Endicott Tufts, of Boston, whose own family had wealth. Apparently, it was not a happy union. Ezra's earlier days of far-traveling had fostered in him a restlessness, and an interest in arcane religious practices and the occult. He'd brought with him a crew of people who'd worked for him years before, natives of mixed ethnicities, "jippsys," as local people mislabeled them. Even including one who was said to have been a cannibal, with teeth filed to sharp points. Rumors floated around about Ezra Bancroft and these people. When citizens in Kingsport made clear they didn't care for his presence, and shunned him, he returned the sentiment with action. He moved to Slate Harbor and had a house built. His wife was in the asylum by then, "hopelessly mad" in the phrase of the day, and Ezra lived on the island with his daughter. He and his "jippsys," it was said, would gather out on the Reach on the nights of full moon tides and practice "heathen rites."

Anji sat back, turning her head to loosen tension in her neck. Sensing she was onto something, she read on, but beyond occasional notations in diaries kept by people of that time, and scant gossip items in newspapers, there wasn't much beyond the suggestion of Ezra's growing involvement in "unholy" practices. Anji found herself reminded of *Heart of Darkness* and its "unspeakable rites at midnight." She sighed. It was speculation and, without supporting data, useless for an article. Jotting notes and questions, she worked through the morning.

On the topic of Clara Bancroft, it seemed accurate to say that no child ever emerged as a known member of the Bancroft line. Like her unfortunate Brahmin mother, Clara did suffer from emotional or mental illness and became a harmless figure in town, pushing the baby pram in all weathers, layered up with tattered shawls and old dresses, existing in a world of her own.

Anji went back to the Miskatonic University Library homepage and through exploring links found reference to an archive she'd missed earlier. Identified as "Old Ones: Shoggoth, *et al*" the entry contained the notation: NO ACCESS. She asked Nessa.

The librarian's lips moved, silently pronouncing the word, but she shook her head. "I don't know. Maybe very rare material reserved only for special clearance?" She said she would contact her counterpart at Miskatonic after the holiday, the university was closed, and get back to Anji.

By three o'clock the day was already graying and the air was colder, giving hint of coming snow. The square was still busy, but the high energy of earlier had a fraying, slightly-desperate quality as dwindling gift options and the press of time took hold. From speakers in one of the open shops Joni Mitchell was plaintively wishing she had a river to skate away on. As Anji moved across the square, heading toward the ferry dock, someone called out, "I thought that was you." Carl Reed. He was coming out of Lovecraft's. She greeted him.

"Two days in the library in a row?" His eyebrow cocked. "I haven't done that since I crammed for the Realtor's exam."

How did he know she'd been there? Then she realized his office looked directly onto the square. "I'm just noodling," she said.

Don't make this adversarial, she told herself. He's a friendly guy. Richard had told her about his one on one conversation with Tom Gayle the night of the dinner, how Tom had hinted that the Realtor didn't care for some of the Bancroft legends. Now a thought came to her. "Carl, in all our excitement of buying the house, one thing Richard and I never thought to ask was how long it was unoccupied after the Bancrofts left."

"Well, that was a long time ago. Offhand, I'm not sure."

"Are records available?"

"I don't...um...some I guess. This part of your research?"

"More personal curiosity, I guess."

"Well...I'm on my way home now but stop by after Christmas and perhaps I can help."

"It's not pressing. I was only wondering."

Behind him, the pub was noisy with pre-holiday frivolity. People coming and going, some calling good cheer to Carl Reed. The man was well known in town. "Are you taking the ferry back?" he asked Anji.

She was.

"Me too."

*

Alone for the day, with his wife over in Kingsport, Richard spent his morning on a webinar, then shut down his "office" and went up to the third floor. He pulled down the folding steps and ascended to the attic. He was dressed for it this time, in a fleece-lined shirt, knit cap, and work gloves, along with safety glasses, ear plugs, and a dust mask. He had run a power cord up from below and clamped a work light clamped to a rafter, angled to illuminate on what he was doing. With the Sawzall he cut sections of the old lath-and-horsehair plaster.

By late afternoon there was just one last section to remove, set in a far angle he had to belly-crawl to get at it. As he worked, the reciprocating saw struck metal—likely an old nail. There was a sputter of sparks and then total darkness as the power went out. *Dammit!* He'd have to go to the basement and reset the breaker. He activated his phone's flashlight. In the broken plaster and sawed-off laths he saw the dull shine of where the blade had cut through a rusted chain. It was fastened to the plank floor by ring bolt. With his free hand he tugged the short length into view...and *jumped!* He smacked his head on a rafter hard enough to ignite a starburst. When his vision cleared, there, amidst the debris, eerily pale in the glow of the light, lay a small human body.

*

Dusk had fallen by the time Anji arrived home. As she approached, it appeared as if every light in the house was on, shining through the mullioned windows, casting lattice patterns on the ground.

The front door swung open and Richard came out onto the granite stoop looking shaken. There were blood spots on his shirt collar.

"Richard, what happened? Are you *okay*?"

He drew her inside and quickly closed the door. He had banged his head, but it was nothing, already taken care of. "But I need you to see something."

She had just time to shed her laptop case before he led her wordlessly up to the third floor. The folding staircase was down. In the attic he guided her to a corner where a work lamp shone. She was glad she'd left her coat on; the air was frigid. "In here," he said. It was the place he'd been working two days ago.

The slope of the roof forced them to kneel and crawl in for a view. It took her a moment to make out a rusted ringbolt and length of chain. She gaped. Something the size of a child's doll lay on its side, facing them. The skin was shriveled, darkened like old leather, dusted now with shredded plaster. The chain was secured to a bony ankle. Anji's questions came in a rush. "What is this? How did you find it? Did you call the police?"

"I've been too freaked out. I'm glad you're home." He fumbled his phone from a pocket. "I'll call now."

Her hand paused him. "Wait. First tell me everything. But..." she cast an uncertain look at the small corpse, "downstairs, okay? It's freezing up here."

He was pacing in the living room when he finished his story. "It's a child, isn't it," he said. "Clara Bancroft's?"

"Is it? At this point, I have no idea."

But that's what they were both thinking. Picturing the small body, shrunken as it was, and sprinkled with debris, making out details was difficult. But what did that matter? The chain, the fact of its being walled in...these suggested abuse, even murder. "That's a crime scene up there," he said. "It's for the police."

"Absolutely, I agree. But hold on. You took photos?"

She swiped through the images on his phone. He'd shot half a dozen, each with only slight variation, one a cramped shot from behind. The narrow space made movement difficult, and he'd been badly unnerved. The camera flash cast the body in stark contrasts. The back was hunched forward in such a way that there appeared to be bony ridges on either side of the spine. Below the shoulders, the arms curled inward to the abdominal area. But it was the head which drew Anji's attention. "Is it really..?"

"A child?" he said.

"There's that, but I was going to say...human."

They studied the images together. The small head was elongated, its tiny ears flat to the skull, the eyes tipped downward and wrung shut.

"It's been up there a long time, through heat and cold," Richard said. "But I don't know. We heard that Clara's baby may have been stillborn. And there was the 'lost' rumor."

"Tom Gayle said there were...stories. Maybe there's another explanation."

He was looking at her with mute alarm. She was starting to recover from her shock, a steadying rationality taking over. "First let's get some of these house lights off. It's like a showroom in here. Then I want to look at that wound on your head."

As he'd said, it wasn't serious. A small contusion. She trimmed some hair away, cleaned the wound, applied antibiotic ointment and a dressing. After, she told him what she'd been learning about Ezra Bancroft and his interest in the occult, his Brahmin wife's being institutionalized, Bancroft's growing isolation from the community, and the odd circle of people from his seafaring days. Finally, she recounted her ride back on the ferry with Carl Reed.

"He opened up to you?"

Actually, after she had shared with Carl a little of what she was researching, he told her quite a lot. But she didn't go into detail now. It needed reflection because, frankly, some of it seemed incredible. "I didn't expect him to be open, but I think he realizes we're not on opposite sides. He said that lately he's felt a 'disturbance in the Force.'"

"He said that?"

"I know, right? He said that out on the Reach, where he lives, he's recently noticed some things that struck him as unusual. Like some people he's never seen before."

"It's remote there, not a lot of people around, especially this time of year. He's noticed some people that don't seem to belong."

"You're sure he's not just a snob? That's a

123

plummy area."

"I didn't get that sense. Maybe he was just being colorful, but he said they seemed like they were from back in the day."

"Hippies?"

"Back in Ezra Bancroft's day. 'Jippsys.'"

Richard snorted. "Sounds like a disturbance in *Carl's* force. But whatever, this is why we need to get authorities involved. This was Bancroft's house."

"And it's our house now."

"Meaning?"

"We *will* tell the authorities, only not just yet."

"Anji, there's a *body...*in *our* attic."

"So let's think this through calmly. Okay? But right now fix us a drink? Please?"

She shed her coat as he poured glasses of wine. Neither offered a toast. "I want to upload the pictures to my laptop," she said, "and take some more. I want to have a working hypothesis before we turn this over to others."

"Isn't that for them to figure out?"

"This has to be part of my story."

"For goodness sake, Anji."

"The Gayles and Carl Reed all mentioned a missing child. There was the stillbirth idea, too. Rumors. But nothing's clear. And there's no ticking clock, no distraught family beside themselves with anxiety and wondering."

"But it's an open case."

"Is it? That's what I want to find out. This is part of a larger story."

He was pacing, sending her uncertain glances, but she was seeing it now, *tracing the line*, in the words of her former editor, familiarizing herself with the scope of the tale. The winding history of the Bancrofts, their rise in the 18th century, knit inextricably with the growth of the new country, the parallels with the development of trade along the Eastern seaboard; then the slow decline of their fortunes, the dying of local fishing by the time Ezra became patriarch. All this was backstory. Wealth, madness, spiritualism, mysterious people and unspeakable rites at midnight. She thought of something she'd read in an old Kingsport newspaper: *And then...the uncanny occurred.* The main story was a century old mystery involving her own house. This wasn't simply a magazine piece. No, it was taking on the dimensions of much more.

Almost certainly a book, perhaps a Netflix series...

"Just so I understand," said Richard, "you don't want to notify anyone?"

"I just want to be surer of what this is first."

"Which an official investigation, with an autopsy, maybe DNA, will tell."

"And when the authorities do get involved, as they must, I know that, it'll be headline news. Snap. Viral. News crews from all over coming in here and sucking all the marrow out of the story that I want. And even if I persist, by the time I get the full story written, no one'll care."

"God, Anji, you're talking like this is a commodity and not a monstrous crime."

"It's both. It's *more*. You have to trust me on this."

He'd quit pacing and sat, in surrender. He drained his glass. "At least let me call the Gayles. They're discreet."

"Tom will be busy getting ready for tonight's candlelight service."

"Carl Reed then."

"Not right now, but you've given me an idea." She rose. "Take a ride with me."

*

Richard drove. The snow that had threatened all day was finally starting to fall in scattered flakes that wisped like confetti in the illumination of the headlights. There were few other vehicles on the road, and those were going not out-island but toward the harbor, where people would be at home, some getting ready for the service at the Congregational church, others cooking, wrapping gifts, watching holiday movies, and later they would nestle all snug in their beds. It was where Richard longed to be. Dully, a headache had begun to assert itself.

The Reach was on the lonely eastern shore of the island, fronting the Atlantic. There were a number of expensive homes, situated among the sand dunes, most buttoned up now, the summer lairs of the uber wealthy, or island people like Carl Reed who had done well. As the houses petered out, a wilder aspect presented itself that now, in the bleak December, felt deserted. A sharp east wind came off the water. It was this remoteness, a vast star-shot blackness over a black churning ocean that filled Richard with a nameless dread. In Manhattan, at least, there had always been people.

Anji took his free hand. "I'm sorry I was snappy," she said contritely. "You know how I get with a story." He did know. He squeezed her hand.

"A good tale is like a mystery," she said, "and I want to follow the clues to find out where they lead."

"What will we find out here?"

"I'm not sure; maybe that disturbance in the force."

They were nearing the point where, absent a dune buggy, they would be forced to turn and head back, when Anji cried for him to stop. She turned, looking rearward. "What's that?"

Off the side of the road stood a boxy old truck. It was hard to make out in the thin, blowing snow but it resembled an image she had seen in one of the old photographs in the Kingsport Library. A "jippsy" caravan. "I'm going to have a look," she said, getting out.

The truck part was clearly antique, but it looked serviceable, the tires intact. Built over the chassis was boxy windowless structure of boards. On the back was a door. She contemplated it a moment, her eyes adjusting to the darkness, then moved around to the far side. No window there either, but there was a faded scrawl of graffiti. Two words, barely legible, but at the edge of her mind something stirred. She had seen the words...*were* they words?...on the website for the Miskatonic University archive. *Cthulhu fhtagn.*

From the darkness beyond came the roaring of surf on the shore. Although this couldn't be more than a mile from Slate Harbor, it had never occurred to her before how distant this part of the island really was. She drew several breaths, trying to steady herself. She had an impulse to knock on the door but now something else unnerved her. Coming from the boxy old caravan was a fishy, ammoniac odor.

In the confusion of their finding the body in the attic she had not told her husband all that Carl Reed had shared on the ferry. He had come out of the brew pub and maybe it was that, or maybe he was in a celebratory mood because the year getting ready to end had been a good one in real estate sales, but as the boat moved toward Slate Harbor he began to talk about the old legends surrounding Ezra Bancroft, including his strange circle, a kind of "palace guard," Carl called them, ready to do his bidding, and like Bancroft himself, acolytes in service to the "deep ones."

At the honk of their car's horn, she ran back and climbed in. "Well?" Richard asked.

"What I said about a good story having mystery. The questions pile up and you look for answers that make sense, but sometimes you find yourself at a dead end, left only with your questions."

Back in the center they passed the Congregational church, the small marquee in front announcing the Christmas Eve service: "Behold, unto us a child is born this day in the city of Bethlehem." The flicker of candlelight inside, prismed through the tall wavy glass said the service was underway.

At home they sat with the tree lights on and drank wine. They tried to watch *The Bishop's Wife*, anticipating Cary Grant's antic ice-skating session with Loretta Young and their taxi driver, but neither was attentive. Richard was yawning, sapped by the exertions of the day. But Anji's thoughts were cycling. Unable to pull loose from the knowledge of what was in the attic and the nagging questions it brought, a new perception began to stir. Yes, there was horror in the idea of a child being confined, chained up like that but what if it had been done for a *different* reason? As an act of desperation, the way a dangerous dog is sometimes chained, to keep it from hurting others. An act performed by acolytes. And now, a new clarity came to her thinking. Richard was right. This demanded intervention, not delay. She would lay out for him what Carl Reed had told her, and together they would go to the police. "Richard..."

He struggled awake. "Huh?"

Exhaustion had overtaken him. She shook her head. "Go on to bed. I'll be right up."

He smiled wearily and touched her cheek. "I love you."

*

In the night, Anji dreamed. Ezra Bancroft was on a remote beach under a night sky. Despite being very old, he stood tall and full-bearded, gripping the hand of a young woman, leading her slowly toward the sea. It was Clara. Had to be. She wore a flowing white dress, her hair braided with small flowers. A full moon made a coppery lattice on the dark water. As they neared the sea's edge, there was a shimmer on the surface. Letting go his daughter's hand, Bancroft raised his arms high and gazing seaward began to chant. Clara was frightened and leaned closer to him, looking for reassurance. The old man's chanting, sounds more than words, got louder...*Cthulhu fhtagn...Cthulhu fhtagn...*

A wind had risen, rustling his beard, Clara's diaphanous gown and woven hair. The surface of the sea had begun to stir as though something unseen were moving beneath.

Cthulhu fhtagn...Cthulhu fhtagn he went on repeating the bizarre, unrecognizable phrases.

Suddenly, the water was alive with the frantic leaping scatter of small fish, as if something monstrous and predatory were chasing them.

...*Cthulhu fhtagn...* Ezra continued.

Dreaming, Anji was ice-cold, fearful, aware she was making unrecognizable sounds of her own, wanting only to awaken but the scene was too powerful and held her submerged beneath its surface.

Cthulhu fhtagn, Ezra intoned, like prayer. *Cthulhu fhtagn...*

Very near the shore, something shattered the sea. It was upright, man-sized, but clearly not human, and in the moonlight, glistening green and brown, it churned forward, seawater streaming from a scaled body. It bore a large pulpy head, and lower down, as the thing further emerged, a writhing cluster of tentacles.

On the beach, Ezra Bancroft's incantations grew more frenzied.

The thing came forth and in its head, clearly visible now, countless eyes were moving, searching, then, from its lower form, tentacles were rising, snake-like and blindly groping toward where the young woman stood in terrified waiting...

With a gasping cry Anji wrenched herself awake. She was in their bed. She sat up. The air was so cold she could see her breath. Gathering herself, she extended her hand to the bed table lamp but it didn't light. "Richard?" she whispered. "Honey." Shaking him.

He wakened. "Wha..?" his voice groggy with sleep.

I had a nightmare. "I think...the power went out."

He collected himself and without complaint got out of bed. She did too. He pulled on a robe, stepped into slippers, got the flashlight he kept by the bed. "I accidentally tripped a breaker yesterday. Maybe it's that. I'll go down. Unusually cold tonight. Get back under the covers and keep warm."

But she didn't. When she heard him descending, she crept to a window and looked out. A hard fear gripped her chest. Below, in the yard, stood the old caravan. Its wheel tracks were just visible in the thin snow, and a set of what appeared to be footprints led away from the cab toward the house.

"Circuits seem okay," Richard called from the landing. "Possibly something outside came loose, maybe a branch took a line down. I'm going upstairs."

"I'll come too."

It didn't take long to discover why the house was so cold. The trapdoor to the attic was open, the folding stairs were down. Richard was confused. Had he not closed up after his discovery? He was pretty sure he had, but the question was moot now as something else took his attention.

The folding steps had slime on them, and the icy air coming from the attic bore a dank, briny smell that Anji knew: the odor from the caravan out on the Reach.

In the attic there was a body. Not the child body of before (which was nowhere to be found), this was adult sized, but odd in its features, although this may have been because the face was shredded as if it had been bitten and chewed by very small sharp teeth. Blood stained the attic floor.

The sight was too much for Richard. His cry made Anji turn to see him scramble for the open trap door, but he appeared to slip and with a scream he went through headfirst, thumping down the steps, landing with a heavy thud. Anji descended carefully. The flashlight had spun away and come to rest sending an elongated glow on the hallway wall. Richard was dead. His neck. She knew from looking but a check for pulse confirmed it.

Somehow, perhaps in one of those states one reads about where, supercharged by adrenaline, people do whatever demands to be done, Anji retrieved the flashlight and made her way to the bedroom and her cell phone. A glance outside revealed the caravan was unmoved. Of course. Its driver, (perhaps alerted to some "disturbance in the force" and come on an acolyte's mission to reclaim the small body...dispose of it...reanimate it?) was now itself a corpse in the attic. Where the original body had gone was not in her mind to know right now. Very little was. In the dark bedroom she sat on the bed, patting the covers for her phone, thinking perhaps to make a call, which she should have done long before but hadn't.

She became aware that she was not alone. Something was at the foot of the bed, something alive. She pointed the flashlight.

What she saw iced the marrow in her bones.

The being was small, the size of a child's doll. But it was no baby. In the light's circle it appeared old, *ancient*. It gazed at her, its eyes a series of opaque bulges. Anji recoiled, rubbing her own eyes, *was she dreaming still?* She pressed back against the headboard.

Reanimated (she had no idea how!) the *being* (she didn't know how else to think of it!) squirmed across the tangle of bedclothes, leaving a glisten of blood and slime. It smiled then, or *seemed* to, its mouth ringed with a jagged circlet of sharp teeth, tinted red at the points.

And Anji knew only that there was still so much more she *didn't* understand. She tried to scream but was able only to manage the weak strangled hoarseness of nightmare. Witless now with terror, she flung out of the bed, stumbling on legs gone numb, and went down on her knees.

She twisted painfully onto her side, retrieved the flashlight. At her back there was a thump, and the faint metallic jingle and a rhythmic *slap...scrape...slap,* as of something pulling itself avidly across the floor. She turned and aimed the light.

It was there, dragging a short length of rusted chain and coming with a blind imperative, and now, from its hunched form, instead of arms, came thin tentacles, rubbery and reaching. She made no effort to scream. There was no use. The thing opened its mouth wide, then wider yet, and from it came a wretched, needing, pitiless sound that locked her spine in ice.

"Maaa-maaaaa..."

The Death Pit

By Colleen Drippe

How long before the Lukurra find me? How long until I share the unmentionable fate of my friend Noah; or his shell shocked uncle Heinrich Fischer? Eventually a neighbor will force the door of my apartment and say, "He has disappeared; that strange, nervous man who had books strewn everywhere. He locked himself in and now...he is gone!"

As the night comes on, with its burden of shadows and the mounting sands of that far and awful place (how I have come to *hate* sand!) even now as I stand on the edge of something far worse than dissolution, I *will* write. So much spirit remains to me. The same spirit that prevents me from slashing my wrists and ending my miserable life. I *will* leave behind a testimony of what I have seen and done, and of the blasphemous horrors reaching out to us from the depths of the past.

First, I must set down the fantastic story of my lost friend Noah Fischer even though it is a narrative so bizarre that even now it may only be a symptom of my own mental breakdown. For I am quite convinced I am mad, as mad as Noah's uncle. If I were to seek help, I would be drugged or locked away and...if I so much as offered or even hinted at proof of what I say, my own people would do away with me.

There is no such person as Noah Fischer and never has been. That is what the doctors said when I asked for him during my recovery from the accident. Head trauma, they told me. False memories that will fade with time.

I wrote to his parents, William and Tabitha Fischer on Spruce Street in the small Ohio town where he grew up. I swear the address was in my address book, though I cannot find it now. My letter went unanswered. I dialed their phone number. I shudder at the memory of the that ringing, as it echoed in some nameless void until I grew afraid that someone or something might answer it after all. But no one did, and I soon hung up the phone.

I flounder in a mist where the real and the unreal cannot coexist. Sometimes it seems as though I should have a choice to accept one or the other, reality or delusion. But in truth there is no choice. No more than there was for that poor man in a story I read once, who thought he had been possessed by a being out of Earth's primordial past. Some strange and conelike thing, a scholar like myself, whose form he had taken in exchange during an episode of supposed amnesia.

I did not quite give up my search. Noah had had a great great uncle, an archaeologist named Heinrich Fischer. If I could prove that he at least was real, then I might find some way to establish the existence of his nephew. Dr. Fischer had led a 1920's expedition to the fertile crescent and had disappeared somewhere in the region about Ur, the ancient Sumerian city state made famous for its death pit. In that awful place where the remains of innumerable victims of human sacrifice lay packed side by side in the royal tombs, he had apparently vanished. And after a fruitless search, the expedition had broken up.

But now I find no record of any of this. Woolley's diggings are well documented, but not the Fischer expedition. For all my research, if there ever was a Heinrich Fischer, he was killed in World War I and never returned to his position with the Deutsches Archäologisches Institut, shell shocked (as Noah told me he was supposed to have been) or otherwise.

The afternoon slipping away into lengthening shadows while the view from my window, other Victorian houses broken up into apartments with Green Valley Park behind them, and a random collection of parked cars, is losing its familiar appearance, taking on the hues of an accursed world that is becoming hideously familiar. A world buried deep in the fogs of a past so terrifying it is better left unexplored. I only wish it had been.

I can write no more today. I must get up and close the blinds. There is a bulb to replace in one of the lamps which I always keep burning these days. There is a night to be got through.

Oh God! How long until the sun will rise again?

*

Later. I have been granted another dawn. As I look over the things I scribbled down last night, I see that I've gotten nowhere. Of what use to anyone are my rambling hints when I should at least set down the facts as I remember them? And so, as daylight leaks once more into my room and I settle myself beside the window, I search for an image or a fact to begin.

And of course I remember Mr. Kane, only I do not believe that is his real name if he even had one, and the Haley Memorial Library. Such an innocuous name, but that is where everything started. I remember the first time Noah and I passed the building, a crumbling relic of an earlier day, surrounded by overgrown weeds, half hidden on its ill kept lot. We passed it more than once on our way to the university where we were both graduate students and teachers and we took no notice until...until one day we did.

Even at the time, I had a half conscious urge to

shun the building, believing that nothing wholesome could find a place on its shelves. But Noah insisted that we go in and, despite my misgivings, we did. Haley Memorial turned out to be a small repository, endowed by an eccentric antiquarian of the last century, who wished to make his collection of arcana available to certain kindred spirits whom he had, apparently, expected to be drawn to his library.

Noah and I must have fit into that category, for we were certainly drawn to the place once we got inside. It did not matter to us that some of the contents were plainly rubbish. Despite his impressive record of scholarship, Haley had also been taken in by a plethora of crackpot theories in the form of crumbling books on everything from lost continents to flying saucers.

The gold made up for the dross. Noah's field was the study of Sumerian language and literature while I am a classical philologist and we began to find books and manuscripts in Professor Haley's collection that the university would have given much to have in its own. Once we overcame an initial repulsion, for the inside of the building was no better than the outside and smelled of mold, we foraged with a certain amount of glee, happy to have this edge over our fellow students who had not yet discovered the place.

Mr. Kane presided alone over the library, and we were at the mercy of his eccentricities. He opened the doors midafternoon five days a week and though we could not take out any of the books or manuscripts, we might browse at leisure, copying what we would, until he locked up sometimes as late as midnight.

He was whimsical, to say the least. For one thing, he continued to use the Dewey Decimal system and there was a physical card catalogue where we could find the numerical classifications of the books we sought. Another oddity was his firm proscription of certain shelves after sunset. Indeed, one entire alcove of ancient history was roped off and left unlighted during the latter part of the evening.

Since this included the 935's, my friend had to scramble to get his work done while the daylight held. I was only marginally more fortunate since I could wander off into the 800's to access literature in Attic Greek or early Latin. But as for studies of the ancient history or studies of the languages themselves, all this was to be found only within the restricted alcove.

You may well ask why we did not question Mr. Kane about his injunction, for which there could be no sensible reason, but we never did. It would have meant a prolonged conversation with him, something we both avoided. Now, in retrospect, I shudder at the memory of his detestable form and wonder that I never saw before how utterly repulsive he was. Mr. Kane was, in short, the one blot on what otherwise seemed a very convenient and useful situation.

As I think back, I find it hard to describe his appearance as I first saw him in the ill lighted galleries of the place. I remember there was a faint effluvium that clung to him, an odor reminiscent of cellars and other places where strange things grew, something fungoid that went with the smell of the building itself. And though I know this sounds fanciful, there was also a false seeming about him, as though he wore his body like an awkward disguise. And yet I ignored these things in my greedy quest for books and manuscripts.

Only later came the thought of his loathsome handprints on the books I consulted and the memory that we had breathed the same foetid air in those dimly lighted rooms. And I wondered how I had borne it.

But now I must set down something about my friend, as though writing about him might make him live again. Noah and I had met at the university where we had each been doing some rather painstaking work on our doctoral theses. We were scholars in the oldest sense, in love with our studies and caring very little for the values of the world outside. Our one shared ambition was to be the top men in our respective fields and we were, God help us, willing to do just about anything to stay ahead of our fellow students.

Over the past few years, we had shared a certain amount of personal history and stayed in touch on the rare occasions when we left to visit our families. Noah had his parents and I, a rather distant father who practiced law. While Noah had mentioned his Uncle Heinrich, there seemed to be no living relatives besides his parents. I, too, was rather lacking in kindred.

I learned more about Noah's uncle on one of our

rare occasions of levity; a celebration, if I remember correctly, of his acquiring a much sought after fragment of manuscript transcribed in cunei

form by a long dead enthusiast of the nineteenth century. Maybe a friend of the eccentric Dr. Haley? Anyway, the achievement seemed to merit something out of the ordinary and we accordingly acquired what was supposed to be some really good weed which we smoked after a meal of pizza and beer.

I don't know how we got off onto the subject of bizarre theories regarding the Sumerians, but I suppose it was only to be expected in light of Noah's acquisition. Because the Sumerian language was an isolate, meaning it had no connection to any known language family, the subject was fertile ground for a lot of crackpot theorizing. I remember we made jokes about von Däniken and his ancient extraterrestrials, though I don't know whether he said anything specific about the Sumerians. After that, we drifted on to the subject of Zecharia Sitchen who had indeed claimed that the Sumerian gods were aliens.

Sitchen's writings, my friend told me, had been full of the Annunaki, whom he claimed had bred the ancestors of our own race to use as slaves. Mr. Sitchin professed to be one of the few scholars who had read and understood the Sumerian and Akkadian clay tablets and it was from these that he had accumulated his "evidence" concerning our own solar system. The aliens were out there, he said, or had been, visiting earth some half a billion years ago to look for gold.

There was a lot more but I don't remember it. The next thing I recall was that our discussion had turned serious.

"He disappeared, you know," Noah said abruptly. "He really did. My grandfather's uncle. On the dig."

I drew my attention back from a beautiful golden pothos which I had growing on top of a bookshelf. In my dreamlike state, I thought the vines were moving about, twining themselves together and then breaking apart as I watched. "Your uncle disappeared?" I repeated slowly, dragging myself back to the conversation.

"That's the story as I heard it. From my father, actually, who had it from his father. Dr. Fischer was his father's uncle."

With an effort, I gathered my wits. "Your grandfather...in Germany?"

Noah nodded.

"But...your multiple greats uncle, then? Heinrich? Your father talked about him?"

"Yes. Uncle Heinrich was never right after World War I."

I had a mental picture. Inspired by a movie, I am sure, of soldiers in the trenches. He would have worn a spike on his helmet. There would be shells and things exploding, enough to send a lot of soldiers around the bend.

"They didn't have much sympathy for disorders like that back then," Noah said as though he had followed my thought. "The head doctors in those days were pretty rough on their patients, especially in Germany. But they got him functional enough that he returned to work as a professor of archaeology and ended up leading that expedition."

I nodded. "And then he got lost?" I was thinking that archaeology was not the safest field back then what with bandits and political unrest. And the middle east was never a very stable place.

"Not lost," Noah said distinctly. "Disappeared." He paused to pass me the joint. "I've been dreaming about him lately. More than I'd like."

I thought about this for a bit, my mind drifting. I wished he hadn't told me that.

But presently he dropped the subject and began to talk about some of his own research. Before I knew it, we were off on another subject, one that fascinated both of us. Time, or should I say, sheer antiquity. Not surprising considering our two chosen fields.

I remember holding forth about the hints in the Iliad of an earlier civilization...small glimpses of assumptions about life and customs that predated the Greeks. We talked a bit about the iron age and the bronze age that came before it. And we speculated on even more ancient things, cracks in the foundations of literature that showed glimpses deeper down the wells of time. He even used the word *antediluvian* which seemed an anachronism itself, meaningless to a modern student.

"But the oldest things," I remember Noah saying, "the oldest actual records we have are mine.

Sumer and Akkad. Older than Egypt even. Your Greeks are nothing but children next to the Sumerians."

This was a crude way of putting it, but I suppose it was true. I was struck by a disturbing impression of sheer *ancientness;* not just as something to theorize about but a chilling reality. And I wondered how much further back we might someday go; all the way to the ice age, perhaps? If only they could speak to us, those old ones.

How foolish we were, how naïve.

But already Noah seemed to be thinking of something else; something that unsettled him and crept beneath the cozy cheer of our little party, replacing it with a sudden, frigid incursion of nameless dread. I believe he spoke again of the vanished archaeologist, of the death pit of Ur. I could almost feel the hot wind blowing sand over the ruins...

I don't remember anything more of that particular evening. After we separated, I did not see Noah again for almost two months.

It was during that time, that the horror began.

*

It is some hours since I wrote the preceding. I believe it is afternoon now, though time gets muddled for me here in my room. I wasn't hungry today and I believe I have been forgetting about food for some time. I seem to have lost some weight. But I went for a dutiful scrounge of the eatables I keep in my kitchenette and found two very elderly apples and a banana which I had better throw away. And I put on the kettle and made tea.

I will not say I am refreshed, but I must go on with this writing. The day has been a gloomy one, murky outside and rainy. It seems as though my fate approaches more swiftly when the sun cannot be seen.

When I was younger I read a story about a book called *The King in Yellow*. Even to read this book brought on a nameless doom, heralded by stranger and stranger happenings until...but I don't remember the actual ending. Yet it is as though my friend and I have read this book or done something like it. I think it was the library that was our undoing. We had passed its accursed doorway and made free of the place and now I am left alone to go through the motions of life as I wait for the unnamable. For, make no mistake, there are things in this world that cannot be handled with impunity and we have handled them.

During the time Noah and I did not see each other, I still had occasion to visit the library. My speculations on the hidden crevasses (for that is how I thought of those openings into the deepest past) had led me into another aspect of my already overly expanded thesis. I was hunting in Hesiod and also among the plays of Aeschylus and the writings of Pindar, sifting long sifted writings for gleams of a time before the time of the writers. Mycenae and earlier into the Helladic period or even the end of the stone age. I wanted to *touch* the hands of the Old Ones, to actually hear their voices.

Professor Haley had left a very good collection of untranslated works and even a few scribbled notes from long dead scholars I had never heard of. It didn't occur to me then, what I was doing. I was drifting into the immemorial past by means oblique and almost underhanded. This was not archaeology; this was something occult.

And so I worked by daylight and Mr. Kane did whatever he did at his desk while I worked. Not for the first time, I wondered why Noah and I had never met anyone else in the library besides ourselves. It was very silent, I remember, with nothing to hear but the ticking of the old fashioned clock. But I put such thoughts aside along with other questions clamoring within my fevered brain and got on with the search.

On this particular day, I had been obliged to ask the librarian for a very old, perhaps Renaissance era copy of a few pages of a Greek play I had seen listed in the catalogue. He had fetched the item for me from some recess in the building. As I took it from him, we neither of us having spoken at all after I had made my request, I had occasion to look down at his hands.

As always, the light was not good. It was already evening and the ancient history niche was duly roped off. I might not have seen what I thought I saw...

It was his hands. He held the manuscript delicately; but shouldn't he, shouldn't we both have worn gloves to handle something that old and fragile? and waited for me to take it.

That's when I looked down at his fingers, really looked at them. They were long and slim, yet not bony at all. Rather they were more like worms rippling as they moved...or some sort of animated fungus. I stared at those fingers, not daring to look up into his face. I had the impression he might be laughing at me and I knew that if I acknowledged that laughter I would go mad.

As I stood, frozen in place, he set down the pages and turned away while I, for I could not seem to help myself, picked them up after all and went back to the table where I had been working. But I could not work. I was trembling so that I could hardly hold my pen. And there was worse to come.

...the Haley Memorial Library. Such an innocuous name, but that is where everything started. I remember the first time Noah and I passed the building, a crumbling relic of an earlier day, surrounded by overgrown weeds, half hidden on its ill kept lot.

When I finally got the pen into my hand ready to transcribe what the librarian had given me, I found to my horror that I was writing in a language I had never seen before. I set down the marks as they came to me, almost as though I were taking dictation from a voice calling to me from across the universe.

I heard a movement at the desk and at this, I woke from the spell that held me. I threw down the pen, snatched up my notebooks, all except the one I had been writing in, lest I manage to decipher the script, and ran from the room. Outside, night had fallen and there was a wind, I remember. The trees thrashed against the sky like great tentacles. Like the fingers of the librarian.

I had been working too hard, you would say. I'm sure the doctors would have said so if I had told them about the incident. And I even said this to myself. What I needed was a drink, I said firmly, and a quiet evening among my own books at home.

The drink became two, which finished the bottle, for I am not much of a drinker and do not keep much in stock. But that was enough to put me to sleep and into a nightmare I can scarcely recall. The only image that remains in my memory is of the Great Death Pit of Ur. All those skeletons snugged together, their finery tarnished and rotted away and the sun of a new world blazing down upon them as Woolley and his men peeled back the earth that had been their covering.

I woke thrashing, reaching for the quilt that had fallen to the floor. My own covering. The aeons that had safeguarded the present, securing it against the immemorial past, all scraped away.

And sand. I had also dreamed of sand.

It was not long after this that Noah came back into my life. He did not say where he had been. I suppose he might have gone off, as he or I sometimes did, in quest of a book or some artifact offered for sale in a neighboring state. But if he had, he did not show me what he had found.

When I saw his lights as I walked past the house (he lived several blocks away in the same neighborhood) I went immediately to see him at his apartment. I don't even know how long he had been back.

When he opened the door, (he did not do so at once, as though he might have been studying me from some peephole to make sure I was a friend),

my first thought was that someone or something had put a mark on him. That he, as well as I, had indeed touched some foul and blasphemous thing. I was thinking that henceforth we were both to be the prey of that which moved in the shadows, nameless and hungry.

And then, as he turned up the lamp, the impression vanished and I came in and saw that he had been unpacking. The place was a mess. We went out for something to eat but I don't think either of us was hungry. Nor did we have much to say to each other. Indeed, we seemed to be spilling over with things we *didn't* say.

When I got back to my own rooms that night, I had a sudden desire to turn on all the lights and to make sure the blinds were down. To check that the door was locked. I did not know what I was keeping out but for a moment it seemed to be Noah Fischer. I wonder if he felt the same way about me.

I fell asleep in my chair and woke myself crying out in my sleep. But as before, all I could remember of the nightmare was the tidy regularity of the dead, the unwelcome sunlight and the sand of that place. Even more of it than there had been before.

I did not go back to sleep, but remained where I was, waiting for the dawn. And when I sat up, I felt something gritty beneath my stockinged feet.

*

We returned to the Haley Memorial Library more than once in the next few weeks. We could not help ourselves, though the noisome stench of the place had grown more intense and I would have turned away from that foul doorway if I could. Sometimes when I looked at Noah, I knew he felt as I did: haunted by a doom from which there was no escape.

We began coming later and later in the day, often arriving after dark. We pretended to work but in truth we were only watching Mr. Kane with a new furtiveness as we drifted closer to the roped off niche. On one particular night, a gibbous moon shone in one of the windows, bathing the books in its eldritch glow. It was so bright I could almost read the numbers on their spines. I knew exactly where to find the 935's which were Noah's and not far from them, the 938's that were mine. At the desk, Mr. Kane never looked up.

I don't know what madness possessed us in the end, to defy his prohibition. It was an unplanned act; or a series of them. Noah asked the librarian for several old copies of *Near Eastern Archaeology*, obliging him to leave us alone while he went to fetch them.

Immediately we slipped over the rope and into the forbidden alcove as though we were plunging into a different world. We were. The moonlight was ghastly, the shelves of books disappearing into the distance as though the place were far larger than it could possibly have been. A vile wind shrieked overhead.

One of us made a small sound almost drowned by that keening. I do not know if it was Noah or I. As I peered down the impossibly lengthened rows, seeing the shelved books change as they disappeared into stygian depths, I felt my mind retreating, actually squirming into this dark place from which I shall never emerge again.

Beside me, Noah had become no more than an amorphous shape, casting a moon shadow along the floor. And that shadow, I swear I saw it, was not that of a man. It was like something from that story I read long ago, a cone shaped being, though I knew it could not be one of *them* because it was too small. I lurched backward, half fainting, falling against a shelf of books...or was it something else? It looked like a leaning block of some cyclopean ruin, half illuminated by the moon. As I fell, I remember stumbling in the sand that covered the floor.

The next thing I remember clearly is someone giving me water from a paper cup. The hand that held the cup was long fingered, fungus colored in the grudging overhead light. I looked away from it quickly and saw that I was propped in a chair in the main section of the library. Across from me, Noah sat in another.

At length, something compelled me to look up into the face of the librarian. For the first time our eyes met and I was not surprised to see within his eyes the same hideous darkness I had seen in the cursed alcove. Around those stygian pools, his features assembled themselves, faltering until they became something roughly human.

"You have done a foolish thing," he said. It was one of the longest speeches I had ever heard him make. For the first time, I realized he had a slight foreign accent; or was it only that he lisped?

Across from me, Noah did not speak but only hunched in his chair. I know now that his mind was far away by then and moving even further into the shadows that waited for us both.

I pushed the cup away and tried to sit up. But I was as weak as a baby and dropped back into my chair. "What do you mean?" I rasped. The words seemed to fall from my lips as though I had forgotten how to use my vocal apparatus.

"You should not have looked into the wells of time," he said. He had turned away and I was thankful that I could no longer see his abominable features. "Did you never think, in your greed for knowledge, that something might look up at *you*?" he asked.

"You..." I managed to stammer. "What *are* you?"

"I am the guardian of this place."

"Guardian against what?" I demanded.

His answer meant nothing to me but for some reason I remembered it. "The Lukurra. The enemy you have awakened." As he turned away, even his walk, I could see clearly now, betrayed the fact that he was no child of our world. In the sudden return of silence, the clock ticked loudly. I remember sitting there, mesmerized by that ticking until the stroke of midnight. At this, Noah seemed to come to himself.

I watched him rise clumsily to his feet and begin to gather his papers. He waited for me as I staggered after him to the door. I did not dare to look at Mr. Kane as we passed him. I was praying I would never see him again.

But the terrors of that interminable evening were not to pass away so easily. For, as we emerged onto the sidewalk, I saw immediately that the very air about me had *changed*. It had always seemed to me such a small thing, that interface between the day and the night, nothing more than the temporary loss of light while the earth turns away from the sun. But for the first time I knew what that really meant...to stare out into the void.

I found myself drifting upward into the very *hugeness* of the cosmos; a cosmos from which indescribable things had made their way into our world. I shrank within myself, and could not go on. I had to close my eyes against the myriad stars and the bloated moon, praying that my feet would stay anchored to the ground.

Silently, Noah guided me along the sidewalk until I found myself at my own door. He came inside with me.

I did not want him to come in. I conceived an aversion to him almost as great as that I had felt for the librarian; perhaps worse. Definitely worse, for horrible as he was, Kane was but a creature sent here from outside to do a job. I did not think he had come here to harm us. But what I had seen in the moonlit alcove when I looked at Noah, was not Noah.

And yet when I glanced up from turning on a lamp, I saw only my familiar friend and colleague. I scrutinized him closely as I half fell into my reading chair, waiting to see if he would let down his guard; if his features would slip into some other pattern than that of our own species.

Noah settled himself on the divan. After the silence, I was startled to hear him speak. "My uncle," he said, "was *taken*." I could see the desperation in his eyes, as though he struggled to speak.

I looked at him in surprise. The word the librarian had used came back to me then and I spoke it aloud. "The Lukurra. Did they take him?"

The effect on my friend was electric. He stiffened and almost came to his feet. For one moment, he looked completely like his old self...and then a change came over him. "Where did you hear that word?" he demanded in a voice that brought shivers to my spine.

"Mr. Kane," I said quickly, watching him. "He is...guarding us against them, I think."

"It is Sumerian," Noah said, sinking back into his seat. He had become himself again. "It is the word for stranger, enemy stranger."

"But the Sumerians are gone," I reminded him. "You told me they were older than the Egyptians, far older than the Greeks. It was all so long ago." I was remembering my dream about the uncovered dead and how I had lost the protection of the insulating ages mounded above the past.

Noah had no answer to this. As I had seen the return of his old self, so I had watched it melt away. When he looked at me now, there was nothing human in his eyes. "I must go home," he said abruptly, shaking himself as though to settle his clothing. I feared it was not his clothing he was

settling, but his human form.

"I will return tomorrow," he said.

I was struck at the oddity of his choice of that word "return." Noah would have said, "come back." I looked away from him. I was remembering his shadow in the library, did not want to risk seeing it again.

Without another word, he let himself out into the night. I remained in my chair until morning. I do not think madness was far off but I really don't remember much about what I thought or dreamed...or saw.

*

Once more, I have had to call a halt to this narrative. Somehow, another day has slipped away and I must get up and check the windows and the door. It is my ritual. All the lights are on, I see, and I have removed the shades from the lamps. In the pitiless glare of the naked bulbs, I scarcely recognize myself in the mirror. How long since I have eaten or slept properly? How long since I have changed my clothes or washed? My face has fallen in, my eyes sunk deep in their sockets. I would not know that wreck if I met him on the street.

As I move around the room, checking the lights, I hear voices, faint and far away, speaking in a unhuman sibilance that chills my blood. I remember the strange script I took down that day in the library. This time, I can almost understand the words.

For once, there is such an urgency on me that I resume writing even though the earth has turned and there is nothing but night outside and the infinity of the stars. To work is better than risking dreams.

I do not think I will have to wait much longer...

*

I see that I left off with our parting for the night, Noah's and mine. He had promised to return.

I will not deny that the thought of his return filled me with dread. But when I heard his knock sometime in the afternoon of the next day, I found myself taking off the chain and unlocking the door as though some other will possessed me.

135

For long moments we regarded one other in silence, he in the hallway, I on the other side of the doorway, holding the knob, blocking his way inside.

"Will you ask me in?" he said and his voice was blurred somewhat as though it had thickened during the night.

I stood there for a moment longer and then stepped aside. "Come in," I said, remembering that in old tales, the daemonic visitor could not enter without an invitation. I had given it. What choice did I have?

He crossed the threshold while I kept moving backward and he followed me into the room. Finally I stopped. "You were going to tell me what really happened to your uncle, Dr. Fischer," I said. It was not what I had intended to say. Perhaps I was only skipping over the hours since the night before, continuing the conversation. After all, wasn't that the crux of the situation? That his uncle had been taken?

He nodded and I cannot describe the utter loathsomeness of that nod, as though some vile thing made use of his body, moving it about according to unnatural laws that had nothing to do with human movement.

"They called it human sacrifice," he said, still making no move to seat himself. "At the death pits. That's what we found. More and more of them, all lying in rows as though they had taken poison and gone to sleep."

I stared at his masklike features, wishing he would go. Wishing he had never come. And why did he say "we?" He had never been to Mesopotamia.

"But I knew they were elsewhere," he continued. "That they had been given new bodies and taken away among the gods." *Zat zey had been given new bodies and taken avay...*

"Among the gods," I repeated. "Sitchin. He said the gods were aliens."

"He vas a fool, zat man."

"What became of Dr. Fischer?" I asked. I had now backed away from him as far as I could. There was nothing behind me now except a wall.

"Zey needed him. He...he vas changed." All the while, his shifting features became at one moment those of an older man, bearded, and sporting a monocle. Uncle Heinrich? Then, in the next moment, those of my friend Noah.

I could not take my eyes from him as he continued to stand; or rather to crouch as his form became less and less human. It was as though he was waiting for something.

But so was I. This was no more my friend than it was a human being and, gathering together the last of my manhood, I launched myself at its throat.

The thing gave an inarticulate cry and shouted something in German. For a moment I could see the soldier with the spike on his helmet and then my hands sank into the pulpy flesh of its throat. The stench was appalling as everything gave way at once. I found myself wallowing in a sort of noisome ichor, the very body before me deliquescing in a hideous and long overdue decay.

I think I screamed, or tried to. Somehow I lurched to my feet and ran out the door, sliding in the formless putrefaction, skidding out into the hall. The stairway yawned and that is the last thing I remember before waking up in the hospital. They said I had been in a coma.

As my memory returned and my broken bones healed, an arm and some ribs, two things became clear to me. First, I knew that some *thing* had taken Noah's form. It was the same essence that had possessed his uncle and which, I hoped, was no longer able to possess anybody. The other thing I realized was that, no matter what had become of the possessor and the possessed, I was a marked man. My only hope was that someone, the police or whoever had found me at the bottom of the stairs, would have seen what lay in the doorway of my room. That even now, it was being studied by competent authorities.

But that hope was futile. For when I returned home, there was no sign there had ever been a struggle and, as I was soon to learn as I pursued my fruitless inquiries. no memory of Noah Fischer or of the Fischer expedition. The only evidence I found was a spray of sand outside my door. The landlady, who helped me up the stairs, complained bitterly that, as often as she swept the hallway, someone kept tracking in more.

That was two months ago, I think. I only left the building once since then when, in a fit of desperation, I sought out the librarian in the hope that, whatever he was, he might have some mandate to protect me in his capacity as guardian.

But even as I made my way to the library, I realized it was far more likely it was the building itself he was guarding and not its victims.

For victims we had been. Our ambitions, our childish smugness, our very curiosity and love of knowledge had all worked against us. I believe now that if I had not been Noah's companion, I might never have seen that library; that the Lukurra had not been seeking me. It was Noah who had been their prey as what had been his uncle began to lose its usefulness. Obviously, Heinrich Fischer, too, had been ensnared all those years ago by his own inordinate curiosity.

I might have saved myself a trip. For when I reached the place where the library had been, I found nothing but an iron fenced lot, a very old cemetery much overgrown with weeds and scattered with the wind blown debris of civilization. As I stood on the sidewalk, staring at the place, I began to doubt myself; to wonder if the whole thing had been a delusion brought about by falling down the stairs.

Oh, that it had been!

For as I shuffled through the weeds, stumbling against weathered headstones, looking for some clue as to what had become of the building, I came upon one artifact, one fragment of the library that had been. It was the notebook I had abandoned when I fled the night I first discovered that the librarian was not a human being but rather some sentient fungoid growth. My find lay in a barren spot, half buried in sand, undamaged by the rain as though it had only just been put there for me to find.

As I lifted it, the cover fell back to show the page where I had taken down that strange dictation. I knew now that if I chose, I could begin to decipher what I had written there. That the strange markings would reveal my fate.

I did not read it, but neither did I put it back. Though it contained my doom, I took it with me, knowing that it was far too late to save myself. Already I stood with one foot in shadow, the other in sand.

And so I returned to my room and have not left it since. I am growing weaker from lack of food and my mind is not clear. Or perhaps it is all too clear. I hear voices in the night and sometimes in the day as well. Noah is not here to translate for me, but I am sure the language is Sumerian.

I have been chosen to serve the Lukurra. That is what they say. Just as my friend Noah and his uncle were chosen. When they have taken me, I will cease to be what I was and I can only hope that my own self consciousness, will be extinguished in the process.

But there is not much chance of that. And the dark is closing in…

The Lovecraft Circle and the Inklings: The "Mythopoeic Gift" of H. P. Lovecraft

by Dale Nelson

1. Introduction: Could/Should Lovecraft Have Been a Mythopoeic Society Author?

In 1967, in the midst of the Hobbit Craze, the late Glen Goodknight founded the Mythopoeic Society in southern California. Bulletins began to appear in 1968, and the Society's journal, *Mythlore*, was first published in January 1969.

Anyone who knows of the Society will associate it with Tolkien's *Lord of the Rings*, C. S. Lewis's Narnian books, and the genre of high fantasy. One might also recognize the Society's interest in the mystical thrillers of Charles Williams, such as *The Greater Trumps, The Place of the Lion*, and *All Hallows' Eve*. The three authors were the outstanding members of the Inklings, an Oxford group whose participants met in pubs and college rooms to critique their works in progress, swallow pints of draft beer, and talk uproariously. Tolkien's dedication statement, for the first edition of *The Lord of the Rings*, included his fellow Inklings.

Early Mythopoeic Society 'zines featured plenty of Inklings related commentary and also art, including drawings by fan favorites Tim Kirk and George Barr. In the first issue of *Mythlore* and the February 1969 *Bulletin*, Goodknight solicited articles on the three Inklings and kindred authors such as George MacDonald and G. K. Chesterton and, surprisingly, H. P. Lovecraft.

Lovecraft! As a dyed in the wool racist, indefatigable atheist, and philosophical materialist writer of pulp horror stories, he was an odd addition to a list emphasizing the Christian Inklings and kindred spirits. And, in fact, so far as I have noticed, no article on Lovecraft appeared in a Mythopoeic Society 'zine until 2018, unless perhaps there were, say, a brief report on *The Dream-Quest of Unknown Kadath** in one of the Society branch reports that used to appear in *Mythprint*.

Goodknight, rightly in my opinion, didn't invite people to contribute articles on Lovecraft's epistolary circle friends Robert E. Howard and Clark Ashton Smith to Mythopoeic Society publications. For one thing, there was already a well established fanzine devoted to sword and sorcery fiction, *Amra*. Although Barr and Kirk contributed art to *Amra* as well as to the Mythopoeic Society 'zines, one wouldn't have expected in *Amra* to see articles on hobbits, the Istari, the Ringwraiths, the Stone of Solomon, Marcellus Victorinus, Simon the Clerk, Meldilorn, Tinidril, and Puddleglum, or drawings of Galadriel and the White Witch; and no more should one have expected articles in *Mythlore* on King Kull, Crom, Solomon Kane, Maal Dweb, Satampra Zeiros, and Namirrha, or drawings of animated corpses far gone in decay, or naked princesses slung over the shoulders of giant ape-gods. Howard's pulp adventures of Conan the barbarian don't qualify as mythic just because they contain gods, dragons, and magicians. As for Smith, he wrote stories in the Howard vein but with the swordsmanship toned down and the weird morbidness cranked way up.

However, it seems that Lewis and Tolkien read Lovecraft and that his work left its mark on Lewis. Perhaps Goodknight's inclusion of Lovecraft made sense. I'll come back to that possibility.

2. The Inklings and the Lovecraft Circle: Any Connections?

Tolkien, Lewis, and Williams and their friends met in person sometimes two or more times a week at the height of the Inklings. Except for his New York City sojourn, Lovecraft lived in Providence, occasionally making bus trips and seeing cronies along the way, but relying on an immense correspondence for most of the contact between himself and members of his circle. I won't attempt to say precisely who was in and who was not in Lovecraft's "circle," but will mention just three of his fellow authors: Howard, Smith, and Donald Wandrei. Lovecraft, Howard, and Smith never met one another.

Devotees of fantastic fiction have wondered if the Inklings knew the work of the Lovecraft circle, and vice versa. Several points of likely or certain awareness may be summarized as follows:

[1] By sometime late in his life, Clark Ashton Smith, short story writer, poet, and artist, had read *The Hobbit* and some of *The Fellowship of the Ring*, according to a posting by "calonlan" (Dr. W. C. Farmer) on 30 Nov. 2011, in an Eldritch Dark discussion thread. "Calonlan" appears to have known CAS personally.

[2] Lovecraft himself had read more than one of Charles Williams's spiritual thrillers. Their orthodoxy spoiled them for HPL. He wrote:

> "Essentially, they are not horror literature at all, but philosophical allegory in fictional
> form. Direct reproduction of the texture of life & the substance of moods is not the
> author's object. He is trying to illustrate human nature through symbols & turns of idea
> which possess significance for those taking a traditional or orthodox view of man's

138

cosmic bearings. There is no true attempt to express the indefinable feelings experienced by man in confronting the unknown... To get a full-sized kick from this stuff one must take seriously the orthodox view of cosmic organization which is rather impossible today."

(as quoted in S. T. Joshi, *I Am Providence*, page 878; I'm indebted to a 21 April 2016 posting by John Rateliff on his Sacnoth's Scriptorium blog for this reference)

Lovecraft could not have read *Descent into Hell* and *All Hallows' Eve*, which contain perhaps the most "Lovecraftian" sequences in Williams's seven novels.

[3] Lewis almost certainly not only read, but was influenced by, a story by Lovecraft correspondent and Arkham House co-founder Donald Wandrei. On one of the last pages in his short novel *The Great Divorce*, Lewis acknowledges his indebtedness to an American science fiction story, the title and author of which he has forgotten. This appears to be "Colossus," which was published in the January 1934 issue of *Astounding*. Wandrei's story plays with the idea of our universe being of subatomic tininess as compared to a super universe; the hero journeys from the one to the other. Lewis's novel involves a bus trip from hell to heaven. In the fiction, "'All Hell is smaller than one pebble of your earthly world; but it is smaller than one atom of this world, the Real World.'" (The availability of American science fiction pulps to English readers is evident from several pages of Arthur C. Clarke's autobiographical *Astounding Days* and other sources).

[4] Tolkien evidently read a 1963 paperback anthology called *Swords and Sorcery*, edited by L. Sprague de Camp, who gave him a copy. The anthology contains Lovecraft's tale in the manner of Lord Dunsany, "The Doom That Came to Sarnath," Smith's "The Testament of Athammaus," and Howard's Conan story "Shadows in the Moonlight." According to de Camp, who visited Tolkien in 1967, Tolkien liked the Conan story.

[5] Ballantine Books, Tolkien's American publisher for paperbacks, released Lin Carter's fantasy anthology *The Young Magicians* in 1969. It reprinted Tolkien's poems "The Dragon's Visit" and "Once Upon a Time." Surely Ballantine would have sent Tolkien a contributor's copy, in which he would have seen Lovecraft's "The Quest of Iranon" and "The Cats of Ulthar," Howard's non-Conan story "The Valley of the Worm," and Smith's "The Maze of Maal Dweb."

[6] It is likely that Lewis read Lovecraft's *At the Mountains of Madness* and "The Shadow Out of Time" in *Astounding*. His reading of American pulp magazines is certain. Below, I'll say something about possible influence of *Mountains* on Lewis's *Out of the Silent Planet* and of "Shadow" on Lewis's *Dark Tower* fragment.

All that doesn't come to a *lot*, but it's more than might have been expected.

Inklings-Lovecraft circle awareness didn't get a good chance really to develop. Robert E. Howard killed himself before the Inklings had produced very much writing. He died in 1936; *The Hobbit* was published in 1937, and Lewis's *Out of the Silent Planet* was published the following year. Lovecraft died in 1937. Smith died in 1961, but it seems that his career as a writer of fantastic fiction had concluded about the same time as the deaths of Howard and Lovecraft. Williams died unexpectedly following surgery in 1945; Lewis died in 1963; and Tolkien died ten years later.

3. Literary Influences: Any in Common?

Tolkien and Lewis on the one hand, and Lovecraft, Howard, and Smith on the other, probably shared an interest in the ersatz myth making of Lord Dunsany. (Dunsany, in turn, was, I believe, influenced by Samuel Taylor Coleridge. I suspect that Dunsany's dream worlds came out of the "deep romantic chasm" of Coleridge's "Kubla Khan." Rather than attempting any longer argument here, I will simply invite the reader to undertake a thought experiment. Suppose "Kubla Khan" were unknown till now, and was published as a newly discovered work by Lord Dunsany. I think you'll agree that it's very "Dunsanian" though Dunsanian *avant le lettre*, as it happens, and better than Dunsany.)

Dunsany seems very important to the American authors but not to the British ones. His cynical outlook would appeal to the Lovecraft circle, not to the Inklings. I see Dunsany as an "anti-Tolkien" because Dunsany flaunts the unreality of his dream worlds. "The Distressing Tale of Thangobrind the Jeweller, and of the Doom That Befell Him," ends, "And the only daughter of the Merchant Prince felt so little gratitude for this deliverance that she took to respectability of a militant kind, and became aggressively dull, and called her home the English Riviera, and had platitudes worked in worsted upon her tea-cosy, and in the end never died, but passed away at her residence." Admittedly, this is an extreme example. (*Mythlore* published two articles on Dunsany in its first 102 issues.)

I have little doubt that all six authors read stories by Algernon Blackwood. Certainly Lewis, Tolkien, and Lovecraft did. Tolkien mentions Blackwood in his "Guide to the Names in *The Lord of the Rings*" (in Jared Lobdell's *A Tolkien Compass,* first edition). In youth, Lewis wrote enthusiastically to Arthur Greeves about Blackwood's *John Silence*, which contains "Ancient Sorceries," mentioned below. Lovecraft praises Blackwood in his survey, *Supernatural Horror in Literature.*

Whether Blackwood influenced any of these authors other than Lovecraft is another question. I have argued for the possibility, for example, that Tolkien's screeching Nazgûl owe something to Blackwood's "The Wendigo." Blackwood's "The Willows" is perhaps the story Lovecraft would most have liked to have written in all the genre of weird fiction: "Here art and restraint in narrative reach their very highest development, and an impression of lasting poignancy is produced without a single strained passage or a single false note." The strange creature glimpsed in the tumbling Vermont flood waters of "The

Whisperer in Darkness" may remind readers of something glimpsed in the swollen Danube of "The Willows."

Lewis esteemed William Hope Hodgson's *The House on the Borderland* and Lovecraft praised it and other works by Hodgson, whose "cosmicism" was probably an important influence on him.

Lovecraft and Tolkien esteemed M.R. James' *Ghost Stories of an Antiquary*. For attestation, see Lovecraft's survey *Supernatural Horror in Literature* and the Extended Edition of Tolkien's *On Fairy-Stories*. There's a strong element of antiquarianism in many of Lovecraft's stories, and the citation of rare occult volumes by Lovecraft probably derives from James, although Lovecraft's grimoires were apt to be invented and James's were sometimes real. I have argued that Tolkien's conception of Gollum may owe something to James's haunter in "Canon Alberic's Scrap-book" (and to the accompanying drawing by James McBryde).

with an introduction by Philip Van Doren Stern

In *Mythlore* #1 (Jan. 1969), Glen Goodknight mentioned Arthur Machen as an author who might be of interest to Mythopoeic Society readers, and Lee Speth eventually wrote about him in a couple of issues of *Mythlore*.

Machen is best known for a few classic weird horror novellas. David Llewellyn Dodds has prepared a so far unpublished edition of the early manuscript commonplace book (Bodleian MS. Eng. e. 2012) kept by Charles Williams with interactive contributions by his friend, Fred Page. An entry (p. 124) citing Machen's horror novella "The Great God Pan" opens up the possibility that Williams entertained the idea of treating Merlin as being the offspring of Pan. It may be mentioned that Machen and Blackwood were involved with the Hermetic Order of the Golden Dawn for a time, and Williams may have been a member too. (The evidence is not certain; see Grevel Lindop's biography, *The Third Inkling*, page 66.) Of the authors mentioned in this paper, Machen, Blackwood, and Williams were (if only for a time) the most interested in organizations devoted to the occult. Machen's beautiful Grail story, "The Great Return," prefigures some of the exalted passages in Williams's fiction, such as the Mass in *War in Heaven*.

Lovecraft and Howard knew Machen's early horror fiction well enough to seek to imitate it: Lovecraft's "Dunwich Horror" is heavily indebted to "The Great God Pan," which it mentions, and Howard's repulsive "Black Stone" seems to owe a lot to Machen's "Shining Pyramid." It's likely Smith had read Machen, but I don't suppose Tolkien had read the Welsh-born author. The 1969 catalogue of Lewis's library includes Machen's novel *The Secret Glory*, which awkwardly combines the Holy Grail and a bitter satire of English public schools. The catalogue includes books that, I'm sure, had been Joy Gresham Lewis's books; it is possible that CSL never looked at it.

H. Rider Haggard may be the author most worthy of exploring by readers who are interested in a literary predecessor who was really important for the Lovecraft circle and the Inklings.

Tolkien, who seems usually cagey about influences, admitted to the importance, for his own writing, of the Sherd of Amenartas in Haggard's *She* as an intriguing device that gets the adventures started. From Haggard and, probably, Haggard's imitators, and from Jack London, Robert E. Howard would have derived the notion of modern protagonists connecting via "racial memory" with heroes inhabiting ancient realms of adventure (cf. Howard's "Valley of the Worm," etc.).

Lewis seems to have read all the Haggard romances he could get his hands on, and is surely recalling *She* in his Victorian period Narnian tale, *The Magician's Nephew*, when he imagines the formidable beauty Jadis creating havoc in London. I will draw upon his provocative review of a biography of Haggard below. Haggard gets name checked by Charles Williams when Roger Ingram salutes Inkamasi, chief of the Zulus, in *Shadows of Ecstasy* (Chapter 4). Lovecraft saluted Haggard's *She* as "really remarkably good" in his *Supernatural Horror in Literature*.

Other predecessors were important to the one group and not to the other. For Tolkien and Lewis: William Morris and George MacDonald. For Lovecraft, Howard, and Smith: Poe.

4. Might Lovecraft Have Influenced Lewis and Tolkien?

Lewis almost certainly read Wandrei's "Colossus" in the January 1934 *Astounding Stories* and may have been an habitual reader of the magazine by then or soon afterwards.

It is entirely possible that Lewis read *At the Mountains of Madness*, which was serialized in the February, March, and April 1936 issues. Where Haggard wrote "lost race" novels about ancient civilizations surviving in remote regions of today's world, in romances such as *Allan Quatermain* and *Ayesha: The Return of She*, Lovecraft, here, sends a Miskatonic University expedition to the most remote region of the earth, there to find living vestiges of a civilization predating the appearance of mankind.

Mountains devotes many pages to the expounding of earth's distant past as decoded by Dyer and Danforth, who peruse wall art created by the non-human Old Ones. The art reveals who the Old Ones were, namely ancient scientists from other worlds, who were responsible for the origin of life on earth. John Garth has argued that Lewis began to write *Out of the Silent Planet* in May or June 1937 and readers may remember how, on a beautiful and ancient Martian island, Ransom puzzles out the primordial history of the solar system by examining carvings. These carvings exhibit the truth of the Christian story of the war in heaven in which Satan was cast out. Writers of adventurous romances such as Haggard could use wall art as a device for hinting at the history of the distant past, but Lovecraft and Lewis use this idea specifically for the depiction of the most antique origins.

There's another incident in Lovecraft's *Mountains* that may have contributed to the first novel of Lewis's space trilogy. Readers of the latter may remember the moment when Ransom, who has sojourned for some weeks among the Malacandrians, sees human beings again, and for a brief moment beholds them through Martian eyes (Chapter 19). In *Mountains*, the narrator comes to the point of imaginatively identifying with a small group of Old Ones, revived after a sleep of many millions of years, and attacked by dogs (which hadn't evolved yet, back in their time), and confronted by human beings for the first time: "frantically barking quadrupeds," "frantic white simians with the queer wrappings and paraphernalia." Of course, just as the carvings that reveal the past may derive from Rider Haggard, the bizarre effect of seeing humans through other creatures' eyes may derive from Gulliver's Fourth Voyage, when the narrator, after his happy sojourn among the Houyhnhnms, sees himself and other humans as ugly Yahoos. And, of course, not every literary effect derives from an earlier one.

In any event, it's true that Lewis never names Lovecraft, but rather Lindsay, Wells, and Stapledon as spurring his turn to writing science fiction; still, such parallels remain striking.

As does the difference in execution. Lewis integrates Ransom's learning of the truth more deftly into the story, while some readers have probably found the many pages about the history of the Old Ones to be tedious. Lovecraft keeps inserting little promises into the narration to assure the reader that frightening events are yet to be related. It is clumsy, but many readers are willing to go along and enjoy those pages for their own sake.

There's a great deal of affinity between Lovecraft and Lewis, though, in that they were writing highly imaginative, and also very literate, romances marked by their beliefs but also notably by their reading. In *Mountains*, the echoes of Coleridge ("Kubla Khan") and Poe (*Arthur Gordon Pym*) accumulate, while *Silent Planet* draws on Milton (*Comus*) and Wells.

What about Lovecraft's other story to be published in *Astounding*, "The Shadow Out of Time"? Perhaps Lewis read that one too, in the June 1936 issue, and if he did, it seems likely that it left marks on his unfinished science fiction novel *The Dark Tower*, which was probably started soon after Lewis wrote *Out of the Silent Planet*.

Lovecraft seems to have aspired, in his last years, to write stories that transcended horror fiction, even if they were meant to have horrifying finales; he hoped to evoke awe and wonder. This is especially true of "The Shadow Out of Time." Conversely, Lewis was writing, in *The Dark Tower*, a story with strong horror elements. We might expect that "The Shadow Out of Time" and *The Dark Tower* would be the stories in which each author was closest to the other, and I think that is what we do find.

In both stories, the framework includes the possibility of explanation of anomalous memories and dreams. In both, a vaguely described device effects a transference of consciousness from our contemporary time to another time. There, the contemporary man's mind inhabits a body differing in degree (*Dark Tower*) or utterly in kind ("Shadow") from his rightful body. This character consults the vast resources of a library seeing information about the place and time in which he finds himself, and learns about dreadful possibilities there. It appears from the *Dark Tower* fragment, and is certainly true in "The Shadow Out of Time," that a threat to our own world is revealed as possible. Unusually for Lovecraft, there's even an element in this story relating to one human being's faithfulness to another (a son's loyalty to his father), while Lewis's story was going to develop Scudamour's love for a worthy woman.

Differences between the stories become pronounced. Lovecraft's narrator has little to do in the remote time to which his consciousness has come but to write, read, and look around. Lovecraft trusts mostly to the innate interest of his "world-building" and his description of exotic scenes to keep the reader paying attention to the many paragraphs preceding the final "shock" (when Peaslee, in our time, finds in an Australian ruin a manuscript written millions of years ago in his own handwriting; it's not a shock because the reader has known all along that Peaslee's dreams and memories of his mental sojourn in the distant past were genuine). The disquisition on the Great Race's culture will seem to some readers to belong in an appendix. I think it is justifiable given the story's supposed nature as a testimony of actual experiences.

In contrast, *The Dark Tower* seemed to have been weaving the narrative and the expository material together more smoothly. We're given brisk, if frightening, accounts of the strange goings on in the Othertime for several pages. Then comes calamity, with a sudden and unplanned swapping of minds between the two times. As soon as Lewis gets Scudamour into the Othertime, the young man finds himself embodied as a Stingingman who is on the verge of stabbing the woman who is the counterpart of Scudamour's fiancée in our world, and Scudamour must act quick-wittedly as his Othertime attendant informs him of a crisis occurring right then, with an attack by White Riders. In fact, Lewis is more like a "pulp writer" than Lovecraft at this point!

Lovecraft's agenda in *Mountains* and "The Shadow Out of Time" includes a depreciation of what he regarded as conventional morality. The narrator in the Antarctic story comes to appreciate that, despite their exotic biology, the Old Ones "were men." That is, they were rational creatures (what the Martians call *hnau* in *Out of the Silent Planet*), actuated by scientific pursuits, but also creators of slaves that are controlled by hypnosis; while the Great Race creatures cull "defectives" and practice "fascistic socialism." Contrary-wise, the morality in *Tower* is Christian, evident in the abhorrence with which the good characters regard the Othertime's Nazi-like use of human beings as subjects for medical experimentation and their conditioning as slaves of the state without wills of their own.

Although Lewis and Tolkien didn't set themselves to write methodical retellings of Christian doctrine and the Bible in the modes of science fiction and fantasy, they wrote from deeply Christian imaginations, and this fact is abundantly evident in various ways in their fiction. For example, in *The Lord of the Rings* Aragorn is an ancient *type* of Christ the Savior; in *That Hideous Strength* corrupt human beings try to raise a new "Tower of Babel."

I don't think that Lovecraft set himself to write a body of stories that systematically mocked and parodied Christianity, but it's reasonable to consider *At the Mountains of Madness* as a discovery of the genesis of mankind that flouts the First Book of Moses, with mankind being evolved from ancestors that were created by the Old Ones; or to consider "The Dunwich Horror" as a parody of the Incarnation; or to consider the various occult books of the Mythos, such as the *Necronomicon,* as parodies of the Bible, with revelations around which cults form, and which hint at eschatological calamities due when the stars are right again. Lovecraft also employed incidental references to the Bible, as when, in "The Colour Out of Space," the weird lights that appear on the tips of tree branches are likened to the tongues of fire that rested on the heads of the apostles at Pentecost.

What about Tolkien, by the way, did he write anything along late Lovecraftian lines?　　　Yes indeed: the unfinished *Notion Club Papers*. Here we have a group of male scholars gathering for cultivated conversation, notably about the possibility of travel in time and space; one scholar theorizes that it might be possible to become "attuned" to a meteorite and become psychically aware of alien worlds, not just in our solar system but beyond. One could easily imagine Lovecraft writing a story developed from just such an idea.

As with Lovecraft's "Shadow," the reality of dream glimpses is basic to the developing story. Notion Club scholars begin to correlate their dreams and nightmares, which, it transpires, are putting some of them into contact with a primordial catastrophe on Earth involving transgressive contact with a superhuman entity called Zigūr. They study fragments of an archaic language that provides hints of a disaster that happened before the sinking of Númenor/Atlantis, and that bursts violently into the modern world of the scholars, unleashing destructive winds that, for most meteorologists, are inexplicable. One recalls the terrible wind forces that Peaslee fears will emerge from the ancient Australian ruins, in "The Shadow Out of Time."

I don't know if Tolkien read Lovecraft's story. It isn't very fanciful to hypothesize that Lewis owned that issue of *Astounding* and passed it on to his friend. Lovecraft would have agreed fervently with

Tolkien's remark, in "On Fairy-Stories," that a story may address the hunger "to survey the depths of space and time" and the wish "to hold communion with other living things." The former desire is one of the main things in Lovecraft's mature fiction, and he put his own spin on the latter in "The Shadow Out of Time," by imagining the members of the Great Race as sending out psychic feelers in order to connect with rational beings of other species. Lovecraft didn't believe in the Creator, but he would have had some respect for Tolkien's notion of the literary artist as "sub-creator," since, like Tolkien, he was at pains to produce a sense of the reality of his "secondary worlds."

I think that, when Lovecraft began to write stories that have become identified as "Cthulhu Mythos" stories, he improvised books, entities, etc. in a fairly *ad hoc* and tongue in cheek manner, but became preoccupied by the possibilities of a corpus of *lore* as he wrote the two stories that this paper has discussed at length. "The Shadow Out of Time" is certainly a sequel to *At the Mountains of Madness*, and, conservatively, it would be easy also to integrate material from "The Whisperer in Darkness" into a scheme of Lovecraftian cosmic lore.

If the editor of *Astounding* had pressed Lovecraft for more novellas and novels, Lovecraft would, I believe, have been likely to have deliberately elaborated and explored a sort of "Cthulhu Legendarium:" grandiose science fiction in which Cthulhu himself might have had little to do. Certainly a fascination with imagined *lore* emerges late in Lovecraft's career. Had Lovecraft lived for several more decades, might he even have run into something like the perplexities of Tolkien, as regards reconciling the "facts" published so far and proposing new ones? We know from *The History of Middle-earth* that Tolkien eventually worried about the Orcs: how could they be a rational but irredeemable species? Similarly, Lovecraft might have become uneasy about the idea of immaterial consciousness in his late fiction; is it possible to square that with strict materialism?

However, as things were, it was easier to write another horror story for *Weird Tales* rather than to write a further story with long stretches of lore. "The Dreams in the Witch-House" and "The Haunter of the Dark" may be better written than some of Lovecraft's earlier fiction, but they seem to add little to Lovecraft's achievement. I'm reminded of Lewis's remark, in "The Mythopoeic Gift of Rider Haggard," that *Ayesha*, the long delayed sequel to *She*, is better written but lacking in mythopoeic power as compared to the earlier book.

5. What About Lovecraft's Literary Deficiencies?

At this point, having contended for Lovecraft as something of a peer of Lewis and Tolkien, I should emphasize that, in important respects, this isn't the case. Lewis's *Experiment in Criticism* helps us to see why it is fair to consider Lovecraft as being, much of the time, a bad writer. The *Experiment* also helps to explain his work's appeal to readers who know, and love, works of high literary quality.

Everyone who cares about literature should read Lewis's book. He asks us to start, not from the idea of good or bad books, but with reading. What are the characteristics of good reading, and what are those of bad?

Bad reading desires the same old thing and yet insists upon superficial novelty (hence, a bad reader prizes formulaic fiction but promptly puts aside a book upon remembering that he or she has already read it); bad reading uses literature as a means to pass the time for want of something better to do, and may use literature to get a train of ego-pleasing fantasies started; it is inattentive to words. The corollary is that those who habitually read badly will be put off by good writing, which invites, requires, and rewards attention.

Lovecraft has often been characterized as a bad writer. One might amuse oneself by critiquing a number of Lovecraft's earlier efforts. Rather, let's take what is probably his best story, "The Colour Out of Space." In this story Lovecraft exercises a grave and effective style, but, to consider just one sentence, he slips here: "It was a monstrous constellation of unnatural light, *like a glutted swarm of corpse-fed fireflies dancing hellish sarabands over an accursed marsh*" (my italics). Here the simile runs away with the story, *weakening* the description of the eerie light pouring from a well because the figurative expression is so distracting. It is tactless to compare a real frightening and bizarre thing to a hypothetical frightening and bizarre thing. And it will be seen that one should *not* read this sentence attentively. If one does really pay attention to what it says, one may reflect that fireflies don't eat flesh. It is awkward to refer figuratively to an "accursed marsh" given that a literal well and a reservoir are so important to the story's plot.

Lovecraft has the bad habit of using an intense rhetoric too soon. In another of his best efforts, *At the Mountains of Madness*, his narrator describes his first sight of the tremendous range: "In the whole spectacle there was a persistent, pervasive hint of stupendous secrecy and potential revelation; as if these stark, nightmare spires marked the pylons of a frightful gateway into forbidden spheres of dream, and complex gulfs of remote time, space, and ultradimensionality." He's over-egging the pudding, as far as that early point in the story is concerned, since so much more has yet to happen; and it's clumsy for him to use the simile about the mountains appearing "as if" they were a gateway into "gulfs of remote time, space, and ultradimensionality," since that's apparently what they more or less turn out to be (Chapter 3, Chapter 12).

Lovecraft also practices a kind of bogus portentousness through a certain overuse of *that* and *those*, which he probably picked up from reading so much pulp fiction. Here are some examples from early in the next chapter of *Mountains*:"that daemon mountain wind must have been enough to drive any man mad," "the hatred of the [explorers' dogs] for those hellish Archaean organisms," "One had to be careful of one's imagination in the lee of those overshadowing mountains of madness," "When we came on that terrible shelter," etc.

And so on. Badness in Lovecraft's fiction may also include inept handling of plot, including supposed "surprise" endings and recycling of situations, and so on. "The Whisperer in Darkness," for example, one of the key Cthulhu Mythos tales, compromises its resourceful use of local color and intriguing recent news (the discovery of Pluto), its uncanny atmosphere and imaginative vistas, with a noticeable prolongation of the final episode that relies on a rather stupid narrator and a disguise that is likely to be obvious to the reader, but, unconvincingly, not to the man on the spot. In *Mountains* Lovecraft awkwardly combines pedantic exposition of the Old Ones' civilization, including conclusions about motives and the like that could hardly have been conveyed by pictorial carvings, with reticences and hints.

Lovecraft didn't finish high school, and his writings occasionally betray the vicissitudes of the autodidact; sometimes extensive learned material that reflects his self-selected studies combines with sketchy or erroneous background. Thus, in *Mountains*, it seems he has got up a lot about geological periods, but may betray a weak grasp of how petrifaction works or the inevitable consequences of aeolian erosion. The narrator and his companion flee over the mountains in an airplane with the windows open, i.e. not a pressurized cabin, at high elevation, and experience nothing worse than cold and racket. When they land, at first Lovecraft remembers to say that they suffer from the rarefied air of a high altitude, but he seems to forget all about this for many pages, and has the two running for their lives eventually. Dyer and Danforth learn that the Old Ones flew to earth from interstellar space by *the beating of their wings.* When Robert E. Howard wrote of the elephant-headed folk, in the Conan story "The Tower of the Elephant," thus flying through space, perhaps he didn't realize the impossibility; but how could Lovecraft have known?

6. Does Lovecraft's Mature Cthulhu Mythos Fiction Partake of Lewis's "Mythopoeic?"

If Lovecraft's Cthulhu Mythos fiction conforms to criteria adduced by C. S. Lewis as qualities of mythopoeia, that might help to show why some readers return to it despite defects that no amount of special pleading can completely excuse. This paper will turn to that task in a moment.

An issue too big to do more, here, than take note of, is whether *mythopoeic* fiction must suggest the *transcendent*. Must not mythopoeia suggest that there exists a realm or dimension that is, somehow, eternal and good, and that underlies or is "behind" the realm of quotidian existence? I see that in the Inklings' Christian convictions, in Le Guin's Taoist sensibility, etc. Science fiction writers may have the hope that humanity will evolve into godhood (e.g. Clarke's *Childhood's End*). But any such things are ruled out, for Lovecraft. *It's just meaninglessness all the way down.* Since ghosts imply a surviving spiritual essence, Lovecraft tended, as he developed his craft, to shy away from them, although he couldn't let go entirely, since the idea of possession by the spirit of a wicked magician or the like was so fecund for horror fiction (e.g. even a late shocker such as "The Thing on the Doorstep")

By "Lovecraft's mature Cthulhu Mythos" fiction is meant "The Shadow Over Innsmouth," "The Whisperer in Darkness," *At the Mountains of Madness*, and "The Shadow Out of Time." This is a very short list compared to what many Lovecraft fans would offer for "the Cthulhu Mythos." They would probably add "The Call of Cthulhu," "The Dunwich Horror," "The Dreams in the Witch House," "The Thing on the Doorstep," "The Haunter of the Dark," and perhaps others, as stories that are casually, if deliberately, related to one another through Lovecraft's use of common references and concepts. The "Mythos" elements in these, however, seem more incidental, or the story seems to lack gravity, as compared to the ones I have selected. Someone new to Lovecraft who reads the four I have cited and wants to read more will probably enjoy these other stories without feeling that they add much to the lore of the Mythos, and probably will feel that they are relatively conventional horror stories by comparison. Perhaps there is more "Mythos" in "The Mound," conventionally regarded as a collaboration between Lovecraft and Zealia Bishop. The detestable subterranean K'nyan civilization wallows in slavery, cruelty, mutilation, etc., so this story is more gruesome than the four stories I've chosen.

I've ignored Lovecraft's "Dream-World" stories such as *The Dream-Quest of Unknown Kadath* and relatively conventional horror stories such as "The Picture in the House," the Ambrose Biercesque "In the Vault," the Poesque "Cool Air," and the Satanist *Case of Charles Dexter Ward.*

Although the term "Cthulhu Mythos" has become widely used, it isn't Lovecraft's coinage, and readers should not assume that he took pains to make everything consistent as between every story that mentions Cthulhu, the *Necronomicon,* etc. However, the details in the four late stories I've focused on are probably consistent. Lovecraft seems originally to have had two motives in repeating names of places, forbidden books, entities, and persons in his stories: to provide a (bogus) sense of "lore," and to amuse himself and his writer friends in a playful in-group way, a little as Lewis did when he alluded to Tolkien's "Numinor" in one of the Ransom books, *That Hideous Strength*.

Tolkien is sometimes said to have desired to create "a mythology for England." Lovecraft evidently wanted to evoke a sort of "mythology for New England," since the Mythos stories usually have connections to that region. For example, if a long quotation may be allowed, here is the opening (following an epigraph from Charles Lamb) of Lovecraft's "Dunwich Horror;" in some moods, the reader may find it to be the best thing in the story:

When a traveller in north central Massachusetts takes the wrong fork at the junction of the Aylesbury pike just beyond Dean's Corners he comes upon a lonely and curious country. The ground gets higher, and the brier-bordered stone walls press closer and closer against the ruts of the dusty, curving road. The trees of the frequent forest belts seem too large, and the wild weeds, brambles, and grasses attain a luxuriance not often found in settled regions. At the same time the planted fields appear singularly few and barren; while the sparsely scattered houses wear a surprisingly uniform aspect of age, squalor, and dilapidation. Without knowing why, one hesitates to ask directions from the gnarled, solitary figures spied now and then on crumbling doorsteps or on the sloping, rock-strown meadows. Those figures are so silent and furtive that one feels somehow confronted by forbidden things, with which it would be better to have nothing to do. When a rise in the road brings the mountains in view above the deep woods, the feeling of strange uneasiness is increased. The summits are too rounded and symmetrical to give a sense of comfort and naturalness, and sometimes the sky silhouettes with especial clearness the queer circles of tall stone pillars with which most of them are crowned.

Gorges and ravines of problematical depth intersect the way, and the crude wooden bridges always seem of dubious safety. When the road dips again there are stretches of marshland that one instinctively dislikes, and indeed almost fears at evening when unseen whippoorwills chatter and the fireflies come out in abnormal profusion to dance to the raucous, creepily insistent rhythms of stridently piping bull-frogs. The thin, shining line of the Miskatonic's upper reaches has an oddly serpent-like suggestion as it winds close to the feet of the domed hills among which it rises.

As the hills draw nearer, one heeds their wooded sides more than their stone-crowned tops. Those sides loom up so darkly and precipitously that one wishes they would keep their distance, but there is no road by which to escape them. Across a covered bridge one sees a small village huddled between the stream and the vertical slope of Round Mountain, and wonders at the cluster of rotting gambrel roofs bespeaking an earlier architectural period than that of the neighbouring region. It is not reassuring to see, on a closer glance, that most of the houses are deserted and falling to ruin, and that the broken-steepled church now harbours the one slovenly mercantile establishment of the hamlet. One dreads to trust the tenebrous tunnel of the bridge, yet there is no way to avoid it. Once across, it is hard to prevent the impression of a faint, malign odour about the village street, as of the massed mould and decay of centuries. It is always a relief to get clear of the place, and to follow the narrow road around the base of the hills and across the level country beyond till it rejoins the Aylesbury pike. Afterward one sometimes learns that one has been through Dunwich.

Outsiders visit Dunwich as seldom as possible, and since a certain season of horror all the signboards pointing toward it have been taken down. The scenery, judged by any ordinary aesthetic canon, is more than commonly beautiful; yet there is no influx of artists or summer tourists. Two centuries ago, when talk of witch-blood, Satan-worship, and strange forest presences was not laughed at, it was the custom to give reasons for avoiding the locality. In our sensible age—since the Dunwich horror of 1928 was hushed up by those who had the town's and the world's welfare at heart—people shun it without knowing exactly why. Perhaps one reason—though it cannot apply to uninformed strangers—is that the natives are now repellently decadent, having gone far along that path of retrogression so common in many New England backwaters. They have come to form a race by themselves, with the well-defined mental and physical stigmata of degeneracy and inbreeding. The average of their intelligence is woefully low, whilst their annals reek of overt viciousness and of half-hidden murders, incests, and deeds of almost unnamable violence and perversity. The old gentry, representing the two or three armigerous families which came from Salem in 1692, have kept somewhat above the general level of decay; though many branches are sunk into the sordid populace so deeply that only their names remain as a key to the origin they disgrace. Some of the Whateleys and Bishops still send their eldest sons to Harvard and Miskatonic, though those sons seldom return to the mouldering gambrel roofs under which they and their ancestors were born.

What may for the sake of convenience be called "Lovecraft Country" is, like Mervyn Peake's Gormenghast, a real addition to the inventory of imaginary places. One might compare to the Dunwich description, the loving evocation of the grounds of Bracton College in Lewis's *That Hideous Strength*. There, of course, Lewis is not playing the ominous organ pedal that Lovecraft foots in the "Dunwich" passage; but in both cases the reader is invited to *slow down* and enjoy the antiquarian description:

> The only time I was a guest at Bracton I persuaded my host to let me into the Wood and leave me there alone for an hour. He apologised for locking me in.
>
> Very few people were allowed into Bragdon Wood. The gate was by Inigo Jones and was the only entry: a high wall enclosed the Wood, which was perhaps a quarter of a mile broad and a mile from east to west. If you came in from the street and went through the College to reach it, the sense of gradual penetration into a holy of holies was very strong. First you went through the Newton quadrangle which is dry and gravelly; florid, but beautiful, Gregorian buildings look down upon it. Next you must enter a cool tunnel-like passage, nearly dark at midday unless either the door into Hall should be open on your right or the buttery hatch on your left, giving you a glimpse of indoor daylight falling on panels, and a whiff of the smell of fresh bread. When you emerged from this tunnel you would find yourself in the medieval College: in the cloister of the much smaller quadrangle called Republic. The grass here looks very green after the aridity of Newton and the very stone of the buttresses that rise from it gives the impression of being soft and alive. Chapel is not far off: the hoarse, heavy noise of the works of a great and old clock comes to you from somewhere overhead. You went along this cloister, past slabs and urns and busts that commemorate dead Bractonians, and then down shallow steps into the full daylight of the quadrangle called Lady Alice. The buildings to your left and right were seventeenth-century work: humble, almost domestic in character, with dormer windows, mossy and grey-tiled. You were in a sweet,

Protestant world. You found yourself, perhaps, thinking of Bunyan or of Walton's *Lives*.

There were no buildings straight ahead on the fourth side of Lady Alice: only a row of elms and a wall: and here first one became aware of the sound of running water and the cooing of wood pigeons. The street was so far off by now that there were no other noises. In the wall there was a door. It led you into a covered gallery pierced with narrow windows on either side. Looking out through these, you discovered that you were crossing a bridge and the dark brown dimpled Wynd was flowing under you. Now you were very near your goal. A wicket at the far end of the bridge brought you out on the Fellows' bowling green, and across that you saw the high wall of the Wood, and through the Inigo Jones gate you caught a glimpse of sunlit green and deep shadows.

I suppose the mere fact of being walled in gave the Wood part of its peculiar quality, for when a thing is enclosed, the mind does not willingly regard it as common. As I went forward over the quiet turf I had the sense of being received. The trees were just so wide apart that one saw uninterrupted foliage in the distance but the place where one stood seemed always to be a clearing: surrounded by a world of shadows, one walked in mild sunshine. Except for the sheep whose nibbling kept the grass so short and who sometimes raised their long foolish faces to stare at me, I was quite alone; and it felt more like the loneliness of a very large room in a deserted house, than like any ordinary solitude out of doors. I remember thinking, "This is the sort of place which, as a child. one would have been rather afraid of or else would have liked very much indeed." A moment later I thought, "But when alone — really alone — everyone is a child: or no one?" Youth and age touch only the surface of our lives.

Half a mile is a short walk. Yet it seemed a long time before I came to the centre of the Wood. I knew it was the centre, for there was the thing I had chiefly come to see. It was a well: a well with steps going down to it and the remains of an ancient pavement about it. It was very imperfect now. I did not step on it, but I lay down in the grass and touched it with my fingers. For this was the heart of Bracton or Bragdon Wood: out of this all the legends had come and on this, I suspected... the very existence of the College had originally depended. The archaeologists were agreed that the masonry was very late British-Roman work, done on the eve of the Anglo-Saxon invasion. How Bragdon the wood was connected with Bracton the lawyer was a mystery, but I fancy myself that the Bracton family had availed themselves of an accidental similarity in the names to believe, or make believe, that they had something to do with it. Certainly, if all that was told were true, or even half of it, the Wood was older than the Bractons. I suppose no one now would attach much importance to Strabo's *Balachthon*, though it had led a sixteenth-century Warden of the College to say that, "We know not by ancientest report of any Britain without Bragdon." But the medieval song takes us back to the fourteenth century.

In Bragdon bricht this ende dai
Herde ich Merlin ther he lai
Singende woo and welawai.

It is good enough evidence that the well with the British-Roman
pavement was already "Merlin's Well," though the name is not found
till Queen Elizabeth's reign when good Warden Shovel surrounded
the Wood with a wall "for the taking away of all profane and hea-
thenish superstitions and the deterring of the vulgar sort from all
wakes, may games, dancings, mummings, and baking of Morgan's
bread, heretofore used about the fountain called in vanity Merlin's
Well, and utterly to be renounced and abominated as a gallimaufrey
of papistry, gentilism, lewdness and dunsicall folly." Not that the College had by this action renounced its own interest in the place. Old
Dr. Shovel, who lived to be nearly a hundred, can scarcely have been
cold in his grave when one of Cromwell's Major Generals, conceiv-
ing it his business to destroy "the groves and the high places," sent
a few troopers with power to impress the country people for this
pious work. The scheme came to nothing in the end; but there had
been a bicker between the College and the troopers in the heart
of Bragdon, and the fabulously learned and saintly Richard Crowe
had been killed by a musket-ball on the very steps of the Well. He
would be a brave man who would accuse Crowe either of popery or
"gentilism"; yet the story is that his last words had been, "Marry, Sirs,
if Merlin who was the Devil's son was a true King's man as ever ate
bread, is it not a shame that you, being but the sons of bitches, must
be rebels and regicides?" And always, through all changes, every Warden of Bracton, on the day of his election, had drunk a ceremonial
draught of water from Merlin's Well in the great cup which, both for
its antiquity and beauty, was the greatest of the Bracton treasures.

Since Lewis has treated us to a couple of invented antiquarian quotations, we may read a bit of pastiche
also from "The Dunwich Horror." Lovecraft's narrator writes:

In 1747 the Reverend Abijah Hoadley, newly come to the Congregational Church at
Dunwich Village, preached a memorable sermon on the close presence of Satan and his
imps; in which he said:
"It must be allow'd, that these Blasphemies of an infernall Train of Daemons are
Matters of too common Knowledge to be deny'd; the cursed Voices of *Azazel* and
Buzrael, of *Beelzebub* and *Belial,* being heard now from under Ground by above a Score
of credible Witnesses now living. I my self did not more than a Fortnight ago catch a
very plain Discourse of evil Powers in the Hill behind my House; wherein there were a
Rattling and Rolling, Groaning, Screeching, and Hissing, such as no Things of this Earth
cou'd raise up, and which must needs have come from those Caves that only black
Magick can discover, and only the Divell unlock."
 • Mr. Hoadley disappeared soon after delivering this sermon […]
 •
A little later in the story, we get this:

151

"Nor is it to be thought," ran the text as Armitage mentally translated it, "that man is either the oldest or the last of earth's masters, or that the common bulk of life and substance walks alone. The Old Ones were, the Old Ones are, and the Old Ones shall be. Not in the spaces we know, but *between* them, They walk serene and primal, undimensioned and to us unseen. *Yog-Sothoth* knows the gate. *Yog-Sothoth* is the gate. *Yog-Sothoth* is the key and guardian of the gate. Past, present, future, all are one in *Yog-Sothoth*. He knows where the Old Ones broke through of old, and where They shall break through again. He knows where They have trod earth's fields, and where They still tread them, and why no one can behold Them as They tread. By Their smell can men sometimes know Them near, but of Their semblance can no man know, *saving only in the features of those They have begotten on mankind;* and of those are there many sorts, differing in likeness from man's truest eidolon to that shape without sight or substance which is *Them*. They walk unseen and foul in lonely places where the Words have been spoken and the Rites howled through at their Seasons. The wind gibbers with Their voices, and the earth mutters with Their consciousness. They bend the forest and crush the city, yet may not forest or city behold the hand that smites. Kadath in the cold waste hath known Them, and what man knows Kadath? The ice desert of the South and the sunken isles of Ocean hold stones whereon Their seal is engraven, but who hath seen the deep frozen city or the sealed tower long garlanded with seaweed and barnacles? Great Cthulhu is Their cousin, yet can he spy Them only dimly. *Iä! Shub-Niggurath!* As a foulness shall ye know Them. Their hand is at your throats, yet ye see Them not; and Their habitation is even one with your guarded threshold. *Yog-Sothoth* is the key to the gate, whereby the spheres meet. Man rules now where They ruled once; They shall soon rule where man rules now. After summer is winter, and after winter summer. They wait patient and potent, for here shall They reign again."

That must be the text that launched a thousand fics; fan-fic efforts, that is. It must be the longest stretch Lovecraft composed as from the *Necronomicon*. In Lovecraft's legendarium, the *Necronomicon* is not only a conjurer's grimoire, but a work of the "real" pre-history of the earth. The latter aspect of it (only that!) makes it akin to Tolkien's *Red Book of Westmarch*.

An important difference between the Inklings and the Lovecraft circle authors must lie in their sense of their audience. Williams's novels were, for the most part, intended as "holiday" fiction, but he didn't write them for pulp magazines. His novels were published by Orwell's publisher, Gollancz, and by Faber, where T.S. Eliot was an editor. Other Williams books were published by Oxford University Press. Lewis and Tolkien were also published by Oxford, and their fiction generally appeared in hardcover book form and from respectable publishers. Lovecraft, Howard, and Smith, however, wrote with hope of publication in pulp magazines, notably *Weird Tales*, with its inevitably trashy cover paintings of plasticine pinup girls threatened by sadistic heathen priests and the like. They'd have known that the majority of their readers evidently wanted crude sensationalism.

From his letters, it appears that Lovecraft liked to shock readers but eventually aspired to something more poetic, as Blackwood aimed for in "The Willows." The conflict can break out into the open in Lovecraft's stories. In "The Shadow Over Innsmouth" he is at pains to create a strong element of regional flavor and a whole implied secret history of an obscure New England port town. One might compare the importance of setting in this story with that in Blackwood's tale of an autumnal French hill town, "Ancient Sorceries." Lovecraft's narrator learns a great deal about the history of Innsmouth, a reclusive Massachusetts town dating to colonial times. But despite his labors over these matters, Lovecraft's inner pulpster will not be suppressed. The narrator questions an alcoholic geezer who imparts swatches of important background information regarding Innsmouth's inhabitants, economy, etc. The scene culminates, however, in the geezer looking past the narrator's shoulder and seeing something frightening; whereupon he screams, and Lovecraft actually *sounds out* the screams: "'EH...AHHHH...AH! E'YAAHHHH...E...YAAHHHH!...YHAAAAAAA!'" One supposes that Lovecraft, if he had known that his story was going to appear in a book published by, say, Knopf, would have caught himself and omitted them. How astonishing it would have been if Tolkien had sounded out the screeches of the Nazgûl. The closest any Inkling comes to transcribing some horrible sound is Tolkien's spelling out of Gollum's unpleasant swallowing noise in *The Hobbit*, where children were intended as his primary audience.

7. Lovecraft as a Mythpoeic Writer Continued: Who Are His Peers?

In several places, C. S. Lewis discussed fantasists who wrote works that are compelling despite serious literary faults. These remarks might help us to understand why readers, perhaps including ourselves, read and reread Lovecraft, despite criticisms of his philosophy and recognition of defects in his style and characterization.

In "On Stories," "On Science Fiction," "The Mythopoeic Gift of Rider Haggard," and other pieces, Lewis championed the legitimacy of science fiction and fantasy. Lovecraft, whom Lewis never mentions, is not a peer of Coleridge ("The Rime of the Ancient Mariner," "Kubla Khan," "Christabel"), Stevenson (*The Strange Case of Dr. Jekyll and Mr. Hyde*), or Tolkien (*The Lord of the Rings*). Lewis cited these as works in which the gift for great fantasy has been complemented by "specifically literary powers." But the mythopoeic gift can exist where an author lacks literary powers or is unwilling to take the trouble to exercise them.

Lovecraft is not a peer of the Inklings. He is a peer of Rider Haggard, the author of the classic of fantastic adventure *She*. Haggard, C. S. Lewis argued, possessed the "mythopoeic gift" even though his literary artistry (like Lovecraft's) was defective.

Lewis bemoaned "the clichés, jocosities, frothy eloquence" in which Haggard (1865-1925) indulged in his romances about Ayesha, "She Who Must Be Obeyed," the beautiful and terrifying queen who has ruled a completely subjugated lost race for two thousand years. Haggard wrote a great many adventures also about an African big game hunter named Allan Quatermain, most of which occur before the time of *King Solomon's Mines*, the first one published. Lewis noted an irony; that Haggard seems amused by the "unliterary" manner of Quatermain's narratives. Lewis remarks, "It never dawned on [Haggard] that what he wrote in his own person was a great deal worse; 'literary' in the most damning sense of the word."

Haggard and Lovecraft both want to induce a mood of suspense and even dread in their readers. A remark that Lewis made about the book *King Solomon's Mines* and a movie adaptation he saw can help us get a handle on a recurrent problem in Lovecraft. Towards the end of *King Solomon's Mines*, the heroes seem to be doomed to starve slowly in a cold, lightless tomb, surrounded by the dead (Chapter 18). Haggard's book, Lewis wrote (in "On Stories"), imparted "a hushing spell on the imagination." Well, this wasn't good enough for the movie, which instead gave viewers an earthquake and a volcanic eruption, with inevitable noise and special effects. This version, Lewis thought, merely imparted a "rapid flutter" of nervous excitement, soon dispelled. Maybe the movie makers figured their idea was better suited to an auditorium full of popcorn munchers.

Something like this distinction about emotional effects applies in some Lovecraft stories. For example, in "The Whisperer in Darkness," the narrator listens to a recording surreptitiously made at night, and then mailed to him, by an isolated, elderly correspondent in rural Vermont. The recording is evidence that beings not of this earth who, moreover, traffic with even darker and more terrible powers, are meeting a human agent and communicating with him in weird, buzzing voices. Lovecraft succeeds in conjuring a sense of dread. But the payoff isn't up to this. At the end of the story there's some rigmarole in which

the elderly correspondent has been impersonated by one of the creatures, using imitation hands and face made of wax, and thus disguised the creature sits in the shadows. This preposterous pulp magazine "thrill" is a real letdown. Lewis praised Haggard: "From the move of his first pawn to the final checkmate, Haggard usually plays like a master. His openings (what story in the world opens better than *She*?) are full of alluring promise, and his catastrophes triumphantly keep it." The same is not true of Lovecraft.

It shouldn't take much argument to convince readers that Lovecraft's literary accomplishment is uneven, whether within a given story such as "The Whisperer," or from story to story. Lewis says something that applies to Lovecraft even though I doubt he had Lovecraft in mind. Lewis wrote, "In inferior romances, such as the American magazines of 'scientifiction' supply, we often come across a really suggestive idea. But the author has no expedient for keeping the story on the move except that of putting his hero into violent danger. In the hurry and scurry of his escapes the poetry of the basic idea is lost. In a much milder degree I think this has happened to [H. G. Wells] in the *War of the Worlds*. What really matters in this story is the idea of being attacked by something utterly 'outside.' As in Piers Plowman destruction has come upon us 'from the planets.' If the Martian invaders are merely dangerous, if we once become mainly concerned with the fact that they can kill us, why, then, a burglar or a bacillus can do as much." The key to the story is that the danger is of extraterrestrial origin.

This is often a problem for a writer such as Lovecraft. He has difficulties contriving what to do, with the mechanics of plots, when probably the real center of gravity is the idea of a "cosmic" weird menace. And so he resorts, once again, to the narrator who is falsely accused of insanity, or who fears that mankind will go mad when it learns what he knows (and which has evidently not caused him to lose his reason) Lovecraft's narrators never, in fact, do go mad. (Perhaps the narrator of "The Rats in the Walls" hallucinates the sound of scurrying rats; if so, the trauma apparently allows him to reason accurately in every other respect) Lovecraft deserves some sympathy for his struggles with the requirements of plot, particularly when writing for the pulps, given that the imaginative center of his stories is often something not, in its essence, narrative in nature.

The mythopoeic gift, Lewis came to believe, is distinct from literary artistry. "This gift, when it exists in full measure [as in Haggard's *She*], is irresistible. We can say of this, as Aristotle said of metaphor, 'no man can learn it from another.' It is the work of what Kipling called 'the daemon.' It triumphs over all obstacles and makes us tolerate all faults. It is quite unaffected by any foolish notions which the author himself, after the daemon has left him, may entertain about his own myths."

And here, from Lewis's "On Stories": "In inferior romances, such as the American magazines of 'scientifiction' supply, we often come across a really suggestive idea. But the author has no expedient for keeping the story on the move except that of putting his hero into violent danger. In the hurry and scurry of his escapes the poetry of the basic idea is lost. In a much milder degree I think this has happened to [H. G. Wells] in the *War of the Worlds*. What really matters in this story is the idea of being attacked by something utterly 'outside.' As in *Piers Plowman* destruction has come upon us 'from the planets.' If the

Martian invaders are merely dangerous, if we once become mainly concerned with the fact that they can *kill* us, why, then, a burglar or a bacillus can do as much." The key to the story is that the danger is of *extraterrestrial* origin.

This is often a problem for a writer such as Lovecraft. He has difficulties contriving what to *do*, with the mechanics of plots, when probably the real center of gravity is the *idea* of a "cosmic" weird menace. And so he resorts, once again, to the narrator who is falsely accused of insanity, or who fears that mankind will go mad when it learns what he knows (and which has evidently *not* caused him to lose his reason) Lovecraft's narrators never, in fact, do go mad. (Perhaps the narrator of "The Rats in the Walls" hallucinates the sound of scurrying rats; if so, the trauma apparently allows him to reason accurately in every other respect) Lovecraft deserves some sympathy for his struggles with the requirements of plot, particularly when writing for the pulps, given that the imaginative center of his stories is often something not, in its essence, narrative in nature.

The mythopoeic gift, Lewis came to believe, is distinct from literary artistry. "This gift, when it exists in full measure [as in Haggard's *She*], is irresistible. We can say of this, as Aristotle said of metaphor, 'no man can learn it from another.' It is the work of what Kipling called 'the daemon.' It triumphs over all obstacles and makes us tolerate all faults. It is quite unaffected by any foolish notions which the author himself, after the daemon has left him, may entertain about his own myths."

In that very valuable late work *An Experiment in Criticism*, Lewis turned to the discussion of myth. Here he was thinking primarily, I suppose, of the ancient stories we usually think of as myths. Again he states that the "mythical quality" may come through despite defects of literary artistry. "The man who first learns what is to him a great myth through a verbal account which is baldly or vulgarly or cacophonously written, discounts and ignores the bad writing and attends solely to the myth. He hardly minds about the writing. ...The value of myth is not a specifically literary value, nor the appreciation of myth a specifically literary experience."

Lewis adds (and this is surely significant for Lovecraft, given the oft-mentioned objection that HPL "telegraphs" the endings of his stories such that what apparently is meant to be a surprise is no surprise), "The pleasure of myth depends hardly at all on such usual narrative attractions as suspense or surprise. Even at a first hearing it is felt to be inevitable. And the first hearing is chiefly valuable in introducing us to a permanent object of contemplation, more like a thing than a narration, which works upon us by a peculiar flavour or quality.... Sometimes...there is hardly any narrative element."

Lovecraft had to write *something* in order to capture the mood of "a strange sense of adventurous expectancy" that he cherished from his dreams; and so also for "cosmic outsideness."

Moreover, Lewis adds, "Human sympathy is at a minimum. We do not project ourselves at all strongly into the characters." Critics may sometimes have condemned Lovecraft's characters for lacking depth and complexity. It would be profitable to ask how much depth and complexity a given character should have for a given story. In "The Shadow Over Innsmouth," we need to be able to take an interest in the protagonist-narrator as a plausible college student because, insofar as Lovecraft pulls off what he is aiming for (cf. Aristotle's *anagnorisis*), appalling moments of recognition for himself and for the reader are supposed to happen simultaneously. In *At the Mountains of Madness* the characters need to be believable as scientists, but that will come primarily by means of the narration's use of geologic, topographic, etc. details which Lovecraft got up conscientiously. Those who have read about how bad Lovecraft's style is supposed to be might read the first few pages of this short novel. They will find that Lovecraft could command a disciplined and specific but haunting style. Thereafter, their feeling about photographs of Antarctic regions may be affected by Lovecraft.

Lovecraft's central characters in the Mythos stories are usually scholarly bachelors. As with M. R. James's antiquarian ghost stories, this is economical and appropriate; the problem arises when too many of the stories are read at the same time so that repetitiveness becomes an issue.

Lovecraft's Mythos protagonists are almost never men of action like Quatermain, although the Antarctic explorers in *Mountains* are sturdy guys. Like Quatermain, or Ludwig Horace Holly in *She*,

Lovecraft's explorers are not themselves "mythic," though they may appear in mythopoeic fantasy. They are people like us, not mythic heroes like Odysseus.

8. What Factors Disqualify HPL (and Members of His Circle) as Mythopoeic Authors Comparable to the Inklings?

I think the essence of the Lovecraftian mythopoeic quality, as opposed to the inevitable trajectory of the stories towards horror, can be stated concisely: *the great secret is that the universe, including this planet, was, and is, haunted* or even "infested."

C. S. Lewis

The logic of Lovecraft's futilitarian mechanistic materialism tended to work against the mythopoeic sense, and this might have complicated things for him if he had lived to keep on writing. Lovecraft said that beholding a glorious sunset could produce in him a sense of "adventurous expectancy." But his philosophy works all the other way. It is reductive. It collapses all experience into something that is "nothing but" something else that is *finally less interesting.* He would have to accept that the sunset that moves him is "nothing but" an excitation of his nerves and a corresponding stimulation of associated memories. If he is to be consistent, the sense of wonder must not be privileged as an exception; he may "feel this way" and it matters to him, but his experience is really no more meaningful or valid than that of anyone else in any state of attention and imaginative activity.

For Lewis, the experience of sudden joy was a pointer to some greater thing. His heroine Psyche in *Till We Have Faces* knows how profound imaginative experience has a beckoning quality that blessedly troubles our everyday moods; and when she enters the realm of the gods, she knows whence that beckoning has come. The mythopoeic sense and the sense of wonder are expansive: *there's more!*, they suggest to us. But mechanistic materialism is reductive: it's all a matter of *nothing but*, it says to us. Lewis found the way to unite his imaginative side and his reasoning side, to their mutual flourishing. Lovecraft must remain inwardly divided.

The Inklings and the Lovecraft circle authors differ as regards the depiction of the horrible. The former are restrained in their presentation of horrible things. Consider Tolkien's Orcs. Really very little is written about their appearance. When Williams wishes to indicate the dreadful judgment that overtakes the wicked Giles Tumulty, in *Many Dimensions,* he writes, "When they found him, but a few moments after that raucous scream had terrified the household, he was lying on the floor amid the shattered furniture twisted in every limb, and pierced and burnt all over as if by innumerable needle-points of fire" (end of Chapter 16). That's about all. Perhaps the most gruesome passage in the writing released by the Inklings in their lifetimes comes in *That Hideous Strength;* the escaped laboratory animals, maddened through Merlin's magic, wreaking the vengeance of the gods upon the N.I.C.E. banqueters. The episode has been too much for some readers. Others find it fully justifiable. In any event, it may be noticed that the emphasis, in Lewis's rendition, is upon the confounding, ruinous movement of the animals and the panic and dismay of the wicked, not upon dismembered bodies.

In contrast, the *Weird Tales* authors exploit the gruesome. One may direct the curious to Smith's "The Vaults of Yoh-Vombis," Howard's "The Black Stone," or Lovecraft's "The Thing on the Doorstep" for samples of these authors' wallowing in revolting detail. To quote Joseph Koerner's recent *Bosch and Bruegel: From Enemy Painting to Everyday Life* on the former artist: "yet hell's gruesome fascinations are the quintessential objects of the mindless curiosity of visual desire. According to its Christian critics (and these were legion), curiosity is primarily about unrest, dissatisfaction, and dispersion, and only secondarily about delight. Saint Augustine wrote that humans evince the vicious lust of the eye, or *concupiscentia oculorum*, not only in face of erotic enchantments but (more inexplicably) in their uncontrollable fixation on the ugly: on mangled carcasses, cruel sports, 'a lizard catching flies'" (p. 186).

H. P. Lovecraft

The Lovecraft story in which some gruesome detail seems most justifiable is "The Colour Out of Space," perhaps his finest, though marginal at most to the Cthulhu Mythos. A meteorite falls and soon living things in its vicinity sicken, become brittle, and die. It seems to me, with its evocation of trouble from the stars, that this story possesses the mythopoeic quality. A genuine element of pathos develops, a remarkable achievement for the author of rubbish such as "Pickman's Model." But that pathos coexists with what may be called a Classical detachment from the sufferers; there is something here that might suggest Sophocles. Edwin O'Brien selected "The Colour Out of Space" for the Roll of Honor appendix to *The Best American Short Stories* for 1928.

The Lovecraft stories in which the mythopoeic quality is minimal or nonexistent, such as "The Tomb," may be entertaining, but if he had written only such thrillers, his reputation would be nothing like what it is.

If Lewis had read Lovecraft's "Colour Out of Space," *At the Mountains of Madness*, and "The Shadow Out of Time," maybe he would have recognized the American author as a peer or near peer of Haggard (not Haggard at his best) as a writer of mythopoeia. It is pleasant to think that there is a very decent chance that Lewis did get to read at least the last two of these stories in *Astounding*, even if it should turn out that he didn't read them in time to be influenced by them.

Lewis's library contained August Derleth's 1948 anthology *Strange Ports of Call*, which reprinted *At the Mountains of Madness*. I presume that the book had been Joy Lewis's. She was interested in science fiction and in America had been a member of the circle around Fletcher Pratt, and when she relocated to England had connected with the London science fiction scene (see John Christopher's "Notes on Joy" in Encounter, April 1987). A shared interest in science fiction must have been one of these things that drew Lewis and Joy together. One wonders if they ever discussed Lovecraft. In any event, Lewis might well have read the Lovecraft novel in *Strange Ports of Call* and found it enjoyable. (For what it's worth, the anthology also includes a science fiction horror story by Smith, "Master of the Asteroid." From its jingly title to its trite conclusion, it's a mediocre thing, but it's probably the Smith story most likely to have been read by Lewis.)

If Lovecraft's Mythos fiction shows such conformity to, or affinity with, the qualities Lewis discerned in mythopoeic fiction, should it have been integrated into the Mythopoeic Society? I doubt that anyone by now will be thinking strongly that it should. After all, Lovecraft always works with the horror story template. Whatever the atmosphere of wonder he engenders, the story must progress towards the evocation of fear, horror, terror. He's writing dark fantasy, not high fantasy.

Tolkien coined the term *eucatastrophe* in "On Fairy-Stories", the consoling happy ending. But Lovecraft's stories end dyscatastrophically. The protagonist, and probably the human race, are worse off at the end than they were to begin with, or realize that they always were worse off than they have suspected till now. The sense is that the best one can hope for is a delay in the inevitable demise. The narrator is confined, under suspicion of madness or murder; or he is physically free but convinced that mass insanity and barbarism, or indeed extinction, are imminent. ("The Shadow Over Innsmouth" may seem to be an exception, because the narrator accepts, at last, that in his veins flows the blood of the hybrids, and anticipates being able to join them in their aquatic worship of Dagon. But however happy the narrator feels when he accepts his destiny, readers are supposed to be horrified. The narrator has impressed upon them the repulsive appearance, foul odor, etc. of the Innsmouthites as their nonhuman genetics become more and more manifest in maturity. Thus, this story too ends dyscatastrophically.) The dyscatastrophic Lovecraft ending is meant to suggest, not consolation, but the brutal exposure of the false consolations of what we have ordinarily thought was life; the more we learn, as we apply the scientific method, the less the universe will appear to us to be a good place.

The Inklings' understanding was radically different. They believed in a beautiful, orderly cosmos that is a radiant hierarchy, where even the least of things has its own beauty and goodness, and which is permeated by divine love. They would have said, of the vision of glory that concludes Dante's *Comedy*, that it errs only in falling short of what the reality shall be.

J. R. R. Tolkien

The Latin motto of the Mythopoeic Society during Goodknight's presidency was *Laeta in Chorea Magna,* "Joyful in the Great Dance," the Great Dance being the image of the beautiful, orderly, living cosmos in Lewis's *Perelandra.* For contrast, in Lovecraft's late story "The Haunter of the Dark," we are offered a notion of the final nature of things that could sound like a dismal parody of the Great Dance. We read there of "the ancient legends of Ultimate Chaos, at whose center sprawls the blind idiot god Azathoth, Lord of All Things, encircled by his flopping horde of mindless and amorphous dancers, and lulled by the thin monotonous piping of a demoniac flute held in nameless paws." Lovecraft was not an appropriate author for exploration as the Mythopoeic Society developed.

Yet it seems to me that when we put Lovecraft's best work alongside Lewis's space trilogy and Tolkien's Middle-earth fantasy, our enjoyment of the work of all three writers may be enhanced because this may impress us again with the capacity they had for the writing of imaginative, and even mythopoeic (obviously, in the case of Lewis and Tolkien; and arguably, in Lovecraft's), fiction. Lovecraft was no peer of Lewis and Tolkien, but of Haggard, and not the Haggard who wrote *She* but lesser works, *Allan Quatermain* and *Ayesha: The Return of She.*

*Some readers of this article will believe that it should have dealt with Lovecraft's fantasy stories such as "The Quest of Iranon," "The Cats of Ulthar," *The Dream-Quest of Unknown Kadath,* etc. They might even hold that these stories, and not the ones I discuss, comprise Lovecraft's best claim to be a mythopoeic author. The "dream" or "Dunsanian" Lovecraft stories may have their charms, but they seem to me decidedly minor efforts in both bulk and literary achievement as contrasted with Lovecraft's mature writings or various books of Haggard. Lovecraft's Dunsanian phase was something HPL had to outgrow before he could write the work upon which his claim to literary importance resides.

**Lewis was writing years before *The Lord of the Rings* was finished, let alone published, so I am not sure that he would always have said MacDonald was the greatest of all fantasists.

SOURCES for Lewis quotations: "The Mythopoeic Gift of Rider Haggard," "On Science Fiction," "On Stories," and "Unreal Estates" in *Of Other Worlds*; Preface to *George MacDonald: An Anthology*; *An Experiment in Criticism*. See also the three volumes of his Collected Letters.

"The Lovecraft Circle and the Inklings: The 'Mythopoeic Gift' of H. P. Lovecraft." Mallorn: The Journal of the Tolkien Society No. 59 (Winter 2018): 18-32.

"The Lovecraft Circle and the Inklings" is a streamlined version of an essay by Dale Nelson published in 2019 in *Mallorn*, the journal of the Tolkien Society. The essay has been extensively edited and revised by the author."

THE SHIP OF ATHERON

by Andrew M. Seddon

Greece, 1938

It had been a hot summer in Greece. Perhaps they always were. And for Howard Arthur Sheffield, once a British Army corporal, but a wanderer since the Great War, it had been a summer occupied visiting various ancient cities including Philippi, Corinth, Thessalonica, and, of course, Athens; major centers of population in Roman times, and notable for their connection to early Christianity. While meandering through mazes of impressive ruins or sitting in deserted theaters, Sheffield had spent untold hours allowing his mind to wander, imagining them in their heyday, when Saint Paul trod their once bustling streets.

Baltasar, his sable Alsatian, endured in stoical silence, no doubt wondering what his human found so interesting. Baltasar lived for work, and in these places there was none.

In between times, Sheffield took such odd jobs as presented themselves, although being a man of simple needs and tastes, his financial requirements were minimal.

He hadn't planned on being here; wherever here was. He'd accepted a ride from a lorry driver who said he was heading west to the coast. The direction hadn't mattered to Sheffield, but being near water was inviting. And so he'd ended up at the seashore, at this small town the name of which he could never get his tongue around; a town which the lorry driver seemed curiously reluctant to enter and eager to leave.

"Are you sure you want to stay?" the man asked as he unloaded his goods outside a shop in the town center. His English was good but limited. "I can drop you off somewhere else."

159

"Here is fine," Sheffield said, scanning the array of quaint buildings clustered around a small harbor. "One place is as good as another."

"Not in my books," the driver replied, slinging bags and boxes from his lorry into an untidy pile.

"What's so bad about this town?" Sheffield asked.

The man shook his head. "One hears things..." He crossed himself. "But do as you wish."

The driver waved him goodbye as he departed.

Sheffield shrugged. No matter; he found the sight and sound of the sea which he could see at the end of a street comforting after months spent among parched land and dusty relics.

"Let's find somewhere to stay," he said to Baltasar.

Directed to a small, inexpensive cottage by a shopkeeper, he found the lodging with ease and set about relaxing.

And if the people inhabiting the whitewashed cottages that clung to the rocky hillside were a little odd...reclusive, taciturn, and with an unusual physiognomy...that was all right with him as well. Since he spoke no more than a handful of words of Greek and many of them spoke equally little English, conversation didn't rank highly on his list of priorities.

Still, although located off the beaten path, the town didn't lack for tourists, although not as many as he might have expected. Positioned on the patio of a small café, his table shaded by an umbrella, Baltasar curled up underneath with a bowl of water, Sheffield would watch them pass by, amusing himself creating stories about them.

The short man wearing a black frock coat was obviously a self-important banker, the attractive, exotically dressed woman with him not his wife.

The lean, withered looking man a lawyer, potentially a crooked one, perhaps hoping to scavenge some business from an unsuspecting mark.

The woman walking two small children probably a nanny, and not one who enjoyed her position or her charges at that, judging from the way she jerked them along.

The furtive chap probably a pickpocket; the beggar too well fed to be truly in need; the retired colonel fleeing an unhappy marriage; the young rakes looking for cheap thrills...and so it went.

Perhaps his guesses were accurate, perhaps not. It didn't matter. In fact, nothing really seemed to matter here. It was a place of lethargy and indolence, a place where one day blended seamlessly into the next, like a stream flowing without a ripple to mark its passing.

It was, Sheffield thought, as lifeless as Zeus and Poseidon and Athena and all the other extinct deities that had once been worshipped in Greece and whose crumbling temples dotted the countryside.

And yet, it wasn't totally lifeless, for every now and then, he fancied that he felt something strange, an undercurrent that he couldn't put his finger on. Perhaps it was an odd glance from one of the peculiar appearing locals, a conversation cut short when he approached, a person changing direction abruptly as if to avoid him. And perhaps it was only his imagination or his digestion. Regardless, it could be unsettling or unnerving.

Generally, though, he was content here, relaxed in his small cottage, happy to sit on the veranda or at the café and watch the fishing boats come and go, their white sails dotting the blue of the sea. He made the casual acquaintance of a few of the other English speaking tourists. A sort of lassitude, or complacency, overcame him.

Perched above the town was a little Greek Orthodox church. He had wandered up to it one day, to find it in a state of neglect and disrepair, a broken lock hanging on the door. The rusty hinges had yielded reluctantly to a hard push and he'd entered the dusty, but cool, interior. Baltasar sprawled in the vestibule while he entered the narthex, where statues and icons looked down somberly from their perches while Mary, St George, St Nicholas, and Christ himself regarded him from faded frescoes.

Forlorn; that was how the church felt.

Forlorn, but almost with a sense of welcome, that it was happy he had come.

He saw no other footprints on the floor, and wondered how long it had been since anyone had ventured inside, since the church had experienced worship, since Mass had been said, and why the church was shuttered.

He sat down on the floor of the nave to absorb the atmosphere, and it was only the fading of the light coming through the cracked panes and

Baltasar's hungry grumbles that told him he had been there for hours.

Over the weeks that followed, sometimes, in the heat of the day, he'd return. There, surrounded by the icons and memorials to the dead, he could imagine himself in the presence of the divine and seek relief from a nagging sense of unease.

Was the time ripe to move on?

Was something expected of him?

Perhaps, perhaps.

But otherwise, he could sit at the café sipping Greek Mountain Tea as he was now...

"Excuse me, sir, may I offer you the opportunity to join an excursion?" The accent was heavy, but the English perfectly understandable.

Sheffield started and half turned to look at the woman who now stood beside him. She wore a mid-thigh length white linen dress fastened over her right shoulder. The left shoulder, bare. A jeweled necklace of unusual design (a stylized sea creature?) sparkled against her bosom. For a moment, with her perfect, well formed figure, he thought he was seeing someone out of Greek mythology. Blonde haired, blue eyed, and...what? Her face should have been as mesmerizing as her figure, but... For a moment, he couldn't put his finger on it, but it was as if something was slightly amiss...

And it wasn't as though her face possessed the odd characteristics that he'd noticed to be universal among the population of the town: eyes slightly too large and unnaturally protuberant; noses broad and excessively flared; ears small and low set, necks thick and slightly webbed.

No, there was nothing amiss with her features.

Perhaps it was the expression in her eyes; a hint of mischief stopping just short of insolence...

"What sort of excursion?" he asked cautiously.

She smiled, revealing perfect teeth. "A boat trip. Sightseeing."

He sighed. "I'm not sure..."

"Bring your wife."

"I'm not married."

"Then your dog."

A strange remark. Sheffield looked at Baltasar where he was lying at his feet. It was true, the dog had been somewhat restless of late. One could never accuse the big Alsatian of complacency. Lying around all day must be boring him to tears.

He was staring at the woman intently, almost in a perplexed manner as if the dog didn't quite know what to make of her.

That made two of them.

"If the lighting is good, you might glimpse the sunken city," she urged.

"There's a sunken city here?" He'd heard of Epidaurus and Archampoli, although he hadn't visited them. He shouldn't be surprised to learn of another one.

"Oh yes. Very ancient. Well worth seeing."

That decided him. "All right then."

"Be at the harbor at daybreak, just as the sun is touching the sea. You will find *Atheron's Desire* moored there."

"What does the excursion cost?"

"Whatever you like. Pay only if it pleases you."

"Not a very sound business practice."

"It is a special promotion."

"Very well, Miss..." he paused.

"Até," she said, pronouncing it as 'Ah-tee'.

"'Ah-tee,'" Sheffield repeated.

Curious, Sheffield thought, as she turned with an elegant swish of her linen dress and departed. Still, he loved the sea; what Englishman didn't? In fact, he'd considered joining the Navy at the outbreak of the Great War, but the Army had a greater need for men and he'd ended up in the King's Liverpool Regiment instead. But for the grace of God he might have been blown to smithereens in the Battle of Jutland, instead of somehow surviving four years of carnage on land. Sometimes he wondered if he had made the right decision.

*

Sheffield wasn't sure what to expect when he strolled down deserted streets to the harbor just as the sky was flush with the early pink of dawn, Baltasar trotting happily beside him. But there, moored alongside the usual array of fishing boats lay a lateen-rigged three-masted xebec, graceful and undoubtedly fast;. The type corsairs would have used to devastating effect in centuries past.

"Welcome aboard," Até greeted, waving to him from the end of a gangplank.

161

Sheffield motioned for Baltasar to precede him, but the big dog hesitated, one paw on the gangplank, his stance rigid.

"Go on," Sheffield said, giving him a nudge. "You've been on boats before."

Baltasar cast him a look full of reproach, then made his way carefully along.

Sheffield stepped onto the main deck, joining a group of people already gathered there. Some of them he recognized from having seen pass by in the streets, a few he had engaged in conversation.

There was the amateur archaeologist, a tall, lean woman equipped with binoculars and camera, obsessed with legends of Atlantis and Mu and hoping to make a great discovery. A dapper French university student engaged on some sort of literary project involving obscure legends. A sixty-something American divorcée plastered with make-up who appeared determined to snare a much younger man...Sheffield was glad that he didn't appear to make the cut and that an immaculately groomed and attired Italian *bon vivant* had attracted her cloying attention. A long haired Spanish artistic type he'd seen painting harbor scenes in a particularly garish and grotesque style. A somewhat rotund former seminarian who'd regaled him for an hour or more in atrocious English supplemented with an overabundance of Latin, determined to make it perfectly clear and obvious that he wanted to live life to the fullest and how inconsequential he now found theological study.

Altogether twelve, including himself. Baltasar appeared uninterested in any of them, his focus more upon the crew.

Até cleared her throat. "Thank you for joining Captain Haralambos aboard *Atheron's Desire.*" She indicated a stocky man standing aft by the ship's wheel. "I am certain that you will have an experience that you will never forget."

"I hope she's right," one of the passengers grumbled. "I've been fleeced out of enough drachmas already."

Sheffield wondered if the man had been offered the same deal the woman had given him.

"It should be a clear day for sailing," Até was saying. "Please enjoy." She moved away to join the captain.

Several deckhands began to hoist sails while others released the mooring ropes. *Atheron's Desire* gathered way quickly and, propelled by a light breeze, steered for the entrance of the bay. Sheffield watched the sailors as they worked. Clad in typical fishermen's hats and cotton shirts and pants, they were indistinguishable from the crews of the local fishing boats. And, like them, also shared in the same odd physiognomy. He wondered why he found that disturbing.

The passengers milled idly around the deck. It hadn't struck him before, but now he realized that there were no couples, only solitary individuals such as himself.

"I can hardly wait to see the sunken city," the amateur archaeologist commented. "I wonder if I'll be able to capture any photos. Do you know anything of its history?"

Sheffield shook his head. "I'd never even heard of it until yesterday. Até might know more."

"Strange name, don't you think?"

"What? Ate?"

"Yes. The goddess of mischief and delusion, of irrationality and rashness. Not a name I would choose for my child. If I had one."

Até, Sheffield noticed, had left the captain and now stood near the bowsprit, almost as if she were a figurehead.

"There's no accounting for taste," he said of the name.

"I suppose not," the woman chuckled. "I'd better check my film, just in case."

Sheffield left her to rummage in her camera bag and made his way forward. Leaning against the portside rail, he watched the cliffs and the town recede and the sea sluice along the side of the hull to foam into a wake. Sea gulls soared above the masts. He inhaled the clean sea air, and felt a renewal of vigor.

In a short while they rounded the headland and entered the azure expanse of the Aegean. Sheffield hadn't gone island hopping, but it might be something to consider.

"Most sunken cities are fairly near the coastline," the amateur archaeologist remarked, joining him. "Earthquakes and changing sea levels account for them. And you wonder who built them, and when, and were their civilizations more advanced than we realize."

Sheffield didn't respond, as the sky seemed to be growing darker, although he hadn't noticed the approach of any clouds.

"I wonder if we're in for a bit of a blow," he said at last.

She looked up. "How very curious...it's as though the sky is changing color...or the sun is fading..."

Sheffield scanned the other passengers. Several of them were also regarding the sky with anxious expressions.

He beckoned to Até, and when she came over, said, "We're wondering about the weather. Should we be turning back?"

She shook her head. "It is nothing. Just a trick of the light. We'll be over Atheron shortly."

But instead of clearing, the sky darkened to grey, shot through with iridescent sheets of multicolored lightning, as if a rainbow were being shattered.

The sea, which had been as smooth and clear as glass began to roil and undulate. The xebec rolled and pitched.

"We're definitely heading into a squall," Sheffield said, holding onto a ratline for support. Baltasar stood braced with his legs widely splayed.

"Captain Haralambos!" he called, but now wind was whistling through the rigging and the captain seemed not to hear him.

"Exhilarating, isn't it?" the amateur archaeologist enthused.

The American divorcée had wrapped a death grip around the Italian *bon vivant* whose expression had turned decidedly sickly.

"Até!" Sheffield shouted, but she had resumed her position near the bowsprit and stood with arms extended, her hair streaming past her face.

And then it was as if the sea opened up, and he was staring down a watery chasm into which the ship plunged as if it had toppled over the lip of an invisible waterfall. Somebody...several somebodies... screamed. At any moment he expected a wave to burst over the rail and sweep them from the deck.

Down and down plunged the xebec, further and further, into the yawning chasm, descending an impossible avenue into the depths.

An illusion. It had to be an illusion...tea and a sesame bread ring for breakfast...that wouldn't account for it...

From far below came a luminescence, but of such a shade that Sheffield was at a loss to describe it. It was blue, but it wasn't. Turquoise, amethyst, azure, sapphire, all of them and none of them. Swirling, mutating, blending, separating, coalescing...a bizarre kaleidoscope that almost seemed as if it were alive...

And perhaps it was, for dark, nebulous forms...or parts of one gigantic form...swam through the shifting colors like sharks circling a prey...but eluding definition...

And then, further down, walls, towers, a citadel gleaming black. Phosphorescence glinting off ramparts and pylons...cyclopean walls formed of immense basalt blocks, blocks so huge that surely no human agency could have maneuvered them into place.

"There it is!" Até yelled, somehow making her voice heard. Atheron!"

The amateur archaeologist shrieked with delight and began snapping photos.

Sheffield tore his gaze away from the city.

Those passengers that weren't huddled on the deck in an extremity of fear clung to the rigging. The former seminarian appeared to be praying; at least his lips were moving. Or maybe he was cursing; Sheffield couldn't tell. The artist stood as rigid as if he'd been subsumed into one of his still life paintings, while the French literature student's mouth hung open, frozen in a never ending scream, insanity dancing in his eyes. Slumped down, the divorcée had fainted, her arms still clutching the legs of the wretched *bon vivant*.

And the crew...was it his imagination or had their facial distortions become more pronounced? And the captain, hunched over the wheel like a giant amphibian, a caricature of a human...

And then Sheffield sensed it.

A feeling. No, a certainty; that something was wrong, that something existed here, something foreign, alien, that didn't belong on this world or any world. Something that had no place here. More than that, Atheron itself seemed to exude an evil, an evil so ancient, so long dormant, that its name had been lost to humanity...something, some entity, imprisoned within those grim walls...and yet that could still reach out even from the confines of its prison...

Something that needed, hungered for, human lives, human slaves, human souls…

Then, suddenly, a voice emerged from the storm.

Step out of the boat.

Did he hear the words, despite the raging wind and sea, or were they in his mind? Was this all real or the worst hallucination he had ever experienced? Had the head injuries he'd suffered during the Great War finally caught up to him?

Step out of the boat.

Sheffield looked around in desperation. It would be certain death, surely, to abandon the security of the ship for the maelstrom that surrounded him. He would drown in minutes.

A third time.

Step out of the boat.

He had an image of Saint Peter stepping out of a boat in the middle of a storm to walk on water, however briefly.

But he was no saint, no Peter.

O you of little faith! Why do you doubt?

The dark towers and cyclopean walls that soared up from the abyssal depths grew larger and larger, filling his field of vision. In a moment, the ship would crash into them; or, as he realized, speed through a massive arch which reared up dead ahead, like an open mouth ready to engulf them.

Até's face shone with malevolent ecstasy, her eyes blazing with blue fire.

Suddenly, his mind was made up.

"Jump!" he shouted to the amateur archaeologist, convinced now it was the thing to do.

"Are you crazy?" she shouted back. "And leave the thrill of a lifetime?"

"It's now or never!"

"Never!"

He lunged for her arm, intending to take her with him, but she spun away.

Baltasar shoved against his leg.

The arch loomed above the masts.

Sheffield placed his hands on the rail. He prayed:

Kyrie eleison.
Christe eleison.

Lord, have mercy.
Christ, have mercy.

Then vaulted over. Baltasar leaped after him.

He slammed into the surging wall of water as *Atheron's Desire* disappeared through the arch and the city vanished into the whirling chaos...

*

...and he was floating in the warm waters of the Aegean, Baltasar dog-paddling alongside. Nearby, a small wooden fishing boat bobbed in the swell.

"Hello!" Sheffield called, waving an arm. "Over here! Over here!"

The two men in the boat exchanged glances, then turned the boat in his direction. Strong arms reached down to raise first him, then Baltasar into the boat.

"Do you speak English?" Sheffield asked.

The men nodded. "Yes."

"That's a relief. That was some storm, wasn't it?"

"Storm?" one of the men frowned.

"Blue sky," the other man added, waving an arm. "All day."

"But...“ Sheffield looked around in confusion. There wasn't a cloud in sight. The sea was still. He saw no debris floating on the water.

Baltasar shook, sending gleaming droplets flying.

"Too much ouzo," one of the men commented. "Bad for Englishman." They laughed.

"I am not drunk!" Sheffield exclaimed. "I was on a boat, *Atheron's Desire,* and a great storm came up...“ He broke off at the startled look on the mens' faces. They were faces, he noticed, that showed none of the unusual features which had seemed to be so common among the villagers he'd seen.

The older man pointed towards the bay. "You come from that town?

"I was staying there, yes," Sheffield replied.

"It is cursed," said the younger man, making the sign of the cross on his chest. "The town and the ship. They worship Nyct..."

"NO!" The older man's exclamation slashed across the word, and the younger broke off. "We do not say that name. Never!" He stared at his colleague for a long moment, then shifted his gaze to Sheffield. "No one who steps on that ship ever returns." He gave a mirthless chuckle. "Either you are a very lucky man, my friend, or God must have been looking out for you. And your dog as well."

Step out of the boat.

"Yes," Sheffield said softly, peering down into the sea where the ship and its passengers had disappeared. "I believe he was."

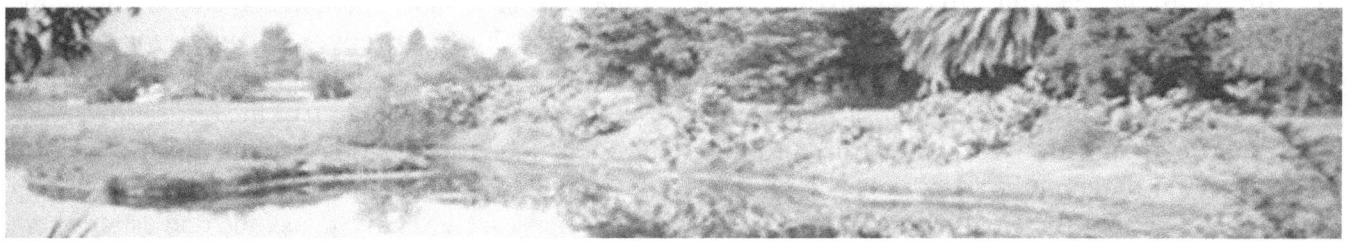

The Thing From the Tarn

by Pierre V. Comtois

Jake Torros congratulated himself on finding the perfect hideout.

At the moment, he was standing in the center of a spacious den with an open hearth on one side and big bay window on the adjoining wall. Outside, a long, unpaved driveway ran through rows of giant maples or oaks or whatever they were, down to the distant road.

Old but comfortable couches and stuffed chairs enclosed the space before the fireplace, where a warm blaze was burning against a cold, overcast November day. The room seemed gloomier than it was due to the dark, ancient wood that covered the walls. A dining area led to a small library that in turn gave onto a living room on the other side of the building.

This portion of the house, according to the real estate agent, was built in the 1700s with others added over the years until it boasted a good twenty rooms, most of them bedrooms. Bedding down in the farthest one was like living in a different county! But it was just the thing for Jake who needed to keep a low profile for a few months until the heat died down.

That armored car robbery he and his partners had conducted went without a hitch and they got away with a cool million easy. They buried the loot in a cemetery outside Dunwich and as agreed, split up until it was time to get together again at a McDonald's in downtown Methuen,

Massachusetts. There, they'd decided if it was safe to recover the money and divvy it up after which, they'd go their separate ways. And looking around the house now, Jake was inclined to return here, outside Prospect, Maine, and settle down. He might even decide to buy the old manse for himself. Pleased with the idea, he passed through the kitchen area, that had been updated to include all the modern appliances of course, and into the narrow space that led to a bathroom on one hand, and a big bedroom that faced the backyard area and the gray, featureless woods beyond. It was the only bedroom on the ground floor and convenient to the kitchen and fireplace so he'd decided to stick close.

He finished his unpacking and studied the woods through the bedroom's paned window. There was a big, unattractive fenced in area where a gaggle of dirty chickens pecked around in the mud surrounding a dilapidated coop. He sure didn't envy those poor buggers. Farther in back stood the forest. He was pretty sure there were no other houses back there as he hadn't see any lights shining among the trees the night before. That was good. One of the attractions of renting the place was its isolation from neighbors. The less anyone saw of him the better even though there was small chance of being recognized as one of the masked gang that robbed the armored car. That was about a week ago and already the news had disappeared from the TV with presidential election and distant wars reasserting themselves on the news casts. Fine by him.

He lit a cigarette and took a satisfied puff. Yeah, things were going smooth, just the way they'd figured it. His only problem now was what to do to kill time until he met the guys again in a few months. He thought of the little library and snorted. Nothing in there more recent than thirty years ago, maybe longer. He'd checked almost first thing. And Prospect, population 422, sure didn't promise any excitement beyond the local yokels jawing at the feed store about the weather and how to keep the pigs warm during the winter.

He fell asleep that night wondering what was going on in the farthest bedroom in the house, miles away it seemed. The next morning, he fixed breakfast and watched some local news. Nothing about the heist. Satisfied, he turned off the TV and considered what to do next. He never realized how empty life could be without even a full time job to help fill up the time. Looking out the window, he saw that the early morning fog that had clung to the distant trees still hovered above the near frozen ground. Vaguely, he wondered how the chickens were doing. Did anyone come by to collect their eggs? Was he supposed to do it? It'd been a long time since he used to do such back home when he was a kid. His parents always had a few chickens around then. With nothing better on the agenda, he decided to go and check.

Shrugging into his coat and jamming a watch cap over his head, he headed outdoors. There, he paused, taking in some lung fulls of air. Nice. Slowly, he began circumventing the house, noting the unplanned nature of the various additions including an unfinished garage large enough for three vehicles. In back, a wooden deck gave onto an in ground pool, long since bone dry with rusty, disused filtering equipment nearby. Pretty depressing amid the featureless sky, fog, and nearby trees dripping with moisture. He reached the enclosure with the chickens about a hundred yards from the house. He heard the chickens cooing and rooting around before he reached it but when he walked up to the fencing, they all stopped what they were doing and stood quietly, eyeing him. He waited for them to get over their surprise but nothing changed. The birds continued to stand and stare. Definitely not ordinary chicken behavior.

He took hold of the wire fence and shook it thinking to startle them into activity but again, nothing.

He found the latch to the gate and let himself in. Making his way to the weathered coop, chickens moved aside for him but made no sound. Inside the coop, there were no eggs. *So much for that*, he thought. Back outside the enclosure, he picked up a stone and threw it a clump of the birds, now angry at their lack of reaction to his intrusion. Still nothing. Their quiet staring was definitely getting on his nerves. He'd have to ask the real estate agent if there was something wrong with them.

Casting one last look over his shoulder, Jake continued past the enclosure, heading toward the edge of the forest farther back on the property. He was about half way across an open field when he noticed that the chickens had come back to life. Turning, he could see movement within the enclosure, cooings and squawks. If there had been a rock around, he'd have thrown it at them in frustration but there wasn't any in that field of long, brown grass that hadn't been hayed before the season ended.

Now the fog cleared a little as he approached the tree line. The first thing he noticed were the stone fences that snaked their way through the woods, marking out former pastures long since abandoned and covered now with second growth forest. He remembered them well from his youth when he and friends would follow the same kind of walls in the New Hampshire countryside where he grew up. He followed one now as it led him deeper and deeper into the woods. Arriving at a juncture, he followed another wall to the right that led to another open pasture. Was this part of his rental property or a neighbors? He saw no posts against trespassing so continued on, entering the new pasture on the crest of a slope. Looking down slope, he spied another stone wall but this one was different from all the others. Curious, he began walking toward it.

As he walked, he noticed that the wall was bigger than he expected, much bigger. And when he finally reached it, was amazed to find that it stood a good five feet high and at least as wide. Big, heavy boulders composed its base with smaller stones stacked on top. Looking at those base stones, Jake had to wonder at the amount of sheer horse and manpower it must have taken to set them in place. In fact, the work that had gone into building the wall seemed far in excess of what was needed to mark off a field or keep cows in and deer out.

After lunch, he followed through with his intention to visit the real estate office and luckily, Bill and Eleanor Riverrun were in.

"Well, hello stranger," called Bill, looking up at

...he noticed that the wall was bigger than he expected, much bigger. And when he finally reached it, was amazed to find that it stood a good five feet high and at least as wide. Big, heavy boulders composed its base with smaller stones stacked on top.

He gazed out over the wall to the land on the other side. It beckoned him to continue on and explore, but he decided to wait on a nicer day. Maybe he'd go into town instead and bring up the subject with the real estate couple from whom he'd rented the house.

On the way back, he passed the chickens again and again, they went silent, just standing and staring. He could see their heads turning as he walked past, their beady, thoughtless eyes gazing but expressing nothing.

Huddling deeper into this coat, Jake passed them by, noting their renewed activity after he'd reached the pool area. Weird.

the tinkle of the bell over the door. "No problem at the house I hope?"

"No, not at all," said Jake. "I just had a question about the property itself."

"Oh?"

"I was wondering how far back it went. I found a big wall way down in back and was tempted to go over it and explore on the other side but didn't want to trespass."

"Not to worry," chimed in Eleanor pleasantly. "Your property runs all the way down to the swamp at the bottom of the slope."

"Right," agreed Bill. "You can wander all over down there. No problem."

"That's good to hear," said Jake. "But what about that stone wall? You know the one I mean? The big one."

"The five footer? What about it?"

"Well, it doesn't look like any other stone fence I've seen. Who built it? Why is it so huge?"

Bill shrugged. "Never gave it much thought."

"Okay. I'll ask around town. Maybe someone has an explanation. Just to satisfy my natural curiousity."

"Sure! Let us know what you find out."

Although his visit with the Riverruns proved to be a dead end wall wise, at least he'd verified that it was safe to walk beyond it without getting a load of buckshot as a trespasser. But it still left the bigger question of the wall itself. For that, he'd have to keep nosing around.

He did some light shopping at Hanneford's and managed to engage a likely looking local in conversation but the man claimed not to know anything about stone walls beyond what everyone else knew. Nevertheless, Jake thought he detected some reticence on the man's part in discussing the subject after learning where Jake lived. Deciding to take the bull by the horns, he went next to the feed store where it was likely he'd find people more knowledgeable about farming issues. He'd use the excuse of looking to buy some chicken feed as his reason for being there. It worked. No one questioned his presence and the proprietor even noted that he was new around town.

"I'm renting the place up at 369 Old Marsh Road," said Jake helpfully. "Nice country out here."

"We like it," agreed the proprietor.

"Was wondering though," continued Jake, "about all those stone walls running through the woods."

"Fences we call 'em," corrected the proprietor. "Stone fences."

"Oh, right. Well, I've seen them before of course, but there was one...well, I have to call it a wall because it was way too big to be just a fence."

"Oh, yeah?"

"It was a good five feet high and just as wide," said Jake, holding his hand up to indicate height. "Never saw anything that big before. Know anything about such things? Why anyone would go to all that trouble to build it? It was way down on a wood lot, not near the street or anything."

Did the proprietor suddenly seem more guarded? Or was it Jake's imagination?

"Down off Old Marsh you say? You must be talkin' about the old Wall of Jericho. Leastways, that's what folks hereabouts been callin' it for years, since before I was a boy. Asked around once but no one remembers who built it. Old man Spencer, must be well past ninety by now, still comes in here for supplies, he used to say the wall was built by Indians. Don't know if I'd put much credence in that though. No one ever knowed Indians to waste time buildin' things in stone. They weren't in one place long enough for that. Then agin', who knows? You could check with Maggie Jones at the historical society. She might know somethin'."

"I'll do that," said Jake, paying for his feed.

Jake found the historical society offices only a few doors down from the feed store.

"It's not unheard of for Indians to build permanent structures out of stone," Jones was saying. "There were plenty of other tribes in the area before the Passamaquaddy. In fact, it was only a few hundred years before the European settlers arrived that the outskirts of the mound building cultures reached into Maine. There are evidences here and there of stone structures or megaliths in New England."

"But did they build walls like the one on Old Marsh Road?"

"That's difficult to tell. Not many architectural peculiarities go into stone fence building, or walls."

"Well, are there any other similar walls in the area? Or even in New England?"

"Actually, no," admitted Jones.

"So is there anything you can tell me about this wall?"

"Only that the folks around here don't like to talk about it much. They'd prefer to forget all about it."

"How come?"

Jones shrugged. "Oh, vague stories about the area being haunted. From records made by Prospect's earliest settlers, Revolutionary soldiers mostly, it seems the stories began among the local Indians who regarded the area down there as taboo, bad medicine you know. But nothing more concrete I'm afraid. Sometimes there's the occasional report from local hunters of strange sounds down there but they've never really been confirmed. Probably coyotes or barking deer."

Consulting old property records dating back to the eighteenth century, Jones found contemporary surveyors' maps showing metes and bounds and when Jake identified the area bounded by the wall, she was unable to identify who exactly owned the land on the other side.

"The real estate agent told me it belongs to the owners of the house I'm renting," said Jake.

"They should know, but there's nothing in these records indicating such," said Jones. But the question clearly piqued her curiousity and she determined to find out more.

Outside of the historical society, Jake was just heading back to his car when an elderly man stopped him.

"Hey, young feller," he hailed. "You the one been askin' about the big wall down Old Marsh Road way?"

Surprised, Jake stopped and regarded the man, who stood on the sidewalk, leaning on one of those rolaters that were all the rage in nursing homes these days.

"Yeah, I am," admitted Jake. Then, taking a stab in the dark: "Are you Mr. Spencer?"

The old man chuckled in his short, white beard. "Good guess!"

"Well, I'm glad to meet you, Mr. Spencer," said Jake. "The guy at the feed store said you knew something about that big wall down behind my place."

"Only what I heered as a youngster," said Spencer. "Namely that it's been there for as long as anyone remembers. And no one remembers or knows when it was built. Not the reg'lar kind of stone fence that farmers have been puttin' up ever since settler times."

"The man at the feed store said that you thought it might have been Indians who…?"

"Don't think. Know. Got it from my grandad who got it from his'n. Likely the story came down to him from the Spencers who first come to this region. Fer as I know, Spencers were amongst the first white hunters out here. Before King Phillips' War when relations betwixt whites and Indians warn't so bad. They talked to each other. That's where the first stories came from I reckon. One of 'em was about that wall. My grandad fer instance, said it was built by the Indians but even they didn't

remember when. It's old, young feller, old! Grandad said it survived all these years, and never got cannabalized fer other construction on account of bein' pertected by secret people."

"Secret people?"

"Supposed to have been a secret society amongst the tribes responsible for the wall," continued Spencer. "They made sure it was kept in repair. Rumor had it that they had their secret signs and handshakes and such. Even made sacrifices on the wall."

"Is there anything that substantiates those stories?" asked Jake, growing more and more skeptical.

Spencer shrugged. "Dunno and don't care. Believe if you wanna or not. Makes no difference these days."

"Well, thanks for letting me know. It's all very interesting even if it's all just stories."

Spencer began pushing his walker along, then paused, saying "Just the same, I'd leave that wall alone...and stay out of the hollow."

Jake smiled in acknowledgment and waved so long, but didn't take Spencer's warning too seriously.

In the end, he returned home hardly any the wiser about the wall but still curious.

With daylight savings time, night fell early and with it, Jake confined himself to the kitchen and area before the fireplace where he sat gazing into the flickering flames. He wondered about the stash of money sitting in that cemetery. What the other guys were doing to while away the time? About the big wall in the lower pasture. And even the weird behavior of the chickens out back. When scrolling through the news feed on his cell phone grew stale, he got up to make himself a cup of coffee. On the way back, he passed the dining area with the door leading to the library in back.

Tired of the cell phone, he changed course and headed to the library. Flicking on the light, he was reminded at how small it was but its four walls were lined with shelves, all filled with books mostly dating back to the time of the Kennedy assassination. Interestingly, he found that many of the books had been signed by their authors, some by gift givers including a couple names even he recognized as well known political figures. Apparently, the owner of the house was connected.

But not finding anything in the library that he wanted to read, Jake passed through to the parlor on the other side.

Its hearth sharing a flue with the fireplace in the den on the other side, the parlor room was crowded with antique looking furniture and framed pictures on tables and walls. And now that Jake took a closer look, all seemed to be of the same man standing with political figures like Bill and Hillary Clinton, Jimmy Carter, and other Democrat bigwigs. There was the same guy with Hollywood types too. Citations and paperwork in a desk drawer suggested that the house's former owner was a Democrat donor or bundler of some sort. Scary. But it was while idly looking through the desk that Jake found a little book of local legends. *Stories and Legends of Old Prospect,* read the title. Just what he was looking for.

Taking the book, he crossed from the parlor, through the little front hall where darkened steps led upstairs, to the den on the other side. He fed more wood in the dying fire and settled down on the couch to thumb through the book. There were the usual tales of first settlers and their family trees, local movers and shakers, the establishment of the Baptist church and even a small but long since vanished colony of Shakers. The town was noted as the birthplace of a state representative and a few famous sons who went on to success in the medical and military fields. But it was the chapter covering the earliest days of the town that interested Jake. There was brief mention of isolated, upright stones that might have been used to mark the seasons; strange lights seen atop hills in the early days, presumably lit by local Indians; encounters with the Passamaquaddy by early white hunters before settlers entered the region. In those days, sometimes, white men would take native wives and become members of the tribe. They learned things not often imparted to strangers and when they returned to civilization, told of Indian ways and beliefs, among them, spirit totems, animal spirits, the gods Wendigo, Ithaqua, Sho-Goth, and entities that roamed the deep forests and mountains like today's Bigfoot that the Indians referred to as the Great Race. And they told of other things, evil things, that seeped down from the stars and to which sacrifices of appeasement were made.

There was the facsimile of a letter written by a nearly illiterate hunter to officials back in the Massachusetts Bay colony, warning of doings among the Passamaquaddy:

Edward Winslow
Hon. Governor
Massachusetts Bay
Plymouth
April, 1633

Honourable Sir, this letter is to inform thee and warn thee of doings among ye natives of this colony. Specifically, ye Passamakuddy. With long experience among ye natives, I have learnt their language and have spoken with sundry of them. They desire peace betwixt our people on condishion they are left alone in pursuit of their heathen ways. They desire that we refrane from sending ye missionaries amongst them as they have their own peculiar ways. Ways that would seem to ye savage and heathen but to them, quite practicle. Chief among these practicalities is a peculiar Order amongst them. A secret Order charged with peculiar Rites intended to protect ye people against unseen spirits. Ye group possesses its own secret language and salutayshions used to identify each other and by these Signs ye shall know them: *Ia Ia phnglui Sho-Goth ythaa*. I do not profess to know what the meaning of this salutayshion is, but feel that it represents something evil and unclean. My warning to ye is to stand guard against this secret cult and to crush it if opportunity presents itself.

I remain your most obedient servant,
Zekiel Spencer

Jake was surprised to note the identity of the letter writer. Clearly, he was an ancestor of the old

170

man he'd spoken to in town and was inclined to give more credence to the man's stories about the wall and the local Indians.

At that point, however, Jake was ready to give up on the book having decided its collection of unsubstantiated local legends wasn't very helpful. But seeing as he was almost finished the chapter, he decided to continue reading about a final legend involving something called "the dirty man" which, so far as he could figure, was a new addition to the area's weirdness, something in the way of a modern urban legend. It seems there had been stories from remote farm houses and others by the occasional kids that had been off parking somewhere, of a human figure that would emerge from the forest. It was never clearly identified but described as being mostly black but streaked with white giving the figure a dirty look as if it had been covered in mud. *Well, it was different than the ax murderer stories that used to go around when he was a kid*, thought Jake.

Rising, he'd left the warmth of the fireplace to replace the book in the parlor when the night was pierced by an unearthly cry from somewhere at the back of the house! Jake froze, listening, as the wail trailed off quickly and ended with echoes that died among the trees of the forest. *What was that?* he wondered, shaken. He was aware of noises in the forest that sometimes could sound like human voices or the wails of animals that turned out to be nothing more than two trees rubbing together in the wind, but this was nothing like that. Whatever had made it, was terrified. He'd never heard anything like it in his life. For the next few minutes, he stood silently, listening, but nothing else came. Gradually, he took hold of his nerves and retreated to his bedroom where he could look out back. Maybe one of the chickens was taken by a fox or something? But he could see or hear no special activity in the direction of the enclosure.

He went to bed not without some trepidation, expecting any minute to hear another agonizing cry in the night. But it was not repeated. In the morning, he decided to go back to town to make some more inquiries. Maybe someone else heard the noise. It'd been loud enough. He breakfasted at the local greasy spoon and made some offhand comments hoping to get some reaction from the other early risers and someone did mention that such sounds

were reported now and then from deep in the hollow. No one, however, had ever really investigated. It was said that the police had once gone to check but never found anything. Just as well. It wasn't healthy to poke around down there anyway.

What he'd learned in town, only increased Jake's desire to check things out for himself. More than likely, he'd find a pool of blood, evidence that a deer had probably been jumped by a puma or mountain lion. There had been occasional reports of the return of such predators to the area. With that in mind, he was careful to bring his .38 Special with him, the one he'd used in the robbery, when he finally set off for the lower pasture. Once again, the chickens fell silent as he passed and the overcast sky threatened rain as it had ever since he'd arrived in Prospect.

He reached the wall he'd found the day before but now it seemed bigger than ever. He could have climbed over it but it would've been a chore. Instead, he chose to follow it for a while hoping to find a break somewhere. Some minutes later, he did.

Watching his step, it wouldn't do to get a sprain this far from the house, he picked his way over the rubble and hopped down into the old, overgrown pasture on the opposite side. Looking around, he decided to head for the distant tree line where some morning fog was slowly lifting. As he went, he noticed many places where the tall, sere grass had been mashed flat, as if whole herds of deer had settled down together. Evidence that maybe he'd been right about suspecting one of them having fallen prey to a mountain lion.

Presently, he reached the trees and moved in among them, careful not to lose his footing amid the undergrowth. Damp, browning leaves carpeted the forest floor and as the land continued to slope downward, he glimpsed the tell tale clearing of trees below that indicated a body of water of some kind. No doubt the pond mentioned by the locals. He made that his goal and continued on. As he went, holding onto trees for support, he began to notice that many were overly large and all had the bark completely stripped from their lower extremities. He knew that moose often rubbed themselves against trees, scraping off the bark, but this phenomenon couldn't have been moose as the scrapings went too far up. Was it some kind of plant disease? In any case, it struck him as odd that the trees had been allowed to grow so large in what had obviously been intended at one time to be a wood lot. He'd still not arrived at a satisfactory answer when he reached the bottom of the slope. There, he was stopped by the edge of a small pond rimmed by thatches of cat o nine tails now gone to seed.

As he surveyed the open water, nothing appeared out of the ordinary. He walked along the edge for some minutes, looking for telltale sign of a struggle. And though he didn't find a scattering of blood, he did come across an area showing definite evidence of having been disturbed, possibly in a violent struggle of some kind. He looked around but found no further disturbance. Again, he turned his gaze out over the water. Something about its calm, placid surface prompted him to break that mirrored sheen. He picked up a rock and tossed it in. But instead of the expected kerplunk, the sound it made was more short lived, almost as if it had struck mud rather than deep water. Curious, he picked up a stick and began poking at it. As ripples began to disturb the surface, his stick met resistance sooner than he'd expected. Frowning, he dug his stick deeper. There was more resistance than he'd expect from simple mud and when he pulled the stick out, he was surprised to find that it was coated in a black, tarry substance.

"What the...?" he mumbled aloud before realizing that the pond was not a pond at all, but some kind of tarn, like the La Brea Tar Pits; except for a few inches of water gathered on its surface, the pond was actually a tar pit formed by oil leaking from the earth and then hardening to a kind of soft asphalt. Suddenly, Jake knew what had caused that wail he heard the night before...and the others heard over the years by locals and before them, the Indians. They were nothing more than animals coming for a drink of water and then getting caught in the tar and being dragged under by their own struggles to free themselves. He smiled. Wouldn't he have a story to tell to the folks in town about the true nature of the hollow they were all so afraid of!

He was still thinking of the pleasure he'd have in filling in the locals when there was a sensation of movement at his feet. Casually, he looked down and was momentarily consternated when he saw that a black psuedopod of some sort had emerged from the tarn and was snaking its way toward him. He stood frozen, unable to understand what was happening. It wasn't until the thing had wrapped itself around his hiking boot and began to tug that he was awoken to the danger that menaced him. Quickly, he resisted the tugging thing but the more he did, the tighter it constricted its hold on him. Then began the pulling, an inexorable tugging that Jake quickly found was impossible to resist. But when he tried, his efforts seemed to agitate whatever it was that had extended the black member. Suddenly, the water over the tarn began to ripple violently, heaving and splashing as something moved in order to form a better grip on its resisting prey.

Panicking now, Jake tugged all the harder to free his leg, but all he succeeded in doing was to pull his foot from the boot, which quickly disappeared into the tarn. The freeing action sent him flailing backward onto his rump where he wasted no time getting to his feet but instead, began to scrabble backward on hands and feet. By that time, whatever had been agitated in the tarn appeared to be unsatisfied with the boot it had taken. Suddenly, whatever it was, reared from the pond, water sloughing from its smooth, black surface. It towered over Jake then came crashing down on the dry land that ringed the pond. In seconds, it had reshaped itself into a solid wave, a moving wall of tarry black that filled the nearby woods with the crackle and snap of the fallen branches and leaves that carpeted the forest floor.

Jake didn't know how or when he'd gained his feet; he only knew that he was running madly among the trees, uncaring about his unshod foot, wanting only to reach the wall, the wall whose size and height now made complete sense to him. It had been built to keep this creature, this thing, from breaking out of the hollow. He only hoped now that it would again this time. He risked a look over his shoulder only to see the thing still surging forward, intent on seizing him and dragging him back with it back to its resting place at the bottom of the hollow. Now he understood what had happened to the bark on the trees; this wasn't the first time the thing had left its hollow. And when it did, its oozing bulk would slither around the trees before reuniting again taking the bark along with it. But that realization didn't help him now. Only flight would. He reached the break in the wall and stumbled over the fallen stones only to realize with horror that the break would also allow the thing to escape the enclosure! He remembered the flattened areas of grass in the pasture and wondered if they could have been made by this thing? But that didn't matter, as he saw it begin to slither past the break and continue to pursue him.

Now the shadows over the property were growing long as the lowering sun marked the shortening days of daylight savings time. Stumbling, running, scrambling past the chicken enclosure and the empty pool, Jake made for the house, his sole intent of the moment to grab his car keys and escape toward town. He had to warn the neighbors. Get the police. But at the house, he fumbled with the storm door. It wouldn't open! With increasing desperation, he yanked until the latch tore loose and he pushed open the inner door before slamming it shut behind him. He only had time for a glimpse outside but it was enough to confirm his worst fear as he saw that the thing was still rolling, still surging in his direction. Outside, he could hear the frenzied cries of the chickens as the thing engulfed them. Then, suddenly, there was a loud thump at the back door where he'd just come in from. Pulling the .38 from his pocket, he gathered his courage to approach a window and saw the black thing crowding against the house. In the shadows there, as the sun continued to sink behind the trees across the street, it boomed against the walls, beginning to roll from window to window, as if seeking entrance.

My God, thought Jake, *does it actually think?*

Seeing it crowd up against the bedroom window, Jake lifted the sash a little, poked the nose of his gun outside and fired a few shots into the thing with no effect. He kept shooting uselessly, emptying the gun before giving up and retreating to the kitchen. Now glass was breaking elsewhere and he knew that the thing would be oozing into the house soon.

The keys! He thought with rising panic. Where did he put them? Desperately, he searched the counters, scattering appliances over the floor. *Where are they?*

But it would have been too late even if he'd found them. Already, the thing was breaking in. And was it his imagination? There was also pounding at the front door and windows being smashed in the parlor and den. Running to the den, he could see human figures at the windows. They were smeared with oil from the tarn but streaked in white as well. *The Dirty Man!*

Now, his mind in a turmoil, he could only go to the stairs leading to the second floor. But his retreat there only offered temporary safety. Already, he could hear noises from downstairs indicating that the dirty men had entered the house. The clumps coming from the stairs told him that they were pursuing him still. He found the door to the attic even as a last minute idea occurred to him. If he could make his way across the attic and into the space over the unfinished garage, he could lower himself down, head off the thing coming up the stairs, and make his way outside again. After that, it would be easy to outrun the thing down the driveway to the road!

As quickly as safety allowed, he negotiated his way across the exposed rafters in the attic, ducking his head here and there, finding easy passage over the occasional sheet of plywood. At last, he reached the space over the garage where fading light streamed through the empty doorways waiting for the overhead doors to be installed. With newfound energy, he eased himself between a pair of rafters and hit the concrete floor below, off balance due to his wearing only a single boot. But he'd no sooner straightened up when he was startled by a stream of dirty white substance that stretched from the attic space onto the floor where it gathered and built up into a manlike shape. It was mostly white now and had no face; simply a featureless template of a man. Slowly, as more and more of the substance leaked from above, the dirty man grew more shapeless, more amoebic, until it grew into a great, heaving lump of protoplasmic bubbles that seemed to glow in the growing gloom. Suddenly, to Jake's horror, the mass split open like a seed pod, revealing a tangled mass of eye stalks, tentacles, and feelers that seemed to pause before suddenly lashing out in his direction...

From the darkness outside the house, Jake's soul chilling scream, eerily like those that had echoed from the hollow, was cut horribly short just as Bill and Eleanor Riverrun drove up to the driveway. Bill pulled up along the roadside and prepared to leave the car.

"We'll have to get a glazier in to replace all those windows," said Eleanor, staring at the distant house, where it sat brooding in the night.

"From out of town this time," agreed Bill.

"Why don't you collect his things and bring out the car. We'll leave it in Belfast for the police to find. They'll think Mr. Torros disappeared himself or something."

"The police will come around looking for clues to what happened to him."

"And they'll find nothing," replied Eleanor.

Bill, preparing to exit the car, popped the trunk. He removed a sign from the back and pressed it into the ground at the end of the driveway.

"You don't think it's too soon for that, do you?" asked Eleanor when Bill had reentered the car.

Bill reconsidered. "Maybe you're right. We're not likely to have those windows fixed before the police drop by. They'll wonder why we didn't report the damage."

He left the car again and plucked the "for rent" sign from the ground and tossed it in the back seat.

As he drove up the drive to retrieve Jake's car, he began to chant, and was quickly joined by his wife:

Ia Ia phnglui Sho-Goth ! Ia Ia phnglui Sho-Goth!

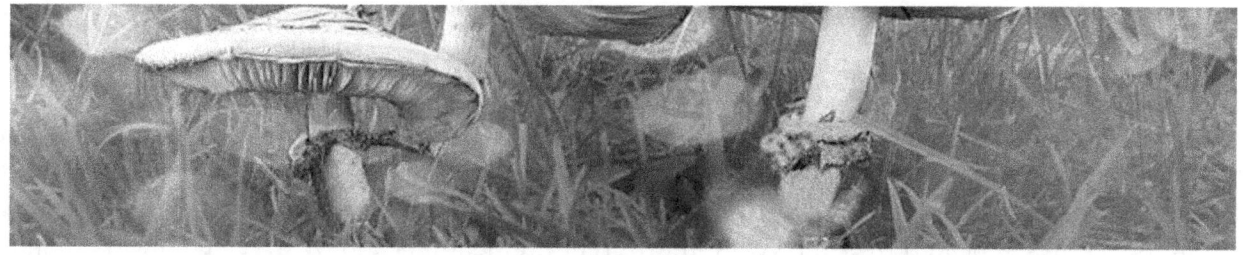

<u>*The Grand Mycelium Says*</u>

Looking for an excuse to re-read the classics?

Then look no further than editor Leslie S. Klinger's *The New Annotated H.P. Lovecraft* (2014)!

An award winning anthologizer, Klinger has edited a number of annotated collections from Sherlock Holmes to Neil Gaiman's *Sandman* comic books. And though it is not clear what credentials he has regarding H.P. Lovecraft (he holds ranking positions in organizations devoted to Sherlock Holmes, crime fiction, and horror fiction in general), it clearly has not prevented him from issuing the aforesaid *New Annotated HPL*.

An 800+ page tome, Klinger's *New Annotated* book covers most of HPL's major stories including "The Call of Cthulhu," "The Dunwich Horror," "The Colour Out of Space," "At the Mountains of Madness," "The Haunter of the Dark," "The Thing on the Doorstep," "The Shadow Over Innsmouth," and others. For fans of HPL, even those who have multiple versions and editions of his tales, non-fiction treatises, and a complete run of *Crypt of Cthulhu*, Klinger's tome is a valuable item to add to their collection. This is largely thanks to its annotations which largely do not step on the toes of the previous, and still final word on such volumes, those of genuine HPL scholar, S. T. Joshi: *The Annotated Lovecraft* (1997) and is followup, *More Annotated Lovecraft* (1999) In fact, you might say the two versions are complementary.

As with Joshi's superb volumes, *The New Annotated* also comes with illustrations taken from various sources from past/present photos of real life locations of Lovecraft's stories to cover illustrations from *Weird Tales* to the latest comic book adaptations. However, Klinger's annotations, as noted in the author's introduction, largely attempt to avoid covering the same ground as Joshi's (thus allowing the collector a free conscience when ponying up for this expensive new volume) Instead, the author seems mostly to stick with geographical, historical, and scientific commentary (marred only by his annoying adaptation of woke science's BCE/CE claptrap instead of the actual BC/AD) However, as if trying to make up for his restrictive annotations, Klinger often goes into vast, if not unnecessary, detail on bio-backgrounds of real life figures mentioned in HPL's text as well as scientific/historical items. Be that as it may, the text of the stories themselves, reliant as much as possible on HPL's intended text as opposed to edited versions that has appeared over the years in different publications and by diverse editorial hands, is a plus as is the larger font (for grateful aging fans!)

All that said, as professional and impressive as Klinger's package is, it's more suited for the general HPL reader looking to tentatively dip his toes into the more esoteric study of the author's work. For a more authoritative look, the discerning reader must still refer to Joshi's in depth annotated editions whose notes represent more of a deep dive into Lovecraftiana including extensive introductions and back story along with the by now expected accompanying illustrations.

And while we're discussing things Lovecraftian (due to the Mycelium's long absence from these pages) might we suggest some independent films based on Lovecraft's stories for the discerning fan? Although the filmic Lovecraft has exploded into a cottage industry lately (with most efforts pretty much junk), there have been several delightful triumphs of late, including *The Call of Cthulhu* (2005) and *The Whisperer in Darkness* (2011) each produced by The H.P. Lovecraft Historical Society, with *Call* succeeding better than *Whisperer* due to the unfortunate choice of the producer to add original material to *Whisperer* that goes beyond the story's actual climactic scene. Otherwise, both these films are among the very best efforts to capture HPL on film and come highly recommended.

The third and best of the three top adaptations however, has to be *Die Farbe* (2010), a German produced film adapting Lovecraft's *Colour Out of Space* that manages to come up with a clever idea to illustrate the impossible...namely, a new color! With rumors of another production by the same team, one only hopes that it arrives soon!

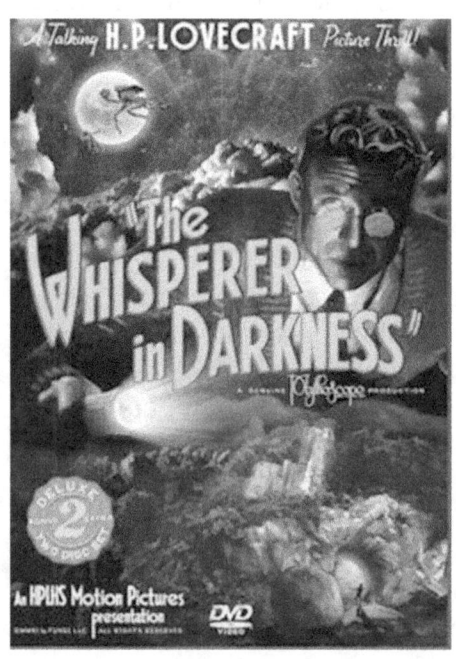

The House

by H.P. Lovecraft

'Tis a grove circled dwelling
   Set close to a hill,
Where the branches are telling
   Strange legends of ill;
Over timbers so old
   That they breathe of the dead,
Crawl the vines, green and cold,
   By strange nourishment fed;
And no man knows the juices they suck from the depths of their dark slimy bed.

In the gardens are growing
   Tall blossoms and fair,
Each pallid bloom throwing
   Perfume on the air;
But the afternoon sun
   With its red slanting rays
Makes the picture loom dun
   On the curious gaze,
And above the sweet scent of the blossoms rise odours of numberless days.

The rank grasses are waving
   On terrace and lawn,
Dim memories saving
   Of things that have gone;
The stones of the walks
   Are encrusted and wet,
and a strange spirit stalks
   When the red sun has set,
And the soul of the watcher is fill'd with faint pictures he fain would forget.

It was in the hot Junetime
   I stood by that scene,
When the gold rays of noontime
   beat bright on the green.
But I shiver'd with cold,
   Groping feebly for light,
As a picture unroll'd…
   And my age-spanning sight
Saw the time I had been there before flash like fulgury out of the night.